# THE LAST
# GREEK

Christian Cameron is a writer and military historian. He participates in re-enacting and experimental archaeology, teaches armoured fighting and historical swordsmanship, and takes his vacations with his family visiting battlefields, castles and cathedrals. He lives in Toronto and is busy writing his next novel.

# THE LAST
# GREEK

CHRISTIAN CAMERON

ORION

First published in Great Britain in 2020
by Orion Fiction,
an imprint of The Orion Publishing Group Ltd
Carmelite House, 50 Victoria Embankment
London EC4Y ODZ

An Hachette UK Company

1 3 5 7 9 10 8 6 4 2

A CIP catalogue record for this book
is available from the British Library.

ISBN (Hardback) 978 1 4091 7659 6
ISBN (eBook) 978 1 4091 7661 9

Typeset by Deltatype Ltd, Birkenhead, Merseyside

Printed and bound in Great Britain by Clays Ltd, Elcograf S.p.A.

MIX
Paper from
responsible sources
FSC® C104740

www.orionbooks.co.uk

*To Giannis Kadoglou, who keeps me faithful to Ancient Greece, and Father William O'Malley, SJ, who led me to the water AND made me drink it.*

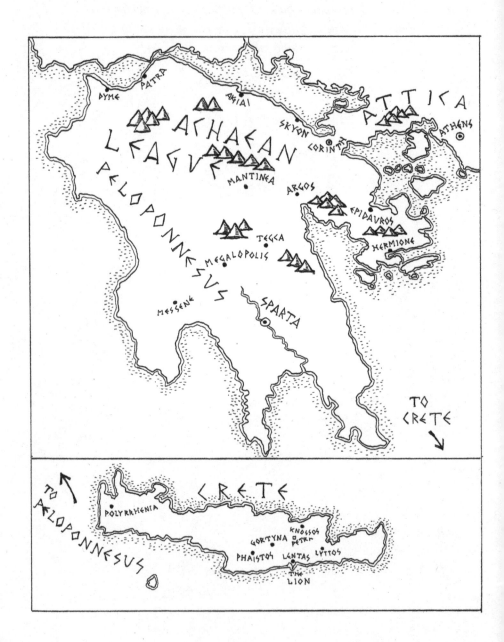

# AUTHOR'S NOTE

Four things I think perhaps you need to know before you read this book.

First, Ancient Greek cavalry did not have stirrups. If you think too many riders are falling off horses here, or if you think that Alexanor has too much trouble mounting, I recommend you go out and ride rough terrain without stirrups, or just stand on flat ground and try to mount a fourteen-hand horse. It can be done, but ancient cavalry manuals (like Xenophon's *Cavalry Commander*, which I recommend to all) are full of advice on mounting.

As a corollary to the first point, wrestling on horseback, which continued to play a major role in mounted combat into the late Middle Ages and the Renaissance, would have been an even more vital part of mounted combat in Philopoemen's time. The press of a cavalry fight could be as close as an infantry fight ...

And my thanks to Georgine and Ridgely Davis for their tutelage and advice on all things equine; and to Elizabeth Usher and John Conyard for their examples.

Second, the calendar used by my protagonists is the Boeotian calendar, which I chose for various reasons, not least of which is that the Argosian calendar was not fully realised. But in brief: every Greek polis had its own calendar; even inside the Achaean League each city probably kept its own calendar. This is because of religion; every city had its own festivals and its own worship dates. Because there was nothing like a religious 'authority' above the level of the polis, there was no one to rectify calendars. This makes dating *anything* quite challenging, and so I freely admit that I have taken some small liberties with the calendar to allow for chapter titles that will, I hope, help the reader sort the pace of the action. Note there are only ten months in the Boeotian calendar ...

## Boeotian Calendar
Bucatios (January–February)
Hermaios (February–March)
Prostaterios (March–April)
Agrionios (April–May)
Homoloios (May–July)
Theilouthios (July–August)
Hippodromios (August–September)
Panamos (September–November)
Pamboiotios (November–December)
Damatios (December–January)

## Attic Calendar
Hekatombaion (July–August)
Metageitnion (August–September)
Boedromion (September–October)
Pyanepsion (October–November)
Maimakterion (November–December)
Poseideon (December–January)
Gamelion (January–February)
Anethesterion (February–March)
Elaphebolion (March–April)
Mounichion (April–May)
Thargelion (May–June)
Skirophorion (June–July)

The third point is about the study of history. When dealing with the ancient world, there are too few facts and too many accepted assumptions. An issue as apparently obvious as the date of the Spartan seizure of Tegea (scholars are divided even on what *year* this took place), or the military effectiveness of various troop types (an area where wargamers have made assumptions that now haunt mainstream history), or what Philopoemen's political ideals really were ... We sift the evidence for pot sherds that we might be able to fit together into a story.

And finally, yes, it's true. I'm not a fan of Sparta. Neither militarism nor brutality appeal to me. You be the judge.

Christian Cameron
Toronto, 2019

# BOOK I

# HIPPARCHOS

# PROLOGUE

———⟨ひひ⟩———

## Epidauros, Peloponnese

### 7 THARGELION (ATTIC) OR 14 THEILOUTHIOS (BOEOTIAN) (EARLY JUNE), 210 BCE

The moment before dawn: the sacred precinct of Epidauros seemed to hang in a timeless darkness, the white marble of the sanctuary's precious buildings mere pale blurs against the stronger shadows; and then, as light touched the rim of the world beyond the mountains to the east, suddenly there was the sound of birds, the lower tones of insects, and the salmon pink of rosy-fingered dawn reached to touch the pillars of the temple, the columns of the *stoa*, the floor and seats of the theatre and the walls and marble roofs of the houses of healing. For a breath, the grey was touched in rose, and then the dawn swept over the sanctuary of the healing god like a reckless pink cavalry charge.

Alexanor of Kos and his wife Aspasia stood at different altars – he at the altar of Apollo, the god himself, and she at the altar of Hygeia, goddess of health – nor did they exchange even a glance, and yet Alexanor was aware of her, and aware, too, of the old priest, Sostratos, watching his every ritual motion, and Leon, his friend and vicar, swirling a censer over the head of the sacrifice.

The bull roared and turned his head towards the incense burner, and in that moment, Alexanor's knife slashed, and the bull's head came down. Blood poured from its open throat and its mighty knees buckled, and then it fell forward even as Alexanor stepped to the side to avoid the splash of crimson blood on his white robes.

The blood of the sacrifice ran like bright red wine in the grooves cut for the purpose, and a dozen under-priests began to cut the dead animal. A thigh bone wrapped in thick fat and tied with bloody tendons was placed on the altar before Alexanor by a stone-faced novice. He raised the thigh bones in supplication and then placed them on the brazier, full of charcoal and burning like an ironsmith's furnace.

The smell of sizzling fat filled the temple, overwhelming the more delicate notes of frankincense.

Alexanor's stomach rumbled loudly enough for Leon to hear it and the two men exchanged a smile. After four days of fasting, the smell of rich animal fat was as enticing as the ritual itself.

One of the local priests frowned, as if the rumble of Alexanor's stomach was an impiety, and Alexanor wondered what was wrong. He'd sensed a coldness from the priests, even some of those he'd trained with.

Across the temple, Sostratos completed his own sacrifice and put the thigh bones of a ram on his lit brazier. At the northern end of the complex, Aspasia and two other priestesses finished their own litanies and placed a series of shaped barley cakes on the fires of their altars, so that the smells of the sacrifices mingled, rising to the gods.

Two junior priests stripped naked, pulling their spotless white *himations* off and laying them over the waiting arms of acolytes, to begin the serious business of butchering the ritual meat. The ram and the bull sacrificed in honour of the birth of the god Apollo would feast every man and woman in the sanctuary, from illustrious guests and healing patients to the newest slaves.

Alexanor and Leon paced down the nave of the temple, surrounded by novices; Sostratos joined them from the second altar, and another priest, Erenida, joined them from the west altar. The numbers swelled until they were a procession of all the priests and priestesses of the vast temple complex; the ceremonial priests and the healers too, and all the novices and many of the guests, the pilgrims, and the sick able to walk. On this, the principal god's birthday, the procession, led by the sacrificers and the incense bearers, made the rounds of the sacred precinct of the whole sanctuary. At the great gates, where travellers and pilgrims were received, a choir of initiates sang the *paean*. At the northern gate, a choir of priestesses sang, their high voices carrying in the clear morning air.

Leon swung his silver censer with grace and Alexanor was proud for his friend, who had once been a slave and now was a senior priest, leading other priests in the most important ritual of the year. Leon walked at the head of the procession with a dignity that those who did not know him might have missed in his day-to-day humour and impatience with authority; in a ceremony, he became a pillar of piety.

Finally, after the procession had blessed every altar, visited every building, it wound its way back to the high altar of the Temple of Apollo where Chiron, the old hierophant of the temple complex, waited on the steps, leaning on his cornel-wood staff.

He intoned the ritual of welcome as they practised it at Epidauros, and Alexanor and a hundred other initiates sang the response. They all lifted their arms and sang the *paean* again, three hundred voices raised together, and the ceremony was completed.

Alexanor caught his wife's eye on him and he smiled, and she returned his smile, turned and spoke to one of the other priestesses, Kleopatra, who grinned.

'After the feast,' she said softly.

Close contact between male and female priests was discouraged, at least in public, and even when they were married. Alexanor deplored the rule, but found the need to communicate secretly with his wife – to flirt with her eyes, to pass messages – had its charms. He grinned, and Leon rolled his eyes, and the two of them carried their ritual instruments out of the crowd. Having completed important parts of the ceremony, they were now responsible for cleaning everything.

Alexanor followed Leon into the *skeuotheke*, the small building that acted as a treasury and a ritual storage house. Inside, amid the hanging lamps of gold and silver and bronze, stacks of silver platters and gold bowls worth a fortune, there was a small, very ordinary wooden table against one of the barred windows. There the two men emptied the precious censer, dumping the hot coals and the unburnt crystals of resin into an old iron pot with a close-fitting wooden lid that extinguished the burning material and rendered it inert.

Leon hung the thurible from a bronze hood near the window, where the hot metal could cool safely.

'Like old times,' he said wryly.

Alexanor returned his smile. 'Better than old times. We're senior priests.'

'We're still polishing the thuribles,' Leon noted. 'And not everyone here loves us. Remind me, why are we here?' he asked quietly.

'We're here because Chiron requested our presence for the god's year-day procession,' Alexanor said.

Leon was busy using a tuft of flax-tow dipped in ash to polish a spot off one of the ritual platters. A long queue of acolytes now stood outside the doors of the *skeuotheke*, with armloads of silver vessels and lamps that had been used for the bull's heart, the ram's heart, the sacred fire, and a dozen other liturgical purposes.

'By my count, this place still has more than seventy initiates, and thirty priests, any one of whom could have conducted the whole blessed thing,' Leon said. 'Sostratos, for example.'

Alexanor went back out to the portico and received another armload of ritual vessels, which he brought in and set carefully on the table.

'Chiron asked for us,' he said.

'Why?'

'I agree that not everyone here loves us,' Alexanor said. 'I assumed some of the juniors were jealous that we were asked to lead the sacrifice.' He shrugged, as if dismissing the subject which was, he thought, unworthy. Seizing the moment, he asked, 'Have you ever considered marriage?'

Leon's hand froze. 'What?' he asked, startled. 'Is this your notion of how to change the subject?'

Alexanor went out, got two trays from a young Gaulish slave, and asked for a bucket of clean water. Then he went back inside, where he began to wipe down the silver.

'Yes,' Alexanor answered. 'That's how I change the subject. I assume Chiron has his reasons, which might be anything from an attempt to improve the unity of the sanctuaries of Asklepios to a friendly desire to see us.' He glanced at Leon. 'And we needn't gossip about the priests.'

'By the god, you are not curious?' Leon asked.

'My curiosity is of a piece with my hunger,' Alexanor said. 'Soon to be assuaged. So why dwell on it?'

'What a Stoic you are, to be sure,' Leon grumbled. 'Philopoemen is rubbing off on you.'

Alexanor allowed himself a smile. 'I'm as curious as you are,' he admitted. He shrugged. 'But my curiosity won't get these platters clean.'

*

The feast was superb, and conjured images of bygone days. Alexanor had spent six happy years in the sanctuary of Epidauros and Leon had spent even longer. The great feast of Apollo had always been a favourite festival, with dancing, abundant food including beef and lamb, and elaborate sweets, amphorae of wine from all over the Hellenic world, and important guests, with speeches, song, and sometimes even presents.

Now, reclining on a couch with Leon at his side, Alexanor remembered his last feast of Apollo, and all the events that followed after it: the attack of the Spartans on the sanctuary, led by Machanandas, and his first sight of Philopoemen as an apparent corpse flung over the back of a riderless horse.

Epidauros was a more conservative temple than Lentas, where Alexanor was hierophant, and he reclined with Leon because men and women feasted separately in Epidauros, even when they were married and shared children. Alexanor could hear the sound of his wife's laughter through the leather screen that divided the hall, and he could hear the even higher laughter of Kleopatra, his wife's new friend.

'I like the procession at Lentas better,' Leon grumbled. 'With all the priests and priestesses from Gortyna, and the cavalry, and the phalanx.'

Alexanor took a sip of watered wine and passed the bowl to Leon.

'It is odd, isn't it? To have the sanctuary so—'

Leon lay back. 'Dominant. I like our balance better.'

Kleopatra laughed again.

'They're having too much fun,' Alexanor said.

'The local priestess of Hygeia is less ...' Leon smiled. 'Less staid than I'd have expected.'

'Aspasia says that she's very well trained and actually lived in Alexandria for three years.'

'What if Chiron wants to send an embassy?' Leon asked.

'An embassy?'

'Don't be overmodest. He sent you to the king of Macedon eight years ago – that's what started all this. Don't be coy. Last year Kos sent you to Philip. Both Epidauros and Kos used you to stay in touch with Philopoemen.'

'I take it we've returned to the subject of why we were summoned here,' Alexanor said.

'You used to be more fun. Shall I tell everyone about how you took Phila's pulse?'

'Only if you want to die in the dining hall at Epidauros,' Alexanor growled.

'Good, good, just making sure you are still in there, because the Stoic Hierophant of Lentas is a dull fellow indeed.'

'I'm thinking of how much of old Heraclitus' river of time has flowed past my toes since I last lay here in this hall.' Alexanor looked up at a line of shields dedicated by the former king of Macedon. 'When last I lay here for a feast, Doson was still king of Macedon. It was after the Feast of Apollo that Chiron sent us to Doson, as you say.'

'And Philopoemen won the Battle of Sellasia,' Leon said. 'Almost single-handed, as I seem to remember.'

'There's a little hyperbole there,' Alexanor said.

*I met Phila. And fell in love with a courtesan.*

'And then he received an ovation at Nemea,' Leon said.

'Doson received the ovation—'

'It was for Philopoemen and his Greeks. I was there. The old king was mortified.'

'He was quite cheerful, really,' Alexanor said. 'All right, I admit it, the ovation was mostly for the Achaeans and Philopoemen.'

'And then Philopoemen declined to serve the king, and then we failed to keep the old fellow from drinking himself to death.'

'We?'

'And then you lured Philopoemen to Crete.'

'What happened to "we"?'

'That was all you. You wanted to be hierophant. I got to pretend to be your slave. You beat me cruelly.'

'You deserved it.'

'You two are laughing too damned hard,' Sostratos said, leaning over their *kline.*

'Have a seat and we'll make you laugh too,' Leon said.

The older priest was laughing already. 'I don't remember you two as troublemakers. Mostly Alexanor pouted and moped and Leon did all the work.'

'Very little has changed,' Leon said.

'So about your marriage,' Alexanor said.

8

Leon whirled, almost dumping Sostratos onto the floor. But he recovered.

'Can you tell us, reverend sir, why the Hierophant has honoured us with an invitation?'

Sostratos nodded. 'I imagine that I could, at that. But I won't, because I'm a cruel bastard. Also because Chiron is old, but I still fear him.' He poked Alexanor. 'The truth is that we all miss you.' He raised an eyebrow. 'Despite everything.'

'And you're finally old enough to actually be a senior priest,' Erenida said, sitting on the low table that was supposed to hold their food. 'When you were here before—'

'Now I remember why I went away,' Alexanor said, clasping Erenida's hand with a laugh. 'How's old Bion?'

'Still hale. A freedman now, of course – he's training initiates.'

'I imagine he keeps them in a state of gentle terror.'

'Pretty much,' Erenida agreed. He frowned. 'It's been a difficult time,' he admitted. 'And you two aren't making it easier.'

Sostratos nodded. 'We're not far enough from Sparta to escape the effects of the new tyrant there. Remember the young scapegrace who tried to invade the precinct? Machanandas?'

'All too well,' Alexanor responded.

'He's the Tyrant of Sparta now. He rules in the name of the young king, of course, but in reality, he does whatever he wants. He's worse than Cleomenes ever was. He has some trumped-up document claiming that the sanctuary is part of the royal domains of the Lacedaemonians – he's demanded a tithe of our treasury.'

Alexanor shook his head. 'You can appeal to the League.'

'The League is a broken stick,' Sostratos said. 'An old dog without any teeth. The wolves don't fear her any more.'

'I thought that's why Macedon summoned Philopoemen,' Leon said.

Erenida frowned. 'Why was Philopoemen of Megalopolis even on Crete? As a mercenary?' He made a face. 'I've heard some nasty tales about him, and I know he's your guest-friend.'

Leon drank some wine. He glanced at Alexanor.

Alexanor smiled. 'The Achaean League sent Philopoemen to Crete to save the League of Crete from the Spartans and the Aegyptians.'

'And the Rhodians and the Romans,' Leon said.

Erenida frowned. 'What?' He shook his head. 'What in Hades does Achaea have to do with Crete?'

Leon nodded over the rim of the *kylix*. 'Everything. Grain, slaves, mercenaries, ties of guest-friendship, and the seasonal winds that blow from here to there.'

'You must know,' Sostratos said. 'Sparta holds cities on Crete.'

'Macedon needed Crete to be stable.' Alexanor said.

Erenida shrugged. 'I'm a simple priest. And I confess I'd heard a very different story from one of the other priests. Of Philopoemen serving as a sort of bandit king, murdering and raping his way across Crete for profit. And sacking the sanctuary at Lentas.'

'Sacking the sanctuary?' Alexanor asked. 'Who said such a thing?'

Leon's vulpine face took on a nasty smile. 'Can't you guess? Someone who hates Philopoemen. And you, too, I would wager.'

Erenida shrugged. 'No friend of yours, it is true. Pausanias of Gortyna.'

'Is he here?'

'He's at Messene, minding the temple there as part of his duties.' Erenida shrugged.

'I replaced him,' Alexanor said. 'I sent him here under arrest.'

'Ahh,' Erenida said. 'I've stepped in it again.'

Alexanor nodded. 'Philopoemen went to Crete at the command of Aratos and the League. With fewer than a hundred men, he retook Gortyna, refounded the Cretan League, built an army, and defeated the oligarchs utterly.' He smiled. 'He's a very able general.'

'And now Philip of Macedon wants him to command the Achaean League,' Sostratos said.

Alexanor nodded. 'Where is this going?' he asked.

Sostratos shook his head. 'The whole world is at war. And the war is coming to Epidauros. Like it or not, you and your friend are players in that war, and we have to take an interest in these events if we are going to survive.'

Erenida shook his head. 'Call me old-fashioned.'

Leon smiled. 'You are the very definition of old-fashioned,' he said. 'When I was a slave, you were the most conservative, most aristocratic novice.'

Erenida raised his eyebrows in acknowledgement. 'Of course. Regardless, we are priests. It is not our business what happens beyond our precinct walls. Let this Philopoemen march about – we should pray, and interpret dreams.' He took the *kylix*, drank, and then rose. 'I'll make sure some other couches have wine.'

When he was gone, Sostratos settled in his place.

'He's not as bad as he sounds.'

'He never was,' Leon said. 'He always spoke like one of the *Kalos Kagathos*, the beautiful people, but he treated me better than most of the other novices. And since I became a priest, he simply assumes I'm a gentlemen. I prefer that to many of the other attitudes I've encountered, I promise you.'

Alexanor looked puzzled. 'Chiron has trusted Pausanias with a temple?' he asked.

Sostratos shrugged. 'Pausanias is a very rich, very difficult man. What did you expect – that we'd execute him?' He laughed. 'I probably have the only sword in the precinct.'

'I have a sword,' Leon said.

'And I, too,' Alexanor said. 'Life on Crete was violent.'

'And that's what's coming here,' Sostratos said. 'The thing that I'm surprised Erenida didn't mention is ...' He looked around. 'You two are quite notorious, these days.'

'Notorious?' Leon said.

'Dissections,' Sostratos said very quietly. 'The open study of internal anatomy.'

Alexanor nodded slowly. 'Ahhh. Now I understand why I'm here.'

'No,' Sostratos said, 'you don't. Chiron approves of your study of anatomy, and anyway, you have the approval of the House on Kos. But the old-fashioned priests are not your friends, and your Pausanias has made you sound as dangerous as he could manage. He's a sly serpent. You should be wary of him.'

'Erenida seemed fine,' Leon said.

Sostratos looked around. 'He's a decent fellow, for one of the very rich. But you need to be wary. Chiron placed you in charge of the ceremony to make a statement – but there are priests here who resent you.'

'We noticed,' Alexanor admitted.

*

Chiron wasn't sitting in his cell. Instead, a brown-clad slave led them out to the second storey of the *stoa*, where the old priest was leaning on the railing, looking out over the distant mountains.

'Well done,' he said, clasping Leon's hand, and then again, when he took Alexanor's. 'Well done.'

'The ceremony?' Alexanor asked.

'Bah. That too. No, your life. The sanctuary at Lentas. Your handling of Philopoemen. The way you both rebuilt the reputation of your temple – everything. Both of you have justified every trust that was placed in you.'

Both of the younger men smiled; indeed, each of them glowed, although in very different ways. Leon, the former slave, grinned from ear to ear, and stood straighter, while Alexanor, the Rhodian aristocrat, gazed embarrassedly out over the valley, an untameable smile forcing itself on his face. Praise from the old priest was rare indeed; such open, absolute praise was worth a decade of work.

'But the reward for all your hard work is more work.' Chiron nodded. He moved stiffly. 'War is coming.'

'Sostratos said as much.'

'I asked him not to say too much.' Chiron made a face. 'For the first time under my rule, I'm sorry to say, there is dissension *inside* the sanctuary. I suspect that many of the younger priests are counting the days until I die and planning for the succession here.' He shrugged, as if this was of no moment. 'In the meantime, gentlemen, I have called on you to ask your political help, and, I think, your medical help as well.'

Alexanor bowed, Leon waved for the older priest to go on.

'A month ago, the Romans took the island of Aegina.'

'We know,' Leon said. 'We passed south of their fleet on our way here. We could see their warships.'

Chiron nodded. 'They are barbarians, not Greeks. They sacked every temple they took. Stripped the altars and the treasuries – looted even the hangings and the bronze decorations on the statues. Aegina! One of the richest islands in the Greek world.'

'And a member of the Achaean League,' Alexanor added.

'This is no longer a squabble between warlords,' the old priest said. 'When Macedon and the Seleucids spar over Syria or Boeotia, they do not sack temples. We are every bit as vulnerable as Aegina. The

Roman fleet could be here at any time. The League fleet is at Corinth, and if they have ten warships I'd be surprised.'

'And the Romans have been joined by Attalos of Pergamum,' Alexanor said. 'Two great fleets.'

'There's a rumour that the Carthaginians have promised Philip of Macedon a fleet,' Chiron said. 'Let me be brief. As long as I have been hierophant, we have tried to stay free of entanglements with politics. But we have always remained *aware* of the world around us. Now I fear we must do more. I want you, Alexanor, to go to the *Synodos* of the Achaean League and speak for us as an institution, almost as if we were a constituent city. I need to know if the League will defend us – fight for us, if necessary.'

Alexanor nodded. 'You want me to talk to Philopoemen?'

Chiron glanced at him, his eyes hard. 'Yes and no. Your friend Philopoemen returns to us with a very ... tough ... reputation. Most of the rich men of the Peloponnese fear him as a radical and worry about him as a potential Macedonian satrap. And even Philip seems to have ... doubts. I am not sure that we can rely on Philopoemen to protect us. On the other hand, your credit must be high with all the Achaeans – you reformed the sanctuary at Lentas and supported Philopoemen.'

'So am I going as an ambassador?'

'A *representative*,' Chiron said, placing particular emphasis on the word.

'What do we have to offer the League?' Alexanor asked.

'Who's going to run the sanctuary at Lentas?' Leon asked. 'I do not mean to be difficult, sir, but we are a joint foundation of Epidauros *and* Kos, now. We cannot just abandon our charges.'

Chiron nodded. 'I'm going to ask you, Leon, to direct Lentas, so that I can have Alexanor for a year.'

'A former slave as an acting hierophant?' Leon asked. 'Now who is a radical?'

'There's more, I'm afraid. I want you to take half a dozen of my juniors and train them in anatomy. And I'll tell you up front that I'm giving you the whole of a faction – a virulent faction.'

'An aristocratic faction?' Leon asked.

'Yes.'

'So, I – the former slave – will be teaching unorthodox medical techniques to men who question my birth and fitness?' he asked.

'Exactly,' the old priest said.

Leon smiled. 'Well, well. You really do think I'm capable. I'm flattered.'

'Leon gets to run my sanctuary while I ride around the Peloponnese nattering with politicians?' Alexanor asked.

'Exactly,' Chiron said. 'Just so.'

Alexanor shook his head. 'Of course I'll obey. But it does seem that Leon will have more fun.' He bowed. 'And may Aspasia accompany me?'

Chiron waved his hand. 'Your wife? No, no. It wouldn't be fitting.'

'Perfect.' Alexanor's bitterness threatened to boil over.

And at the end of the interview, when they were alone in the great *stoa* of the temple's headquarters, Alexanor glanced at Leon.

'Was I too happy?' he asked. 'I have a house. A family!'

Leon put his hand on his friend's shoulder. 'Brother,' he said, 'I think our mentor is trying to tell us that the whole of the Greek world is under threat.'

'I understand that,' Alexanor snapped. 'My utterly unworthy thought is that I've done my service ...'

Leon smiled.

'I'm not even sure how to tell Aspasia,' he said. 'Damn.' He looked over at Leon. 'I'm being difficult. Congratulations, Leon. You fully deserve to run a sanctuary. You'll probably be better at it than I was.'

'It's only temporary.'

Alexanor shook his head. 'No, Chiron wants me to leave Lentas. I suspect ...' He looked out into the evening light. 'Never mind. Now you should consider marriage.'

'Why do you keep harping on about marriage?' Leon asked.

'Because it's so—'

Leon laughed. 'Wonderful? I can hear your baby cry, brother, and you and Aspasia seem to manage a spat a day. No thanks.'

Alexanor shrugged. 'You're wrong. The fights are nothing. The companionship is everything.' He looked at his friend in the failing light. 'If you are to be hierophant, you'd find it useful to have a companion that you trust.'

'Are you matchmaking?'

'Aspasia is,' Alexanor admitted.

'Someone I know?' Leon asked. 'Not Kleopatra!'

'She's incredibly well trained. She's not just a midwife. She's—'

'The perfect recommendation for a wife,' Leon snapped. 'She's a fucking aristocrat, the daughter of Arkadian nobles, she's almost half my age, and I can't stand her laugh.' He snorted. 'And she has flaming red hair.'

'You're right, that clinches it,' Alexanor said. 'By the god, I don't want to tell Aspasia ...'

'She's a tough nut. Although it suddenly occurs to me that she won't be coming with me back to Lentas.'

They stood at the edge of the portico, watching the night fall across the sanctuary.

'I knew when we were summoned that it was all going to change,' Alexanor admitted. 'I brought the children because I suspected I wouldn't be coming back.'

And in his heart, he had imagined riding with Philopoemen.

'You will be at the centre of events,' Leon said. 'Honestly, brother. You like it that way. And Chiron probably intends you to take over Epiduaros.'

Alexanor nodded. 'Think how popular I'll be here.'

'You and me both,' Leon said, and they clasped hands.

And later, they lay on *kline* with wine in the priest's quarters – a small tiled courtyard behind the theatre where man and wife could share a cup of wine without scandal. Leon sat on the other couch, while Kleopatra lay on her stomach, watching a beetle on the tiles below her.

'So I will live ... here?' Aspasia asked.

'Here or Rhodes,' Alexanor said.

Aspasia laughed. 'No contest, love. On Rhodes I won't see you for years. Here I won't see you for months.'

'I'll get back as often as I can.'

'You'd better,' she said.

'You are taking this well,' Alexanor said.

Aspasia lay back and looked at the stars above her.

'Three years ago I was the wretched possession of a man who stole from his friends.' She rolled over and looked into Alexanor's eyes. 'I'm not a delicate flower, love. My life is exciting and worthy. I can handle some separation.' She made a face. 'I worry for the children, a little.

There are so few young people here. It's so quiet, and the children are so loud.'

'Perhaps we should buy a house outside the sanctuary,' Alexanor allowed.

Kleopatra began to laugh. Her laugh was much larger than she was herself – not a feminine giggle but a raucous, full-throated laugh. Leon was leaning over her, laughing just as hard, if more quietly.

'Well, well,' Aspasia said, well satisfied. 'Don't worry so, love. It will all work out.'

'I was happy,' Alexanor said.

'You were beginning to be bored,' Aspasia said. 'Anyway, riding will be good for you. You're running to fat.'

'I am not!'

Aspasia laughed, and the night was young and beautiful.

# CHAPTER ONE

∿

## West of Megalopolis

### 24 THARGELION, 210 BCE

'Sometimes I forget how rich he is,' Alexanor muttered.

He glanced at the slave his wife had purchased, a Persian boy of fifteen years who said nothing and flinched when anyone moved too quickly.

Philopoemen's magnificent farms now had two enormous stone barns and a fish pond, and his stone-built fortified house was complete, stuccoed and beautifully finished, a jewel set on the green hillside. There was an arcaded porch, with a red tile roof, so big that it was better than the *stoa* in many small towns.

Alexanor's thighs burned; he was, as his wife claimed, sadly out of shape. He missed her, and he missed Leon. His acolyte and servant, Kritias, was too young and too arrogant to be a good companion.

But he made himself sit up and move with his horse, sparing a thought for the magnificent beast who'd died in the campaigns on Crete. His current mount represented everything that the priests at Epidauros thought about horses: old, calm and boring. But as he moved with his animal, the horse's gait improved, and the two of them were moving together as they entered the white marble gate of Philopoemen's estate.

They were expected. Four young men were holding the gates open, and Philopoemen himself, dressed as a priest of Zeus, stood on the stone steps of his entry hall, with Dinaeos and Kleostratos on either side of him and another man Alexanor didn't know. Dineaos was dressed in fine wools, a buff-coloured *himation* with a very expensive ruby-red border worked in silk; Kleostratos wore a magnificent *himation* of imported Indian work, covered in dense embroidery in twenty colours. The slightly garish garment went with the whorls of tattoos that ran up his arms to his neck. He was Thracian, even when he dressed in the most expensive, aristocratic clothes.

Alexanor dismounted and the new slave slipped from his mule to take Alexanor's reins. In his hurry to perform his service well, he tripped Kritias, who fell in the dust of the yard. The young novice leapt to his feet and his hand shot out; the blow was not light, and it staggered the slave.

'Watch where you're going,' he said casually, as he dusted himself off.

Alexanor noted it all, but he was not going to spoil his best friend's welcome invocation. He went up the steps, and Philopoemen nodded, and two young Thracians brought a ram from a shed, and Kaeso, the Roman slave, brought the animal to the altar set into the steps.

They sang an invocation to the gods, all together, and Alexanor joined in as soon as he caught the tune; then they sang a hymn to Zeus, all together, and Philopoemen sacrificed the ram, the sharp knife cutting the animal's throat effortlessly, the blood pouring into a bowl held by Kaeso. Then, as the animal slumped, the two Thracians lowered the dying ram onto the altar, as neatly as temple attendants at Epidauros.

And then, the ceremony over, the men embraced.

'It has only been a few months and it seems like years,' Philopoemen said. 'I know it is unmannerly of me, but what are you doing here?' He was grinning from ear to ear. 'Not that I'm sorry to see you.'

'He's bored out of his skull,' Kleostratos said.

'We were afraid he'd start building another barn,' Dinaeos said.

'Or maybe just raise an army and attack Sparta.' This from the stranger.

'Not funny,' Philopoemen snapped.

'See?' Dinaeos shrugged.

'Come inside,' Philopoemen said. Remembering his manners, he introduced the shorter man. 'Simmias of Megalopolis.'

Simmias bowed. 'I rode with Philopoemen in the war with Cleomenes. My brother and I are hoping—'

'To make war on Sparta!' Dinaeos shook his head. 'Revenge. So Greek.'

Simmias frowned.

Philopoemen raised his hands like a priest, or a man about to speak in the assembly.

'Gentlemen! Let us go inside!' He smiled at them. 'Where, if we grow snappish with one another, at least it won't be in front of the troops.'

'Troops?' Alexanor asked.

Kleostratos made a face. 'All of his household are organised and trained as cavalry,' he said. 'We drill every day.'

Alexanor shook his head. 'Do you ever just ... sit and drink?'

'Guess.' Kleostratos said. 'Before we had word you were coming, we were packing to visit his farms in Attica and Lesvos. An inspection tour.'

They climbed the steps and entered the foyer – a tiled entry hall with a mosaic floor that was cool and yet light and airy after the sun-drenched heat of the courtyard.

'No one is snappish,' Dinaeos said. 'Except you.' He nodded at Philopoemen. 'I'm married, by the way. I expect it was all the domestic felicity I saw on Crete that did it.'

'He means you,' Philopoemen said.

Kleostratos shook his head. 'I'm sure he only did it to save money.'

Dinaeos wrinkled his brow. 'I can't see how. She's only sixteen. She knows nothing of running a household, and so far mostly she spends money instead of ...' Slowly, his face flushed from the roots of his red hair to the neck fold of his *himation*. 'You bastard,' he hissed.

Simmias, who until that moment had seemed very dour, burst into laughter. Aside, to Alexanor, as if they were old friends, he said, 'Teasing Dinaeos was the chief obsession of our whole school when we were boys. I'm happy to see the grand tradition lives on.'

Alexanor decided he might have to like Simmias, even if he wanted revenge, a concept that Alexanor thought empty of *arete*.

Philopoemen laughed with the others. 'And this is my "tiled room",' he said.

A massive embroidery frame sat against the wall; on it was a piece of woven wool as tall as a man, the wool so fine as to be almost transparent, in a milky white, with very narrow black borders. The floor was done in mosaic, and a magnificent mosaic: men hunting stags and lions. And there, on one side, was a woman mounted on a horse and carrying a spear – Phila herself.

Alexanor felt his heart give a lurch.

'Is Phila here?' he asked.

Phila, the most famous courtesan in Athens – once Alexanor's lover, and then Philopoemen's. Alexanor was married to the love of his life, but Phila was still palpable to him; he could feel her slight figure in his arms, smell her hair . . .

'No,' Dinaeos said. 'If she was here, would Philopoemen be planning to visit his foreign farms?'

'With a side trip to Athens?' Kleostratos asked. 'I assumed the whole bloody trip was just an excuse for us to visit her.'

Philopoemen winced. He raised his hands, as if to say 'You see what I put up with?'

Simmias smiled. He nodded to Alexanor.

'Of course, teasing Philopoemen was always fairly entertaining, if you could penetrate all that perfection.'

'I see that you are richer than Croesus and surrounded by friends,' Alexanor said. 'But she was here?'

'She's come twice.' Kaeso handed Alexanor a cup of wine. 'Welcome, sir.'

'I freed him,' Philopoemen said. 'It's ridiculous having a gentleman as a slave. Actually, the whole of slavery is ridiculous. You can't *own* a person.'

'Yes, you can,' Dinaeos said. 'I own more than a hundred of them. So do you. You only think of Kaeso differently because he's a cavalryman like us.'

Kleostratos crossed his arms. 'Philopoemen is joining Phila's anti-slavery campaign.'

'By my lord Apollo!' Alexanor said, with more dismay than he'd intended. 'Philopoemen! They already fear you as a radical—'

'And now they'll fear me more,' Philopoemen said. 'Honestly, friends, there is no chance whatsoever that I'll get a political career here. So who cares if I turn against slavery?'

'What of your own slaves?' Alexanor asked.

The wine was excellent. His heart was slowing from its encounter with Phila, but he kept glancing at her embroidery as if she might step from it.

'I plan to free them, a few at a time, and make them into paid retainers,' Philopoemen said. 'I'll see to it that their children are citizens of the League.'

Dinaeos shrugged. 'As long as you don't expect me to follow you in this. I sank almost every drachma we made on Crete, loot and all, into my farms here. The slaves alone cost me half my winnings.'

'The silver you made taking other men's cattle?' Philopoemen asked with an easy smile.

'I earned it!' Dinaeos spat. 'Damn, why does he always make me feel like I'm wrong?'

'Aren't you glad to be back?' Kleostratos asked.

'Like I never left,' Alexanor said.

'But why are you here?' Philopoemen asked.

Alexanor smiled. 'By the way, this is my new novice, Kritias. His father is Cronan of Corinth.'

Philopoemen offered his hand.

'Would you really free the slaves?' Kritias asked. 'They can't be citizens – they can't *do* anything. They're not like us!'

'Are they not?' Philopoemen asked. 'How did you get here, young man?'

'On horseback, from Epidauros.' Kritias managed to sound aggressive and sulky at the same time.

'And if a Spartan took you on the road and sold you to Rome, or Aegypt, or Carthage?' Philopoemen said. 'Are you then rendered unfit for citizenship by having been a slave?'

'We have guards,' Kritias said, as if the mere fact of having bodyguards made slavery impossible. 'And anyway, my father would ransom me.'

Kleostratos smiled. 'It is possible that someone might pay to be rid of you.'

Simmias laughed aloud. 'I, too, have a son,' he muttered.

Kritias frowned. He looked at Philopoemen. There was a brief silence.

'Won't you reprimand this ... *Thracian*?' he asked.

Philopoemen nodded. 'No.'

'I'll excuse myself, then.'

The young novice looked like he'd smelt something foul, and he left the room.

'Where did you find *him*?' Dinaeos said.

'Chiron assigned him to me,' Alexanor said. 'He's part of a group that have been making trouble at the temple. Aristocrats. Hereditary priests.'

'Everyone is a hereditary priest,' Dinaeos said.

'Everyone rich and well born, you mean,' Kleostratos said. 'Alexanor, where's Leon? He wouldn't put up with that entitled brat for a moment.'

'Leon has his own temple now.'

'Where?' Philopoemen said, his eye suddenly kindling.

'Lentas,' Alexanor said.

'Your Lentas?' Philopoemen asked.

'It was never mine. It is the god's. I have been called to Epidauros.'

Philopoemen raised an eyebrow.

'Fine,' Alexanor said, throwing himself onto a low couch, a *kline*. 'Fine. I'm annoyed, to say the least. My wife is in a strange house in the port of Epidauros with two children and Chiron didn't give her a thought, although she trained for a year to be a priestess of Hygeia.'

'That's terrible!' Dinaeos said. 'You built that place from nothing!'

'So did Leon,' Alexanor admitted. 'And life is like being a soldier. You obey, yes?'

Philopoemen glanced at Dinaeos, who grinned.

'Not always,' Dinaeos said.

'Yes, we do,' Philopoemen said. 'We do what we're told, and when Philip of Macedon passes us over for some incompetent, we sit on our farms and say nothing.'

'You mean he recalled you for nothing?' Alexanor said. 'I confess, I was hoping for your influence when I approached the *Synodos*.'

'Perhaps if I were to propose that you be refused admission, it would help you be admitted,' Philopoemen said. 'I'm told that my very success on Crete is an offence to the party in power. Remember Demodokos?'

'No,' Alexanor said.

'The perfect revenge. He was *Hipparchos* when you ... *arranged* that I be sent to Crete.' Philopoemen smiled slightly.

'Fat? Given to snide remarks?'

'The very man. He is now the head of Aratos' party. The Macedon party. The oligarchs. He is telling people that I weakened the League by going to Crete and that I'm a mere mercenary. He'll be the next *Strategos*.'

'I've heard a theory that Macedon recalled Philopoemen here to get him out of Crete before they made him king,' Dinaeos said.

'As if I would ever accept being a king,' Philopoemen said.

Simmias looked meaningfully at his wine.

'As if Philip of Macedon would believe that anyone, anywhere, was less ambitious than he is himself,' Alexanor said.

'Well put,' Philopoemen agreed. 'So you are going to the *Synodos* of the Achaean League on behalf of Epidauros?'

'Yes,' Alexanor agreed. 'Since the sack of Aegina—'

'Absolutely,' Philopoemen said. 'We are at war with Rome. All the useless clods in Aratos' old party seem to miss this one salient fact. By being clients of the Macedonians, we are enemies of Rome. When the Romans signed a treaty with the Aetolians last autumn ...' He shrugged. 'Our lease was up, so to speak. Macedon is a tough nut to crack, even with the Roman fleet combined with the Pergamene fleet. But we're right here. Elis is a day's sail from Italy. The Aetolians can raid across the Gulf of Corinth and be home for dinner with their wives.'

'Or our wives,' Kleostratos muttered.

Two house servants came in with stacks of barley rolls and more wine. Philopoemen began building a map with bits of barley roll.

'Here's Aegina, now a Roman fleet base. Maybe sixty stades from Epidauros.'

'Less than a day's sail,' Dinaeos put in.

'And so we have Romans to the east and west, Spartans to the south and Aetolians to the north. Combine that with no cavalry, no infantry, and no fleet ...' Philopoemen smiled grimly. 'Philip is sacrificing us. And we're not even going to defend ourselves. It's pitiful – the self-serving crap, the aristocrats who won't serve or pay their taxes. Greed triumphs over everything, and the magnates seem to believe that, worst case, they can be rich under the Romans.'

Alexanor shook his head. 'It can't be that bad.'

'The Romans sacked Aegina to provoke us to surrender,' Philopoemen said.

'And the fat fucks in the *Synodos* aren't even smart enough to sur-render,' Dinaeos said. 'My wife hates it when I swear, so I save it up for here. Speaking of which, I should get home.'

'So early in the day?' Kleostratos said. 'What can you possibly need to be home for, at this hour?'

Dinaeos turned to Alexanor. 'I appeal to you, brother. When you wed, did we stand around making salacious jokes?'

'Yes,' Alexanor said. 'You especially.'

Dinaeos paused. 'Did I?'

'Weren't you the one under my marriage bed playing a flute until we poured wine on you?'

Dinaeos feigned surprise, and then bent over laughing. 'You didn't know we were there!'

'I think that might be considered obvious.'

Alexanor was remembering Aspasia's laughter at discovering that there were two drunken wedding guests under their marriage bed. Her reaction – laughter, not rage or shame – was one of many things he loved about her.

Himself, he'd wanted to kill them both – Dinaeos and Lykortas too. Drunken fools.

'Let me get this right,' Alexanor said, turning back to Philopoemen. 'The League cannot protect Epidauros?'

'I doubt the League can protect our farms,' Simmias said.

Alexanor swore, and then sat back. 'It can't be this bad,' he repeated.

Philopoemen stood up and put an arm around Alexanor. 'It's that bad. If Sparta doesn't attack us this summer, I'm a Syrian horse trader. They won't attack until they're sure of their allies. Sparta is too weak to take us by themselves, which tells you how pitiful they really are.'

'Brother, I need to know … are you just mouthing off? Is this bitterness? Or simple fact?'

'I won't pretend I'm not bitter, as I was promised the command. But it would have been a near-impossible task – we're surrounded, and we haven't men, nor arms, nor will to fight. When I say that Philip is sacrificing us, I mean it, exactly the way a desperate general will allow an enemy to loot his camp to get the enemy drunk and laden with plunder. And we're to blame! As it is, the oligarchs will elect one of the servants of Master Macedon, and Rome will kill us, and the Spartans and Aetolians will feast on the corpse of our freedom.'

Alexanor hung his head.

'More wine?' Philopoemen asked gently. 'Remember Cercidas?'

'The man who commanded your phalanx at Sellasia? Of course. He hates you too.'

'He hates the oligarchs more. He writes poetry … You know he's a follower of Diogenes. A Cynic.'

Alexanor had forgotten what a whirlwind Philopoemen could be.

'I know nothing,' he said.

'You need to know all this if you are going to face the *Synodos*. He and Kykliadas are the leaders of the anti-Macedon party. Except that they're not *against* Macedon. They're against the corruption of the oligarchs, the rampant enslaving of our free farmers … He wrote a very nice piece against Xenon, and another against Conan of Corinth who he calls a "greedy cormorant gulping our wealth", and some other good bits. The problem is that they want to *cut* the military budget to pay for other reforms. I've talked to Cercidas – I like his ideas. We're not exactly friends, but … he's now the best hope.'

'Gods!'

Alexanor didn't often blaspheme, but the image of Cercidas, the worst *strategos* Alexanor had ever seen, as the best hope of the Achaean League …

'See why I freed young Kaeso?' Philopoemen said. 'I'm hoping he'll put in a good word when the Romans march up to the door.'

'Worst master ever,' Kaeso said. 'Burn everything.'

There was a little silence.

Philopoemen got up and left the room.

'The Spartans burned everything here,' Alexanor said quietly. 'Murdered his wife and all of his children.'

Kaeso turned as red as Dinaeos had. 'Damn it! I'm an arse,' he said in his Latin accent. He looked around. 'You all make these harsh jokes …'

Dinaeos clapped a hand on the young Roman's shoulder. 'Philopoemen is not so tender as he used to be, laddie. Don't worry. He'll probably just beat you for a few days.'

Indeed, the former *Hipparchos* of Crete returned with another tray of wine cups and more wine in an antique *krater*.

'If I'm going to liberate my slaves, I'll have to learn to serve my guests,' he said.

'Maybe it'll be like a campfire in an army camp,' Dinaeos said.

'I always assumed that the *andron*, with the couches, was supposed to be like a feast in the Trojan War.' Alexanor looked around.

Simmias glanced at him. 'I never thought that,' he said. 'I like it.'

'The things you think about,' Dinaeos said. 'I'm for home. Don't get up to any trouble, and for the sake of all the gods, don't let Philopoemen involve you in some sort of plan to save Greece. My hope is that we get the assembly in Megalopolis to vote us enough money to raise a squadron of cavalry. That's the Megalopolitan assembly! Screw the League. It's dead. We'll save our own farms, at least from the Aetolians and Spartans.' He kissed Alexanor on the cheek. 'Don't despair. We'll get through this. Think of what we accomplished on Crete.'

'There speaks a man with a young, pretty wife waiting at home,' Philopoemen said.

'She's pretty?' Dinaeos looked surprised. 'I hadn't noticed. She's good at embroidery, that's all I know.' He smiled and reached for his cloak.

'Drill in two hours,' Philopoemen said.

'Maybe.' Dinaeos grinned and went out.

'Do I drill too?' Alexanor asked.

'It wouldn't hurt you,' Philopoemen said. 'You should run with me in the morning.'

'Ouch.'

Philopoemen shrugged and looked away. 'Kaeso will show you to your rooms,' he said. 'My house is yours. I'm sorry to be the bearer of so much bad news.'

Alexanor rose and put a hand on his friend's shoulder.

'You are drinking too much,' he said.

'I have all sorts of good reasons,' Philopoemen said, with more of a whine than Alexanor had ever heard from him.

'I'll run with you in the morning if you'll put that wine cup away.'

'If you knew ...' Philopoemen said, but he put the wine cup down.

'If you only knew what a drunkard's liver looks like compared to a healthy liver,' Alexanor replied.

'Ouch, as my friend Alexanor likes to say,' Philopoemen drawled.

Alexanor went out after clasping hands with Simmias. He resisted the temptation to pause and look back to see if Philopoemen was drinking the rest of the wine.

Kaeso led the way from the front of the house to the tiled court in the middle of the four arcades that defined the main house. It was cool under the arches.

'If you are free,' Alexanor asked, 'why not go home?'

'I will,' Kaeso said. 'I'm waiting to see if those of us who were captured are to be punished. My father warned me of some such. And I like it here. I tell myself that I'm learning to be a better cavalry officer. Here's your rooms, sir.'

'Thanks, Kaeso. Congratulations on your freedom. Would Rome really punish you for surrendering?'

'Oh, yes. We're very good at that sort of display of piety. Usually we punish foot soldiers. I'm from a knightly family – unlikely that they'll punish me.' Kaeso smiled bitterly. 'A year in this house, and I'm going to be as much of a radical as *he* is.'

He bowed and went out, leaving Alexanor to his rooms. He had three rooms, and there was a bathhouse; he asked the Persian boy to prepare him a bath.

When the boy was gone, he turned to his acolyte, who was reading a scroll.

'What is my slave's name?' he asked mildly.

'No idea,' the young man said from his couch.

'Best learn it,' Alexanor said. 'He's Dariush. He is a human being with feelings. If you hit him again, I will hit you just as hard.'

The young man looked up. 'You must be joking, and your joke is in poor taste. You cannot hit me.'

Alexanor smiled, the Stoic in him rising to prevent the instant action.

'In fact, I can hit you. As I'm a trained *pankrationist* and former Rhodian Marine, I suspect I can kill you. I doubt you could do much to stop me.'

'My father ...'

Alexanor smiled pleasantly. 'Your father would never even know.'

'For a fucking slave?' the young man said. 'Are you insane? All that mucking about inside men's intestines has made you—'

Alexanor shrugged. 'Very well, I've tried to be mild. Let me be direct. Modify your behaviour or be punished. Treat the slave – all slaves – with the consideration you would treat any other person.'

'Or you'll kill me? I think you are insane. Slaves are just property. They cost money and can be replaced.'

Alexanor wondered why he had been assigned this particular novice. Or rather, he knew that the young man had been one of the ringleaders of a near revolt, but he wondered why it was his own fate to deal with so much ignorance and will.

He kept his face impassive. 'It matters little to me what you think. You should want to treat everyone well – as a matter of leading an excellent life. I mean, since you are reading Aristotle, there.'

He pointed at the scroll that the young man held, somewhat defensively, in both hands, as if Aristotle would protect him. The young man glared at him.

'Bath is ready, master,' said the Persian boy from the doorway.

'Thanks, Dariush. Go and get fed, now.'

'Yes, master.' The boy bowed and vanished into the garden.

'And what if I want something?' Kritias asked.

'You would need your own slave for that,' Alexanor said. 'It happens that Dariush is my slave, not yours. If you only place value on property, as you implied, then you should respect my property. I don't let you wear my shoes or ride my horse – why would I let you beat my slave?'

The young man smiled. 'Take me to court, then,' he said. 'I do what I want. And my father ensures that whatever you try, you lose.'

Alexanor knew when an adolescent was talking to hear himself talk. He nodded.

'I believe you've heard me. Let me be clear, Kritias. If you misuse my slave, there will be consequences.'

'So you say,' Kritias said.


That afternoon, Alexanor rode with Philopoemen's cavalry troop, despite his travel-worn muscles and his layer of middle-age fat. He rode in the rear ranks, and met Simmias' brother Polyainos, who seemed to him the very epitome of a Peloponnesian gentleman: he could ride, hunt and wrestle, and had no further thoughts in his head.

That evening he wrestled with Kaeso and with Kleostratos in the beautiful *palaestra*, and fought with wooden swords and cloaks, until he could barely hold himself upright. The next morning, cursing, Alexanor rose before dawn and ran with Philopoemen. Kaeso was there, too, and a dozen other young men: farmers' sons; retainers he'd seen in the cavalry drill; Polyainos but not Simmias; and Dinaeos, naked and heavily muscled.

'Kleostratos doesn't run?' Alexanor asked.

Dinaeos laughed. 'He's a Thracian,' he said. 'He'd rather die.'

They ran forever, or so it seemed to Alexanor. Most of them ran barefoot; Alexanor had to wear sandals.

But in the end, he felt wonderful, the elation of spirit that inevitably follows heavy exercise. He lay on a stone table in the arcade off the *palaestra* and a tall woman massaged his weary muscles while a heavyset man massaged Philopoemen and Kleostratos drank wine.

He poured a cup for Philopoemen, but he raised a hand and turned it away.

'I have a new bargain with my physician,' he said with a smile. 'I don't want to turn into a Thracian.'

Alexanor was polite to Kritias; he asked him to run, and to come to the other exercises.

'If I'd wanted to be some sort of *athlete*, I'd have stayed home and paid my own trainers,' the boy said.

Alexanor went through his own bags and found two books, in eight scrolls – books from Alexandria.

'You should read these,' he said.

'Bah. I'm not some sort of *techne*. You know, what's wrong with your kind is that you want us to become craftsmen, like leather-workers. We're not. We are priests – god-born. We are *born* knowing what we need to know to teach lesser men. The proper study of mankind is man. Man is the measure of all things.'

'Really?' Alexanor asked. 'Make that up yourself?' He smiled. 'And if man *is* the measure of all things, perhaps you should learn something about men. Herophilus might teach you a few things. The other text is Erasistratus—'

'I have Aristotle, thanks,' the young man said, with his nose literally in the air.

'Aristotle was a brilliant man, for certain, but he thought that the heart was the seat of human intelligence, when it's obvious the brain is where we think,' Alexanor said. 'Herophilus proved that.'

Kritias was silent for a moment.

'I'll just leave these here.'

Alexanor dragged his weary frame back to the exercise field.

They had a small dinner with excellent wine, and he collapsed into his bed.

The third day was the worst. It took an effort of will to rise in the morning, and every single muscle in his hips and legs seemed to hurt, and Alexanor had to confront, for the first time, the reality of the ageing of his body. It hurt. It all hurt.

But he made it out to the road, where all the young men were gathered around Philopoemen. Most of them were kind enough to look sympathetic. Polyainos, whom he had taken for an empty-headed country squire, put a hand on his shoulder.

'Don't worry; we'll go slow!'

Philopoemen slapped his back. 'You are feeling it. I understand – this is what I go through every time I take a bad wound. But look.' He pointed out over the valley, to the east, where the sun was rising over the mighty mountains of Arkadia. 'Come, brother. The world is full of beauty, despite our sagging flesh and aching muscles. Let's run to the sun.'

'Sagging flesh, my arse,' Alexanor muttered.

Philopoemen looked like a Titan from myth; a head taller than most men, his muscles appeared to be carved from tanned ivory, and when he ran, nothing sagged.

'I hope we run as short today as we did yesterday,' one of the young men said.

Alexanor thought about that for a few stades and then pushed himself to run beside Philopoemen. He tried not to pant when he talked.

'Did we run short yesterday?' he asked.

Philopoemen nodded. 'Yes. I don't want to break you. We ran about a *parasang*.'

'And today?'

'The same. For a week. And tomorrow you should rest. Indeed, we will all rest. I'm giving a dinner party.'

'A dinner party?'

Alexanor tried not to sound as if his lungs were about to burst out of his chest. He failed, but everything hurt too much for him to worry much about the impression he was making.

'A political party. As usual, you come and awaken me from a stupor. I was surrendering. That was wrong. Instead, we should fight.

When I told you about Kykliadas and Cercidas, I realised that instead of bemoaning their lack of foresight, I should be converting them.'

Alexanor shook his head. 'And so you give a dinner party?'

'For them, and for you. We'll talk politics like gentlemen. Maybe we'll convince them that we need to have an army.'

Alexanor knew that Philopoemen could manipulate men with his charisma, and with rhetoric. But somehow he was surprised to find him giving something as intimate and overtly political as a dinner party.

'Will there be flute girls?' he asked.

Philopoemen laughed and they came to a steep uphill stretch, and for a stade there was no conversation. And then, at the top, the whole of Arkadia seemed to be laid out below them. Alexanor could see the magnificent central agora of Megalopolis, so far below them that it seemed to be a toy.

'I can't imagine that Aspasia approves of flute girls,' Philopoemen said. 'And everything I ever knew about giving one of these parties, I learned from Phila.'

'Of course.' Again Alexanor felt that pang – jealousy, or something like it.

'I wish she was here,' Philopoemen said.

Alexanor looked at the warrior's magnificent physique in the light of the ruddy dawn.

*I don't*, he thought.

Alexanor awoke the next morning feeling better than he had for weeks, and although his muscles were sore, a massage before some stretching made him feel like a younger, fitter man. He and Kaeso went for a walk on the shepherds' trails on the mountain behind them; they visited the shrine to Zeus and prayed there, and then walked along to the taverna at the head of the valley for a cup of wine before walking home. Alexanor learned a great deal about Rome and Romans that day – sometimes very like Greeks, and sometimes utterly alien. He heard about Kaeso's family and friends and his plans to be wed and a hundred other things, and while he listened, he also thought about Greece: about Aspasia and her house; about raising children; about being an ambassador.

'I thought you might be late for dinner,' Philopoemen said when he greeted them on their return. 'Did you have a good walk?'

'Superb,' Alexanor said.

Kaeso smiled.

'He's an excellent guide,' Alexanor said.

'I get lost all the time. Eventually, I learn where I'm going,' Kaeso said.

'Hurry and bathe. Guests will arrive soon.'

Alexanor thought Philopoemen was anxious – a very unusual occurrence.

An hour later, clean, neat and better dressed than he usually managed, Alexanor went back to the *andron*. Philopoemen stood with Dinaeos, and the two of them were sharing a small Boeotian cup of wine.

'Too much damned reform,' Dinaeos said. 'If he stops drinking, we'll have no fun at all.'

'This from a newly married man?' Alexanor asked.

'She asked to come,' Dinaeos said. 'I thought about it. The truth is, I agree with Philopoemen. And Phila. Phila changed my mind about women. She's a better politician than I'll ever be, and men who say that women can't understand politics are ... fucked in the head.'

'Always so well put,' Philopoemen said.

Dinaeos shrugged. 'If you swore more, people would like you better.'

Philopoemen raised an eyebrow. 'Really? Anyway, I wish you had brought her,' he added. 'I've yet to meet her, and gatherings of men can be deadly dull.'

'Shall I send for her?'

In that question, Dinaeos revealed that perhaps there was more to his story than met the eye. Perhaps the young woman had been angry ...

'Absolutely,' Philopoemen said. 'If Phila were here she'd have reminded me. And your acolyte, Kritias?' he asked Alexanor.

'Possibly still reading Aristotle and thinking about how superior he is.'

Philopoemen smiled.

Cercidas was the first to arrive. He rode to the courtyard like a country gentleman, and came up the steps. He made a small sacrifice to the household gods and then gave Philopoemen a long, cool look before taking his hand.

'So,' he said. 'I take it we're going to start again?'

'I'm willing if you are, sir,' Philopoemen said.

Cercidas laughed. 'This man once called me a fool to my face,' he said to Alexanor.

*I was there.*

'But I'm sure he's not the only one,' Cercidas said. 'Never mind. Mayhap I was a fool at that. What are we eating?'

'Bread. A little *opson*.' Philopoemen smiled. 'Maybe a single cup of watered wine.'

'Damn, lad, you read my poetry?' Cercidas asked.

Philopoemen shrugged. 'Our city doesn't produce so many good poets that I'd ignore one, sir.'

'And you ...' Cercidas looked at Alexanor. 'I know you, I think.'

'Alexanor of Kos. I'm a priest of Apollo and Asklepios at Epidauros.'

'You were at the League meeting, back in Aratos' day,' Cercidas said. 'From Kos, you say. My wife went there for healing after our second child.'

'I hope she was well treated.'

'Brilliant. And one of the best elements of your temples, if I may say, is that they treat rich and poor alike. When I think of the way the oligarchs fleece us and pretend that the rich are a different breed from the poor ...'

'All are equal before the god,' Alexanor said, hoping that he didn't sound altogether too pious.

'I wish more men believed that. What brings you here?'

Alexanor smiled. 'Philopoemen is like a brother to me.'

'Gods, it always warms my heart to hear that,' Philopoemen said. 'He's here to talk politics, Cercidas. We all are. Ah, here is Dinaeos, with his wife.'

'A woman!' Cercidas paused. 'Of course, I should have known. Should I have brought my wife?'

'Would all Megalopolis have been scandalised?' Philopoemen asked.

'Perhaps. Damn me, Philopoemen. You are a radical.' The politician smiled.

'Yes,' Philopoemen said simply. 'I am. And thus your ally, if you'll allow me to be.'

Alexanor saw the exchange, and watched Cercidas' face change. The man's face warmed up; he smiled, a real smile, not a political smile.

In one phrase, no more complex than a simple attack with a sword, Philopoemen had won the man over. Alexanor had seen him do the same thing on the *palaestra* – a single, brutal move, and his opponent was down.

*We could cancel the party now*, he thought.

But instead, Dinaeos came up the steps, followed by a small woman in a long veil. She impressed Alexanor immediately; despite her minute stature, her head was up, and she met his eye and the eyes of the others, and greeted each in a firm voice.

'Thank you so much for having me,' she said to Philopoemen.

'*Despoina*, I beg your pardon for so forgetting my own principles that I didn't invite you. I can only claim that we hadn't been introduced.'

She smiled, and her smile was infectious.

'I'm going to be the scandal of the neighbourhood,' she said.

'Let me begin by introducing her.' Dinaeos was grinning. 'My wife is Hediste, daughter of Nikophoros.'

'I know your father,' Cercidas said. 'A good man, Hediste.'

'Call me Alethea,' she said. 'Everyone does.'

'Her mother called her Alethea as a pet name because it is very hard to lie to her,' Dinaeos said. 'It's true, I assure you.'

They all laughed, and Philopoemen took his guests inside and seated them on the *kline* of the *andron*. He put a hand on Alexanor's shoulder.

'Would you attend them while I wait for the last guest?' he asked.

Alexanor was perfectly capable of functioning as the host, and he made sure that wine was poured. Despite being a free man – or perhaps because of it – the Roman, Kaeso, poured perfectly, and then put out the mixing bowl, the sieve, and the wine amphora for Alexanor to mix the next bowl.

'Is it true that you cut up people's bodies?' Cercidas asked.

Alethea gave a little shudder. She was experimenting with lying on a *kline*, the couch for dining. Women usually sat in chairs, but Philopoemen's house didn't have a single chair. Phila always managed to lie with both dignity and a certain allure; Alexanor hadn't given it much thought.

'Within the prescriptions of the laws,' Alexanor said carefully, 'I have been learning anatomy.'

Cercidas nodded. 'We live in interesting times. The assumptions of the past are not going to survive the modern age.'

Alexanor was mixing wine. The amphora, a fine one from Lesvos, had a rich purple wine in it, but there were twigs and bits of sediment and he was straining the pure wine before mixing the water. Motion in the doorway caught his attention and he looked up.

It was his acolyte, Kritias.

'I assume I was invited?' he asked haughtily.

Alexanor nodded. 'Of course. Friends, this is Kritias, son of Cronan, of Corinth.'

Kritias sat down on Alexanor's couch. 'Who is the woman?' he asked. 'An entertainer?'

'My wife,' Dinaeos said.

'Oh. You,' Kritias said, as if Dinaeos had just proved himself beneath contempt.

Alexanor thought to intervene, and then thought again. But the dinner was so important to Philopoemen.

'You are not a friend to women?' Cercidas asked.

'All very well in their place,' Kritias said.

Dinaeos' bride leant forward. 'What would that place be?' she asked breathlessly.

Kritias ignored her. 'I'd like some wine.'

'Your father is Cronan of Corinth?' Cercidas asked. 'The slave dealer?'

'My father is a gentleman. He is not in trade.'

'Nonsense,' Cercidas said. 'He is the largest dealer in slaves in Corinth.'

'You are mistaken,' Kritias said.

Cercidas laughed. 'Boy, people like your father always try to hide behind their gentility. I'm sure he owns the slaves through intermediaries. But I promise you, he's the dealer.' Cercidas nodded. 'One of my inveterate foes in the Assembly. Why are you here?'

'He is my acolyte,' Alexanor said.

'I have been forced to come,' Kritias said. 'I should be with my initiates at the temple, but the senile old man there has some notion of punishing me by sending me into the wilderness—'

'This young man attempted to foment rebellion inside the Temple of Apollo,' Alexanor said, handing a fresh bowl of wine to Dinaeos. 'I'm taking care of him.'

Cercidas laughed. 'I told my wife this evening would be dull. How wrong I was.'

Alethea laughed with him. She glanced at Kritias and her eyes seemed to skewer him. With a drawl that was almost flirtatious, she said, 'And to think that I was worried I was too young and immature to appear in public.'

Her barb hung in the air for a moment. Then, suddenly, Kritias flushed, and Cercidas lay back and roared. Dinaeos laughed, and Alexanor laughed.

Philopoemen came to the door. 'You are having too much fun,' he said severely. 'That kind of laughter is for the fourth or fifth bowl.'

'Excuse me,' Kritias said. 'Your guests are rude and this woman is inexcusable.'

Philopoemen looked at Alexanor.

'For my part, I apologise,' Alexanor said.

'You are apologising for your friends?' Kritias asked.

'No, lad, he's apologising to us for you.' Dinaeos smiled. 'In other company, if you insult a man's wife, you're likely to be killed.'

'Oh, reeeallly?'

'Really,' Philopoemen said in a voice of steel.

Kritias rose from his couch, tossed his head like a young horse, and walked out of the room.

'By all the gods,' Dinaeos said.

Philopoemen whistled. 'Where did you find him?' he asked, and then went back to await his last guest.

Cercidas waved away Alexanor's apologies.

'I know a dozen like him right here in Megalopolis,' he said. 'I'm sorry to say it, but those are common attitudes among the rich. Especially the very young rich. They've never known anything but money and idleness.'

'If the Romans come they'll be taught to dance to different music,' Dinaeos said.

'That's just it,' Cercidas said. 'Many of them imagine that they'll still be rich and powerful under the Romans.'

Dinaeos shook his head. 'Sad.'

Philopoemen reappeared, this time leading a mature man, younger than Cercidas, older than Alexanor, with a neat beard and a long *himation*.

Cercidas rose. 'Kykliadas!' he said.

The two men embraced. Philopoemen introduced the others, and Kykliadas smiled.

'Now I wish I'd brought my wife,' he said. 'I could be so modern.'

'That's what I said,' Cercidas put in.

Wine circulated, and Cercidas asked Alexanor a dozen questions about the temple complex at Epidauros and the practices at Kos and Lentas.

'All this new learning is so important,' he said.

'Not everyone would agree,' Alexanor said. 'My acolyte thinks that we should stay with Aristotle.'

Kykliadas laughed. 'I enjoy his *Ethics*. But a great deal of his work is nonsense.'

'Are you a Cynic like Cercidas?' Alethea asked.

Kykliadas laughed. 'I think I'm more of a Stoic. Indeed, I think I mix and match the philosophies to match situations. After all, I'm a politician.'

They all laughed.

'You read my poetry, *Despoina*?' Cercidas asked in a courtly voice.

'I've read a few of them,' she said. 'It makes a change from Xenophon.'

'I think we're being mocked,' Dinaeos said. 'I warn you, she has a sharp tongue.'

Alexanor was lying next to Philopoemen and he raised an eyebrow.

'Xenophon wrote a book on how to train young wives,' Philopoemen said.

'I thought he was a cavalry officer?' Alexanor asked.

Philopoemen nodded. 'I suppose a man can be a cavalry officer and a husband.'

'I hope that he was a better horse-trainer than he was a woman-trainer,' Alethea quipped. 'Oh dear. I said that out loud. Too much wine.'

'It's all lies,' Dinaeos said. 'There's not a copy in the house.'

'Dinner,' said Kaeso.

A dozen young men carried in a haunch of steaming venison, as well as trays of bread and oil, sweetmeats, small fish fried in olive oil and a dozen other dishes. Each guest had a small table by their side, and the servants cut up the haunch of venison and placed a dish beside a gleaming pyramid of barley rolls and little dishes containing the other *opsons*.

For long minutes, as long as an orator would give a speech timed by the water clock in Athens, there was no conversation, but only the sound of chewing, interspersed with comments like 'delicious', and 'marvellous' and 'Is that coriander?'.

Alexanor was as hungry as three wolves, and he ate his bread and all the meat placed by his table.

'You are eating my venison,' Philopoemen said.

'And very good it is too,' Alexanor said.

'No, I mean you have filched my piece, brother.'

'Damn,' Alexanor admitted. He *was* eating Philopoemen's venison. 'It's all the exercise,' he replied weakly.

Philopoemen laughed, drank a gulp of wine, and rose to prepare more. Kaeso brought him a small silver box, and he added spices to the wine, and the fragrance was like the inside of a temple.

A fine and antique *kylix*, a shallow cup, was brought out.

'This was made in Athens in the time of Pericles,' Philopoemen said. 'As you can see, it depicts Odysseus on his return from his travels.'

'What a precious thing,' Kykliadas said. 'Two hundred years old!'

'And the painting is beautiful,' Cercidas added.

'Not everything old is bad,' Philopoemen said. 'And Pericles knew a thing or two about democracy and aristocracy and the relations between the two.'

'And about women,' Dinaeos said. 'Didn't you tell me he lived with a courtesan and she joined him at parties?'

Alexanor laughed. 'Trust you, Dinaeos, to remember that one fact about Pericles.'

Dinaeos smiled. 'To each his own.'

His wife wriggled, trying to hide her laughter.

Philopoemen cast a mild eye over his dinner party. 'My father preserved this, to remind him of the greatness of Athens, and I brought it out tonight because, in the spirit of Plato and his books, I wanted to talk of great matters after dinner, like the ancient Athenians. I want to speak of the coming *Synodos* – and of the Roman war.'

Cercidas nodded. 'I knew I'd have to pay for dinner.'

Philopoemen filled the beautiful black *krater* and handed it to Cercidas.

'No. I'll let you speak first.'

Cercidas drank a long swallow from the bowl, and passed it to Kykliadas.

'In all honesty, I'm not sure what to say. When I look at you, Philopoemen, I see a man constructed like a Titan. More, I have seen you on a battlefield, riding your warhorse like some demigod of the Golden Age – fearless, your face aflame with passion, while I was afraid to lead my men across the river, afraid to fail, afraid to die. No, listen – nothing but truth tonight.'

He bowed to Alethea where she lay on her couch, propped on one elbow, and she flushed slightly. He shook his head, and then struck a classical orator's pose.

'You are a rich mercenary who craves war to make his fortune. You are a desperate man who seeks war with Sparta to avenge his fallen family. You are a radical who consorts openly with a foreign courtesan and would undermine family values.' He shrugged and smiled ruefully. 'I only say what men will say to you at the *Synodos*. Aratos worked very hard to blacken your reputation, and you made your own, very rich, enemies on Crete. To be honest, I began to like you better when I saw who hated you. Men like Xenon here in Megalopolis and that sprig's father, Cronan, loathe you. You undermined the super-rich and raised up the lesser men, and while I may find reason to love you for that, we live in an age of clay when money, not excellence, determines how men act and vote.'

He spread his arms. 'I'm prepared to like you. But your military reputation is at odds with our intentions, which is to find reasonable men in Sparta and Elis and Aetolia to negotiate us a truce so that we can rebuild our economy. We need to build ships, not for war but for trade. We need to improve our industry – not just at Corinth but in all our ports and towns. We need roads and wells and cisterns, not fortress walls and mercenaries. Much as I would like to be your ally ... I can't see how we can co-operate.'

He sat on his couch.

Kykliadas rose to his feet. 'I am likely to be our party's candidate for Hegemon and *Strategos*.' He smiled at Cercidas. 'I agree with most of what Cercidas says, and yet ...' He looked at Philopoemen. 'For my part, I took for granted that you were Philip of Macedon's man. In fact, Demodokos claimed that Philip would have put you over us as a military satrap, and only Aratos prevented it. Demodokos was Aratos' right-hand man – I had no reason to doubt him. And you went to Crete as a mercenary, or so men say, and that will count heavily against you. On the other hand, despite the objections of my worthy colleague, I see almost no possibility that we can make some sort of truce with the Spartans and the Aetolians. To me that is magical thinking, the sort of imagining that allows idealists to wish away the worst of their practical difficulties.'

Cercidas wriggled.

Kykliadas glanced at him. 'You said it was a night for truth, and I agree. You and I have our disagreements, and this is one. I see war. The Romans have utterly destroyed Aegina. You might agree that not a single real Achaean lived in Aegina and I agree – but set against that, once we accepted Aegina into our League … we owed them the same protection that we owe Megalopolis. And if Sparta were to march tomorrow, my friends, Megalopolis would be exactly as well protected as Aegina. Men of my generation seek a return to the power and prestige that Achaea enjoyed in our youth – when Aratos was in his prime, and seized Corinth, and when we had an independent foreign policy and we were not a tool of Macedon and a foil for Rome and Aegypt. But for all I love you, Cercidas, I see a poor, weak federal state and I wonder, despite some misgivings, if a brilliant soldier isn't exactly what we need to provide the security at home that would be the foundation for all of our other reforms.'

Cercidas looked stunned. But the rules of a symposium were fixed, and he held his peace, and the wine bowl circulated.

Dineaos rose to speak. 'Friends, and from this evening, I will count you two as friends – who knew you were real flesh and blood? I've been gone a long time, and both of you were names, political names, and who gets to really know a politician?' He waited out the laughter. 'And I won't take up time defending Philopoemen. He's a great man – my best friend. But never mind that. I'm a farmer, and sometimes a cavalryman. I am here on behalf of your citizens. You in the political class, whether you affect to hate the very rich or love them, you are not like us. We have to work. We build barns and till fields and press grapes and olives. We don't have fortunes in art or in coin or in ships on the sea. Our fortunes are right here, and when the Spartans or the Romans burn their way down this valley, we will lose everything. So will all the men I grew to manhood with – so will every woman, yes, and every slave. No party, no faction, should ignore us. Philopoemen, for all his riches, is one of us, and we will follow him. We don't have to "militarise" Achaea, but we need a working, professional force to defend our farms. I liked what Kykliadas here said – I might vote for him. Let's be secure, and on that foundation, mayhap we can have all the rest of the reforms that Cercidas dreams of.'

He sat, and his wife looked at him as if she'd seen a new man. Alexanor reached out a hand to him.

'I think that is the longest speech I've ever heard you give,' he said.

'He loves his farm,' Alethea said with a smile. 'And Philopoemen.'

Alexanor took the wine bowl and drank deeply. Odysseus had a wonderful face: thoughtful, a face that had seen many sorrows and acquired wisdom. Alexanor chose to take it as a sign.

'I am a priest of the god Apollo, and of Asklepios the healer, too,' he said. 'While I was born on far-off Kos, I have come to think of Achaea as a second home. The hierophant of my temple sent me to visit you and to attend the *Synodos* on behalf of our temple, and in the hope of rallying some of the other priests and temples of Arkadia and Achaea. The temple at Epidauros is rich – richer than the richest man you have ever heard of. I'm quite sure that Epidauros would consent to some contribution, if there were promises of protection. I will not hide, since we are speaking the truth, that the destruction of the temples of Aegina, just fifty stades away, is a terror to us. We could see the fires when they burned. Perhaps here in Megalopolis, in the centre of the Peloponnese, Aegina seems far away, but I assure you that on the beach of the port of Epidauros, it is very close.'

He looked around. His mention of the riches of the temple had, indeed, struck home with Cercidas.

'And while we're discussing the power of temples,' he said with a smile, 'I too will be honest. I have several times functioned as the ambassador of my order to the king of Macedon. Indeed, I was briefly a physician to Doson. I know Macedon well.' He glanced at Cercidas, to whom this was clearly news. 'I think that perhaps you gentlemen spend too much time thinking of yourselves as the opposition to the party of Aratos and the alliance with Macedon.'

Cercidas frowned, and Philopoemen winced, but Alexanor knew his subject and was sure of his people.

'You will run a slate of candidates at the *Synodos*, all known and probably disliked by Macedon, and you will lose.'

'Ouch,' Philopoemen said.

But Kykliadas was nodding.

'I promise you that Philopoemen would be acceptable to Macedon. I'll go farther. Philopoemen, and the promise that Achaea would attempt to protect itself without help from the king, or with minimal help, would very likely win you the election.'

Cercidas could not restrain himself.

'It might win Philopoemen the election,' he spat. 'It wouldn't help us at all!'

Alexanor had planted the seed. He bowed and handed the beautiful black *krater* to Philopoemen.

'I think that what my friend means,' Philopoemen said, 'is that I'm a famous cavalry officer, and I have, under my hand, at this moment, the best troop of cavalry in Greece. My ideals, and my plans, are broader than mere military plans, and I assure you that they are as radical as my other ideas. But for the moment, I will speak purely of military realities. We are surrounded by a ring of foes – famous enemies! Sparta, Rome, Pergamum, Aetolia! And every one of those four states is more powerful than we are ourselves. We will need every turn of Tyche on our sides, and determination, and action, to make it through this autumn and winter unscathed. But there is a way, a military solution. I will not run as *Strategos*. I will run as *Hipparchos*, the second position, meaning that your candidate for commander will outrank me and you will have control of the government. For my part, I'll reorganise the federal cavalry. We'll levy a contribution on the temples and the very richest class, force men who want to avoid military service in the cavalry to pay for the privilege at the rate of two professional troopers per rich avoider, and I promise you that before winter we'll have a cavalry force to be reckoned with.'

He took a breath, but Kykliadas was sitting up on his couch.

'I hadn't expected such a direct and *practical* symposium,' he said. 'I want to ask questions.'

Cercidas shook his head. 'I'd like to believe in this. Not least because we never thought of taxing the temples. That is well said, Alexanor.'

'Ask what you will.' Philopoemen gave the bowl to Kaeso, who filled it.

'Cavalry,' Kykliadas said. 'My father would say that cavalry doesn't win battles. Flashy, rich boys who ride away when anything goes wrong. How is reforming our cavalry going to help us deal with Sparta or Rome? They have the best infantry in the world.' He smiled, as if sorry to dampen his own enthusiasm.

'Your father is a wise man,' Philopoemen said. 'But the bigger horses of the last generation and the *xyston*, the heavy lance, have given cavalry some power on the battlefield that they lacked even two generations ago. That said, however, if we do this, I will try not to fight any battles. Listen! My sole claim to fame is that I won on Crete. I learned so much there ... I learned that, like Alexanor and his anatomy challenging the assumptions of medicine, we need to challenge our assumptions about war. War does not work the way it did a hundred years ago, or two hundred years ago, but we keep acting as if it does. Listen, my friends. If the Romans land on the coast and march up the valleys towards Megalopolis, they'll burn some farms. But they will only actually hold the ground they stand on. With a strong cavalry force – something they will *not* have – we can cut them off from their ships, kill their foragers, deny them food, perhaps even water, until they retreat to their ships.'

Cercidas shook his head. 'This is war?'

Philopoemen nodded. 'The brain, not the heart, is the centre of the intellect. Aristotle was wrong. Likewise, war is not fought for honour and glory. Nor is it settled by the last state whose citizens are willing to push hard in the phalanx. Rome can lose fifty thousand men in a single battle ... Kaeso here is a survivor of such a disaster. We don't even *have* fifty thousand fighting men. Not if we armed every citizen in Achaea. Look at their war with Carthage! Look at their wars with Pyrrhus! We will not win by fighting battles settled by heralds on open battlefields. We will win by making war in the mountains of Arkadia too difficult for even a rich state to endure. A cavalry force that can operate here, moving rapidly from threat to threat, will be worth five phalanxes.'

'Heavy cavalry?' Cercidas asked.

'For actual combat, yes. I can provide most of that – a few hundred is all we'll need. For the rest, we need expert riders on small, hardy horses.'

'Cattle raiders,' Dinaeos said.

Philopoemen smiled.

'Really?' Kykliadas asked. 'Sorry, what I mean is, will they actually raid cattle? Will the war ... pay for itself?'

Philopoemen laughed. 'You were the one who used the phrase "magical thinking". War is very expensive. I learned that on Crete, too. No, it won't pay for itself, but if we're very lucky, our troopers might make enough in loot that they'll be eager to serve again next year, because I promise you, my friends, this problem is with us for years. Unless we surrender to Rome, in which case, we'll immediately have to face Macedon.'

'A strong, mobile cavalry, raised from the rich and forcing the rich to pay for it,' Alexanor said.

Kykliadas looked at Cercidas. Cercidas wasn't quite nodding. He was staring at the elbow rest of his couch, deep in thought.

Finally he said, 'It helps your argument, Philopoemen, that your friends are likeable men. They love you, and that makes me see you in a new way. I confess that I thought of you as a character from Menander – a mercenary, a blowhard.' He shrugged. 'But I do not trust you. You could still be the satrap of Macedon, and all this a trick to ensure your election to office.'

'Philopoemen refused to be the satrap,' Alexanor said. 'I was there.'

'You went to Crete for him!' Kykliadas said.

'Aratos sent me! The League voted!' Philopoemen protested.

'Again, I was there,' Alexanor said. 'And Cercidas, you were there too. When Aratos promised him the command.'

Cercidas paused.

'In the temple grove of Zeus the Unifier. At Aegio. I believe that Aratos had just been elected to the ivory chair for the thirteenth time.' Philopoemen leant forward. 'Demodokos was there with you and Aratos.'

'Damn it!' Cercidas said. 'I remember, although I had no part in the discussion.' He shook his head. 'So maybe you aren't a tool of the king of Macedon after all.' He smiled, got up, and offered Philopoemen his hand. 'I'm prepared to trust you.'

'I'm prepared to offer my life for Achaea,' Philopoemen said. 'I'll earn your trust.'

Cercidas nodded. 'I fear you, Philopoemen. You have something in you that is more like a Titan than a man. I want men to rule themselves. I don't want Achaea to have a tyrant.'

Kykliadas shook his head. 'I do *not* fear you, Philopoemen. I will be honoured to have you as my *Hipparchos*, if we can gain the election, and I, for my part, will listen to your military advice. I was at Sellasia – I was in the *Epilektoi*, and I crossed the stream to fight the skirmishers. It is my only experience of warfare, except for running away from the Aetolians.'

Cercidas nodded. 'Aratos used the Macedonians to protect us for ten years,' he said. 'Our young men have never seen a war.'

'War is the king and father of all. It makes some men kings, and others slaves,' Philopoemen said, quoting Heraclitus of Ephesus. 'Like it or not, war is coming to us this summer. If you will have me, I will give with both hands. Money? I have it. Are there men who can be bought?'

'Dozens,' Cercidas said. 'Most of them can be bought, but then they don't stay bought. We have always preferred men who believe.'

'We've always lost,' Kykliadas said. 'Philopoemen, I agree. I too have some money. Shall we buy whomever we can?'

Alexanor leant forward. 'Gentlemen, may I make a suggestion? I know that Philopoemen's ideals are ... very modern. And I suspect that Kykliadas is of the same stamp. But with our ... Macedonian connections and with Cercidas' financial policies, can we not appear as defence-minded moderates?'

Kykliadas smiled like a fox, an animal he was said to resemble with his red-brown hair and long face.

'I can, and will, begin a whispering campaign supporting a moderate faction that offers protection to property,' Alexanor said. 'The temples would support such a faction.'

Kykliadas shook his head.

Cercidas said, 'It's all too good to be true. Do you think we could actually defeat Demodokos and win the election?'

'I think we will win.' Philopoemen rose. 'Give me terms and I will swear by them. My only goal is to save what can be saved of the Achaean League, and Greece.'

'No terms,' Cercidas said. 'If you agree that Kykliadas is to be *Strategos* and I am to be Treasurer, then we have the power to unseat you if we must, and that satisfies me. I'd rather say, let us save Achaea and bicker afterwards.'

'I agree,' Kykliadas said. 'Let us let go of our differences until we are free of the Romans and the Spartans.' He smiled. 'For my part, I have no objection to having women at parties.'

Alethea smiled. 'I have said nothing because I am a young woman, and the bowl was not offered to me. But as an outsider, a person who has no vote, and yet who can be raped, murdered, sold as property if your policies go awry, I beg you to succeed. It may be sufficient for some rich man like Cronan of Corinth, behind high walls, to allow Achaea to be sacked, but in the name of women and children, I beg you to stop it.'

She too had risen to her feet, and she was breathing hard: nerves, at speaking so much in front of men – and youth, too. Had she known it, she had never appeared more impressive; beyond beauty, she seemed to embody Achaea.

'For my own part,' she went on, 'I can ride a horse and handle a bow. Scythian women fight. I would do my part.'

Alexanor glanced at Dinaeos, willing him not to make a derisive comment, but the man was gazing at his young wife with unalloyed admiration.

'Damn me,' he said.

'I believe you,' Philopoemen said. 'I suspect that we'd have a revolution if we attempted to arm a squadron of women, but your words are beautiful.'

Then he smiled around at them, and put his hand out, the way a priest would at an altar.

'I swear,' he began.

Kykliadas put his hand atop Philopoemen's. Dinaeos put his hand on theirs, and Cercidas, and Alexanor, and then, after a hesitation, Alethea's small hand rested on his.

'We swear on this wine and the hospitality of this house, before Zeus and Apollo and all the gods, to save the League of the Achaeans, to offer our lives and our fortunes and our sacred honour to save our altars, our farms and our people.'

Alexanor founds that tears were running down his face.

'Perhaps,' he said slowly. 'Perhaps we will die in the attempt. But let the cup be kept safe, so that men in later years will remember us.'

Outside, on the steps a couple of hours later, the moon shone like a white torch in a starlit sky. Kaeso had gone for Cercidas' horse, and the politician stood waiting for a slave to bring his cloak.

'He is more like a demigod than a man,' Cercidas said.

'And at times, he is very human indeed,' Alexanor said. 'When his wife and children died, he learned to close himself.'

'I hear what you say,' Cercidas said. 'But when he proposed that oath, his voice was not human. I fear him. But I believe, tonight, now, under the moon of Artemis, that we have a chance. I will take that home to my wife and cherish a little hope.' He leant over. 'You offered money from the temples. I'm going to inherit a large military budget and an empty treasury. I hope you meant what you said.'

'Every word,' Alexanor said, hoping that the old priest would back him.

'Well, that was the best dinner I've been to in some years,' Cercidas said. When Philopoemen came holding his cloak, the two men embraced. 'Odd, finding a friend where I expected a foe. I almost didn't come. Curiously, it was my wife who made me come.'

'Perhaps we are both different men than we were when Doson was king,' Philopoemen said.

Cercidas gave him a wry smile. 'Maybe. Regardless, thanks for dinner, and thanks for the ration of hope. I'll go home and start counting votes.'

He went down the steps chuckling, mounted his horse, and clucked.

Kykliadas came out next.

'I'm ... amazed,' he said. 'When I came here, I thought to beg you to help us plan a military strategy. I considered offering you money. I beg your pardon, that's the sort of man you've been portrayed as.'

Philopoemen winced. But he embraced the other man.

'We'll win,' he said.

Kykliadas laughed. 'Indeed, I think we will. That's what I'm afraid of. One thing to sit on the benches and complain about the corruption of Aratos and his flunkies. Another thing to govern.'

'Yes,' Philopoemen said.

'You are not afraid?' Kykliadas asked.

'No.'

*He ruled Crete, or close enough. But let them learn that in their time.*

Kykliadas laughed again, embraced Alexanor, Dinaeos and Philopoemen, bowed to Alethea, and rode away into the starlit darkness.

When he was gone, Dinaeos sighed.

Alethea turned. 'That was lovely,' she said. 'But, as I have drunk too much and I'm so bold, I have to ask. Can you do it? Defeat Sparta and Rome?'

Dinaeos put an arm around her waist. 'We took Crete with sixty men,' he said.

'We had a great deal of help,' Alexanor said.

Philopoemen nodded. 'That's it exactly. We can do this. But it will be like farming – to do a job, usually first you have to build a building and make a new tool.' He grinned. 'Yes, we can do this. But we'll need a great deal of help.'

# CHAPTER TWO

—ᴗᴗᴗ—

## Aegio, the *Synodos* of the Achaean League

HOMOLOIOS, (SPRING) 210 BCE

Alexanor waited with three hundred other men for the sacrifices to end and for the formal proceedings of the Assembly of the League to begin. He had not been invited to officiate, which was probably unimportant; most of the representatives didn't know him.

He stood with Lykortas, who, despite years spent in Athens, had been returned for Mantinea, and Aristaenos, who had led the League's federal troops on Crete and was now well launched on his own political career, despite having almost lost them the Battle of Gortyna.

'I always thought Philopoemen would return to Achaean politics,' Aristaenos said.

Lykortas glared at him. Alexanor, more pious, or perhaps just bored with the sheer pettiness of politics, strained to hear the invocation. Euryleon of Sicyon was the outgoing *Strategos*, and as he was also a priest of Zeus, he was the celebrant. With him stood Demodokos, the outgoing *Hipparchos* who was now standing for *Strategos*, or head of the League. Ancient laws forbade any man from serving in the same office two years in a row, although the rule was sometimes waived for the treasurer, who was inevitably someone very rich who ended his term in office much richer.

Euryleon had made hundreds of ritual sacrifices, but he was nervous, or perhaps the gods took a hand; either way, it took him three cuts to kill his ram, and the animal died bleating, a shocking state of affairs. Euryleon himself was covered in blood, as was Demodokos.

Despite that, Euryleon finished the ritual, and then delivered an opening oration, besmottered with the blood of his botched sacrifice. He spoke of the importance of continuity and the sheer complexity of directing a federal state.

After him, Demodokos rose. The brown bloodstains on his white *himation* made him look as if he'd been wounded, and he didn't have a good voice for orations. He began by discussing the empty treasury, and ended with a suggestion that the League needed to appeal to Philip of Macedon immediately for military support. Those listening to his low-voiced and somewhat rambling oration heard him claim that the Tyrant of Sparta, Machanandas, was raising mercenaries. That set the benches to rumbling.

When he was done, he didn't introduce the next speaker, as was customary, but rather stepped off the *bema* as if expecting to be voted in unopposed. Or perhaps he'd only forgotten.

Kykliadas didn't walk to the rostra. He sprang onto it with an energy that the assembly of the Achaeans hadn't seen in twenty years.

'Greetings, Achaeans,' he said.

He had a beautiful voice, and it carried. At least one older man in front of Alexanor woke up.

'My colleague Demodokos,' Kykliadas said, 'offers you another year of the same – low taxes and the protection of Macedon.' He looked out over the Assembly and this morning he was more an eagle than a fox. 'Unfortunately,' he continued, 'this year, nothing will be the same. This year, the Romans have burned Aegina. This year, Philip of Macedon is not conquering Illyria – instead, he is fighting for his kingdom. This year, the treasury is empty, we have no army, and we are ringed by foes – Rome, Sparta, Aetolia, Elis, Pergamum. We're like a sheepfold full of fat, indolent sheep surrounded entirely by wolves. My esteemed opponent claims that the wolves, whom he admits are there, will be kept at bay by his well-known military expertise and some powerful wishful thinking.'

There was a growl, almost a roar. Demodokos had made a serious mistake in admitting that Sparta was arming, and Kykliadas was capitalising on it.

Demodokos was on his feet now, calling out something about his military reputation.

'Demodokos says that he has a military reputation, and I can't help but agree. He's run away from the Aetolians and the Spartans and now hopes to practise the same tactics on the Romans!' Kykliadas laughed, and a great many of the representatives laughed with him. 'I won't hide it from you, friends. I shouldn't mock! I ran too. I was there.'

Silence.

He looked out over them again.

'Listen, friends. The time for vague promises is over. The wolf is at the door – we have nowhere to go, and Macedon won't be coming to save us this winter, not even if one of my rival politicians offers Philip his wife.'

This was a particularly nasty, and juicy, attack; it was common knowledge that Philip of Macedon had seduced Aratos' son's wife while a guest in her house – a shocking impiety.

Into the shocked hush, Kykliadas spoke with force.

'Rome is coming. Sparta is coming. The Aetolians and their Illyrian pirates are coming. You can vote for Demodokos, and watch your farms burn, but by the gods, your taxes will remain low. Or you can vote for us. We have a plan to face Sparta and even, if the gods wish it, the Romans. We have a plan to rebuild the army, and indeed to fund it.'

'How in Hades will you do that?' some backbencher called.

'We'll tax the temples and the richest men,' Kykliadas said. 'They can either serve in the *hippeis*, the cavalry, or they can pay.'

'The temples?' shouted another.

'The temples of Corinth and Epidauros have already promised five *talents* of gold each, if we promise to use it all on the army,' Kykliadas said.

Silence. Men visibly measuring the possibility of a new government. A murmur.

'And we won't hand this new force to Demodokos so that he can run away,' Kykliadas said. 'We're going to raise the strongest cavalry force in Greece, and we'll put it under the best cavalry commander in Greece.' He paused, and let the moment build.

No one spoke.

'Philopoemen of Megalopolis,' he said into the silence.

Close to the front, a man dropped a cloak and stood up. Philopoemen was so tall that even standing under the *bema*, his head was almost as high as Kykliadas.

'Philopoemen is our most famous soldier,' Kykliadas said. 'He has offered to serve for nothing, lest some among you call him a mercenary. He will raise a hundred cavalry from his own people, at no cost to the state.'

There was shouting, and some catcalls, but most of the sound was cheering. More than a few Achaeans called 'Achilles!'

'Gods, they still love him,' Lykortas said, breathing a sigh of relief.

'They're desperate,' Aristaenos said. 'It's like drunkenness. Later, they may wake up sober and remember that they fear him.'

'I thought you were his friend?' Alexanor asked.

'I am. And I'll vote for him and for Kykliadas, but ...'

Whatever else he might have said was drowned by another electoral roar.

'Cercidas swears that come what may, he will end his term as treasurer of the League no richer than he is now, a claim no other League treasurer could make!' Kykliadas waved at Cercidas. 'Gentlemen, we have the ability to form a government of competent men who will prosecute the war as it must be fought. We will do our best to save your farms and your homes, and we will not make you pay for it. Let the rich pay.'

Close to the rostra, a man stood.

'Why should we pay?' he demanded. 'It's our money!'

Kykliadas opened his mouth to speak, but Philopoemen had stepped up to the man. In a voice like thunder, he said, 'Will you serve in the cavalry, sir? You appear wealthy enough.'

The man shook his head. 'I'm not some sort of ... warrior!'

'Then you can pay,' Philopoemen said. 'Because that is the *law*.'

The man, who was none other than Cronan of Corinth, had mistaken his audience. He had few of his peers in the assembly, and most of the men there laughed at his discomfiture.

'Pay! Pay! Pay!' they chanted.

'Beware!' Cronan roared. 'These are levellers, who will try to bring down the best men to be level with the worst! All your property is threatened.'

Kykliadas laughed. 'Why don't we defeat Sparta and Rome,' he said. 'Then we can argue about whether we're social levellers or not.'

'Pay!' shouted the assembly.

'You're all fools!' roared Cronan.

Cercidas pushed through the crowd to stand beside Kykliadas. Philopoemen joined them. He beckoned, and Alexanor wondered if his friend was waving at him, but Aristaenos grew an insufferable smile.

'I'm to be *Navarch*,' he said. 'A small office, but a good start.' He walked forward, grinning.

'What a prick,' Lykortas said. 'Despite which, he brought us twenty-three votes and some assurances. I hope that he stays loyal to Philopoemen.'

'Have we won, then?'

Lykortas smiled. He waved out at the Assembly.

'First ballot,' he said. 'Kykliadas was brilliant, but he needn't have been. Demodokos spoke badly and offered no hint of a plan. And when he admitted that Sparta was arming, he undercut his own position. They've been in power so long they can't imagine ... Anyway, we probably had the votes walking in. People are frightened.'

'Gods,' Alexanor said. 'It's happening.'

'It is,' Lykortas said. 'Like old times. But better, because we're going to repair our own home, instead of helping some foreigners fix theirs. You play this game well, by the way. As if you were born to it.'

'I was. Rhodes is no different – even the parties are the same. So is the Order of Asklepios, really. People. They argue, they make factions, they vote.'

'They also fight and make love. Don't forget that.'

'I'm a physician,' Alexanor said. 'I wouldn't forget.'

'Good, because men don't think rationally. Men think with an odd, elliptical semi-rationality.' He was quiet for a moment; there was applause. 'I think we're going to vote.'

Alexanor nodded.

Euryleon was clearly angry. He let his anger show, and he harangued the Assembly for too long, claiming that Kykliadas was incapable of governing, claiming that Macedon would desert them and that the Romans would destroy them.

'Kykliadas is not acceptable as a candidate to the king of Macedon!'

Kykliadas rose. His voice carried despite the roars.

'I might ask why any candidate for government in Achaea must be acceptable to the king of Macedon!' he called. He waited for a lull in the roar, and then shouted, 'But I am a realist, and I call on the ambassador of the king of Macedon!'

Behind Alexanor, a tall man in a purple-edged cloak pushed through.

'Make way, make way,' he said in a Macedonian accent.

Alexanor didn't know him, but he knew the cloak – an officer of the Royal *Hetaeroi*, the king's companions.

'Kykliadas and his *Hipparchos* Philopoemen are more than acceptable to the king of Macedon,' the officer called.

A stunned silence fell.

'The axe,' Lykortas said quietly. 'Phila's work.'

'Gods!'

'Phila,' Lykortas said. 'Sometimes, she is more powerful than the gods.'

Philopoemen came back through the crowd as the voting began.

'You think we've won,' Alexanor said.

'Yes,' Philopoemen said. 'There's irony that we had to spend our treasure and take risks so that we could *be allowed* to wager our lives and save our country. But we've won.' He embraced Alexanor. 'Now,' he said, 'we work.'

Alexanor had never heard him sound happier.

That night, there was a symposium at Philopoemen's house, a town house with a magnificent courtyard fountain that Alexanor had never seen before.

'You are very rich, brother,' Alexanor commented as he waited for the sacrifice to be brought forward.

Philopoemen smiled. 'I won't be in a year. I'm buying four hundred panoplies of horseman's armour from Macedon. I'll be selling this house, but I thought it would be nice to use it to celebrate victory.'

Cercidas laughed. 'I think we're lucky you are on our side, Philopoemen. You are as rich as Cronan.'

'Richer,' Philopoemen said in his offhand way.

Alexanor winced; sometimes his friend seemed to have no notion of how arrogant he could be, but Cercidas was too happy to notice, or care.

'What do four hundred panoplies cost?' Cercidas asked.

By the gate, Kaeso was struggling to bring a black ram into the courtyard.

'More than five talents of gold,' Philopoemen said. 'In fact, more than ten talents of gold. And we still need a thousand good horses. And another thousand small, tough horses. You're paying for those.'

Cercidas nodded. 'Yes.'

Philopoemen smiled. 'Just one word? Yes? No prevarications, now we're in power?'

Cercidas shook his head. 'No. We're in for the horses. We knew we were. Where are they coming from?'

'My *hyperetes*, Kleostratos, will be leaving for Thrace in two days,' Philopoemen said. 'We'll buy the whole horse market at Byzantium. If he has to, he'll go into the Euxine – even as far as Olbia and Tanais.'

Cercidas shook his head. 'It's hard to believe that an officer of the federal state has to go as far as the Euxine for horses—'

'We don't just need horses,' Alexanor put in. 'We need stock and farmers to raise them, so that ten years from now we have remounts and our own sources.'

Cercidas watched the ram being tied to the altar.

'I wonder if we can turn that to our advantage,' he said pensively.

Then all the guests fell silent as Alexanor sang the invocation. His knife was sure, and the ram slumped away, bleeding out silently over the altar.

Men cheered – the pious ones who'd been concerned by the bad sacrifice earlier in the day.

Kykliadas put a hand on Alexanor's shoulder when he'd finished singing the invocation.

'You are a good priest,' he said. 'I could never handle a sacrifice so well.'

'Practice,' Alexanor said pleasantly.

There was something about Kykliadas – too bright, too cheerful, that made him seem false, or possibly just too good to be true. But Alexanor wanted to like him and wanted him to prove to be everything Philopoemen needed him to be.

Philopoemen had a dozen huge salmon, imported from Athens by a fast ship and run across the Isthmus – the sort of party trick that the very rich used to impress their inferiors, but as Philopoemen had two hundred of the League's representatives in his courtyard, it was more of a public culinary miracle. There was plenty of bread, both barley rolls and good wheat bread, jars of fine oil with a little salt, roast lamb from the sacrifice, fine sauces for dipping the bread, and sweets: almonds in honey, figs and raisins. There was a rich lentil soup and another with rabbit in it.

As men took their share from the loaded tables, Philopoemen stood up on a stool. It took a little time for the guests to fall silent.

'I hope that you are enjoying the food,' he said.

Men cheered, because that's what you did when rich politicians put on a feast for poorer men.

'I hope you enjoy it especially, because we will not eat like this when we are in the field, facing the Aetolians and the Spartans,' he said.

Then he had real silence.

'Friends, I will start training the new federal cavalry of the League tomorrow morning. I will start with the *hippeis*, the cavalry class of Aegio, our hosts in this federal capital.'

The natives of Aegio groaned.

'But in truth, gentlemen, every one of you here meets the property qualification to ride as a cavalryman. So why not rise early tomorrow and join me for a day of training?'

'We're the government!' shouted one man. 'We need to be in the Assembly, voting.'

Philopoemen nodded. 'The *Strategos*, Kykliadas, tells me that if I need a training day, he will put off the Assembly until the day after tomorrow.'

Kykliadas sprang up. 'I usually serve as a hoplite, but in this case, I'll take a training day with our famous master of war.'

Cercidas grimaced, but said the same, and soon the room was shamed into agreement.

Philopoemen grinned. 'Don't drink too much! Now enjoy yourselves.'

The sun was just peering over the rim of the world to the east. Naupaktos was just visible across the Gulf of Corinth, in the direction of the rising sun – the new Roman fleet base.

There were four hundred horsemen on the beach. Most of them

had cloaks and a spear or two. It took Philopoemen, with Lykortas, Dinaeos, and a dozen professionals, almost an hour to line them up in four ranks.

'There they are!' Philopoemen called, and every one of them could hear him. 'If they leave port, you can see them set their sails. If they row, you can usually make out the flash of oars. There are the Romans. From there, they can land almost anywhere on our coastline. In an hour's march, they can come at most of our farms and properties, our temples, our monuments. And behind them, the Aetolians, eager for revenge, and the Spartans, and the men of Elis. And on our other coast, more Romans, and Pergamum. So, let's drill, under the very eye of the enemy.'

Alexanor glanced at Kaeso, who was, after all, Roman. Kaeso sat easily on horseback, swatting flies with a horsetail whip.

'Incredible,' he said. 'It's just like a muster day in Rome. Useless fucks. Send them all home and hire mercenaries, that's my advice.'

Alexanor looked at the young Roman.

'Oh, I'm mocking, but I assure you, the *equites* of Rome and its allies aren't much better.' He shrugged. 'My pater says it's always thus – you take out the whole draft, fight a battle, the most useless die or fall off or run home, and then you train the survivors.' He shrugged. 'Or take their money and horses and hire Tarentines or Numidians.'

Alexanor could barely stand to watch. Every man was wealthy enough to be in the cavalry class, and the very wealth that put them in the cavalry made them fractious, independent and unruly.

Philopoemen had asked Lykortas to ride through the muster, checking each man's equipment. There wasn't a League standard, and Lykortas was a man of some political standing, so the assembled *hippeis* or cavalrymen didn't precisely ignore him, but very early in the process, when he asked a very rich man where his breastplate was, the man raised an eyebrow.

'I'm not required to have a breastplate,' he said. 'Or a helmet. Show me the law.'

Lykortas shrugged. 'Of course, you could die,' he said.

The man shrugged. 'Can we get on with this? I have work to do.'

Most men did, in fact, have helmets, usually very old and polished to perfection – some so polished that Lykortas could push a finger through the bronze. He did this to one old helmet and got a lungful of Achaean invective from the owner for 'ruining a perfectly good helmet'.

'I'll go to the law!' the man insisted.

But for the most part, it was horses that were bad.

'Is this the horse you intend to take to war?' Lykortas asked a particularly rich grain merchant, Nikos of Aegio. 'And do you own a helmet?'

'You don't expect me to ruin a good horse, do you?' Nikos said. 'War kills horses, young man. Your father should have taught you that. You don't wear good clothes to whitewash a house, and you don't ride a good horse to war.' He shrugged. 'Helmets are recommended, but not required. They're expensive. I didn't get where I am today, young man, by spending my money on foolish baubles.'

Lykortas made a note on his wax tablet.

'Thanks, sir,' he said.

Philopoemen rode in among them constantly. He didn't harangue or argue; he merely directed, cajoled, joked. But he and his captains had magnificent horses – big horses, often three hands taller than the horses other men rode. They also had beautiful equipment: good stout bridles, long military cloaks, and Philopoemen had a magnificent helmet with three huge plumes in blue, yellow and white. Dinaeos had a very similar helmet, covered in repoussé, and both of them had elegant breastplates with matching backplates over embroidered *chitons*.

'He dresses better for war than for a party,' Cercidas said.

After another hour of very simple manoeuvres, Lykortas waved at Philopoemen, and he nodded sharply. His dozen professionals rode into the ranks, becoming file leaders of every fourth file, and for the next three hours, Philopoemen led them up and down the beach.

Horses became exhausted.

So did riders. At the end of the second hour, a dozen men, greatly daring, simply rode out of the ranks and dismounted, sitting on rocks on the edge of the beach. As the hours passed, more and more of them dismounted, until Philopoemen was leading only about a hundred and fifty men, mostly the youngest men on the freshest horses. Alexanor was pleased that he had only a little difficulty in keeping up. He rode through the whole exercise, so that by evening, when the hundred or so survivors were capable of manoeuvring in a rhomboid and changing directions at a shouted command, he was in the third rank with Dinaeos. His hips hurt and he knew he'd pay the next day, but he was with the riders to the last.

Philopoemen and his professionals looked as fresh as they had in the dawn. Their fine tunics were still bright; their horses weren't even sweating. Most of the rest, even those who'd dropped out earlier, looked as if they'd already been in a war – sweat-stained, on jaded horses.

But the hundred or so men who'd ridden all day had a little pride in their accomplishment, and Philopoemen addressed them.

'You should be proud. That was a hard day. Twenty more hard days like that and you will be cavalrymen. Then you will have to learn to cook and stay clean and take care of your horses while we move every day.' He looked them over. 'This isn't going to be easy. Young men think war is about fighting. The truth is that almost anyone can fight. War is about being well slept and well fed on the day when you have to fight. War on horseback is about being well fed and well slept on the back of a rested, trained, well-fed horse. But by the gods, friends, if you came through today on your mount, I know you can do this.'

He smiled and saluted the men sitting along the beach on their rocks. Dozens had gone home; more of them had waited.

Philopoemen didn't stop to talk to them. He waved, and rode off the beach.

The next morning, the Assembly met – the full *Synodos* of the Achaean League. There were a great many sore muscles, and some groaning, but on balance, the Assembly was cheerful. They buckled down to the legislation that the situation required: a dozen votes on taxes and expenditures; a vote of thanks to the temples who volunteered a contribution; a set of increasingly severe penalties for men who chose to avoid military service.

They also voted to send a delegation to the Romans, and another to the Spartans, offering to mediate a peace.

It was an agreeable morning, and the slaves bustled about, serving a light lunch, and the men chosen for the *Synodos* congratulated themselves on a job well done.

After lunch, Philopoemen rose, walked to the *bema*, and addressed the *Synodos*.

'Well, friends, I learned almost as much as many of you learned, yesterday,' he said, and they laughed. 'I have certainly trained citizens before this. Perhaps I had forgotten exactly what it was like, or perhaps our Achaeans are a trifle ... more difficult than Cretans.' He was smiling broadly. 'Regardless, I will ask you to pass a few of my notions into law to help me as I train the new federal cavalry.'

Men nodded agreeably.

'First, I would like a law legislating a set of minimum equipment that is acceptable in the federal cavalry. Second, a law concerning the inspection and valuation of horses and the appointment of inspectors, with a "rider" about those who raise and farm horses, and the rewards they can expect from the state in exchange for breeding horses for war. Third, a regulation for the duration of training days and the penalties for failing to attend, or for dropping out of the training before the *Hipparchos* or his appointed officers so direct. And last, a law allowing the *Strategos* and his *Hipparchos* to appoint officers to command the federal troops.'

The Assembly sat in stunned silence.

'What I learned yesterday is that there will be an element of compulsion to service,' he said. 'I learned that you, the leaders of the state, were capable of arguing against your own best interests. Gentlemen, when the Aetolians come, when the Spartans come, when the Romans come, I promise you, we have to have the *best* cavalry, or all this is for nothing.

'Finally, I am *asking* you for these acts, rather than simply ordering them. The federal officers need to have the backing of the Assembly, not its hostility, or really there's no point. You might as well have elected Demodokos and hope that the gods ordain that the Romans be destroyed by a miracle.'

Kykliadas was shaking his head; he had clearly not approved Philopoemen's speech. But he rose and spoke in defence of the new laws. Cronan of Corinth spoke against them, which was helpful ... to Philopoemen.

The acts were carried. Alexanor could see that a great many men voted for them because they were ashamed to be seen to vote against them. He wondered if this had been the purpose of Philopoemen's drill day for the Assembly all along.

But the Achaeans were better than the sum of their complaints. Nikos, the richest man in Aegio, came up to Lykortas when he was sharing a sausage with Alexanor.

'I reckon I'll have to buy a new helmet.' He grinned. 'No hard feelings, lad?'

'None, sir.' Lykortas smiled after the older man, and then looked back at Alexanor. 'Just when I'm ready to be overwhelmed by cynicism, men like that ruin it for me.'

The next afternoon, Lykortas, Dinaeos, Simmias and six more of Philopoemen's friends were appointed League officers.

'Here we go,' Lykortas said. 'He has a plan, and now I think he may pull it off.'

'How's that?' Alexanor asked.

He was gathering up his belongings preparatory to returning to Epidauros, where he would have to sell the temple hierarchy on the donation of five gold talents.

'He's dividing the whole League into military districts and appointing officers and inspectors for each,' Lykortas said. 'He's going to visit every district and train fifty men – the picked men of the district – and they are to train the rest. And then we'll inspect them, and he'll come back again, and again, working on whatever they need.' He shook his head. 'This winter is going to be harder than the labours of Herakles.'

# CHAPTER THREE

—✤—

## The Achaean League

### WINTER, 210 TO 209 BCE

The autumn began well for Alexanor. Chiron felt that he had done well in helping Kykliadas win his election; Leon had taken the trouble-makers east to Lentas, and Kritias, left to himself, couldn't do much more than mope and complain.

In fact, Alexanor knew that the young man could have left him in Aegio. His father had been there, vocally; yet Kritias hadn't run to his father. Alexanor suspected that the rich, well-born youth had reported certain conversations to his father; but for whatever reason, he'd stayed with Alexanor and the temple.

Aspasia had a fine house with a new innovation – a rooftop garden with a tile roof. Even in late autumn, the climate of Epidauros was sufficiently mild that a man and woman could sit on a rooftop garden in perfect privacy, discussing the events of the world.

'It's much nicer than living at the temple, love,' Aspasia admitted. 'And Chiron thinks he's so modern, but he can't imagine that I want employment, and keeps encouraging me to have more children. I suspect he can't see much use for women beyond that.'

'I fear you are right, my dear. Despite which, he's the best leader for the temple that I can imagine.'

She shrugged. 'Oh, of course. It's just infuriating to have spent so much time in study, and then to be ignored!' She frowned. 'He turned down my request to study in the library. He said that I would be "too distracting".'

'I'll see if he can be convinced,' Alexanor said.

'At the same time, it is pleasant to be here with the children, to watch my garden and oversee the food and listen to the gossip of the agora. Which reminds me – do you know that Philopoemen is coming here?'

Alexanor sat up. 'What?' he asked.

'I think he intends to surprise the local gentry,' she said, smiling. 'But in truth, someone has leaked his itinerary, and the locals all know he's coming. Anyway, he's to be here in a week. Shall we invite him to stay?'

Alexanor nodded. 'He may own a house here, for all I know.'

The day before Philopoemen arrived, Alexanor had an ugly incident. He'd been watching Kritias carefully; most of the boy's friends had been sent with Leon to Lentas, but a few remained, and Alexanor didn't want a renewal of their plotting.

He wasn't exactly spying on Kritias, but he made it his business to pass the young novice at least twice a day, to know where he was working, or, as was more usual, not working.

He was on his way to his own afternoon bread and olive oil when he heard the sound of sobbing. Entering the herb garden, he found Dariush on one knee. Kritias was nursing his right fist; he'd obviously just punched the slave in the gut.

'When I ask you to tell me something, I expect—' he was saying, and then he saw Alexanor. His face changed.

Alexanor ignored any remorse the boy was feeling.

'You were warned,' he said.

He hit Kritias in the side of the head, with his fist. The novice fell to his knees. Alexanor collected his slave and walked away.

'He tried to make me say things ...' Dariush said. 'And do things.'

Alexanor thought he knew what the boy was talking about – the usual torments that young men like Kritias devised.

And he didn't ask the right questions.

As it proved, Philopoemen didn't stay with them; he had a hundred cavalrymen with him, in the red cloaks of the federal cavalry, with

Polyainos carrying a small red banner on a crossbar and Simmias commanding his escort. As soon as Alexanor saw them, he knew they were Philopoemen's own people, his servants and retainers and the Thracians he'd purchased and freed.

But the local Epidauran citizen *hippeis*, even if they were fore-warned of the great man's arrival, had no way of knowing that the hundred beautifully mounted, well-armed men weren't the norm of the Achaean cavalry. Epidauros was a rich town, with almost a hundred and fifty male members of the *hippeis* class, and one hundred and thirty of them turned out for the muster; twenty of them paid the fine in advance and stayed home.

Alexanor joined the citizens, many of whom were well known to him: the grain supplier to the temple, and a man who owned the big bronze-smithing sheds where dozens of artisans, slave and free, worked; the two men who owned the shipyard, and a dozen prosper-ous gentlemen-farmers. All were men he'd worked with at the temple, or in several cases, healed.

Philopoemen had moderated the first training day; it was nowhere near as difficult as the first day on the beach at Aegio had been. But Lykortas rode through the whole muster, judging horses and equip-ment. Even with new cloaks made by their wives and all their panoplies newly polished, the citizens of Epidauros left a great deal to be desired in terms of both equipment and performance.

A man fell off his horse the first time Philopoemen ordered his newly formed four-deep rectangle to advance. Another man swayed, gave a yell, and thumped on the stony ground when they began to practise forming column from line and line from column – basic manoeuvres performed at a walk.

As the day went on, it became clear that the local farmers and their sons could mostly ride adequately, but the city men, despite a few of them having better armour and finer horses, couldn't really ride over difficult ground or stay in formation.

Philopoemen's tone never changed. He was cheerful, and he rode beautifully, so that as he dashed up and down his column as it jogged through the countryside east of the temple complex, he seemed to be one creature with his horse. Men said it was like having a riding lesson just to watch him.

Sostratos came out from the temple, mounted on a mule, and followed the column.

'We paid five talents of gold for this?' he asked. 'We could protect them better than they can protect us. And by the time this drill day is done, we'll have a lot of work. There's a broken collarbone, and that fellow must have a sprain at least – look at the size of his ankle.'

Dinaeos rode up and Alexanor reintroduced the former mercenary to the Achaean officer.

'Oh, sir, I remember you well,' Dinaeos said. 'You and your archers probably saved my worthless carcass from being dragged off by the Spartans.'

Sostratos smiled. 'You'd do better to take their kit away and hire Cretans,' he said, as one of the younger men slumped on his horse's neck, already too tired to sit upright.

Dinaeos nodded. 'I admit, it's more of a challenge than I expected,' he said. 'It's not just that our people are bad. It's that they've forgotten *why* we train. The best of the young men still think this is all a game where you get to wear your best *chiton* and some fancy armour.'

Sostratos watched the column turn down a side road. The simple turn required the files of each section to hold, as the column went from four men wide to just two men wide.

As he watched, Philopoemen roared an order, and then two files turned into an empty field and began to form a front. The files behind came up and formed to the left of the first files, so that in moments, a sizeable body of cavalry was arrayed in the field, ready for anything. Except that one of the hurrying cavalrymen lost control of his horse in the entry to the field and blocked the files behind. He was thrown, and knocked unconscious, and the whole back of the column collapsed into anarchy. Men went to rescue their friends, crashing through the roadside brush; one daring soul put his horse at the stone wall that bordered the field and leapt it.

Simmias shook his head. 'We're all going to die,' he said.

Sostratos nodded. 'That's my prediction, yes.'

But Lykortas, Dinaeos and Polyainos were in the gateway, sorting men out, giving orders, and in some cases, taking men by the bridle and riding them back to their places.

Philopoemen had ridden up to the youth on the fine gelding who'd leapt the wall.

'He's for the Agema,' Dinaeos said with satisfaction.

'Agema?' Alexanor said. 'I know that word. Philip of Macedon has an Agema.'

'So do we, now – our elite cavalry. We're taking the picked men of each district and making them into full-time cavalrymen. They get the new panoplies and the warhorses that, if Poseidon wills it, Kleostratos is bringing home to us from Thrake. We'll use Philopoemen's troop from home as the basis.'

'If you take the best men out of every district, won't you render the rest of the cavalry less competent?' Alexanor asked.

Dinaeos nodded. 'Yes. In some districts. In others, it won't make so much difference. But Phil's sure that men live by ambition and emulation, and they'll all want to be as good as the best. I suspect that some of these fellows will be just as happy to watch the firebrands ride away ... Never mind. I'm an old pessimist.'

'I think you aren't pessimistic enough,' Sostratos said. 'One whiff of a real enemy and this assembly of local squires will worship the god Panic and vanish into the hedgerows.'

Dinaeos grinned. 'You keep saying what I think. But Phil doesn't hold with us constantly voicing our views.' He looked around. 'He claims that he encourages dissent, but ...'

Alexanor laughed. 'You were in Crete.'

'I know,' Dinaeos said. 'This is going to be worse.'

And that night, at a dinner given for all of the men of the *hippeis* in the *stoa* of the town, Philopoemen shared his *kline* with Alexanor.

'I have to thank you for riding with the cavalry today,' he said when the speeches were over.

'Why?' Alexanor asked.

'Because with you, I knew that I had one actual soldier. When is the last time Epidauros' men saw action?'

'There were more than a hundred hoplites at Sellasia,' Alexanor said. 'But no cavalrymen. In fact, I can't remember the last time the *hippeis* was summoned, and neither can anyone else.'

'Well,' Philopoemen said, 'it's not all bad. Lycurgos, the Epidauran *archon*, is totally competent. So is the *Hipparchos* out of Hermione, Aristides. How he picked up so much tactical acuity as a merchant I'll never know, but he has the touch. And I saw some excellent horses today, and tomorrow I'm touring the horse farms. There are a dozen really good riders. Young Kleander knows his stuff – excellent horse, rides like a Centaur. I wish I had more like him.'

'Will you take them away to be part of your picked men?'

'Someone's been talking ... but yes. I will. The ones who ride with me all winter will actually be fully trained by the spring. Every man we train now can help us train more in the spring. It's a little like a man lifting himself by the straps of his own sandals—'

'You know that doesn't work,' Alexanor said.

'It's an expression.'

'So right now, the entire cavalry of the League is your hundred mercenaries, who are wolves in League clothing?'

'Yes. Now I have almost thirty picked men training with Lykortas, every day.'

'Thirty? The Romans must be shaking in their military boots.'

'I never said this would be easy,' Philopoemen said. 'Cercidas is making trouble about money already, and I know the men I fine are paying because I usually escort the money myself.'

'Escort the money?'

'The Spartans have so many bandits on the roads that it's like a state policy, which, I admit, some of my friends claim it to be. Dinaeos' father thinks that the Lacedaemonians are sending their helots into the hills to rob travellers. Certainly a surprising number of travellers have been killed, so watch yourself if you have to go anywhere this winter. I'm trying to clean them out as I go – it's excellent practice and it bloods the new men.'

Alexanor flinched at the casual cruelty of using highway thieves as practice. Philopoemen saw him flinch, and he nodded.

'I know,' he said. 'But they have to go. And some of these young men have never even *seen* a fight.'

'If we make them adept at killing, won't they bring that home?' Alexanor asked.

'If we survive the Romans and the Spartans, I'll give that some thought.'

The next morning, they threw javelins for hours. Philopoemen's household troopers had straw targets which they hung from olive trees and from signposts, and then men would ride along, thrusting or throwing their spears into the targets, a few on each side, and then more, and then even more. At first each man had just one javelin and one target; by afternoon, most of the men could ride with three javelins, throwing into two targets and thrusting into the last two.

When men fell, Alexanor tinkered up their bruises and handed them over to Arkas, now an officer, and the Thracian prince Dadas, who were running an impromptu riding school, where the men who fell, and those who'd raised their hands when asked if anyone just wanted to practise riding, went round a ring, first on a lunge line and then without. As the day went on, the riding school filled up, until half the *hippeis* of Epidauros was in the riding school. Dadas and Arkas seemed equal to the challenge, and they had a dozen other trained troopers helping them, so that the poorest riders were receiving individual instruction.

But the winter wheat was in the ground, as was the third crop of barley; it was a slow time, and the third day dawned cold and clear, and the cavalry school went on like a circus of equine education. Men sparred with wooden swords, on foot and horseback. Men strove to unhorse each other with staves the length of javelins. Dinaeos and Philopoemen himself began to instruct the Epidaurans in wrestling on horseback.

'*Pankration* is useless,' Philopoemen said. 'No, I don't mean that precisely, but there's no use in teaching it as if it was military training. I'd rather that they can actually ride in formation and keep their place in a rhomboid. But ... in a cavalry fight, a few simple moves can be life or death. Men don't always think of wrestling when mounted, especially the men whose riding is the weakest. But if they learn three attacks, they'll be better than most cavalry in a really close press.'

'You are, as far as I have been able to observe, the best *pankrationist* of our generation,' Alexanor said. 'And I have most certainly watched you use your skill to winnow men like ripe wheat on the day of battle.'

Philopoemen shrugged. His calm arrogance said that what applied to other men might not apply to him.

'I get them for twenty days,' he said. 'Twenty days a year, and that's an imposition to most of them. The lads who ride away with me will learn a great deal of *pankration*. The rest of these ...' He looked at Alexanor. 'How much *pankration* could you teach me in twenty days?'

'Quite a bit. But I take your point. It's time better spent throwing javelins.'

'Even that,' Philopoemen said. 'I'm sure it is gross heresy against the gods of war, but I don't think that an individual's weapons skill is as important as how well he rides and what orders he can obey. Give me a thousand fine horsemen, well mounted and trained to my hand, against a thousand Spartan champions, every one of them a master of the sword, the spear, and *pankration*, and my thousand will ride over them like so many weeds under the scythe.'

'You exaggerate,' Alexanor said.

'I do not,' Philopoemen said. 'If war was an Olympic sport, it would be a team sport, not an individual contest.'

'He's going to ruin war.' Thodor, one of the Thracian captains, was scathing. 'I've said it before and I'll say it again. All this drill … anyone will know how to do things! Everyone will do things the same way! No easy victories, and no plunder.'

'I'd like to ruin war so people don't fight them any more,' Philopoemen said. 'I don't see much chance of that happening, to be honest.'

Over the course of the week, men graduated from the riding school. Arkas would walk up to a man, pat him on the shoulder, and send him back to the drills or contests. Alexanor was constantly impressed by how well the young man and the Thracian prince worked together – how seldom they lost their tempers, and how thorough their lessons were.

'I thought it took a lifetime to learn to ride?' Alexanor asked.

'Yes,' Arkas admitted. 'But we don't need them to ride well enough to fight, at least for now. Just well enough to spend the winter practising. If they ride all winter, they'll be better in the spring.' He pointed at Lycurgos, the local commander, who jumped a low wall without changing his seat. 'See?'

'They're already better,' Alexanor said.

'Yes,' Dadas said with real satisfaction. 'For Greeks, I mean.'

That evening, Alexanor and Aspasia had Philopoemen to dinner. He was a gracious guest, bringing a dozen amphorae of excellent wine, and he lay with Dinaeos, and Lykortas shared his *kline* with Arkas. The rest of the officers ate with the troopers in the town. Many of the town's cavalrymen had joined the temporary messes and were sitting by campfires in their own market square.

'Will we be ready in the spring?' Alexanor asked.

'No,' Philopoemen said. 'No, we will not be ready. But we'll be readier than if we hadn't done this. Cercidas is putting signal stations along the coast, so that we can respond to raids. We don't have to win every engagement. We only need a little luck, a mere nod from *Fortuna* – kill an important Aetolian, capture a Roman officer, and they will back off. But that's a secret. What I want the world to see is our "extensive and professional preparations". That's a quote from the Ambassador to the League from the king of Pergamum.'

'He said that?' Aspasia asked.

'He wrote it in a letter to his king, which I opened and read,' Lykortas said.

'Shame!' Aspasia said. 'Now we read people's letters?'

'He was sent as a spy,' Philopoemen said. 'So we spy on him in turn.'

Alexanor sighed. 'The world is a very dark place, sometimes.'

'Darker if you are poor and sold into slavery,' Philopoemen said.

'While we're on that subject, where is Kaeso?' Alexanor asked.

'I sent him to the Roman consul, Galba. He went with our emissary, along with my promise to free any other Roman soldiers I found enslaved. I pointed out that there are more than a thousand of them at Sparta.' Philopoemen shrugged.

Lykortas barked his sharp laugh.

'Fomenting dissension?' Dinaeos asked.

'It shouldn't be hard. Machanandas isn't a subtle, sly fox like Nabis. He's more of a brutal, self-serving tyrant, and he's not anyone's friend.'

Philopoemen spoke with unaccustomed heat. Alexanor knew that Machanandas had been directly responsible for the deaths of Philopoemen's wife and children.

'I confess that any time I can do the Spartans a bad turn, I will. But likewise, Lykortas says that anything we can do to establish a rapport with the Romans will only help later.'

'Later?'

'If we survive this spring, eventually the war will end. Macedon is reaching military exhaustion. Rome is still fighting Carthage. We are a sideshow. There *must* be a path to peace, even for a few years. We cannot fight Rome. We can face Sparta – Sparta and Elis. If we push ourselves to a great effort, we can face the Aetolians. Rome ... Rome has sent thirty warships to face us this year, and two legions, plus their allies. Twenty thousand men.' He shook his head. 'This while they face Hannibal in Italy. How I would love to go to Rome. I want to see this awakening giant.'

'But Macedon!' Alexanor said.

Lykortas spoke up. 'Macedon will struggle to put fifteen thousand men in the field this year, and pay another five thousand mercenaries and garrison troops. I know – I have someone in the Macedonian tax secretariat.'

'By Apollo!' Alexanor swore.

He was used to thinking of Macedon as a leviathan; it was almost painful to imagine Macedon as a mere local predator.

'And as Philip grows desperate, he is inclined to desperate measures,' Lykortas said. 'He's funding piracy in the Aegean. He's sending his own ships to take cargoes – especially Rhodian cargoes.'

Alexanor shook his head.

Philopoemen sipped his wine. 'That's why I begin to believe that the Spartans are actually sponsoring this land-piracy, this brigandage. We are in terrible times, when states once famed for their nobility stoop to such tactics.'

Lykortas laughed. 'States have no morality. No *polis* has the morals of a four-drachma prostitute or a pickpocket. They, at least, are nice to their friends.'

Aspasia mimed putting her hands to her ears. 'This is why women don't go to men's parties. I'm not sure I want to know all this. It's all terrible.' She glanced at Lykortas. 'But since we have you here, how are the collections of taxes going for our state?'

Lykortas grimaced. 'That's the state of modern war – nobility is out, and taxes are the sinews of Ares. Our collection is going badly. Most of the citizens don't seem to be paying. It's possible that it's just winter, but there are rumours that a great many of the smaller states in the Federation are considering pulling out and making a separate peace.'

'And Machanandas is ready to march,' Dinaeos said. 'We sent scouts into the north of Lacedaemon. Machanandas has almost four thousand men in a camp, ready to march, and they are better supplied than the citizens in his city.'

'And the Aetolians sent two shiploads of cavalry into Elis,' Philopoemen said. 'It will be a bloody spring.'

'I have five talents of gold for the League,' Alexanor said. 'Will you take it away?'

Lykortas winced. Philopoemen looked around the room.

'We're going west and south,' he said. 'And what we're doing is risky. I recommend you take it north yourself.'

Aspasia put her hand in Alexanor's and squeezed.

'I was afraid you'd say that,' he said.

'I'm going back for the winter session of the assembly,' Lykortas said. 'I'll ride with you.'

'I can spare ten new troopers – they'll make a good show.' Philopoemen gave a wry smile. 'And protect you. And you, in turn, can see what's happening with Kleostratos.'

'Kleostratos?' Alexanor asked.

'We have moved the League treasury to Sicyon,' Lykortas said. 'In fact, we're moving it around. There's a strong possibility the Aetolians are planning a raid on Aegio.'

'So as you pass through Corinth, see if there's word from Kleostratos. I'll meet you in Megalopolis in a month.' Philopoemen glanced at Lykortas, but his words were for Alexanor.

'It's almost as if you are giving me orders,' Alexanor said.

'You are the temple's representative to the League, are you not?' Philopoemen said. 'And I'm quite sure that you, a man of property, reported for duty at the muster of your city.'

'I knew that was a mistake,' Aspasia said. 'I'm not even sure we're citizens here.'

Philopoemen smiled. 'If you were not before, you are now. I'll meet you in Megalopolis in a month.'

Lykortas smiled. 'Welcome to the Argonauts,' he said. 'Don't ask questions. Just keep rowing.'

'I'll take Dariush,' Alexanor said to his wife, who lay with her head on his shoulder. 'And, unless Chiron tells me not to, I'll take Kritias.'

'That arrogant twit,' Aspasia snapped.

'I suspect there's more to him than his arrogance.'

'I beg leave to doubt it. So, you are off to war? I thought we would at least have the winter together.'

'I admit that I hadn't expected to be under orders quite so soon. And it is clear to me that Philopoemen left a great deal unsaid. They must be desperate for hard currency, or they wouldn't be asking me to move five talents of gold across Achaea in winter.'

'You heard what Lykortas said.'

'I heard him, but I didn't fully believe it. Now I do. What Lykortas and Philopoemen left unsaid is terrifying – the League could fall apart this winter.'

'Can the cities make separate peaces with Rome or with Aetolia?'

'No, love. But we can scatter like sheep, and the wolves will pull us down one at a time. The cities of Arkadia and Achaea banded together in the first place because they were too weak to face Sparta or Athens one by one. Now, a hundred years later, the situation is different, yet the same.'

'Such a cheerful future for all of us. What can I do? I used to be content to keep house and avoid my husband, but you've unleashed me. I don't want to sit at home. I want to *do something*.'

'Write letters to everyone you know and get us news from Rhodes and Athens.'

'I can do that!'

'Write letters to Leon, to Kos, to every sanctuary of the god. Feel free to explain our situation. Visit Chiron – get him to participate. Perhaps in the process he'll learn that you do more than make babies.'

'Bless you, love. I'm glad that I can do more than make babies.'

'I didn't mean that as an insult.'

'I know.' Her hand travelled across his stomach. She wriggled. 'War has one positive consequence.'

'What's that?' he asked, aware that his wife was moving with purpose.

But he never did learn what she was going to say.

# CHAPTER FOUR

———✦———

## Achaea

### WINTER, 209 BCE

'By Hera's fulsome tits!' Lykortas roared.

The wind blew through the pass, carrying a heavy load of blowing snow, and it was so cold that the flakes cut exposed skin like so many tiny knives.

Alexanor's new red cavalry cloak blew straight out behind him, and with it his pocket of warmth. He was wearing three woollen *chitons* and tall boots, and nothing seemed to protect him from the bite of the wind.

The mountains rose on either side. It made no difference that the sea was only ten stades away to the east; the Korfos Ridge towered above them, and on the landward side, the precipice above was lost in clouds.

The wind ripped at them again and every cloak blew out, so that their scarlet cloaks stood out behind them in the wind. The young troopers put their heads down and rode on; but one young man's cloak pin failed and his cloak went sailing off on the wind, and Kritias lost his broad-brimmed wool *petasos* hat.

The flying cloak was intercepted by Dariush, Alexanor's slave, and the flying hat was plucked from the air by Kleander, the newest recruit into the Agema, eager to prove himself. Too eager, in almost every way.

'Poseidon's swollen member!' Lykortas swore.

'Your language has taken on a new richness,' Alexanor said with a frozen smile.

'I live with soldiers,' Lykortas said. 'And the Thracians are the best … or the worst.' He grinned. 'It keeps you warm.'

Alexanor tried to smile but he felt as if his face had frozen into a mask of immobility. He didn't think he'd ever been so cold.

They were almost at the top of the pass. Alexanor looked back at the three mules carrying the gold, and then forward, where Dadas, the Thracian prince, was waving from the marble marker at the top.

'Almost there,' he said.

Something metallic winked on the hillside above them.

'There are men on the hillside,' Alexanor said.

Lykortas looked up. 'Ganymede's ruddy arse!' he snapped. 'Ride for it!'

Dadas was also aware. He was coming back.

'Don't stay to fight!' Lykortas shouted. 'They'll never catch us!'

'Unless they've blocked the pass ahead,' Alexanor said.

'Damn!' Lykortas said.

The wind blew, a huge gust that swept their cloaks up again.

'They have a crossbow,' Lykortas said.

'I saw it,' Alexanor said.

The *gastraphetes* made a distinctive wooden *clack* when it was loosed; Alexanor hadn't heard it, but he'd seen the man shoot, and watched the bolt vanish in the wind.

'Ride for it!' Alexanor said. 'If there's a roadblock, attack it. Go!'

Lykortas nodded. 'On me!' he roared.

The young troopers gathered around him, and the ten of them raced up the pass.

'Stay with me!' Alexanor called to Dadas.

Kritias was white – fear or cold or both combined. Dariush had the mules, and at a nod from his master, began cantering along behind the cavalrymen.

'We are the rearguard,' Alexanor said. 'They have a *gastraphetes*. Don't stop moving.'

Even as he spoke, the thing loosed another bolt. This one went through calmer air, and slammed into the bags on one of the mules. The animal began to bleed, drops of purple-red brilliant on the snow.

'Go, go!' Alexanor shouted at Dariush.

The mules broke into a clumsy run. Alexanor followed them, watching the hillside above him.

Suddenly he was face down in the snow. He never saw the arrow that killed his horse – an unlucky shaft, loosed from high on the hillside and plummeting straight through the animal's neck. His horse bled out in the snow, and he was soaked, and wiping the snow from his face.

Kritias wheeled his horse, and it reared, and he stayed on. He reached out a hand and Alexanor took it the way a drowning man might seize a piece of timber, and the younger man swayed him up behind.

The horse was warm after the snow.

'Thanks!' Alexanor managed.

Whatever Kritias' other failings, he was a superb horseman. He said nothing, and his heavily burdened horse ploughed along over the uneven ground. Ahead, the mules were still moving, one of them with a *gastraphetes* bolt standing out of his load like an extra tail.

Kritias reined in. 'There they are.' He sounded more angry than afraid.

There was a barrier of felled trees, and the red-cloaked cavalrymen were attacking it. Two were already down, their blood bright as their cloaks on the snow.

'Let's go!' Alexanor said.

Kritias bit his lip, but he didn't urge his horse forward.

Alexanor looked back. The men on the hillside were coming down. An arrow vanished into the snow by his dangling boot.

'Damn it!' Kritias said. 'That could have hit me.'

Alexanor ignored him, rolled from the horse's warm back into snow up to his crotch. He almost shrieked at the cold, but instead he pushed himself up and bounded forward. The felled trees were downhill from the top of the pass, and the men behind the barrier were mostly archers, not swordsmen; their ambush had been badly sited, with too little time with their quarry in their field of fire. But now three of the young men were down, and the mule continued to colour the snow purple-red.

Alexanor drew his sword. He got onto the path in the middle of the road, and slipped; the packed snow was slippery as ice under his riding

76

boots. He got a knee under himself, cold forgotten, and went forward.

The young men were trying to climb over, and through, the branches of the felled trees. Lykortas was down, curled in a ball; the other two were youths. But the archers had trouble shooting through the tangle of branches.

Kleander was bellowing, cutting branches with a long Gaulish-style sword, clearing a path through the *abattis*.

Alexanor took a different course; he slogged back into the deep snow, running around the end of the *abattis*, vaulting one of the trunks, and then ...

There they were. Ten men in furs and coarse woollens and felt cloaks, with red faces and heavy bows. They even had a firepot to keep their bows warm.

Alexanor let his soaking wet cloak fall onto his left arm and he went forward onto the packed snow behind the felled trees.

The nearest archer, a small, tattooed man in a Scythian hood, was just putting an arrow to his string. He turned and drew, and Alexanor raised the wool cloak in a swirl. He was too far to avoid the arrow, and it punched through the heavy cloak and fell into the snow.

Alexanor roared and plunged forward, the daemon of combat forcing his limbs through the snow. Again his smooth-soled boots betrayed him and he skidded, and an arrow went into his felt hat.

The tattooed man in the Scythian hat turned and ran. His mate, taller and more confident, pulled a long knife from his belt. Alexanor deceived it, encouraged a counter-cut by flapping his cloak, and then he stabbed, low to high, in under the man's ribcage with his narrow-bladed *xiphos* and the man fell dead. Alexanor dropped his cloak, plucked the dying man's long knife from his grip as he went down, and tossed it to catch the hilt blade-down in his fist. He turned to the next archer, who assumed that he could get one more arrow into the oncoming cavalry *epheboi* and died for being incorrect.

And then, in panic, they all came for Alexanor: four men with various weapons – a spear, two swords, and a club. The first thrust of the spear took Alexanor by surprise; the man was better trained than he expected, and his arrogance cost him a deep cut all along his left forearm.

But now time was against the ambushers, as the young men were finally through the web of branches and thorns. The spearman thrust again, and this time, despite the blood dripping into the snow, Alexanor used the heavy knife in a sweep, moving the spear's point well to his left, and he stepped in, cutting with the *xiphos*. It wasn't really a cutting weapon, but the blade hurt the man's numb fingers on the spear, severing one and damaging others, and he dropped his spear. Alexanor stepped in again, stabbing with the *xiphos*. It went home, and Alexanor left it there, threw the heavy knife left-handed, and scooped the spear out of the snow.

One of the survivors took the moment to burst past him, and the second man cut at him with the club, landed a piece of a blow on his left arm, numbing it. Alexanor had made a poor choice with the spear; he was too close. He tried to shorten his grip, but the man pressed in, and Alexanor dropped it to wrestle, kicked the man with a snap to the shin and knee ...

Suddenly the club-man's mouth opened, showing broken teeth, and then a gout of blood over the stumps of his teeth, and he fell face forward into the snow. Kleander stood behind him, pulling a cavalry javelin out of the man's back.

'Good throw,' Alexanor managed. 'Who's watching the gold?'

'Shit!' the younger man spat.

'And our horses,' Alexanor said.

Kleander had, with remarkable courage, cut a path through the *abattis*, and Alexanor followed him, trying to ignore the drip of blood from the slash on his left arm. He could see that Dariush still had the mules, and the enemy on the hillside were keeping their distance, because Dadas had a heavy bow and had already knocked one down at a long range.

'Get the horses!' he roared – his full Rhodian Marine voice, as his wife liked to call it. 'Kritias, move your arse! Now!'

He knelt by Lykortas, who was rolled into a tight ball in the snow.

'Let me see it,' he said.

Lykortas had an arrow deep in his right bicep, just above the elbow. Alexanor breathed a sigh of relief.

'Can you ride?' he asked.

Lykortas nodded.

'Get up! You're just getting cold and wet.' He turned to one of the *epheboi*. 'Put your cloak on Lykortas. Good lad. Get mounted. Now, now.'

An arrow flashed by with a buzz and then rattled among the branches of the roadblock.

Lykortas flinched.

Alexanor nodded. 'This is going to hurt,' he said. 'Lean over. More. There.'

He rested the shaft, where it protruded, against the trunk of one of the felled trees making up the *abattis*.

'Get me that hand-axe,' he called to Kleander.

The young man plucked a hand-axe off the belt of a dead man and tossed it to Alexanor, who popped the bone axe-sheath off with his thumb, and cut. He severed the arrow shaft cleanly just behind the tiny bronze head, and then pulled the shaft out of the wound.

Lykortas gasped, but he didn't scream.

'Let it bleed a little and then we'll wrap it,' Alexanor said. 'Get mounted, now. Come on, my friend.'

'Having trouble thinking ...'

Lykortas had blue lips. Alexanor knew this reaction well – combat, wounds, confusion, with cold added in.

'Kleander, get him mounted.'

Another arrow, and then two more, and Dadas loosed a shaft with a grunt; his horn bow was both heavy and cold.

Alexanor knelt by another downed man – a boy, perhaps seventeen, lying in the snow, his jaw torn away and lying a few handspans from the boy. He was the victim of a thrown spear which lay by him. The boy was very much alive, and all too aware that, despite the relative light injury, it was a death wound. A man without a jaw could not eat or drink easily – or at all – or talk.

Once, Alexanor would have wept. Instead, he went back across the *abattis*, picked up his cavalry cloak from where he'd dropped it, the heavy knife that he had thrown in the fight, and plucked his own *xiphos* from a dead man's abdomen. He wiped both of them on the clothes of the dead, and he took the scabbard of the heavy-backed knife from his second victim.

And then, without an apparent qualm, he knelt by the jawless ephebe and cut his throat, exactly the way he'd perform a sacrifice. He held the boy as he bled out, and the life went from his eyes. The boy didn't weep, or scream, and his eyes remained open to the last, as if to savour his dying moments.

Dariush had the mules past the *abattis*. It was an incredible feat of horsemanship – or mulemanship – but he never panicked the stubborn beasts, and they worked with a will.

'Master, I could use the beasts to move the wood,' he called out. 'The tree. The trees. We have rope.'

Alexanor might, under other circumstances, have smiled.

'No,' he said. 'Keep going.'

'Yes, Master.'

Dariush tapped his heels to his horse, which sprang forward.

Alexanor caught the dead boy's horse, a small grey with a noble head. He swung onto her back, feeling every minute of his years, and pointed at the spear.

'Toss me that,' he called to Kleander, who was standing by the dead boy.

'We should take his body,' Kleander said.

Alexanor looked back.

Lykortas nodded. 'Philopoemen would,' he said through clenched teeth.

'Get them moving,' Alexanor said. 'Kleander and I will get him over a horse.' He slid down, loath to relinquish the relative warmth of the horse now that post-combat reaction was setting in. 'Kritias!'

The novice was staring at the hillside as if in shock.

'I ...' he began.

'Get over here. Now. You have the best horse.'

Kritias looked back at the hillside and swallowed heavily.

'Yes,' he said, and brought his horse competently along the trail.

Kleander and Alexanor lifted the ungainly bundle of the dead boy and slung it over Kritias' horse even as he protested.

'It will slow me down. Apollo! Disgusting! *He's bleeding on my horse!*'

'He was a man, and he's dead, and you, my dear boy, are alive. So kindly shut the *fuck* up and ride!' Alexanor said savagely.

As he picked his way around the snowdrifts and the felled trees one more time, Alexanor counted. Eight ambushers dead; he had been too thorough and all his victims were dead. Eight men dead, and two run off down the pass – perhaps as many again behind them.

When he caught up with grey-faced Lykortas, he said, 'That was a big ambush. Fifteen, or even twenty men. Fine weapons, well cared for. This little axe – it had a bone sheath for the blade. Here. And look at this spear.'

Lykortas, despite his wound and the added misery of the cold, looked at him sharply.

'Mercenaries,' he said.

'They weren't bandits,' Alexanor insisted. 'Bandits don't have an expensive crossbow and fifteen men with good kit. Those were Cretan bows.'

'I know,' Lykortas said with a weak smile. 'I have an arrow in my arm. Every time I look at it, I think, "Cretans".'

'We're five hundred stades from Sparta,' Alexanor said. 'Machanandas' arm is long indeed if he can reach here.'

Lykortas glanced back over his shoulder at Kritias.

'Not impossible, if someone told the Spartans when the gold was moving.'

That hit Alexanor harder than the wound in his arm.

'Kritias is a fool,' he said, 'but not a traitor.'

Lykortas shrugged. 'I have no evidence,' he muttered. 'Except the way he behaved in the ambush.' He winced, closing both eyes. 'Where can we stop?'

'It's ten stades to a farmhouse,' Alexanor said. 'Even that ... two of them ahead of us and more behind. If they are not bandits—'

'Then maybe we aren't done.'

'Exactly.'

Dadas rode back to them. 'There's a farm ahead,' he said. 'Stop there?'

'Not much choice,' Alexanor said. 'But the farm could be held by the enemy.'

Dadas nodded. 'I'll look. Kleander! On me.'

'I can't believe that mule is still moving,' Lykortas said.

They followed the bleeding mule along the track, down a long, steep valley and up the other side. The single farmhouse with its high-walled farmyard and red-tiled roof was visible from five stades away, and so was the trickle of smoke emerging from the louvre in the roof above the hearth. It gave Lykortas hope, and the boys perked up. They were very silent.

There had been a lot of blood in the snow, and the dead boy, with his jaw ripped away, had been the very figure of the horror of war.

Dadas emerged from the low door and waved.

Lykortas seemed to deflate.

'I'm barely keeping it together,' he warned.

'I've got you.' Alexanor put an arm around the wounded man.

'Thank the gods for you. Always befriend a doctor …' Lykortas muttered. His voice was thickening.

'Big fire, hot water,' Dadas said. 'Come on!'

There was a dead man in the gateway, face down, with Dadas' heavy spear in his back.

'One of the men who ran,' Dadas said. 'No idea where the other man is.'

Alexanor paid the dead man little attention. He was eager to look at Lykortas' arm.

The doorway of the farmhouse was barely as high as a man's chest, and he had to help Lykortas down from his horse and then carry him through the door.

'The peace of the gods on all here,' he said.

A tall man stood by the hearth with a *kopis* in his hand. Behind him, on the other side of the raised stone hearth, were three women, all armed, and behind them an older woman.

'You are welcome if you bring no evil,' the man said.

'My friend says there is hot water,' Alexanor said. 'I need to wash this man's arm.'

'I'll bring you hot water,' the man said. 'I'm Athenasios,' he added carefully, as if he didn't speak often. 'This is … our … farm. You are welcome, but if you do harm—'

'We will do no harm. We are officers of the Achaean League. I am a priest of Asklepios and Apollo from Epidauros, and we'll happily pay for your time and food and shelter.'

Athenasios unbent immediately, and Alexanor placed his wounded friend on a low bench that was built into the wall by the hearth. Someone handed him a hot, wet linen cloth; he used it to wash the blood away from the wound.

'I feel like a coward,' Lykortas said. 'I took this little wound and lay down in the snow.'

Alexanor grunted. 'Don't be a fool.'

'Glaukon is dead. He was an excellent young man—'

'Lykortas, please don't take the weight of the world on your

82

shoulders, or who will provide us with snappy remarks?' Alexanor got the wound clean, and watched it, even pressing at the entry and exit wounds with his thumbs, watching the flow of blood. 'You are lucky. Unlucky that you were hit at all, but lucky that the head was small and the arrow went ... between some of the muscles, or so it seems to me. Surprisingly little blood – I have so much to learn about the mechanisms of the shoulder and arm. Regardless, I don't see any immediate danger, unless there's poison or infection.'

He sang an invocation while he pressed the pressure point above the wound, and then another. He prayed for guidance from his god, and then wrapped the wound loosely with dry linen.

By then, the small farmhouse had eight men inside in addition to the family and their slaves. The room grew much warmer, and the young men grew noisier.

'Where is Dadas?' he asked one.

'Outside, sir. Someone has to be on watch. Dadas and Kleander are taking the first watch. Here is a cup of wine for you, sir. Eupolis there had a skin of wine and he's sharing.'

'Tell him that he's a fine man,' Alexanor said. 'Anyone cut? Anyone injured?'

'You, sir,' Eupolis said.

'How's the mule?' Alexanor asked. Indeed, his left arm was covered in blood, and the left side of his *chiton*. 'Damn,' he added, as the reaction hit.

Eupolis laughed. 'The mule is fine. The arrow went through a wine skin.'

The boys laughed a little too hard. They were brittle – unsettled.

He was unsettled himself. After combat, the world always seemed ... unreal, or like a dream, and he'd always been this way. As if combat revealed a gate to another place, and it took time to find his way home.

But there were present crises tying him to the here-and-now. The cloth he'd used on Lykortas was bright red, and he looked around for another and found a middle-aged woman holding out another linen rag.

'You'll run me out of old *chitons*, at this rate,' she said.

'Thanks, *despoina*,' he said.

She smiled. 'Here, let me do that. Are you a real doctor?'

83

'Fairly real,' he said, as she cleaned his wound. It hurt, but somehow he felt better immediately. He dipped the rag in wine and ran it along the wound. It burned. 'Do you have honey?'

'Are we Achaeans?' the woman asked. 'Athanasios, get the man some honey.' She leant over. 'Do you know anything about women's complaints, priest? My daughter—'

'My wife knows more, but I'm not unversed,' he said. 'Let me see to all these soldiers and then I'll be happy to look at your daughter.'

'I'll have to be present,' the woman said. 'You being a man and all.'

'Of course.'

An hour later, he'd bandaged several cuts; the worst was across Kleander's left hand, where he'd apparently grabbed a blade. And he'd been able to assure Andromache, his hostess, that her daughter was perfectly healthy, and simply late coming to her full womanhood.

'I was married by her age,' Andromache sniffed. 'Now my man is dead and my son isn't as swift as my man was.' She looked around. 'I need her to marry.'

The young woman in question was perhaps twelve. She was very pretty, in a childish way, and Alexanor doubted that she'd have any trouble finding suitors.

'I need a man who can run a farm,' Andromache said. 'Get the pot off the hearth, Athenasios. There's a good boy.'

Alexanor had experienced this before; the woman clearly felt that, having consulted him as a physician, she could expect him to find a mate for her daughter too.

He smiled. 'I recommend that in the spring you bring her to visit the Temple of Apollo at Epidauros,' he said. 'Perhaps you will receive a dream from the god about her future husband.'

*Or perhaps we'll just have a few handsome young sprites hanging about the place.*

'Never been as far as Epidauros,' Andromache said. 'I'm a farmer, not a gadabout.' She smiled. 'Still, it's a nice thought.'

'It is only forty stades.'

'Cows don't milk themselves, nor goats. But I'll see. And I promise you and your soldiers a good meal. You ain't like the mercenaries of my youth, I can tell you. Right bastards, every one. My pater killed one – he's buried out back. Tried to make trouble for Mater.' She nodded. 'I have to be looking after dinner. Men may work from sun to sun, but women's work is never done, and I seem to do the men's work and the women's.'

She moved to the hearth, and Kritias sat heavily on the bench by Alexanor. It was almost private, and Lykortas had moved to a bed.

'I should have helped you with the wounded,' he admitted.

'That would have been useful,' Alexanor said carefully.

'I ... That ...' The young man turned his head away.

'Have you eaten?' Alexanor asked.

'Of course I've eaten, do I look like a fool?' the young man snapped.

Andromache came back with a wooden cup.

'Try our wine. And thanks for looking at my daughter.' She glanced at Kritias. 'You're a pretty one.' She smiled. 'Know anything about farming?'

Kritias made a face. 'I know it's brutal hard work that only fools and slaves engage in.'

Andromache looked at him for a moment, and then laughed.

'Oh, I see,' she said.

'Who is that horrible old woman?' Kritias asked.

Alexanor sighed. 'That woman is not even ten years older than I am,' he said carefully. 'And she runs this farm.'

'Oh,' Kritias said. 'She's cooking. I thought she was somebody's slave.'

'Where is Dariush?' Alexanor asked.

'How would I know?' the novice replied.

'I find it interesting that you, a well-born formally entered novice in the service of the god, seem to have no interest in the conduct of those mules and the years of sacrifice they represent, while my body slave watches over them day and night.'

'I find it interesting,' Kritias said, 'that a mature man like you imagines that I care what happens to the temple or anything else.'

Alexanor smiled. 'I don't imagine any such thing. I am aware that you care nothing for these things – for ideals, for other people. I find that interesting. It is a malady. I seek to cure you of it. Sometimes I think that only age and maturity will cure you.'

'You think I am sick?' Kritias was, for once, stung out of his arrogant indifference and his adolescent posturing.

'You claim to love Aristotle. Do you seek to lead an excellent life? Do you imagine that this selfish insularity bears any resemblance to such a life? Let me offer you my medical opinion,' he said, talking over Kritias' attempt to interrupt, overriding him. 'Either you are too stupid to understand Aristotle, which seems unlikely, or you have a malady of the mind that allows you to believe one thing and do another entirely.' He smiled. 'Either way, I will work to make you better.'

'I could have died today!' Kritias said suddenly.

'Yes,' Alexanor said. 'Glaukon did die.'

Kritias looked away.

'Lykortas believes that you betrayed us to the Spartans.'

Kritias shuddered.

*So ... it is true.*

'I told my father,' he said suddenly. 'And ...'

He looked stricken. For the first time that Alexanor could remember, the young man's face betrayed great emotion. He couldn't control it, and it worked, as if all the muscles of his face were in revolt, so that his jaw moved, and his eyes seemed to flicker.

'There's a man. At the temple ...' Kritias paused. 'Damn it! I didn't mean any of this to happen ...'

Suddenly he burst into tears.

Alexanor reached out and put an arm around the young man's shoulders.

'They will kill me,' Kritias said.

'The *epheboi*?' Alexanor asked. 'They'll kill you if I tell them tonight, I agree.'

'The Spartans!' Kritias spat. 'Oh, gods, I've done everything wrong.'

Alexanor wanted to laugh because he'd spent his entire adolescence thinking he'd done everything wrong.

'Are there more ambushes?' he asked.

Kritias shook his head violently. 'I don't *know*.' He looked at Alexanor. 'This isn't what was supposed to happen. I was a fool, I admit it. I shouldn't have ... Oh, gods.'

Alexanor nodded. 'Eventually, Lykortas will have to know. But I won't speak out for now.' He considered the moral ramifications of his next statement, and shrugged. 'But I think it is time you made a decision. If you are really against us, then leave us at Corinth.'

Kritias was biting his lip.

'If, on the other hand, you'd like to try again, then from here on out I'll expect to see some changes.'

'Fuck,' muttered Kritias.

'Well?' Alexanor asked.

'I want to try—'

'Don't try. Do it. You can help by fetching firewood from outside for the "horrible old woman". When you're done, take Dariush's place on guard and send him in to get warm.'

Kritias slumped miserably.

'And, Kritias … the man you want to be needs to learn to do these things for himself, not to be instructed. Don't wait for me to tell you what to do.'

Kritias stood up. 'I'll do it,' he said, with a trace of a whine.

'Good. Wear a cloak. Don't be a martyr.'

Alexanor sat back. His arm was beginning to throb, as was his conscience.

In the morning, well fed and rested despite having kept a watch all night, they rode out into a snowy morning.

'How's the arm?' Alexanor asked Lykortas, as the column made its way up the next pass. Kleander was waving at Andromache.

So was Kritias.

Lykortas shook his head. 'My whole body hurts. I feel like an idiot. I lost a good boy and almost lost the gold.'

Alexanor looked around. 'Kritias confessed to me last night. He says there's a Spartan agent at the temple.'

Lykortas winced. 'Of course there is.' His face grew red.

'Don't,' Alexanor said. 'He made a mistake and I think he wanted to make it right.'

'He could have killed us all!'

'Hush. He could have. Instead, he killed Glaukon, whom I suspect he rather liked. And I want to redeem him – indeed, it is no more than my duty. But …' Lykortas still had a hand on his sword hilt. 'But on a practical note, if we keep him alive, we can learn a great deal about his contacts.'

'True,' Lykortas admitted. 'Gods, my whole body hurts. This from one slim cane arrow?'

'Yes. That, and other things.'

That day they rode along the coast, and the winter wind came off the sea – warmer but stronger. As soon as they were down at sea level, the snow turned to rain, and it was, if anything, worse.

But the *epheboi* had had their lesson and they patrolled relentlessly, riding off the road into the brush to look behind stone walls and under coverts.

Dadas chose them a large travellers' inn at Kalamaki – an old establishment that catered to visitors to the Isthmian games and the religious shrines in the area. Four of the young cavalrymen rode ahead and inspected the inn, and the mules toiled up the endless switch-backs, slipping on the omnipresent ice.

'Why do we imagine Hades as hot?' Lykortas spat. 'Ares' shrivelled dick, cold and wet is the worst.'

'Do you just make these little sayings up as you go?' Alexanor asked.

'Sometimes. I have a good education – I need to use it for some-thing.' Lykortas smiled.

'Aphrodite's fecund cunny?' Alexanor asked.

'Oh, that's good. A little technical.'

'Ariadne's clever fingers?'

'Too practical. Good swearing involves either copulation or diges-tion.' But Lykortas was laughing, hard.

'Goodness. Do the gods even have digestion?'

'You are hurting me. No, it's true – laughing hurts my arm.'

'Poseidon's dripping beard?'

'Possible. Not really puerile enough.'

'Poseidon's wrinkled scrotum?'

Lykortas started to bark like a dog. His laughter echoed off the walls of the precipice on their left.

'Of course, it's possible that the sea god has a perfectly smooth scrotum—'

'Stop!'

'Or it is possible to imagine the gods as being as flawed as human beings. Perhaps—'

'Stop it!'

'Perhaps the smith god is flatulent—'

'No!'

'Hephaistos' stinking gas!' Alexanor said.

'You are killing me!' Lykortas said. 'I thought you doctors cured people!'

Lykortas was still laughing when they rode into the courtyard of the inn. It was so much warmer here that their breath didn't steam in the air, and the inn's slaves weren't wearing cloaks.

Lykortas waved to Dariush. 'Put the bags in my room,' he said. 'Alexanor, stay with me. We're almost there – if they're coming, they'll come tonight.'

'Agreed.' Alexanor put a casual hand on Dariush's shoulder. 'I appreciate how hard you are working.'

Dariush smiled hesitantly.

'Is Kritias treating you better?' he asked.

Dariush frowned. And said nothing.

The inn was an old building – really, a complex of well-roofed stone buildings constructed over more than a hundred years. They were all connected, but perhaps men had grown or shrunk in stature over the years; the connecting doorways never seemed to line up well, and hallways always seemed to have a step up or a step down. Most of the buildings were very cold, although the main hall, built like an old megaron, had a huge hearth and a fire of whole oak trees that blazed like a small sun. But Alexanor needed all three of his cloaks to sleep, even pressed against Lykortas. Dariush lay on the floor with the bags of gold and didn't complain.

At some point Alexanor woke. He'd reached the age where he usually woke in the night. He denied nature for a little while and then rolled off the bed. Pulling his cavalry cloak around him, he went out into the cold moonlight of the central yard.

A horse nickered.

And then another.

He was looking for the back gate, which in daylight he knew led out to the privy. In the dark everything was harder. There were no torches lit in the courtyard.

The back gate was open. That struck him as odd.

Just outside, a man struck a light; in fact, he pushed the end of a resin torch into a firepot, and it burst into bright flame. The man with the torch was Scythian Hood. Alexanor knew him instantly in the burst of flame. The hood showed a dull red, the golden ornaments glittering like a warning from the gods.

'Who's that?' another man shouted.

'Alarm! *Alarm!* Alexanor roared. He was unarmed. On the other hand ...

He charged. Scythian Hood flinched, and Alexanor had him. He grasped the torch hand, pulled to break his opponent's balance, punched his right hand across the man's face, kicked him in the back of the knee and threw him over his outstretched leg.

There were a dozen men outside the back gate, or more, and the gleam of bronze and iron.

Alexanor kicked, hard and high, pivoting on his weight-bearing leg so that the whole weight of his kick went into the second man, who doubled over. He had a sword by his side on a rope over his shoulder. Alexanor drew it from the scabbard, pommelled its owner on the back of the head, and retreated into the shadow of the gate-tunnel.

'*Alarm!*' Alexanor roared.

There were shouts behind him, and he could hear Kleander coming. He retreated rapidly. The back gate had a pass-through like a tunnel under the back wing of the inn, between the great hall and the *andron*. Alexanor went back as far as the doors that allowed guests to pass from the great hall to the dining area, and waited in the near complete darkness.

No one followed him. He could hear the *epheboi* arming behind him, and he could hear the mercenaries arguing in front of him.

'Guard the gates!' Alexanor called. 'Front and back!'

Dadas appeared out of the darkness; he was a head taller than most men, and his tattoos showed even in the moonlight.

'I want a prisoner,' Alexanor said.

Dadas nodded. 'Lykortas is staying with the gold,' he said. 'Kleander has the main gate.'

'Ten men out there,' Alexanor said.

Dadas shrugged. 'Here's Eupolis. Let's get them.'

The men at the back gate were not as surprised the second time, but they clearly hadn't expected to be attacked, either. Most of them had moved away; looking for another way in. Alexanor found three of them when he burst out.

More by instinct than skill, he parried a spear thrust with his stolen sword. Eupolis thrust over his shoulder and missed, and Alexanor caught another spear by the haft and pulled, struggling with the owner for possession of the weapon. Dadas stabbed the man over his locked spear, and he screamed. Alexanor broke free and slammed the blade of his weapon against the head of a third opponent.

'Prisoners!' he called.

They had three: Scythian Hood and two more. The rest were riding off into the darkness; Alexanor could hear their horses.

'I swear, we're getting better at this,' Lykortas said into the darkness. 'By Apollo, my arm is barely working. That hurts.'

'If I hadn't needed to urinate,' Alexanor said slowly.

He was fogged with combat and still heavy with the last remnants of sleep, battling with the rush of spirit of fighting for his life. He was unhurt, and yet he felt heavy.

He took his own pulse, and took stock of his faculties, interested in the ebb and flow of spirit brought on by danger. Then he looked at Lykortas' arm; it was bleeding. Again.

'We could pursue them,' Dadas said.

'No,' Lykortas said. 'We have a prisoner and we have the gold.'

The owner was out in the yard, with a long Galatian sword in his hand and a good helmet on his head; behind him, three servants, or slaves, stood uneasily with spears.

'Bandits,' Alexanor said. 'They attacked us two days ago in the pass.'

The innkeeper shook his helmeted head. 'If'n this crap don't end, I'm goin' a lose my place here. Fuckin' helots are always thievin'. Out o' work mercenaries. Eh, you got one? Let's fuckin' string the bastard up.'

A gust of wind hit, carrying rain from the sea.

'Best get under cover,' the innkeeper called.

Lykortas set a watch and they all went back to bed.


Kleostratos had taken over a waterfront taverna on the Aegean beach of the port of Corinth. He had thirty Thracian troopers hired in the east and a dozen actual Scythians: small men, most of them, although one was tall and blond and three were young women.

Kleander's eyes all but popped out of his head as a bare-chested woman of perhaps fifteen years threw back a cup of wine and bellowed for more.

'Getae and a handful of actual Sakje,' Kleostratos said with satisfaction. 'Best horsepeople in the world. Ours now.'

He ruined the commanderly effect of his pronouncement by

belching. It was the middle of the morning watch and all the Thracians and Sakje appeared to be tipsy at least.

The taverna-keeper approached with a deep bow and a flinch, recognising that Alexanor was at least a fellow Greek, and probably a gentleman.

'Please take them away,' the taverna-keeper begged. 'I can't keep them. Oh, lord, please save me. They have drunk all my wine, and last night the … older lady … with the knife … She threatened me—'

'I said I'd cut off his balls!' roared the tattooed women in question. 'I need another pouch!' She flourished the leather pouch around her neck and made a rude gesture.

'I had to buy wine from a rival!' the man cringed. 'I'm ruined.'

Alexanor had coin in his purse. He took a gold daric that he kept for emergencies.

'This should keep the wolf from the door,' he said and tossed it.

The innkeeper caught the coin from long practice and brightened up.

'Good wine,' Alexanor said.

'Immediately, my lord,' the man said.

'Dickhead,' Kleostratos said. 'It's all crap. Philopoemen gave me coin. Sakje only deal for hard currency. But we're staying here until the horse-ships come in. I have six hundred of the best horses in the world out on that storm-tossed-black water and I'm fucking petrified.'

'Six hundred!' Alexanor whistled.

'And I brought another three hundred overland,' the Thracian said. 'Through the hands of a Macedonian army and without losing one to the fucking Bastarnae, either.'

The man seemed proud, and Alexanor whistled; it was an epic achievement. It made Alexanor think, too, that the fate of the Achaean League wasn't on battles, but on deeds like this: on the willingness of taverna-owners to pay their taxes; on the goddess Fortuna and the god Poseidon and a shipment of horses on the high seas.

'How many ships?' Alexanor asked.

'Seven big and three little,' the Thracian said, counting on his fingers. 'The little and one of the big ones are Philopoemen's. The rest I hired.'

Lykortas put a hand on the Thracian's hand.

'And you have a new tattoo,' he said.

Kleostratos beamed. 'I do. I wed a Sakje battleaxe – that old harridan over there.'

The woman with the broad smile and the pouch around her neck waved.

'The Sakje are hers – her war band,' he said. 'It's a long story.'

'So you are like Jason?' Lykortas asked. 'You went to the Euxine and came back with an eastern wife and her warriors?'

Kleostratos shook his head. 'I know you Greeks like Jason. But fuck no. What a dick! And he ditches his wife as soon as he's home. And if Medea had been a Sakje, she wouldn't have killed her children – right, Kau-Ippa?'

The tattooed woman laughed. 'Fuck yes. Kill the bastard, not the kids. That's just fucked.' She licked her curved knife.

'Kau-Ippa, this is Alexanor, a *baqsa* of healing.' Kleostratos twined their hands together – a curious gesture.

'Not *baqsa*,' Kau-Ippa said. 'I tell you this before, mate-of-mine. *Baqsa* is outside of all – outside world. Not man, not woman, not alive, not dead. Also not priest.'

She smiled at Alexanor. She had more muscles in her upper arms than Alexanor had ever seen in a woman, and despite her facial markings, she was attractive. She was also extremely graceful, like a dancer, which seemed to be at odds with her constant swearing. She was very dark-complexioned, with odd bronze-coloured hair, dyed red at the ends, and she had two knives at her elaborate belt, covered in bronze plaques and some colourful beadwork. She was the very essence of a barbarian, but her smile was genuine.

Alexanor bowed. 'I am a priest,' he said.

'Exactly,' Kau-Ippa said. 'I am also priestess. Well met. Husband-friend is my friend.' She clasped his hand, hard, and kissed him on both cheeks.

Alexanor stayed up too late, drank too much, and was late rising the next day. The sheer amount of wine that the eastern horsepeople could drink was staggering – the youngest, slightest girl was capable of drinking more than him – and they drank it unwatered.

Alexanor and Lykortas were barely human until they'd been on the road for an hour. Kleander had what appeared to be the first hangover of his life. Kritias had not one, but two black eyes. Alexanor caught Dariush smiling a secret smile. Alexanor rode up next to Kleander.

'Anything happen that I should know about?' he asked.

Kleander spat. 'No,' he said, sullenly.

Alexanor had never known the boy to be sullen. But he let it go.

Unmolested by bandits, they rode into the temple complex, the capital of the League, in time for the opening of the winter Assembly. With an incredible sense of relief, Alexanor handed over the five talents of gold to Cercidas.

'By Zeus, Alexanor – this is literally going to save lives. And change the financial markets. God sent, indeed.'

Alexanor received the public praise of the League in a unanimous vote of the Assembly.

'Now you are immortal,' Kykliadas joked.

'Immortal?' Alexanor asked.

'Of course. Your name and the vote will be carved in the stone of the amphitheatre.'

Alexanor kept himself from pointing out how often old stone was cleaned and repurposed. But he was touched by the honour.

'Will you stay for the Assembly?' Kykliadas asked.

'Yes – that's my role. But then I must hurry to Corinth and help one of Philopoemen's officers move horses—'

'Gods!' Kykliadas groaned. 'Those horses! A thousand horses. I thought he was joking. The whole League treasury!' Kykliadas was no fop; he was a farmer. 'And we'll have to feed them, and half of them will die in the cold.'

'I doubt the last. Most of the shipment is Getae ponies – hardy as goats.'

'Interesting,' Kykliadas admitted. 'Listen, Alexanor ...'

He put a hand on Alexanor's shoulder. Alexanor had known a few politicians, and his father; he was instantly on his guard.

'What's he doing in the south? A great many men think he's provoking Machanandas.'

Alexanor wanted to refuse to discuss his friend, but he understood the situation politically.

'According to our scouts,' he said carefully, 'Machanandas has an army of almost five thousand mercenaries encamped in the north of the Lacedaemonian lands, at Pellana, south of Megalopolis.' He glanced at the *Strategos*. 'Also, we have a prisoner. He's talked. He was paid by Machanandas to attack us. Parade him in front of the Assembly. The Spartans are literally paying their mercenaries by sending them to attack travellers inside the League.'

'In the winter?' Kykliadas asked. 'Gods. That's bad.' But then he smiled. 'But the prisoner? That's brilliant. I assume it's true?'

Alexanor almost smiled. 'It is true.'

'Even better. You know they say that power corrupts?'

Alexanor smiled this time. 'They do.'

Kykliadas nodded, looking out over the winter sea. 'They're right. The desire to achieve something, the endless compromise, the endless temptation to lie ...' He shook his head. 'What's Philopoemen going to do?

'I can't speak directly for my friend's intentions, but I can guess that he wants Machanandas to know that we have forces ready to react.'

'But we don't!' Kykliadas spat.

Lykortas had been silent until then, but now he smiled wolfishly.

'We've done our very best to convince the Aetolian ambassadors, the Romans, and the Spartans that we are stronger than we look.' He smiled at Alexanor. Behind him stood one of the Sakje men, a beardless youth in a foreign kaftan and un-Greek boots. 'The horses landed, and as ordered, the captains sailed them right past the Roman fleet. Every one of our enemies knows that we just brought in a thousand horses.' He smiled.

Kykliadas nodded. 'I hadn't seen that dimension. But we're playing with fire here – half the benches are men who'd do almost anything to avoid war.'

Alexanor nodded.

'Can I tell them that Philopoemen won't cross the Laconian border?' Kykliadas asked.

'Yes,' Alexanor said.

Privately, he thought, *You can tell them that ...*

Seven days later, and Alexanor had spent one of those days riding with the Aegio *hipparchy*, which was coming along well – more than a hundred troopers who looked the part and could ride. Alexanor noted more than a dozen new helmets and half the men had different, better horses, and despite a biting wind, most of them rode all day. Lykortas led the drills, and his dozen *epheboi* became leaders, which they, as very young men, thoroughly enjoyed.

The day after the drill at Aegio, Alexanor rode east along the road to Corinth, this time without Lykortas, but still leading Kleander and his *epheboi*. He told Kritias, Dariush, Kleander and Eupolis the tales that Philopoemen had told him, about the gods and demigods and their games with the land and sea of the northern Peloponnese. But the weather was cold and rainy, and they were all happy enough to see the fortress of the Acrocorinth above them and to ride into the town itself. Alexanor took his slave and his novice and spent a night at the temple. Kleander found the *epheboi* shelter with one of Philopoemen's friends.

Alexanor was giving his novice every chance to go home to his father and report all he had heard at the Assembly. Cronan had not attended, and there was a rumour that he was on Aegina, talking to the Romans, which was not *quite* an act of state treason.

But Kritias didn't leave the sanctuary. And when they left for the mercantile beaches, he seemed eager to go.

Dariush was equally eager.

Alexanor decided to let it go, and he rode into the yard of the beachside taverna with two very willing young men who competed to curry horses and rushed in to get themselves beds.

Kleostratos embraced him. 'Just in time. And I need help – even these beardless boys. A thousand horses! In winter!' He shook his head. 'How in fifty frozen Sakje hells do I find fodder for a thousand horses between here and Megalopolis?'

'With money,' Alexanor answered.

They spent the evening plotting it out; four of the boys were sent off as messengers. Kritias sat through most of it, and finally couldn't contain himself.

'My father has a huge farm right here,' he said, pointing to the plain beyond Isthmia – one of the difficult areas. 'I can guarantee there's enough fodder in our barns ...'

Alexanor looked at his novice. 'Even one night's fodder for a thousand horses is a sizeable sum of money,' he said.

Kritias nodded. 'I'll answer for it. Send me now. I'll be ready.'

Alexanor just looked at him – a long, steady look, the look a physician gives a patient who might be lying about his diet or his exercise regime.

'I won't fuck this up,' Kritias said.

'If we had them well fed at Isthmia,' Kleostratos said, 'we could probably make it across the passes.'

*Or he could run off, arrange an ambush, and take something worth far more than five talents of gold.*

*On the other hand, as a practical matter, whoever attacks us has to defeat our* epheboi *and another thirty veteran horse-nomads.*

'Go, Kritias, with my blessing.'

He didn't say *if you betray us, may you be cursed for eternity.* If you are going to place trust in someone, there's no point in threatening. Alexanor learnt that in the Rhodian marines, and it was Philopoemen's code, too.

'If you sent Dadas with me, I could send him back to say the fodder was ready,' Kritias said.

Dadas looked stunned.

'Done,' Alexanor said.


Dadas was gone less than a full day.

'Barns bulging with grain and hay,' he said. 'It is as he said. All is prepared.'

The horse herd looked like an army. The whole beach was covered in horses, some of them the ugliest horses Alexanor had ever seen, vicious steppe ponies with nasty tempers and big, bony heads. But the foreigners knew how to handle them, and before Alexanor and Kleostratos were done arguing the exorbitant taverna bill, the whole herd was moving. Hundreds of ship owners, *navarchs*, sailors, oarsmen and slaves stood in crowds to watch the horses trot past into the snowy distance.

'I liked how he "forgot" that you'd given him a gold daric,' Kleostratos said.

'I liked how he pretended that we'd somehow hurt his business,' Alexanor said. 'Full up for nineteen days ... in winter?'

They rode on in the shared annoyance of those who have been cheated at an inn.

'Anyway,' Dadas said, 'it's not our money.'

That made the Getae laugh. It was clear to Alexanor that the new mercenaries viewed all of Greece as a 'land of war' to be plundered, and that they'd have to be watched. The Sakje were different; Kau-Ippa held them in an iron fist, and anyway, they seemed more prepared to be delighted and awestruck than the Thracians.

The gates opened at Cronan's Isthmia estate and twenty male slaves helped get the horses under cover and fed. Alexanor had nothing to complain about, and even less the next day when the same slaves helped load fifty horses with bales of good spring hay. The foreman, an old Gaul with as many tattoos as Kau-Ippa, nodded sagely.

'You'll get over the passes, unless there's a storm,' he said.

They made sacrifices, ate well and moved on. At Kleostratos' orders, no wine had been made available. The Sakje were fractious; the Getae were despondent.

Kritias left with them. He looked to Alexanor for approval, but also to Kau-Ippa, who beamed at him.

'You are a good boy,' she said.

Dadas nodded sagely, like a much older man.

'Kritias is in love with Kuka, the war-maiden who has not yet earned her full name,' he said. 'But he is wise enough to seek Kau-Ippa's good approval, so the maiden will think better of him.'

Alexanor glanced at the Thracian prince. 'So wise, prince!'

Dadas laughed. 'I watch Kritias like a hawk. But you do well with him. You are like the old men who straighten bent arrows with heat and skill. I honour you.'

Alexanor flushed at the younger man's praise.

'You Thracians say things ...' he muttered, embarrassed.

'We speak truth. You Greeks are embarrassed by truth, even when it is your friend.' Dadas shrugged. 'When we want to fuck, we say we want to fuck. When you want to fuck, you mutter odd things and flail about with your hands and smile too much.'

Alexanor laughed at the image.

'True,' he said.

Dadas smiled. 'On the other hand, I would have killed Kritias the moment I knew he had betrayed us. Oh, yes. Lykortas told me. I guessed, anyway. We Thracians are difficult to deceive.' He paused and then muttered, 'And he rides well.'

Dadas said the last as if the way a man rode might compensate for a life of crime.

Alexanor watched Kritias, who was receiving a mounted fighting lesson from Kau-Ippa.

'But I would have been wrong. I have learned from Philopoemen that just killing is without worth.' Dadas nodded, as if this was a profound thought.

And Alexanor thought of his year as a shipboard marine.

*Maybe it is a profound thought.*

They had lost thirty-six horses by the time they had them in the pens behind Philopoemen's great stone barns. Most of them were gone forever in Arkadian snows, and despite that, the losses were lighter than any of them had expected. They spent two brutal days getting the horses warm and fed. More than a hundred of them had to be brought indoors, and four of them were in Philopoemen's hall, standing quietly by the hearth, when the *Hipparchos* returned from his long absence on their third day on his estates.

He embraced Kleostratos like a long-lost brother. Outside, through the open door, Alexanor could see two hundred men dismounting in the dirty snow. They looked happy, but then, anyone who has mounted a winter campaign looks happy at the prospect of warmth.

'Were you successful?' Alexanor asked.

Philopoemen grinned like a boy with his first sweetheart.

'Well,' he said. 'We didn't catch any of these mysterious bandits—'

'That's fine,' Kleostratos said. 'Alexanor and Lykortas did that.'

Philopoemen's grin widened, if that was even possible. 'I need to hear about that.'

'You first,' Alexanor said.

'Well. Not much to tell. We didn't get into any fights – we burned nothing.'

'Why does everyone look so smug?' Kleostratos asked. 'You all look like you slept with the innkeeper's daughter and no one knows but you.'

'Speaking from experience?' Kau-Ippa asked.

Philopoemen bowed. 'And this is?'

'A war-leader of the Royal Sakje, and my wife,' Kleostratos said. 'Her name is Kau-Ippa.'

Philopoemen kissed her on both cheeks. 'Isn't that "white mare" in Sakje?'

'Oh! Husband, we have to watch our chatter with this one! Yes, War-leader, I am the White Mare.' She grinned. 'My enemies shit themselves when they hear that the White Mare rides.'

Philopoemen shook his head. 'Legends come to life. Kleostratos, you *did it*! I want to hear your story.'

Alexanor shook his head. 'No. The whole League is waiting in suspense for news of you.'

'We're all fine.'

'But no combat,' Alexanor said.

Dinaeos came through the door.

'Nay, we never so much as drew our swords.' He was also grinning. 'On the other hand, friends, if there's a single horse anywhere in northern Laconia, I'll be a helot.'

'Horse?' Kau-Ippa asked. Without a word spoken, they all drifted to the doorway.

And there, just outside the gates, the roadway was jammed with horses. Hundreds and hundreds of small, sturdy Greek horses.

'We found some cattle, too,' Dinaeos cackled.

'They followed us home,' Philopoemen said. 'What could we do? I wouldn't want to live in Sparta, either.'

Alexanor blinked. 'You went into Laconia on a *cattle raid*? Machanandas will declare war!'

Philopoemen nodded. He was slapping his sheepskin mittens against his thigh.

'He probably will,' the *Hipparchos* said. His grin was undeterred. 'He always meant to, anyway.'

'But now he'll do it without a cattle herd for food, and without any cavalry at all,' Dinaeos said.

Early spring in Arkadia: driving rain; ice in the passes. Only a fool travelled.

Or the *Hipparchos* of the Achaean League.

The first buds struggled to reach the weak, watery sun, and winter still ruled the high pastures – even in Megalopolis, there was snow under the west end of the great *stoa*, where the sun didn't reach. But Philopoemen led the *hippeis* of the League from Dyme to Patras, from Pharae to Boura, from Sicyon to Argos, and everywhere he held a drill day, in freezing rain, in driving snow, in frozen sunlight. He visited every town at least twice, and a few towns he visited six times – Argos, which he had to pass through repeatedly, and Patras. And he left a few of his precious Agema in each town; sometimes as many as ten men.

And he appointed a great muster at Megalopolis for the end of spring. At the end of every drill, his godlike lungs would bellow:

'At the Noumelion of the Corinthian month of Gamilios, the Attic Elaphebolion, the Delphic month of Herakles, I command you and all the youth of the League to assemble at Megalopolis with your horse and arms, to defend the commonwealth with your lives, to rescue our liberty, and prove your worth!'

Every time he roared it, they cheered. And as the winter went on, there were more of them, and they were better mounted, with more armour, on better horses. Men sat better; fewer fell off. Riding classes with the Scythian women were especially popular with the younger cavalrymen.

At Megalopolis, a dozen women of the *hippeis* class rode to the weekly muster with their fathers and husbands – a piece of enormous daring. Philopoemen gathered them together and gave them a speech that no one else heard, and sent them away.

The early spring stuttered and then came on, the buds swelled, and the horse herd began to put on weight. Coats grew less full; the bigger horses began to shine in the sun. Philopoemen had a long, private conversation with his former servant, Arkas. Alexanor knew he gave Arkas a large sum of money. And Arkas, who had known Alexanor for years, joined him on the wooden balcony over the courtyard – a balcony that would probably have held the women, if there were women in Philopoemen's house.

'Do you know where he's sending me, sir?' Arkas asked.

Alexanor always smiled to be called 'sir' but he shook his head.

'No idea. Macedon?'

It was a shrewd guess; there was already talk of requesting armed help from Macedon.

But Arkas shook his head, leant close, and whispered, 'Crete.'

Alexanor's eyebrows shot up without any volition on his part.

'I'd take a letter to Lentas for you, if you gave me one,' Arkas said.

'You are a fine young man. Give me an hour. Does Philopoemen—'

'He said I could tell you, sir.'

And the next day they rode out together. Alexanor rode back to Epidauros when the passes opened. Arkas came with him as far as the port of Epidauros. There was a fast trading galley there, with a

Corinthian crew. Alexanor watched the young man board and the vessel was off the beach and underway in minutes.

Alexanor went home and embraced his wife and for two weeks he did his duty at the sanctuary. It was a pleasant time and a difficult time. The place was almost empty due to the snow and ice, but loads of food and rare spices and drugs were coming into the port and the whole temple complex was working hard to prepare for the rush of pilgrims in the full blossom of spring. Chiron placed him in charge of the restocking of the sanctuary, and he worked from dawn until dark and then on by oil lamp, and he understood the level of trust placed in him.

And every traveller brought a story of preparations for war – from distant Macedon, from Epiros, from Athens and Thessaly to nearby Sparta – and among the guests at the sanctuary, all the talk was of war, and the rumours of war.

# CHAPTER FIVE

## The Achaean League

### PROSTATERIOS (MID MARCH TO LATE APRIL), 209 BCE

Argos was the city and the district that Philopoemen had visited most often during the winter – not because the *hippeis* there was good, but the opposite. Perhaps because Argos had so many Spartan exiles and sympathisers; perhaps because the oligarchs there, the very rich, had an impregnable citadel above the plain and had little to fear from Romans or Aetolians. They didn't like to drill and they didn't seem very interested in purchasing better helmets or better horses.

The district was the responsibility of Aristaenos, and the failure of the local *hippeis* drill made him angry.

It was raining; late spring. Forty of Philopoemen's Agema sat comfortably on their heavy warhorses, their postures expressing their contempt for the four-score young men who had actually showed for the drill.

'Why don't we execute a few?' Dinaeos said with an easy smile. 'Just to encourage the rest, so to speak?'

Alexanor knew that Argos was just the very tip of an ugly problem; for every success they'd had in training, there was also a failure, and a dozen towns had refused service altogether.

'Why execute the ones that have actually come out in the rain?' he asked.

'Because they are so very fucking useless,' Aristaenos said bitterly.

'Philopoemen, I accept full responsibility, but damn it, what am I to do?'

Philopoemen nodded, the wet plumes on his magnificent helmet nodding and shedding water.

'Don't let it trouble you,' he said. 'Set a drill date a week from today, and let's do what we can with those who have come.'

'You have a plan?' Aristaenos asked.

Dinaeos laughed. 'He always has a plan,' he said with a grin. 'Let's work these bastards a little. It'll be warmer.'

They rode up and down the plain of Argos until the local gentry were too tired to complain. At the end of the day, Philopoemen gave his usual speech, and ordained another drill day for a week later.

'Financial penalties for non-attendance will be doubled,' he said.

There were some rumblings, but nothing more.

A week later, Alexanor saw the *hippeis* of Argos assemble on a fine sunny morning. It finally felt like spring; there were flowers on the hillsides, jasmine and broom bloomed everywhere, and the ground was beginning to dry.

The *hippeis* of Argos showed no signs of the joy of spring. Only about thirty of them had made the new red cloaks; the same thirty, about a fifth of the whole, had helmets and breastplates and good swords. The rest had very little and stood by bony horses and spoke loudly.

Philopoemen had brought a smaller escort than usual – just twenty cavalry, who sat well up the ridge behind him, mere spectators.

He paraded the Argos *hippeis* and they rode up and down the plain in sullen incompetence for an hour.

Philopoemen smiled.

He trotted to the front of the formation, a living Centaur, his scarlet cloak flowing in the breeze like the banner of a victorious army, his plumes nodding. He smiled, as if at some private joke.

'I think ...' he said slowly, and then he raised his voice. 'I think perhaps you would benefit from watching the manoeuvres of a better trained cavalry troop.'

He waved at his escort. They came down their ridge at a fast walk, and manoeuvred from a file into a column of fours while coming down the ridge; the column wheeled smartly as they passed Philopoemen and cantered away across the plain. Almost at the edge of vision they wheeled about and formed a single line, and then the line seemed to vanish; in fact, they reformed into a single file.

One rider galloped from the head of the file, put javelins into two prepared targets ...

And then another ...

And a third ...

'That's all nice,' mocked one man. 'But those are professional cavalrymen. Mercenaries. We won't look like that in a month of feast days.'

Philopoemen said nothing.

The last troopers in the file were now galloping along the plain, their horses moving so fast that it was difficult to follow their actions.

The last rider put three javelins into the same target.

'So what?' spat an angry man.

'You think we're going to be like that?' said another.

'I do,' Philopoemen said.

He raised his hand, and the line of his escort came forward at a fast trot and arrived in a cloud of dust. It took a moment to clear.

'Gods!' spat the loudest complainer. 'They're all women!'

Alethea sat her horse like the natural rider she was, in a leather breastplate and a red cloak, and behind her was Simmias' wife Heraklea and two dozen more young women. A few – the ringers – had facial tattoos and other indications of their Thracian or Sakje origin, but more than a dozen of them were obviously Greek women.

'That's disgusting!' barked the loud man of Argos.

'What's disgusting,' Philopoemen said, 'is that these women began training *after* you began. Heraklea there didn't know how to *ride* four months ago.'

'You lie,' growled the Argosian.

Philopoemen rode up close to the man. 'You are a soft-handed coward. Unfit to serve your country, unable to even understand the duties of a man—'

The man lashed out with his fist.

Philopoemen took his fist out of the air and threw him from his horse. He glanced around, his face stern, even menacing.

'I will give you gentlemen one more chance to be prepared to train as cavalrymen,' he said. 'If you are not ready, I will assess every one of you for the maximum fine *and I will field these women as the* hippeis *of Argos*. It amuses me that you see this as a mortal insult, because of the "well-known inferiority" of women. It amuses me, because right now, anyone in Greece can see that they are more fit for war than any of you. You are dismissed.'

'I will sue you in the courts!' ranted the man on his back in the mud.

And the local *Hipparchos*, Memnon, spat as he passed.

Philopoemen looked down. He shook his head, touched his reins and rode away, his contempt palpable, as visible as his scarlet cloak.

'That was risky,' Alexanor said, a day later, at Philopoemen's table.

Lykortas agreed. 'We really don't need Argos to lead the secession of the dissenting cities of the League,' he said. 'It is the strongest city after Corinth—'

Philopoemen sat back, swirling watered wine in a beautiful Aegyptian glass.

'What would you recommend that I do?' he asked.

Alexanor waved his hands. 'I have no idea. But shaming men with the learning powers of women is somehow both trite and unfair. Unfair to women, as we all know they can learn as fast as men – indeed, I'm not sure they are not better horsemen.'

'Horsewomen!' laughed Kleostratos.

'But mostly because those women want so desperately to participate. They crave the opportunity to contribute ... anything.' Alexanor shrugged.

Philopoemen smiled.

'I have fallen into one of your philosophical traps,' Alexanor said.

'Yes,' Philopoemen said. 'I'm savouring it. I catch Dinaeos all the time, but catching you—'

'Stop gloating and speak plainly.'

'The men of Argos shouldn't need any greater motivation. You say these women are highly motivated? Why? Are they fighting for their lives and their honour? Are they fighting to preserve their entire way of life? Because *the men of Argos are*. If they choose to forget that, they cannot blame the women of Megalopolis for remembering it.'

'Good gods!' Dinaeos interjected. 'You're not going to put my wife in a battle line.'

Arkas came in. He bowed his head slightly and handed a slip of papyrus to Philopoemen, who glanced at it and raised his eyebrows. Then he turned back to Dinaeos.

'I'm certainly going to put Kleostratos' wife in my battle line,' he said. 'But not Alethea, I admit it. I'm a radical but not a fool. If I sent your Alethea and her girls on a cattle raid, the reaction of the male Greek world would hurt us for a decade. I'll merely add that I'm quite sure that Alethea and at least six of her women are better troopers than some of those men at their best. Viewed rationally—'

'Oh, gods, here we go ...' Dinaeos shook his head.

'The horse makes us all equal.'

'Crap,' Dinaeos said. 'I could kill my wife in a single pass.'

'Ouch,' Alexanor said.

Dinaeos shook his head. 'No, I stand by what I said. I'm bigger and stronger and I know more about fighting.'

'I think if my wife were here,' Kleostratos said, 'she'd say that the horse *and the bow* make men and women equal.'

Dinaeos thought for a moment. 'Yes,' he agreed, finally. 'Yes ... I can see that.'

Philopoemen smiled. It was a thin smile, not a grin – a smile of fatigue and perhaps frustration.

'Well,' he said. 'I did what I could. The Argosians will never get another drill day.'

'Apollo's rod! Why not?' asked Lykortas.

Philopoemen turned his thin smile on his officers. He waved the papyrus.

'Kau-Ippa says the Spartans are marching. Six thousand hoplites and *peltastoi* will cross the frontier tomorrow or the next day.'

'Poseidon's sacred horses,' muttered Dinaeos.

'Light the signal fires,' Philopoemen said. 'No. The general muster is less than a week away. Let's let the Spartans imagine we're unprepared.'

The next two days passed in a whirlwind of preparations. All across the southern marches of the League, farmers moved their winter grain stores, or whatever they had left, into the fortresses and the stronger positions. It had all been planned since the autumn, and while there was grumbling, the borderers knew exactly what happened when a Spartan army came through.

During those two days, Alexanor ran a dozen errands, visiting farms that lay along the border to make sure they had complied with Philopoemen's orders, or posting guides for the movement of herds to the north, or, finally, commanding a detachment of excited *epheboi* watching the passes south of Gefyra. He also watched a perfectly competent midwife deliver a baby and didn't interfere. All in a day's work.

The Spartan army moved with professional caution. They left their winter camp and marched, first east, and then very slowly north.

'Machanandas is fighting the wrong war.' Philopoemen sounded different – superior, arrogant, perhaps even smug. 'Or, gods! I hope he is.' He seemed to deflate.

'Brother, I worry that your hatred for this man will in some way blind you,' Alexanor said. He said it in gasps because he could barely breathe.

They were on horseback because they were living like Scythians, eating on horseback, riding all day and even catching naps on horseback. They were watching the Spartans march through the defile of Kamaritsa.

One of the many difficult features of the days on horseback had been that the new Achaean cavalry, or at least the Agema, seemed to think that they could ride up and down mountains, over cliffs and up gorges. Alexanor was in a state of nearly constant fear just staying mounted. Some of the climbs might have given him pause on foot; on horseback they seemed insane. And downhill was worse than uphill – hills so steep that he had trouble staying on his horse.

The climb up the Kamaritsa ridge had been one such nightmare. Philopoemen was calmly watching the Spartan army, which seemed vast, while Alexanor tried to steady his pulse. Around them, a dozen young men seemed indifferent to the height and the climb they'd just made. Alexanor wondered if he was lacking something, or perhaps they were all insane.

'I do hate him,' Philopoemen said.

There was a long silence.

Below them, the Spartans filed off from the right, so that their phalanx narrowed for some indeterminate number of files – perhaps three hundred – to just two. A few tiny figures ran through the gorge below, and then a few more, and then more, and finally a respectable company was formed for battle on the far side. Only then did the main body begin to pass the defile.

Dinaeos nodded as if he'd been answering questions from the *epheboi*, and perhaps he had.

'So, why not just stop them in the defile?' he asked. 'I think I know, but all the boys will want to know too.'

Philopoemen was still watching the Spartans perform their passage of the defile. They did it well. It was a formation change that Alexanor had seen practised on Crete and he knew that it took time and discipline to learn which file to follow, to keep the even flow that he saw below.

'The Spartans want a battle. They expect one,' Philopoemen said. 'They have the very best heavy infantry, at least in this part of Greece. A fight in a narrow defile would be perfect for Machanandas.'

Dinaeos was nodding.

'What do we want?' Alexanor asked.

'Wings?' Philopoemen said. 'A Macedonian phalanx?' He shrugged. 'Right now I'd settle for knowing that my trained cavalry were actually going to be at the rally point in five days. My worst nightmare now is that everyone tries to make a separate peace and all the city cavalry stays home from the muster.' He smiled, but it was a wintry, fragile smile.

Alexanor was watching the Spartans. 'We can't ... fight that. With cavalry.'

Philopoemen nodded. 'I hope that Machanandas thinks the same. Come on, I know how much you enjoy riding down a steep hill. And if we get cut off and captured, only Machanandas will laugh.'

They plunged down the hill, and Alexanor thought that either he'd plunge over his horse's ears to his death, or perhaps the animal would fall and he'd fall with her. He prayed to Apollo and to Poseidon all the way down. Perhaps because of their intercession, he arrived on the valley floor in one piece and followed the Achaean cavalrymen over a low hill, through the new grass of spring, to a tiny shrine of Herakles where two dozen Agema waited with a pair of Spartan helots they'd taken prisoner.

The two helots sat on the ground. They didn't appear to be afraid, and Alexanor watched them with the curiosity that most men would have for a bear-baiting or a dogfight.

Philopoemen questioned them at length and then ordered them taken to Megalopolis.

'What will happen to them there?' Alexanor asked.

'They'll be manumitted by order of the League and they will be free men,' Philopoemen said.

'Free to starve, maybe,' Dinaeos said. 'I hope someone hires them as farm labour.'

It had started to rain; the veterans all had wide-brimmed *petasos* hats and they pulled them onto their heads. A few of the *epheboi* had cloaks which they pulled over their heads.

Philopoemen made a face and then looked at Dinaeos.

'As usual, you put your finger on the problem,' he said.

'It's my major talent,' Dinaeos agreed.

'Enemy cavalry!' a voice barked, and Philopoemen took one glance and nodded.

'Let's get out of here,' he said in a conversational voice.

The Achaean cavalry withdrew, although they easily outnumbered the handful of Tarentine mercenaries coming up the valley behind them.

They rode north until they crossed the boundary stones of the League, and then they halted. The rain had become a downpour – a rare occurrence in late spring in Arkadia – and one that was clearly slowing the march of the Spartans behind them.

But an hour later, wet to the skin, the forty of them watched the Spartan vanguard cross the boundary stones and halt. An officer in a scarlet cloak was already laying out a camp, and more than a hundred helots went to work gathering brush and cutting it with hooked knives.

Philopoemen left Lykortas with a dozen of the younger Agema cavalrymen and, after a short speech and a broad smile, he took the rest of the tired troopers and rode north on the road to Megalopolis.

Alexanor had seldom seen his friend so withdrawn. The moment Philopoemen was done smiling at the scouts he was leaving behind, he folded that smile away and rode with a face almost devoid of emotion, a mask.

Alexanor left him alone for a while and rode with the *epheboi*, chatting with Kleander. But when Philopoemen turned and glanced at him, he pushed his horse to a trot despite his reservations about the narrowness of the trail. He was beginning, after many years as a hesitant rider, to trust his mount; if his gelding believed that he could pass another horse, Alexanor had to fight the urge to interfere.

'So ...?' Alexanor said.

Philopoemen didn't answer with his usual smile. In fact, he didn't turn his head.

Alexanor almost made the mistake of smiling. 'You, my friend, are afraid.'

'You are so fucking helpful. Is this some sort of medical achievement? You can identify fear in a close friend?' Philopoemen was savage.

Alexanor bit his lip. 'What's wrong?'

Philopoemen glanced at the valley below them.

'The Spartans are invading the League, and right now, the whole League army is on this hillside.'

'Surely it's not that bad.'

Philopoemen glanced at him, and he saw the blankness in his friend's eyes, the tightness in the corners, the pinched look of his nose.

'I am no doubt being foolish, but until I see the cavalry at the muster, I can only think of how many cities were claiming just two weeks ago that they would secede from the League and make their own peace. And I watch the Spartans coming with confidence, and I wonder what Machanandas knows. Perhaps he's talked to Tegea – certainly he has agents in Argos, probably even in Megalopolis.' He smiled bitterly. 'I just keep imagining the drill field empty.'

Alexanor shook his head. 'You ...' He was thinking, trying to imagine what was going through his friend's mind. 'They'll be there. Dyme, Epidauros, Hermione, Corinth, Patrae, Aegio ...'

'I know,' Philopoemen said. 'No, I lie. I *don't know*. I felt this way in Crete a dozen times, but ...'

Alexanor reached out.

'But sometimes I just have trouble breathing. This isn't Crete. This is *my home*. And I failed ...' He breathed in and out. 'I failed before. I lost my ...'

Alexanor put a hand on Philopoemen's shoulder. 'They'll be there.'

'Thanks,' Philopoemen said. 'I'm ...'

They rode on in silence for a while and Philopoemen said, 'Yes. I'm better. I *hope* that they are there.'

Alexanor looked away. It was too raw.

*He'll go and fight the Spartans by himself.*

'What's next?' he asked.

'Assuming there's someone at the muster?'

Philopoemen was fully in control of himself; the mask was gone, and his face was relaxed. But the corresponding smile was still bitter.

'Sure, assuming that,' Alexanor said.

Philopoemen looked behind them, then up at the hillsides, shining wetly in the sun, with the roar of the temporary waterfalls loud in their ears.

'We invade Sparta,' he said.

# CHAPTER SIX

---

## The Achaean League

### AGRIANOS (MID APRIL TO LATE MAY), 209 BCE

The muster of the federal cavalry of the Achaean League was an event that resonated throughout the Mediterranean. Lykortas had done his homework. All the spies of all the major states had managed to attend, so that the inn on the Argos road, where Leon and Alexanor had stayed their first night, years ago, returning from a winter in Macedon, was packed with foreigners.

'If we burned that taverna,' Lykortas said, 'we'd be killing intelligence services from Pergamum to Aegypt.' He smiled with satisfaction.

The satisfaction was general among Philopoemen's staff. The Spartan invasion had, in fact, alarmed the whole League. There were more than a thousand cavalrymen camped across Philopoemen's farms, eating his grain stores at a prodigious rate. And more were coming in from the north, and from the east coast. By the stone barn that Philopoemen had built with his own hands, Aristaenos and Dinaeos were fitting men for their panoplies, choosing the best riders and the best horses to get the heavy armour. Alexanor stood with Kleander, among the now-expanded Agema – two hundred cavalrymen who stood in their ranks, wearing red cloaks and bronze breastplates that shone in the sun.

'You did it,' Alexanor said to Philopoemen, who had just finished adjudicating a squabble between two contingents over their position in the battle line.

Philopoemen nodded. 'Can I confess to you my least favourite element of command?' he asked quietly.

'Tell me anything.'

Alexanor was always fascinated by how Philopoemen's mind worked.

'I effortlessly replace one crisis with another. We have done nothing yet.'

'Nonsense,' Lykortas said. 'Forty rogues and intelligencers are even now scribbling their secret messages on hidden tablets to their various masters. In a week, every warlord in the Middle Sea will know that Achaea has a brilliant general at the head of a mighty force of cavalry.' He grinned. 'Aetolia won't dare invade.'

Forty paces away, the contingent from Dyme wheeled by sub-sections. One of the section leaders fell off his horse and the whole column disintegrated into a rising chaos of dust and horses.

Philopoemen winced. He trotted forward to help the officers sort out the Dyme cavalry, and behind him, Lykortas shrugged.

'Or maybe they'll underestimate us?' he asked hopefully.

The next morning, after a brief speech by Kykliadas, the entire force rode south. Before the sun was high, Alexanor could see the rising columns of smoke like funeral pyres where the Spartans were burning Achaean farms.

Philopoemen sent the Thracians and Scythians out on a reconnaissance and then called for his officers. Alexanor wasn't sure of his status, but he had a breastplate and Dariush handed him a fine helmet, care of his thoughtful wife, and he followed Lykortas. The helmet was like an old friend; the weight settled on his neck muscles and the extra weight of the horsehair crest was there too.

Inside his mind, he knew what the helmet meant. He suspected that the helmet made him a different man. Not a doctor. Not a priest.

A killer.

He released a pent-up breath and joined the officers.

No one dismounted. The officers gathered in a circle of mounted men: Lykortas and Dinaeos, Aristaenos and Kleostratos and six more, leaders of the largest volunteer contingents; Alexanor knew Aristides of Hermione and Lycurgos of Epidauros; Simmias and his brother Polyainos were there as messengers and bodyguards to the *Hipparchos*. Aristides was, at least temporarily, in command of all the 'coastal' *hippeis*.

Alexanor nodded to Simmias, whom he hadn't seen for months, and the man walked his horse over and clasped hands with him.

'I knew you were a fighter,' he said.

Alexanor frowned. 'Not by choice.'

'Only my brother fights by choice,' Simmias said quietly.

Philopoemen spoke calmly; he sounded like everyone's favourite tutor, gentle but firm.

'The Thracians will locate an isolated Spartan detachment. The Agema will envelop it and destroy it, and the federal cavalry will cover us.'

'What form does this "covering" take?' Aristides asked. His tone was light – ironic. If he was racked with nerves, he wasn't giving anything away.

Philopoemen smiled grimly. 'We'll sit here on this ridge and do nothing.'

'We?' another officer asked – a thickset man in a beautiful breast-plate covered in snakes and Gorgons' heads.

'I'll be right here with you,' Philopoemen said. 'Dinaeos will command the Agema.'

Dinaeos grinned. 'Thanks, boss.'

'What we want here is to pluck the lowest hanging fruit,' Philopoemen said. 'We don't want a fight. We want a massacre or a rout. Am I clear?'

Dinaeos nodded. 'Absolutely.'

A quarter of an hour passed, and then a rider came up the ridge at a full gallop. Even far away, Alexanor knew it was Kau-Ippa. She rode a white mare, and she didn't look much like a man, and she rode better than anyone he'd ever seen – better even than Philopoemen.

'Fucking cowards!' she spat as she rode up. 'All my life I hear about these "Spartans" and now they are running for home.'

Philopoemen shifted and his horse felt his unease and took several steps.

'Tell us,' he said with firm control of his voice.

'As soon as they saw you on the ridge they turned the whole column south,' she said. Then she smiled, and it was like a wolf looking at a long lamb on a hillside. 'But their Spartan cavalry is in the rearguard, and they are being humiliated by my people.'

Philopoemen nodded. 'I think you are brilliant.'

'I am the White Mare. Listen. Greeks think women are useless, so nothing makes them angry like a band of adolescent females killing their officers.' She barked a laugh. 'We will draw them away from their main body slowly ...' She pointed towards the distant mountains. 'Maybe at that wood – on the second ridge.'

'I see it,' Philopoemen said.

Alexanor wondered if his eyesight was fading.

Dinaeos nodded. 'I think I see it. Stay in touch, Kau-Ippa.'

Kleostratos turned his horse. 'I'll keep you linked.'

'Agema!' Dinaeos called.

A thrill ran through the ranks of the elite cavalry; even the horses seemed to be excited. Kleander's horse gave a curvet.

'And the federal cavalry?' Aristides asked.

Philopoemen was gazing over the ground – three ridges, thickly inhabited, with farms along the bottom land and grazing and wood-lots along the tops of the ridges. They were on the highest ridge for miles, so that the next three looked like massive waves about to crash on a beach; pale green waves, in spring. In a month they'd be parched orange-brown.

Philopoemen nodded sharply. Alexanor knew of old that he had made some decision; the head nod was his private acceptance of the moment.

'We will move up behind the Agema,' Philopoemen said. 'If something goes wrong, we will be in close support.'

'That's more like it!' Lycurgos said. 'I don't want to sit here and do nothing.'

'I like that man,' Lykortas said.

'Alexanor, stay with me,' Philopoemen said. 'Listen, all of you. If I send Alexanor to you, he speaks with my voice. Understand? Obey him!'

Dinaeos raised his arm in the old Olympic salute.

'I do whatever he says anyway,' he grumbled.

Lykortas nodded.

Aristaenos frowned. But that was his way.

'On me.'

Dinaeos led the Agema away at a trot down the ridge.

They crossed a ploughed field, which cost them time, but the out-riders led them through a gap in the field wall and then they reformed on the distant road, flowing like water.

'Damn, they're good,' Aristides said.

Philopoemen raised his hand. 'We'll follow the road,' he said. 'Keep together.'

He set off at a walk. The column marched behind him. The road they were on, the main road west from Megalopolis, ran along the ridge for stades, but before they'd gone three hundred paces a small farm road ran south and Philopoemen found one of the Thracians there. The man waved and galloped away down the road.

The column followed Philopoemen down the ridge, into the valley at their feet, and almost immediately lost their eagle's eye view of the three ridges and the rising columns of smoke from the farms in the valleys.

At the base of the ridge they crossed a stream on an ancient, high-arched bridge.

'A thousand years old,' Philopoemen said. 'Or so my fathers used to tell me.'

On the far side was a rich farm – or what had been a rich farm. The stone barn was smouldering; three dead men lay in the yard, all slaves. The house was afire, and there was a smell of burnt pork.

'Apollo!' spat Alexanor, who knew the scent of burnt human flesh all too well.

'Ride on.' Philopoemen's face was closed; eyes narrowed. He was giving nothing away. 'They will be avenged in half an hour.'

The column started up the next ridge.

Philopoemen waved the column on and then rode aside at a sacred grove – a dozen tall cypress trees and an altar. He looked back down the ridge. The volunteers were spread out almost all the way to the top of the first ridge.

'Oh, gods,' he muttered.

Men had stopped to gaze at the fires, and a small party was trying to get water on the house. A jam of horses and men at the bridge was preventing the column from moving.

'You go on,' Alexanor said. 'I can fix this.'

Philopoemen nodded. 'Do it. I might kill someone.'

Alexanor could hear the suppressed anger and the fear. He tried to sound positive.

'Never mind—'

'This is how disaster starts,' Philopoemen said very quietly. 'Get them moving.'

Alexanor turned his horse and rode down the ridge. He stayed off the road and trotted down a farm trail he'd seen, over a culvert and then back towards the road at the bridge. By ill luck or perhaps something worse, the contingent stopped at the bridge was that of Argos. Alexanor rode in among them.

'Back to your ranks, gentlemen,' he said. 'You need to cross the bridge in two files.'

'Who the fuck are you?' shouted one of the Argosians.

The priest of Asklepios slipped away, and the Rhodian marine took over.

'Someone who outranks you,' he said, his voice flat. 'Next time, I'll hit you in the head. *Look at me! All of you!*'

The Argosian cavalry shifted and muttered, but every head turned, and there was silence.

'*You and you follow me!*' Alexanor had not used that particular voice for a long time, but it was still there. '*Form two files on those men and don't fuck around!*'

He turned his gelding and trotted across the high bridge and the two men followed him.

'Column of twos!' he called in a normal command voice.

They were moving. So were the eastern League cavalry behind them – the men of Hermione and Epidauros.

He plunged into the men at the farmyard.

'On your horses,' he called.

'There's people in the house!' a man cried.

'They're dead. Philopoemen says we can avenge them in half an hour, but only ...' He looked around. 'Only if we're an army and not a mob. Mount!'

Looking sheepish, most of the men mounted. A few hung back, and Alexanor ignored them. There are always limits to an officer's authority, and sometimes, as he knew all too well, it's best to ignore the shirkers.

'Move it!' he snapped to the *Hipparchos* of Dyme.

'I thought ...' the man began.

He was *someone* in the hierarchy of the League. Alexanor had seen him before – at the *Synodos* and at the temple of Olympian Zeus at Aegio.

'Never mind what you thought!' Alexanor snapped. 'Get your men up the ridge, in order.'

'Yes, sir,' the man answered and Alexanor almost smiled. *Sir.* He shook his head as he rode away.

He turned aside and looked back. The Dyme contingent was shuffling into motion; the front of the column was a full stade separated or more and the gap was widening, and the Dyme contingent had stopped the Argosians from getting across the bridge. It was sorting out, but the column was effectively broken in half.

Alexanor didn't want to be in charge of anything; he'd had enough of war. But he understood certain necessities and he'd had an idea. He crossed the shuffling river of horsemen and rode back down the column to where the last of the Argosians were finally clearing the bridge and found Aristides.

'Aristides!' he called. 'Follow me!'

Aristides turned his head. A couple of the rear files of the Argosians trotted over.

'No! You go with your own unit!' he shouted.

They turned away, shaking their heads.

'What?' Aristides asked.

'Follow me. With your men.'

Aristides looked at him a moment, tempted to ask questions.

'I'm taking you around the logjam on the road,' Alexanor said.

'Ah!' Aristides said. 'Bless you, then. Let's go.'

The coastal horse, led by the Epidaurans, turned off the road and went up the farm track. They had to go in single file, but they were better riders than they had been in the autumn and they managed to make speed – somewhere between a trot and a canter – once they were out on the fields. The track was very narrow, with deep, ploughed mud on either hand, but the Epidaurans were equal to the job at hand. In minutes, they were passing through the sacred grove at the crest of the ridge.

'Column of fours!' Alexanor ordered, and then cringed. 'Apologies, Aristides.'

Aristides shrugged. 'No problem,' he said, indicating that he was, perhaps, offended.

Regardless, the column formed on the move and continued along the road, having completely passed the Dyme and Argos contingents. In fifteen minutes they had caught the front half of the column just as they passed the top of the second ridge, which also had a small grove of sacred trees and a dozen stelae and a monument – a sleeping lion.

'The League fought Sparta here – fifteen years ago,' Aristides said.

'More like twenty,' Lykortas said. 'Well done, Alexanor. Philopoemen sent me back to find you. Halt and dismount as soon as the unit in front is halted – tight order, ready to remount and fight. Water your horses if you are close enough to the stream. Got all that?'

Aristides nodded. 'Halt when these ahead of me halt. Water my horses if I can get it done fast.'

Lykortas nodded. 'Excellent. Alexanor, with me.'

The two of them rode forward up the column to Philopoemen, whose fancy, Italian-style plumes set him off from the other red-cloaks from two stades away. He was watching the next ridge, where the occasional glint of bronze or red gave away the position of the Agema, who were climbing the ridge through the woods.

It was a little like watching a really good play, or perhaps the end of a really excellent race; as soon as Alexanor understood what he was seeing, his heart was beating fast, and he felt a little like he was choking. There, almost at the top of the next ridge, was the Spartan cavalry. They were formed in a dense block, but in front of them, some were skirmishing.

Below them on the ridge were a handful of fast-moving figures – Centaurs, at this distance.

'The Sakje have killed someone important,' Philopoemen said. 'And now the Spartans are trying to recover the body. I swear, I will sacrifice a bull to Poseidon and another to Zeus. Oh, gods ...'

The Agema were coming up the ridge on the flank of the Spartan block.

The Spartan cavalry charged the Sakje and the Thracians. The steppe cavalry turned and ran, changing directions like a flock of birds, all together. Even from four stades away, Alexanor saw the sparkle of javelins and arrows.

The Spartan commander was no fool. He drove the Thracians off their victim and then halted to rally his squadron.

The first Achaean Agema troopers emerged from the woods behind him and began to form on the road.

'Damn it!' Philopoemen said. 'So close.'

A minute earlier and the Achaeans would have struck the flank of the Spartan cavalry. As it was ...

'No sense in waiting,' Philopoemen snapped. The Aegionian contingent was at the front of the column. He motioned at their *Hipparch*, Nikos. 'Forward.'

Nikos, the older man who hadn't owned a helmet, smiled.

'Come on, lads!' he shouted, and buckled the cheek plates of his helmet. The Aegionian cavalry gave a cheer. The whole column began to move forward.

'Lykortas, ride down the column and tell them this is for real, and forget watering their horses. Alexanor ...' He was watching the hillside. 'Go and get your friend Aristides and see if you can follow that track over there.'

'Into the flank of the Spartan woods?'

'Exactly.'

Philopoemen was staring at the ridge opposite. The Achaean Agema was still forming on the road, and the Spartans were trying to turn to face them. The Thracians and Sakje were already back, harrying the defenceless rear of the Spartan horse. A red-cloaked Spartan trooper fell, a spear in his back.

'That's Nabis.' Philopoemen was smiling. 'Here we go.'

If it was Nabis, he wasn't giving in easily. His rear files turned about *again* and charged the Thracians, who melted away. His front files started up the ridge in good order.

The hastily formed Achaeans above them charged.

Alexanor couldn't stay and watch. He was already headed back north, looking for Aristides. But his last glance over his shoulder caught a glint of metal in the fields beyond the trees; something was on his projected line of march. Helots? Psiloi?

He drove his heels into his horse and forgot that he didn't like to gallop. He reined in by Aristides. Behind him, the coastal cavalry were mostly standing by their horses; a few men were watering in the stream.

'Me again. We're going to try and flank the Spartans to our left. Understand? They're on the crest of the next ridge.'

'I understand,' Aristides said.

'Get mounted. I'll be back in two minutes.'

Alexanor tapped his heels to his mount and rode away to the east, following a footpath. It petered out at an irrigation ditch and he had to come back and try another, and then a third, while the Epidaurans watched him and returned to their ranks.

The fourth track led across the first field and through a gap in the boundary wall.

It was the best path he was likely to find, and the field beyond was rocky, more a grazing field than a barley field.

'On me!' he roared, and waved.

The Epidaurans were all mounted – a couple of latecomers from the watering trotting up from the back – but they were *moving*, and they turned off the road and began to cross the field. Alexanor was stunned to see Kritias riding with them, in a breastplate and helmet.

Aristides ordered them into two files.

Alexanor rode away, pushing his mount to a gallop. He passed the wall and slowed to cross the next field, which was indeed rocky, but firm under his horse's hooves. The track continued, muddy but firm, over the ridge and down the far side – a wide field of tiny flowers, the full glory of Greek spring shining, still wet with dew in the shade at the edge of the field and baked dry in the late morning sun at mid-field.

Off to his right, the Agema was head to head with the Spartans. The numbers were equal; the Achaeans had the hill behind them and the Spartans were probably veterans.

Alexanor had the sense he'd had years before as a marine; the fight to his left was not his immediate problem and he ignored it. His immediate problem was a path up the next ridge, and the possibility of an enemy resistance. He glanced back, made sure that Aristides was still following, and then he went down the field of flowers. It was steep, but days riding with the Agema had freed him from some of his fear of steep slopes. His horse had no problem; he rode easily down to the banks of a spate-stream. The little stream was nearly empty, with just a trickle of clear water flowing past his gelding's hooves, and the horse picked his way across with ease. There were trees and shrubs all along the watercourse, and he had to push through a screen of foliage to see the field ...

On the far side of the trees was another field, also unploughed, and in it ...

Was a squadron of Tarentines. Perhaps two hundred cavalrymen, all well mounted, with big round shields. Italian professionals. They were waiting in four ranks, their officers watching the fight on the road.

Heads turned, and men saw him.

Alexanor cursed.

*There's no way the Epidaurans can match these*, he thought.

But in the same moment, he saw a dozen of the Epidaurans burst out of the brush along the stream, led by Aristides.

*Too late to back away.*

'On me!' he shouted. 'Form on me!'

Aristides saw the Tarentines, but he obeyed, turning to his right and trotting along to where Alexanor sat. Another clump of Epidaurans crunched out of the brush and trees and moved to join them.

The Tarentines were splitting off a troop on the ground above them. But wheeling took time.

'Good quality professional cavalry,' Alexanor said.

Aristides looked at them.

'We're going to charge them,' Alexanor said.

'What?' Aristides asked.

'*Prepare to charge!*' Alexanor roared.

'I thought you were a priest,' Aristides said, but he smiled.

They had about sixty men.

'Stay here, and gather the next group to cross,' Alexanor said to Aristides. 'Charge behind me.'

'But—'

'Just do it.'

'Why?'

'They're mercenaries, far from home.' Alexanor shook his head. He hoped that's how the Tarentines felt about it. He held his spear over his head. 'This is what you came to do!' he roared. 'We are not spectators! We are not in reserve! You saw the dead women they burned in their houses. This is your country. This is your hour. Up the hill and over these mercenaries!'

They cheered. It was a lusty cheer – the wild shout of young men who have no idea what war really is.

'Forward at the walk!' he called.

The Epidaurans, all those who'd made it across the stream so far, started forward. Their formation was terrible, far too open. They were going uphill into superior troops who outnumbered them, and it was all insane.

'Close on the centre!' Alexanor called.

It was no use; a handful of well-mounted men on the far left burst out of the brush and went straight forward. His little *taxeis* was more like a wild horse herd.

The Tarentines above them on the hillside threw their javelins. One man went down with a spear through his body, and two more went down with spears in their horses. Another young man fell off his horse in the shock of the moment, and yet another lost control of his mount, who bolted, riding west, towards the fight on the road.

Alexanor took this in at a glance and saw no point in trying for a better order.

'At them!' he roared. '*Now!*'

The Epidauran cavalrymen put their heels to their horses and charged up the hill. They were too raw, too untrained, to know that what they were doing was stupid. They began to scream, the high ululation of the Arkadians.

The little knot of riders who had swept off to the left turned inwards like a fish-hook, hooting like hunters.

The Tarentines threw their second javelins. Now a dozen men fell, some screaming, but the charge was not stopped. It was the Tarentine horses who flinched. Their horses were smaller than the Achaean horses – smaller and less well fed – and they began to flinch under their riders. They didn't run ...

Alexanor threaded between two Tarentines, his horse at full stretch, and his spear-stroke was too *slow* to take either one because he was too surprised that he was suddenly *there*, in among them. But he used his haft, sweeping a man from his mount, and then there was a close press and then closer, a meadow full of close-packed horses and desperate men.

Alexanor caught a man's spear in his bridle hand, pulled the man off balance and then, his legs locked on his own mount, he used the man's weight against him. He turned his horse and threw him to the ground and stabbed him with his own spear. He missed as the man squirmed, and then slammed his spear haft into the man's helmet as he tried to rise, knocking him unconscious. Then he'd lost his spear, wrestling with a man who didn't know as much as he and died for it. He left his *xiphos* in a third. Turning, looking for his people ... A heavy blow against the crest of his helmet, and he was staggered. Another blow and he almost fell, leant so far forward that he got a mouthful of his horse's mane, and then he was out of the press, alone.

He was fifty paces from the second troop of Tarentines. He couldn't really take in what he was seeing, and he shook his head, which hurt. Something bad happened when he shook his head, and a big piece of his scalp seemed to be hanging in front of his eyes, and he closed his eyes and opened them and his horse was falling.

He rolled off his dying mount's back by instinct or training and rolled to his feet. And then the dizziness made him drop to one knee.

It wasn't his scalp that was cut. It was the whole horsetail crest of his helmet, which had been cut loose from the crest box and was flapping around. He took that in as if it had happened to someone else.

The Tarentines to his front had killed his horse; it lay next to him, looking like a spear target on drill day.

Three of the Tarentines burst out of their formation at a gallop and came for him, cantering easily over the beautiful flowers. Alexanor found his spear on the ground, blinked, and used the spear to parry the first thrown javelin, batting it out of the air from a low guard, as Xenophon taught. He flicked his spear up and then plunged the weapon into the man's groin – a killing blow that also took him off his horse. He did it all without a moment's thought or planning.

Alexanor lost the spear, but the other two were past him; a tumbling javelin suggested that they'd tried to bring him down with throws.

The screaming man on the ground tried and failed to keep his horse's reins. It was like a gift from Poseidon. Alexanor snagged the reins from the dying man's hands and mounted ... tried to mount. His knees weren't working perfectly; something was wrong, and he couldn't get up on the horse. He slid back down as the two Tarentines turned, but now the dead man's horse was between him and them. They were circling him, but behind them it was obvious that the first Tarentine troop was having second thoughts about the combat. Men were turning away, and a dozen Epidauran riders burst out of the melee ...

Alexanor tried to mount again ... This time, after a ridiculous struggle, he got his far leg over the horse's back as it turned under him.

His two immediate adversaries turned away at a gallop, abandoning the hunt. As if they were giving a signal, the whole of the Tarentine troop broke, leaving six dead men on the ground, and as many again as prisoners.

Alexanor untied his cheek plates and tugged at his helmet even as Aristides approached from one direction and Dariush, unarmed, trotted up from the other with a fresh horse.

'Apollo – you look like death,' Aristides said. 'It's amazing you are alive.'

'What ...?' Alexanor was looking at Dariush. 'You need a spear, at least.'

He had trouble forming words, and he slurred everything.

'With pleasure,' Dariush said. 'Your head is all blood.'

Ever the perfect servant, he produced a towel.

Alexanor touched his head with it. It felt mushy. He looked at the helmet on his knee; the whole right side was crushed, the repoussé ruined.

'Fuck,' he managed. He couldn't see properly and nothing made sense. 'Take ... command ...'

Aristides nodded. 'Yes.'

Alexanor knew too much medicine to allow himself to do what he wanted to do – sleep. He blinked and blinked again, trying to fight the nausea; failed, and threw up, which his new horse tolerated.

Dariush had a second towel.

Alexanor managed a deep breath, and then another, and the world began to clear a little. Aristides was rallying the victorious Achaeans. They'd lost more men than the Tarentines; on the other hand, more and more of the coastal cavalry were coming over the stream behind and filtering through the scrub and brush to join the fight, so that the force forming on the site of the combat was now double the size of the Tarentines – almost five hundred horsemen.

Alexanor had a terrible thought: that if the Tarentine officer got over his paralysis and charged *them*, they'd be routed, caught against the stream and destroyed. He suspected this was what would happen.

Men sag after a successful combat. He knew that all too well. He was sagging himself.

On the other hand, often in wrestling and *pankration*, the first man to deploy a technique was the winner, when everything was on the line.

He put a hand to the soft spot on his head.

'Charge them again,' he said to Aristides.

'You think so?' the man asked.

Alexanor shrugged. 'Do ... you ... a better ...?'

'Shouldn't you lie down?' Aristides asked.

'No,' Alexanor said.

'All right. It's ... all a matter of spirit, isn't it?'

'Yes,' Alexanor agreed.

Aristides leant forward, and his horse advanced a dozen steps. He turned.

'We're going to charge again!' he called. He sounded confident, and Alexanor knew in that moment that they would win.

The Achaeans cheered. Alexanor, who could barely stay on the back of his horse, saw Kritias cheering, and beyond him, one of the men of Argos, who'd become intermixed, or just followed the wrong file leader, and over to the left, men of Hermione and even Corinth.

The charge never happened. The Achaean cheer decided the Tarentine commander; his men turned and rode away. They were quick; they knew how dangerous a retreat could be, having pushed many into routs themselves.

Aristides needed no urging.

'*Forward! Forward!*' he roared.

The whole line of eastern volunteers rolled up the hill – 'line' was too proper a word, as they were more like the tangled mane of a wild horse. But they had twice the numbers of the enemy, and they swept up. Men fell from their horses, or slowed; horses went lame, or bolted.

It didn't matter. Once they started to retreat, the Tarentines had no intention of turning on their foes. Rather, they moved at a fast trot themselves, trying to stay ahead of the Achaean javelins.

The Achaeans drove them over the crest. There was no sign of the original Spartan cavalry, unless it was half a dozen red-cloaked bodies that might have belonged to either side, lying in the road.

Alexanor rode along with the front ranks. He was feeling better as they went, and he drank a long pull of water from his miraculously unbroken pottery canteen and his brain suddenly clicked on, as if something broken had been repaired. He could see; he could see the Achaean horse flowing over the stream below him, and he could see Philopoemen to his right, on the road, waving.

But nothing the *Hipparchos* shouted made sense, and Alexanor ignored him, riding over the crest.

Then training told, and experience. On the far side of the crest was a low stone wall, not even tall enough to restrain sheep. The Tarentines flowed over it, most of them jumping it.

The Achaeans balked, and moved to the openings at either end. The Tarentines threw a dozen javelins, killed a man, and then suddenly broke into a gallop and vanished into the olive grove on the far side of the wall, leaving the Achaeans at a stand.

'And *that's* how you break contact,' Philopoemen said, riding in among them.

Polyainos was right behind with Philopoemen's personal standard. Simmias was nowhere to be seen.

Philopoemen raised his spear.

'Halt! Halt! Well done! Brilliant, friends! Now, no farther!' He turned to Alexanor. 'I told you ...' He reined in. 'Gods! You're all blood.'

'I had a towel,' Alexanor said, making little sense, even to himself.

'I thought it was my job to get wounded and your job to heal me.'

Philopoemen was as fresh as the spring flowers around them; he didn't even have blood on his sword hand. He hadn't been in either fight. Philopoemen waved to Aristides.

'Back to the other side of the crest,' he said. 'Just in case Machanandas decides he wants a battle.'

Aristides was smiling. 'Wasn't that a battle?' he asked.

Philopoemen glanced back at the road. 'Not even a skirmish.'

'You seem happy, brother,' Alexanor managed.

'Oh, it was perfect.' Philopoemen broke into a grin. 'We captured a dozen Spartiates and an officer – someone important. We broke their cavalry—'

'We have a dozen Tarentines,' Aristides said. 'Alexanor here brought down their officer. He's alive.'

'You see?' Philopoemen said. 'You are the hero. I just give the orders.'

His smile was as bright as the midday sun.

The aftermath of the skirmish at Choremis vindicated all of Philopoemen's predictions. Machanandas retreated out of the League's territories and requested a truce and the return of his dead.

'He'll be back in a month,' Philopoemen said. 'If we let him.'

'So we accomplished nothing?' Dinaeos asked.

He had a cut on his bridle arm that, when Alexanor had first looked at it, showed bone at the bottom. He'd stabilised it as best he could; remarkably, Kritias had cleaned it and then sewn it up, demonstrating patience and skill. If it hadn't been for the ringing in his ears and the piercing headache, Alexanor would have been happy.

'Oh, no,' Philopoemen said. 'No, the League has decided, on the basis of the world's smallest military victory, to make a stand. The Attalid ambassador to the League told his prince that our cavalry is as good as the best Macedon or Persia has – clearly an excitable man with no cavalry experience. With a little luck, the Romans think the same. But it is our own people who we've affected the most. The League cavalry know they are heroes, and the Agema fought and beat veterans.'

Alexanor smiled. 'So did the Epidaurans.'

Philopoemen smiled thinly. 'That was foolish. I know why you did it, and you did it well, but it only worked because your troopers were too inexperienced to know that it was impossible.'

Dinaeos grinned. 'Veterans would have told you to fuck off. Me, for instance.'

'So will you accept Machanandas' truce?' Aristaenos asked.

'No,' Philopoemen said. 'We were lucky, and now we press it home.'

The next morning, just after dawn, the Thracians crossed the boundary stones, followed by the eastern coastal cavalry, with the Agema as a rearguard. About half the League cavalry was left at Megalopolis as a reserve, in case of disaster, with Lykortas and Aristaenos in command.

But the rest plunged like a dagger into Lacedaemon. They bypassed Machanandas' fortified military camp, and Philopoemen cut them loose, and they spread across the Vale of Sparta, burning the farms, taking the cattle and anything else they fancied. He kept only half the Agema under his hand, and the rest rode off down rocky tracks and hit isolated farms, rich manors and little hamlets. Barns burned; olive trees were girdled.

'This is a terrible way to make war,' Alexanor said, watching the hillsides of the valley of Sparta. It was night, and as far as the eye could see, there were fires.

'This is what Sparta has done to Megalopolis for two hundred years,' Philopoemen said.

'Why don't the Spartans come out and fight?' Dinaeos asked.

'Come out where? Fight what?' Philopoemen asked. 'This is what I learned in Crete. Battles are fought by *consensus*. I can just ride away and burn something else. If I just burn Sparta with my cavalry, Machanandas is going to have a hard time chasing me with his *infantry*.' His smile was ugly, feral, delighted by the chaos and horror he was causing.

'You would destroy Sparta?' Alexanor asked.

'I have told you before,' Philopoemen said. 'I *will* destroy Sparta. This is only the beginning.'

'You have given this a great deal of thought, haven't you?' Alexanor asked.

'Years. Remember, before you judge me – Sparta attacked us, not the other way around. Sparta initiated this war. I sat quietly on my farm and waited for them to do this and treated them like neighbours.'

'Because the Spartans behave like animals, must the League?' Alexanor asked.

'If I can bring Sparta to its knees without losing a single young man of Epidauros or even, gods with us, Argos, I will do so,' Philopoemen said. 'My duty is the defeat of Sparta at the least risk to the League, is it not?'

But on the third day of the raid, the captured Spartan officer approached Philopoemen. He was a tall, handsome man; he had ruddy brown hair and something of the look of Dinaeos. They might have been cousins.

'*Hipparchos*,' he called. His voice was strong; he was not afraid, or if he was, he hid it well. 'I am Timolaos, son of Leonidas. Will you hear me?'

Philopoemen nodded. 'Speak,' he said formally.

'*Hipparchos*, I have come to beg on behalf of the citizens of Sparta. You are making war on the ... the Spartiates. On my people. You burn our farms – you kill our cattle.'

'Yes,' Philopoemen said.

'*Hipparchos*, in this ... you are wrong! Machanandas cares nothing for us. He steals our wives – he taxes us to hire mercenaries. He cares nothing for our traditions. He has never passed the *agoge*, he does not know the sacred dances. You are killing the only people who could govern a Sparta that you would have as a neighbour, and you will leave only helots and *periokoi* who will do whatever the tyrant demands.'

Philopoemen looked at Timolaos for a long time. The Spartan officer bore his regard without fidgeting.

'Is this why he isn't even sending his mercenary cavalry out to contest the countryside?' Philopoemen asked.

'Yes, *Hipparchos*. You are doing his work for him. Either way he wins – you kill his political opponents, or you drive them to support him. I promise you – I speak for the Spartiates. He exiled my brother! I am serving under Nabis with my children as hostages!'

Philopoemen nodded slowly, and then, suddenly, nodded sharply.

'Call in the raiders,' he said.

And later, over a campfire, Philopoemen handed Alexanor a full horn cup of very good wine.

'I think I'm so smart,' he said bitterly.

'Why didn't Lykortas know all this?' Dinaeos asked pettishly.

'Who said war is simple?' Alexanor asked.

'Yes,' Philopoemen said. 'And it is much harder to hate Spartans when they turn out to be good men.' He spat.

'Hate is a useless emotion,' Alexanor said.

Philopoemen looked at him across the fire. And then looked away.

The next day they withdrew up the valley. They had a brief and very one-sided fight with some Greek mercenary cavalry in the saddle of the pass and then they skirted Machanandas' camp again. They saw a screen of the Tarentines at a distance, but not a single javelin was hurled.

That evening, they met up with Kau-Ippa and the Thracians.

'Well, there is a silver lining about our rapid withdrawal.'

Philopoemen was reading from a wax tablet that Kleostratos had given him.

'What's that?' Alexanor asked.

'The Aetolians have invaded the League. I had hoped that if I beat the Spartans fast enough the Aetolians would stay home.'

'So?' Dinaeos asked.

'So now we get to do it all again,' Philopoemen said.

Dinaeos shrugged. 'This time, the horses are all worked up, and the men are already together.'

Alexanor looked around. 'Won't they …? Eventually, don't all these men need to go home?'

'One of the many advantages of employing the cavalry class,' Philopoemen said. 'These men don't work their own farms or sail their own ships, like the hoplites. I don't want to keep them out all summer. But if we have to, we can.'

'We may have to,' Lykortas said, the next afternoon. 'The Roman fleet is at sea. Kykliadas has sent messengers to Philip begging for support.'

'At best, a month away,' Philopoemen said. 'And our farmers are getting worried. We'll go west in the morning.'

'Everyone?' Aristaenos asked.

'Everyone,' Philopoemen said. 'This isn't decadent Sparta. This is the Aetolian League.'

'And Rome,' Dinaeos said.

'You are so cheerful,' Lykortas said.

Dinaeos shrugged. 'I love all this.'

Philopoemen glanced at him and the two men exchanged smiles.

'Any time I can go back to being a priest, you just tell me,' Alexanor said.

Dinaeos nodded. 'Sure. You keep telling yourself that. You love this as much as we do.'

At Megalopolis, the League had summoned the infantry, and they had begun to march in. There were already almost three thousand hoplites, most armed as *thureophoroi*, with little armour, long, narrow shields and a variety of javelins and spears depending on their region's taste. Most had helmets, but these varied from Boeotian dog-bowls to elaborate styles or old Phrygian helmets. There was no uniformity, and some men came in traditional hoplite equipment with the old-style rimmed *aspis*.

Philopoemen paraded the League cavalry opposite them mostly to make a show – fifteen hundred horsemen, most of them with modern equipment. During the campaign – or rather the raid – into Sparta, he'd taken the time to organise the unarmoured men as light cavalry, and he'd handed the entire formation over to Kleostratos and Kau-Ippa.

She frowned. 'Among my people, the very *best* are the first to fight. The scouts, the raiders, the—'

Kleostratos put a hand on her tattooed arm.

'We need more horses,' he said. 'We outride our enemies. We need two or three horses for every rider.'

Philopoemen glanced at Lykortas. They were watching the end of the parade; the hoplites were feeling outclassed, and grumbling.

'Our so-called phalanx hasn't got any better since Sellasia,' Philopoemen said to Kykliadas, when he walked over to his *Hipparchos*.

'Philopoemen, the cavalry is ... incredible.' Kykliadas' smile was genuine. 'I'm ... impressed. And perhaps a little frightened.'

'Don't be,' Philopoemen said. 'It was all luck, and Alexanor here.'

'I'll see to it that your name is mentioned in every temple and theatre,' Kykliadas said.

'I'd rather you didn't,' Alexanor said.

But then he thought ... *My wife will hear my name. Hmm. She might laugh aloud.*

'*Strategos*, we were just discussing a problem our light cavalry are facing – we have too few remounts. I wonder if you would allow us to distribute the Spartan horse herds we ... took. To the Light Cavalry.'

Kykliadas ran his fingers through his beard. 'I have to ask the treasury,' he said. 'Don't bark at me, Philopoemen. The herds you seized are all the funds we have just now.'

Kleostratos grew red in the face, which accentuated his tattoos.

'We took them,' he said.

Philopoemen raised a hand. 'Gentlemen. Let's ask Cercidas before we disagree among ourselves.'

Kykliadas nodded, and sent a slave for Cercidas.

Kleostratos shook his head. 'We took those horses and those cattle. If I tell my people that none of them are ours—'

'By the gods,' Kykliadas said. 'I didn't realise your mercenaries were quite so rapacious.'

Philopoemen put his horse firmly between the two men.

'Gentlemen,' he said. 'Kleostratos, he has no idea what he's saying. Kykliadas, this Thracian is my lifelong friend. He is serving for free, and he is in fact an officer of the League under your authority.'

Kykliadas considered anger. It was written on his face; he didn't want to back down, and he had ideas about mercenaries ...

He swallowed them. 'I'm sorry, sir.' He extended his hand to Kleostratos.

Kleostratos, for his part, had his mouth open to say something. But he didn't. Instead, he took the other man's arm in a Thracian handshake.

'Cattle are very dear to my people,' he said. 'We can be greedy – I own it.'

Alexanor willed Kykliadas to say something amusing, or to say nothing.

'Here's Cercidas,' Philopoemen said after an uncomfortable pause.

The League treasurer was well armed, in a fine bronze panoply in the Macedonian style. He wore the traditional transverse plume of a senior officer. As he came over, he pulled off his helmet and handed it to a slave to hold.

'*Strategos!*' he said. '*Hipparchos*, you are making us look bad.' He said that with a smile, however. 'Damn, the Agema look like Centaurs. Even the badly armed cavalry look good.'

Philopoemen liked praise. He beamed. 'Thanks, Cercidas,' he said.

The treasurer shrugged. 'We need to work on our infantry, but by the gods, you gave us teeth in one winter.'

'Cercidas, Philopoemen wants to keep the Spartan horses for his cavalry,' Kykliadas said.

'Gods, he just robbed the treasury bare for a thousand horses!' Cercidas said.

Philopoemen nodded. 'We only got about seven hundred. And we need more, and then more again. And still more, in mares, so we can breed still more. Gentlemen, we lost more than a hundred horses in our first *three weeks* and we didn't fight a major action.'

'Gods!' Cercidas said.

'Friends, this is why minor states do not possess powerful cavalry. I told you ...'

Cercidas waved his hand. 'You tell me this is necessary?'

Philopoemen looked at Kleostratos. He nodded.

'The younger men, the poorest cavalrymen have the worst horses.' Kleostratos looked around. 'Sometimes they are the best riders, but bad horses are slow, unreliable, death in a skirmish.'

Lykortas spoke up. 'And, gentlemen, the financial risk of losing a precious horse can cause a man to be ... skittish ... in a fight.'

Cercidas shook his head. 'We need money. If you take the Spartan horses ...'

Kykliadas looked at Philopoemen. 'Gods. We're fighting for our lives. We'll just make it up as we go along.'

Cercidas sighed. 'I know you are right. Very well. Take the horses.'

Reports came in from the Macedonian garrison in the border fort at Alipheira, and Kleostratos left that same day with all five hundred of the unarmoured cavalry. Many of the local contingent commanders expressed their dissatisfaction as having their 'rear-rankers' taken away; some contingents lost up to half their riders. The commander of the Argosians, Lysander, expressed the views of a dozen officers.

'You will take our men away and leave us without commands, even though we are the elected officers of our cities and you are merely appointed officers of the League.'

He would not sit down. Thirty officers were sitting or reclining on couches in the garden of Philopoemen's red-tiled arcade, the magnificent courtyard behind his farm.

'We won a great victory,' he went on. 'We won it – the cavalry of the cities. And yet you want to take our young men under foreign officers and barbarians.'

'And women!' another officer shouted. 'One of the barbarian officers is a *woman*.'

Servants bustled about serving more wine.

Philopoemen rose. 'This is not a simple matter—' he began.

The man who'd shouted about women shouted again. 'It's fucking simple!'

Philopeomen nodded. 'No, it is not, and if you shout again, I'll have you removed.' He looked around. 'Listen, gentlemen, while I tell you some unkind truths. When you get medical attention, do you want an untrained priest or one with a record of healing? When you

135

go to buy fish, do you buy them from a leather-worker?' He looked around. 'None of you are soldiers. And no, I'm sorry, the League horse performed well the other day, but the heavy fighting was done by the Agema, who are the closest thing to professional soldiers we have, under professional officers.'

'Bullshit!' roared the loud man. He stood up. He wasn't as tall as Philopoemen.

'Really, Tiraeseus?' Philopoemen asked. 'Your men were wilting from lack of water. You didn't know to keep your horses out of the river when the fight was over and two of them died. You don't have a clue how to picket horses. The state of your own armour speaks of the material readiness of your entire detachment, and you have failed to provide guards for the rota—'

'No one needs your fucking idiot guards! No one is going to attack us in Megalopolis!' Tiraeseus shouted.

There was silence.

'You are loud,' Philopoemen said. 'But you are not competent to command troops in battle, and shouting will not change that.'

'You're finished!' Tiraeseus roared. 'You're too fucking arrogant to command Greeks. We're free men and we won't stand for this sort of tyranny …'

There was no grumble of assent, and Tiraeseus realised that he was not supported any more.

Lysander, of all people, turned. 'Don't be an idiot.'

Tiraeseus sat down.

Philopoemen didn't gloat.

'Listen, friends. By the end of the summer, every one of you will be a competent cavalry officer, and I will see to it that you have commands. Real commands. Listen to me! You think that I don't understand that it is on military success that our political careers depend? Do you really think I am so alien that I would ruin you, the very men who brought their contingents to training?'

He looked them over. Alexanor knew he'd hit the nail on the very head.

'I ask you to trust me. We need to win. Right now, that means that I need to break up some of your contingents to get efficient squadrons. I promise in turn that by the end of the summer, every one of you will be in command of a contingent as big or bigger than your city provided – and we will win. Listen! You have to know how popular we are right now – you must have been cheered riding by some farmstead. Do you think I won't share the glory?'

Alexanor looked around. *That's what they fear. Whereas what I fear is that you are too good at this.*

Philopoemen waved at Tiraeseus. 'I mean what I say. And I hear you, despite the insults. So I suggest that five of you volunteer – five good riders who want to learn to be officers of our new Light Cavalry. Five men who will, at least temporarily, take orders from a Thracian and a Scythian woman.'

Astoundingly, Lysander raised his hand. So did Aristides, and some others Alexanor didn't really know.

Lykortas rolled over on their couch.

'Damn it, he's terrifying,' he said.

'I've never known a man with so much charisma,' Alexanor agreed. 'I pray he uses his powers for good.'


No one was precisely hungover when the cavalry column rode out in the dawn. Alexanor was aware that Philopoemen and some of the officers had gone from campfire to campfire, visiting the men who were awake, but the *Hipparchos* looked fresh and titanic in his full armour polished like the sun.

Alexanor was a little surprised to see Aristides with the column.

'He volunteered …?'

'He's too good,' Philopoemen said. 'I've seen this before. On the drill field, he was just another merchant. In battle, he became a leader. Or he always was one. Either way, he's one of us now.'


On the march, as they passed west towards the border between the League and the Olympic state of Elis, Philopoemen wrote out a detailed set of orders on a wax tablet, riding with one knee cocked up over his horse's back. Then he had a long discussion with Lykortas.

'Politics?' Alexanor asked when Philopoemen sat by him on a mossy rock.

It was midday. There was a smell of smoke in the air; scouts had reported enemy cavalry off to the west.

'Politics,' Philopoemen said. 'Here, read it.'

On the wax, he'd redivided the whole cavalry of the League into four *taxeis*: the Agema, the Light Cavalry, the Eastern Division and the Western Division. Aristaenos had the Westerners; Dinaeos had the Agema; Kleostratos had the lights with Alexios …

'Alexios?' Alexanor asked.

'The Tarentine officer you captured,' Philopoemen said.

Alexanor blinked.

'He asked to join us. Lykortas has some hopes he'll suborn the entire Tarentine detachment with the Spartans.' Philopoemen nodded.

'Me?' Alexanor asked.

'You and Aristides together,' Philopoemen said.

'I annoy him,' Alexanor said. 'And I don't want to be a cavalry officer. I can barely ride.'

'You are not the best rider, and perhaps it is a measure of my desperation that I rank you among my best officers just now,' Philopoemen said. 'But, brother, although you hate it, you … know how to get it done. And most of these men do not.'

'By it, you mean the bloody business—'

'I do.'

'I hate it,' Alexanor said.

'Good. I know you are a moral man, and I, in some ways, am not. I keep you around to remind me that other men do not love combat as I do.'

'Other men are not as tall as a Titan, with armour made by the gods.'

'Point taken.' Philopoemen glanced at him. 'Will you do it?'

'For a while,' Alexanor said. 'Not forever.'

'I know …' Philopoemen put a hand on his shoulder. 'I know this is not what you want. That for you, this is looking backwards, not forwards.'

'Yes,' Alexanor said, his voice thick.

'Help me until Aristides can command on his own.'

Alexanor felt as if he was signing his own death sentence. He tried to find any part of the peace he felt in the grove at Epidauros, or at the altar at Lentas.

'You are asking a great deal.'

'I know,' Philopoemen said. 'I'm asking anyway.'

'You know I can't refuse you.'

'Yes, you can. Almost alone of men, you know how to tell me

no.' Philopoemen nodded. 'As more and more power comes into my hands, I will need to be told "no". I am not a god. Already—'

'Oh, shut up.' Alexanor put an arm around Philopoemen. 'You know, and I know. And don't short Dinaeos or Lykortas. They also know. We won't let you become a tyrant.'

'Good,' Philopoemen said. 'Because honestly, I can already see some advantages to absolute power.'

# CHAPTER SEVEN

———ᐁᐁᐁ———

## The Achaean League

AGRIANOS (MID APRIL TO LATE MAY), 209 BCE

The hills were full of desperate women, and the roads were crowded with refugees moving east, as the wave front of the Aetolian raiders pushed deeper into the western demes of the League.

'Aetolia must be empty,' Dinaeos muttered. He took a long drink from his canteen and spat.

'They are very good at this,' Philopoemen agreed.

'It's their whole way of life,' Lykortas said, bitterly. 'They make me wonder if this is all there is when we sing about Achilles and Troy – just a mob of vicious thugs with horses, raiding, raping and burning.'

'And stealing cattle,' Philopoemen added. 'They're not all Aetolians. The pack that Kleostratos caught yesterday were men of Elis.'

'All our neighbours are vultures,' Lykortas said.

'We showed weakness,' Philopoemen said. 'Greeks don't have the unity that Persians have, or, from what Kaeso has told me, the Romans have.'

They were on yet another hillside. The season was unusually wet, which was making the campaign even more miserable for the horses. The hills of western Arkadia were still green when in most years they'd have been brown; the crags still showed sparkles of water in spate-streams.

'I feel that we're swatting houseflies,' Lykortas said. 'We never get to the nest.'

'Our opponents are not like the Spartans,' Philopoemen said. 'They're expert horsemen and they have no more interest in a battle than I did in Lacedaemon.'

'And we know how tough they are,' Dinaeos muttered. All of them had faced Aetolian cavalry in Crete.

'Well,' Philopoemen, 'look sharp today. I'm laying a trap. Damophantos is their commander, according to the prisoners. We'll see what Damophantos is made of.'

The Aetolians charged the Thracians, and the Thracians broke, running like deer from a predator, and the Aetolians flowed over the ground after them. Alexanor saw it all from a tiny shrine to Herakles high on the mountain above the stream sparkling in the sudden sun. The Aetolians had 'caught' the Thracians watering their horses, and now they were in hot pursuit down the valley, and their hoots and whoops carried in the still mountain air.

Alexanor watched from concealment as the Thracians rode recklessly along the stream bed and then turned west up a side road that ran through a swale between two peaks. The Aetolians were closing the distance ...

A whole troop of the Agema came over the swale at the trot and charged. Alexanor turned to his own cavalry.

'Ready!' he shouted.

The Aetolians still couldn't see the trap, and Alexanor was impressed by Philopoemen's thoroughness.

'Forward!' Alexanor shouted.

His troop of eastern cavalry trotted down a trio of narrow tracks, down the steep hill to block the road behind the Aetolians.

It was neat, and Alexanor felt the joy any soldier feels at an easy victory. He was watching the Aetolians to his right as they understood their peril and tried to decide which direction to go to escape.

There was an equine flash to Alexanor's right, and Philopoemen burst through the thick cover at the edge of the little stream. He was waving his spear.

'Run!' he roared.

Alexanor didn't understand for a long moment.

'Ride clear!' Philopoemen roared. 'It's a trap!'

*Of course it's a trap,* Alexanor thought. Then he saw the brown-cloaked riders crossing the stream behind Philopoemen were not Agema. They were Aetolians.

Alexanor was tempted to charge them; they were in more than a little confusion crossing the stream, and there were only half-a-hundred or so.

'*Run!*' Philopoemen demanded, and Alexanor obeyed.

'Run!' he called, and turned his horse. 'No order. Ride for it. Back up the farm trails, go! Go!'

The Eastern League cavalry were not professionals. They were amateurs who'd been lucky once, and they took far too long to turn. The men at the front had nowhere to go ...

'Follow me!' Alexanor called.

He had perhaps thirty men with him; the rest were finally scrambling up the steep sides of the valley that should have been the scene of *their* trap. He had no idea what was going on, or how the Aetolians had countered their trap, but now there were enemy cavalry *pouring* over the stream, hundreds of them, and he only had a third of the Eastern troopers; the rest were away north with Aristides.

He pointed his horse at the original Aetolian raiding party and gave his gelding his head. There were a hundred Aetolians who had been the intended victims – far too many to overcome with his thirty, but far better odds than facing the five hundred or more Aetolians cross-ing the stream, or just waiting to be captured.

He caught them at a stand, and he put down their officer, a short, swarthy man with a magnificent helmet. Alexanor ducked under his javelin throw, took his arm and threw him, and his troopers widened the gap. Alexanor saw Kritias cover a javelin thrust, and then another, and then break out, opening a road to freedom for the men behind him. Dariush stayed at Alexanor's side, thrusting inexpertly, and then suddenly he was gone, and Alexanor turned his horse with his knees and lost his spear as another man in a fine corselet stabbed him in the wrist. It was a remarkable blow, the sort of thing Philopoemen did. Alexanor was shocked as his hand opened and the spear fell from it, and then the man turned his weapon with elegant expertise and swept Alexanor from his horse.

Alexanor landed badly, twisting his ankle, and went for his sword. The other man was staying above him, and he thrust, scoring the bronze of Alexanor's breastplate and knocking him into the mud, but

Alexanor rolled and got the *xiphos* clear, parried a spear thrust, tried to get to his feet ...

He was alone, surrounded by mounted men. The man who'd put him down had his spear cocked back.

'Drop the sword,' he said. 'We'll ransom you, laddie, never fear.'

'Nice horse!' shouted another with his terrible Aetolian accent. 'Nice armour too.'

'Nothing to die for here, laddie,' the big killer said. 'Eh?'

Alexanor dropped his sword.

The big man nodded.

There were six prisoners from Alexanor's troop and two from the Agema, and almost a dozen dead or badly wounded, including Dariush.

Alexanor was having a hard time not sinking. Sinking all the way.

But Dariush was his own, and might be savable. The rest of the wounded men were either barely hurt or waiting to die.

'I'm a priest of Asklepios,' Alexanor muttered.

He'd been stripped to his *chiton* by his laughing captors, big men with bright eyes and bushy beards who spoke a barbaric Greek and seemed to find everything funny, including their own dead and wounded. So he made himself get to his feet, and he dragged his twisted ankle to where the big man who'd dropped him was sitting with his cronies, drinking wine.

'Eh, the officer,' the big man said. 'Thoas, come and meet the man who didn't kill you.'

The thickset man frowned. He had large moustaches, like a barbarian, but otherwise looked Greek.

'Eh,' he said. 'He was lucky.'

'No, I was lucky,' the big man said. 'I got my spear into his wrist.' He smiled at Alexanor. 'I'm Damophantos, sir. *Hipparchos* of Aetolia. And you?'

'Alexanor of Kos. I'm a priest of Asklepios. I'd like to see the wounded.' He made himself say the words. 'Yours as well.'

Thoas laughed. 'You've already worked on me,' he said. 'I wouldn't let him near our wounded.'

Damophantos made a face. 'Don't be a fuckwit, Thoas. He's a priest of Asklepios.' He smiled. 'Be my guest, priest. Kos is a long way away. What brings you here?'

Alexanor shrugged. He wasn't going to say 'Philopoemen is my best friend' and raise his ransom. Nor was he going to provide information.

'I like a fight,' he said.

'A mercenary priest of Asklepios?' Damophantos asked. 'Nay, laddie. I'm going to guess that you're Philopoemen's man. We've heard of you. Rhodian marine, eh? You fought against my brother on Crete.'

'Hoot, hoot,' laughed Thoas. 'There's a few mina of silver, standing before us.'

Damophantos smiled wickedly. 'Or we can just take him home and tell Philopoemen to desist or we castrate his boy, eh?' The Aetolian commander smiled. 'Or would that even interfere with his fun, Rhodian?' He slapped his thighs. 'Oh, don't look like that. None o' my business, eh, lads?'

Alexanor ignored the humour. 'May I look at the wounded?'

'Be my guest,' Damophantos said. 'We ride in an hour, maybe less.'

Alexanor walked away, feeling them watching him, and he heard Thoas mutter something. But his head was working, even if his ankle wasn't. His wrist hurt, but the needle-thin spear-tip had thrust between the bones like a nail, severing nothing. He kept working it despite the pain, flexing it constantly.

There were two wounded Aetolians who were savable, and Dariush, who had not one but three deep cuts on his arm and a spear thrust through one cheek.

'Master,' he croaked, and spat blood. He'd lost teeth, too.

'You don't know me,' Alexanor said. 'Understand?'

'Yes, mast—' Dariush blinked. Spat blood. 'Yes,'

Alexanor hobbled out onto the battlefield, where the Achaean dead lay unburied. There was young Pyrrhos, dead with a javelin through his helmet and head, and there was Nikophantes, his neck broken.

Alexanor faced the reality of their deaths and took their *chitons* anyway. They'd been stripped, but not very thoroughly; the *chitons* were good cloth. Nikophantes' fingers had been cut off to get his rings – a vain and wealthy young man. Alexanor thought of Kritias and was glad he'd escaped.

He tore the cleanest parts of the *chitons* into strips and used them to bind the various deep cuts on the Aetolians. He limped back to the enemy commander.

'If you had wine and honey I could do a better job on all three men,' he said.

Damophantos frowned, but he nodded. 'So you're the real deal, eh? Sure. Thoas, give him whatever he needs.'

Alexanor did an odd thing. He spread honey on the corpse of one of the dead Aetolians – just a little, with many a backward glance to see if he was watched. Then he spread more on the cleaner cloths and began to work on Dariush.

'We're riding as soon as everyone is mounted,' Thoas said. 'Who's this bastard?'

'Someone's *hypaspist*,' Alexanor said. 'I thought he was one of yours.'

'Nah.' Thoas slapped at a big yellow wasp. 'Apollo, god of pestilence, the fucking carrion insects come too fast. Move it, priest. You're the most valuable thing we've found in this wet country.'

Alexanor made a show of working on the dead man. The honeyed corpse gathered hornets and wasps at an astonishing rate, and Alexanor worked among them as fast as he could, filling the wine amphora he'd already emptied into the cloth.

Filling it with wasps.

Rhodian marines made grenades by gathering wasps into clay amphorae. It was a punishment detail and Alexanor had been punished often enough in his ephebe years.

He checked the wounded again and hobbled back to the command group, who were all wounded.

'If you leave the wounded, they'll all live,' he said.

Damophantos shrugged. 'Do I look like a give a shit? Man goes raiding, has to take whatever comes. But yes, I'm leaving them, and no, I'm not leaving you.' He chuckled. 'Better wash the honey off before those wasps eat you.'

Alexanor had been stung a few times, and the stings hurt; his wrist hurt, and his ankle was worse for his hobbling around.

One of his father's friends had been taken by pirates, twice. And escaped both times. His wisdom rang in Alexanor's ears.

*You either get free in the first half an hour, when they're in the slump after fighting, or about four hours later, when all they can think of is food,'* the man had said. He'd said it often enough, as well as his usual joke: *captured by pirates once could happen to anyone – twice seems somehow like carelessness.*

Alexanor was not thinking his best, and a pair of Aetolians followed him as he went back and forth between the ageing plug they'd given him to ride and the men he'd tended.

'I'd be sorry to have you beaten and tied over that nag,' Damophantos said. 'But ye're holdin' up the whole force and I weren't born yesterday, laddie. Get yer arse on that horse or take what comes.'

Alexanor plodded back to his worthless horse and had to ask one of his guards for help to get mounted. He almost dropped the wine-jar full of wasps he had in the belly of his *chiton*. He couldn't believe they didn't see it, since he looked as if he was pregnant, but they were in a hurry to get some loot and one of them gave him a casual shove. He got a leg over the old horse and then they called out that they were ready to ride.

The Aetolians were good at what they did. Alexanor saw that the last thing Damophantos did was to call in his pickets. A dozen men on fast horses came down the two big crags on either side of the crossroads and reported.

'Them fucking Thracians bastards is just the other side o' the swale,' one man shouted. 'Some little filly put a shaft into Brasion. He's in Hades.'

'I'll put a shaft in her when I catch her,' said another picket. 'Fucking Thracians!'

'Let's go!' Damophantos called.

To add to the joy of the afternoon, clouds settled in as they rode west. All the farms were burnt, and bodies rotted on the roads.

One of Alexanor's guards looked at him. 'You stupid fucks should just surrender and pay us tribute,' he said. 'You know the Romans are landing at Corinth? Your League is over.'

The other laughed. 'Where's your precious king of Macedon now?' he gloated. 'We're going to pick this country clean. And leave you some sons who will be men. You Achaeans are soft.'

Alexanor didn't need to do much acting to sink into the role of the helpless, beaten prisoner. He hunched over, rubbed his wrist, and tried not to meet his captors' eyes.

The rain hit at mid-afternoon and his captors cursed a great deal and asked aloud why anyone would live in Achaea. The rain grew stronger. Rain didn't go with Alexanor's plan for the wasps; he'd never seen a wasp fly in rain, especially a downpour like this. His misery increased ...

But he was at the four-hour mark, and his captors were as miserable as he was. Both men had spears which they carried under their thighs, trapped against the side of the horse, and heavy *kopis*-style slashing-swords on their left hips. They wrapped their big unbleached wool cloaks around them and huddled, and as the rain went on, they leant together for warmth. His father's friend was right. Neither man was paying him any attention at all.

'Fucking hungry,' said the smaller man, who seemed to be in charge.

Alexanor's right hand was so stiff in the rain that he didn't think he could even hold a sword.

It wasn't going to work.

'We're fucked,' the smaller captor said. 'We've lost the column.'

The three men stopped. The rain was so heavy that a spate-stream, which flowed across the road through a stone channel, was over its banks and slowly flooding the barley field on their side. Visibility was about two horse-lengths.

'Ares, I'm fucking tired of being wet,' said the bigger man. 'How many talents are you worth, Rhodian?'

'I can't feel my right hand,' Alexanor said.

'Don't die on us! Damophantos won't like that,' said the smaller man.

'We passed a barn, or what's left of one. Let's go to it and wait this out.'

'It can't rain like this long or we'll all turn to fish and drown.'

'We won't turn to fish *and* drown, you fuckwit.'

'Sure, it's an expression, arsehat.'

The three of them rode back in the rain, which was slightly lighter. Visibility was perhaps ten horse-lengths, and the misery was epic. There was water passing straight down Alexanor's back, and because he kept slipping the cork on the amphora to keep the insects alive, he'd been stung another half a dozen times.

Nonetheless, this was the moment, and he made his plan and steeled himself. He wasn't going to be a prisoner to be traded. Or sold as a slave.

He got his nag to trot. The old horse went willingly enough, sensing the relatively dry darkness of the ruined stone barn as a safe haven.

He got under cover a full horse-length ahead of his captors and turned the nag.

'Fuck!' he spat. 'Fuck!'

He tried to act like a man not in control of his horse.

The two men didn't care about his acting; they just wanted out of the rain. Alexanor's horse pushed in between them, and Alexanor slammed the jar of wasps into the head of the larger man as his left hand closed on the smaller man's *kopis*, because they were pressed left arm to left arm. He drew clumsily and cut the smaller man on the draw.

The larger man already had his arms locked around Alexanor. The blow to his head hadn't done anything.

Alexanor killed the smaller man anyway, a clumsy left-handed blow with the heavy weapon that bit deeply into the man's skull.

The big man threw Alexanor from his horse, dragging him backwards and then dropping him as wasps stung both of them savagely.

Alexanor fell flat on his back and the wind was knocked out of him. He lay, stunned, as the big man fought the wasps. His horse was stung and stung again, and finally bolted out into the curtain of the rain with the man on its back screaming.

Alexanor took far too long to rally his senses and what was left of his strength, but he had the *kopis* in his fist and the smaller man's horse was huddling at the far corner – a good horse. And the wasps were dispersing a little, and Alexanor couldn't stop for them. Flat on the floor, they'd ignored him, and he made himself crawl across the wet muddy floor to the horse, which didn't like the look of him. A long negotiation followed. Alexanor was a better rider now than he'd ever been, but he lacked the kind of horse-charm that ingratiates a human to an equine, and the horse's ears went back and stayed back for a long time. He smelled of blood; the wasps were buzzing.

Finally, Alexanor snatched the reins.

And in that moment, the big man burst back into the barn. Whatever his plan had been, he caught his far leg on a protruding beam of the ruined barn and almost unhorsed himself coming in the opening too fast. He was roaring with anger and fear.

Alexanor, prodded by desperation, leapt onto the horse's back.

Big Man turned his horse in the ruined barn and threw his spear and missed. Alexanor killed him while he was failing to find his sword.

'Fuck!' Alexanor said, and gave himself over to the shakes. He thought of his wife, his children, and the temple at Epidauros. 'Fuck!' he said again, which was a sort of soldier's prayer to the gods.

And then he closed his eyes and made a real prayer to Apollo, and then he went and took the dead man's cloak and the scabbard of the *kopis*, all of which meant he had to face mounting again. This time he walked up an old wall and dropped onto the horse.

He got the horse into motion. He had the presence of mind to get the nag's reins wrapped around his mostly non-functional right hand. He'd been stung so many times the right hand was hugely swollen and he was having trouble seeing, and everything seemed very distant. He pulled the cloaks as close as he could ...

He had very little idea where he was, and he had had no food, and he suspected he'd reached a point of wet and cold that was very dangerous. On the other hand, he was on a good horse and the heavy rain was going to buy him a head start.

He rode back recklessly. He pushed the horse, and twice in the first thousand strides his mount slipped dangerously on wet rocks and mud, but he came to the crossroads where he estimated his captors had gone wrong. He turned east and pushed his horse to a gallop. The old nag didn't want to gallop, and the reins tightened to the point where he was almost unhorsed, but the old scoundrel finally agreed to the speed and they passed east along a road that had become a flooded stream bed.

After perhaps five stades the rain began to let up. The visibility increased, and then became better again. A patch of blue sky appeared to the west, and then there was an evening sun peeping around the shoulder of the local mountains and Alexanor began to feel that he might live. He turned in to a grove of trees that held the terrible sweet smell of rotting human flesh; there were a dozen slaves and two naked women dead there, all of them terribly mauled.

He watched his back-trail for a while, and considered the likelihood of finding food anywhere, and then he rode on before his horse could cool too much.

Another hour and he was passing over the site of the ambush. He thought of dismounting to eat the last of the honey in the pot he'd abandoned just a few hours before, but he wasn't at all sure he'd get back on the horse.

'I'm sorry, lady,' he murmured to his new horse.

She was a big mare, a Greek horse, and she had good manners and had been well trained. He was killing her, riding her past her endurance.

'Lots of dead already,' he muttered to himself.

So he turned away from the spectacular sunset and headed farther east, up the swale that should have been the scene of their triumph. An hour later, before darkness could fall, Kau-Ippa's arm was around him, and one of her head-hunting adolescent girls was cooing at him, and they laid him down by their campfire and fed him soup.

'You are fucked up,' the girl said. 'I help.'

'Save my horse!' he whispered.

'Of course save horse. Good horse. Stupid man.'

Alexanor was asleep before she could come back with more soup.

# CHAPTER EIGHT

—⟡—

## The Achaean League

AGRIANOS (MID APRIL TO LATE MAY), 209 BCE

Alexanor woke alone by a nearly cold fire pit. The only horses picketed were the Aetolian mare and the old plug. Everyone else was gone, but there was a delicious chunk of roast lamb wrapped in bread and then in damp leaves that had been put in the coals.

He was chewing on it when the command staff of the League cavalry trotted into the clearing.

'The longest day of my life.' Philopoemen embraced Alexanor for the third time. 'Damn it. I thought you were dead, and there was nothing we could do. And then Kleostratos rides in and says—'

Dinaeos also wrapped him in a warm embrace. 'That of course you rescued yourself,' he said. 'Because you are a demigod.'

Alexanor's darkness was largely banished by his friends, who greeted him with so much warmth that he wasn't really able to appreciate it. Some layer of aristocratic reserve blocked him from accepting all this love; when Kleostratos kissed him, as Thracians were wont to do, he flinched and Lykortas laughed.

As usual, he took refuge in facts.

'I met Damophantos,' he said.

'Gloating?' Dinaeos asked.

'No. But he's the calm professional – like the best priests at

Epidauros. Strictly business.' Alexanor nodded at Philopoemen. 'He's as big as you, or bigger.'

'I know,' Philopoemen said. 'I spent quite a bit of time running away from him.' He wasn't bitter; he too was strictly professional.

'What were you doing on the Aetolian side of the stream?' Alexanor asked.

Philopoemen shrugged.

Dinaeos shook his head. 'About half an hour before the ambush, he rode off.'

'Something was wrong. I suddenly realised that I hadn't put a watch post up on Megaron, the big hill to the east ... and that was foolish. As it proved.'

'So you went in person to look ...' Lykortas gave a dramatic sigh.

'Spare me!' Philopoemen said. 'I know. It is a sad fact of war that, like *pankration*, you learn more when you lose than when you win. I got dropped on my metaphorical head there. But since my neck didn't snap, we'll do better next time.'

'I got the sense that the Aetolians have been at this kind of raiding so long that they take elaborate precautions automatically, almost like an animal instinct.'

'I think you are correct,' Philopoemen said.

'Damophantos set a watch while his men looted our dead,' Alexanor said. For a moment he was right there with the corpse of Pyrrhos.

Philopoemen winced.

'On the other hand, they hate the rain and they think our weather is outrageous. And they're short on fodder for their horses – I'm guessing they expected less resistance.' Alexanor powered through the sick feeling by talking about the facts of the raid.

'Aristides and Aristaenos took more prisoners – mostly men of Elis – while we were getting beaten like a drum,' Philopoemen said. 'We lost a skirmish, not the war. Today we rest. Tomorrow we are going after them – north and east.'

'The Thracians are looking for them,' Dinaeos said.

The wound on his hand was infected, and he could barely hold the reins, but the big Aetolian mare was quite friendly after she'd been fed.

'One of the Scythian girls talked to her for an hour,' Kleostratos said. 'Horses love them. Trust me, I know this.'

Alexanor thought perhaps it was just the regular supply of food, but the Aetolian mare was all his.

Dariush, looking pale, came as the cavalry was mounting and forming ranks. He had an armload of bronze armour.

'We keep taking Elisian prisoners,' Lykortas said. 'No reason why they should keep their armour.'

Alexanor chose a cavalry panoply that had probably belonged to someone very rich indeed; the shoulder scales on the *thorax* were silver, and the Gorgon's head in the centre of the breastplate was also silver, as was the edging on the repoussé helmet. The crest was red and white.

Lykortas handed over a fine red cloak. 'My spare,' he said.

'Of course you have a spare,' Alexanor said.

'You up to this?' Lykortas asked, looking at the sky as if to deny responsibility for his words.

Alexanor shrugged. 'I can't fight. I can probably give orders. You know what Philopoemen says about how he'd rather have a squadron that obeys orders than a squadron of brilliant swordsmen? We're about to explore that theory.'

They rode east on the same trail they'd taken three days before and then, in the valley of the ambush, they went north instead of east.

'Aristides is just the other side of that mountain,' Philopoemen said.

Alexanor still had more than a hundred troopers, and they were the rearguard. He rode up the column to Philopoemen from time to time, but otherwise he was the very last man in the column, watching behind them. Twice, when he didn't like the look of the ground, or when he saw dust behind, he formed his hundred across the road and waited.

After midday, an ephebe from the Agema galloped up to say that the advance guard was in contact with the enemy.

'The *Hipparchos* says to keep watching our backs. He says, sir, that the battle is spread over three valleys and he can't promise that there aren't Aetolians behind us.'

'How far away is Philopoemen?' Alexanor asked.

The ephebe shrugged, a very adolescent shrug. 'Three stades?' he suggested, but his facial expression robbed that distance of meaning.

Alexanor turned his horse and looked all around. He was in a small valley with two barley fields, both walled with ancient stone boundaries, and a burnt house. On the hillside above, to the north, was a small shrine; to the south, where the road ran over a ridge, was a cluster of grave stelae, and the mountain to the east was covered in olive groves.

He had Kleander as an under-officer and now he used him.

'Take these six files,' Alexanor said. 'Stay by the farmhouse. Assume that you are being observed from the south. Watch the road, but also the hillside and the olive groves.'

Kleander nodded. 'I get it. You're going to cover me?'

Alexanor might have smiled, but defeat was too close. 'Yes,' he said.

An hour later, they might have been in a different plane of existence from whatever battle was happening. There were no signs of a fight except that an increasing number of carrion birds were gathering to the north.

Alexanor's men, almost five score, were dismounted among the olive groves on the northern hill above the shrine, which proved to be a shrine of Hera. Alexanor prayed, made a small sacrifice of a barley cake and then sat between the pillars of the portico watching his outpost.

Nothing happened, and the nothing caused him increasing unease. He sent a young Epidauran off to the north for news, and then he ate olives. After a while, he took the time to unwrap Dariush's wounds and clean them, and then he had a moment with Kritias.

'You fought well,' he said.

Kritias shook his head. 'I was too interested in breaking free,' he admitted.

'Lykortas says you worked on our wounded all afternoon.'

Kritias nodded, eyes bright. 'I felt as if I had no idea what I was doing. But most of them are better.'

'Welcome to medicine,' Alexanor said. 'You did well.'

Kritias frowned. And then smiled. 'Thanks!' he managed. 'I'm still not sure I'm on the right side. What if the Aetolians break us?'

'What indeed?' Alexanor asked.

Half an hour later, Alexanor's messenger hadn't returned. He sent Kritias over the mountain at their backs to find a route on the sheep tracks. He no longer trusted the ground to the north and he put out more pickets.

He came back with two of the Scythians – a young girl and an older man.

'Big fight and who will win?' the man said. 'And fucking enemy everywhere. Yes?'

He and the girl drank water from the spring by the Heraion and then rode off to the east along the army's back trail.

Time passed slowly, and Alexanor's unease increased. It actually made him angry.

*I didn't want any part of this. Why me? Why the hell does he have to use me as an officer? Who is looking after the wounded?*

He knew in his heart that such thoughts were the children of fear, but the annoyance persisted.

And then a rider appeared on the far eastern ridge. The rider came down the hill quickly, but raised little dust, and Alexanor thought it might be the Scythian girl.

The lone rider stopped at the ruined farm ...

'Come on,' Alexanor begged.

... and then started up the mountain with the Heraion.

'Mount up!' Alexanor said. 'Don't show yourselves! Keep your cloaks over your armour!'

Men had been asleep. Alexanor wished he had been one of them. He was exhausted by a morning of fretting.

Dariush hobbled along the picket line, passing the word, and after a moment, Kritias went with more speed.

Alexanor got onto the mare's back and adjusted his reins.

It *was* the girl. She came up quickly, but not so fast as to raise dust; it was clear she was picking her speed and her horse's gait very carefully.

'Aetolians,' she said, pointing east. 'Some, and then many.'

'Some, and then many?' Alexanor said. 'How far apart? The some? And then the many.'

'Yes!' she said, with a brilliant smile for his understanding. 'Like ... from here to the house.' She pointed at the ruined house in the valley.' She swept her arm as if she was unhorsing an opponent. 'They go ... out. Far.'

'Wide?' Alexanor asked.

Again the brilliant smile. 'Wide! To *take* Philopoemen.' She smacked her fist into her palm.

Alexanor looked down into the little valley, and then he looked at his troop – almost ninety men, mostly from Epidauros, but a handful of Corinthians and men of Hermione.

'We will get one charge!' he called out. 'It has to be perfect. Do not *twitch* until I order it. Then everyone forward. We will cut down whatever we can and then ride all the way back to here. Understand? Here. At the Heraion. Kritias, you will remain here with your file, ready to lead us over the mountain. Understood? Everyone?'

He tried to imagine *exactly* how long his men would take to charge all the way to the burnt house.

So much that could go wrong. Kleander might decide to abandon his post; who would stay and fight? But Kleander had to have understood that he was bait ...

Or Kleander's whole command could be overwhelmed before he sprung his charge.

*I hate this.*

'Ready!' he called.

The Aetolian scouts came over the far ridge.

Then they took what seemed like an hour to decide what they could see.

Three of them rode back out of sight.

'Do not twitch,' Alexanor ordered.

All his men, without exception, were sitting mounted in the hot sun with their cloaks wrapped around their armour, their helmets in their laps. Sweating like pigs. Most of them had a fold of their cloaks over their horses' heads.

'Come on,' whispered Kritias.

And then they came – a long, sparkling line of Aetolian raiders, perhaps a hundred. They came over the crest like a wave and then they were galloping down through the olive groves as if they were galloping along a flat valley.

'They ride well,' the Scythian girl said, as if it was the highest compliment she could pay a person.

Kleander's men ran out of the house and dashed about in confusion like ants in a disturbed nest.

Then they mounted. It seemed to take forever.

The Aetolians began to whoop their long, drawn-out whoops.

Alexanor was watching the ridge behind them.

'Ready!' he called.

Kleander's cavalry began to ride away along the route that the army had taken early in the morning, headed north over the shoulder of the ridge.

The Aetolians shouted like hunters on a chase and went to full gallop at the base of the ridge. The best riders on the north end of the skirmish line were already trying to cut Kleander's men off from the shoulder of the ridge.

Alexanor looked all around one more time – at the ground behind the ridge, at the ridge top. So far, all clear.

He looked right and left.

'In and out!' he roared. 'Everyone drop *one* man!'

They raised their spears and let fall their cloaks, so that the line sparkled in the sun, and...

'*Go!*' he roared.

They were away.

The whole line went down the lower slope of the mountain below the Heraion. They did not ride as well as the Aetolians; two men lost their seats on the hillside and one of Kritias' friends, in his excitement, failed to duck a branch and was swept off his horse.

But the rest of them burst out of the fringe of trees on the edge of the barley fields. The stone walls were so low that even the League riders passed them without breaking ranks. They were thirty wide and three deep, and there were huge gaps in their formation, but they were still much more closely formed than the Aetolians.

The Aetolians at the south end of their skirmish line had all the time in the world to turn and ride away. Forty of them rode clear of the trap easily. Some even tried to skirmish against the closing jaws of the League line, to distract the amateur League cavalry from their prey.

But the League troopers were too inexperienced to feel threatened, even when one middle-aged man fell with a javelin in his gut and another went down, his horse dead.

The Aetolians in the middle of the line were milling around the burnt house, and those trying to close the end of the valley never had time to turn – the more so as Kleander's men turned like falcons and fell on the end of their line, hunted to hunters in the time it took a priest to slit a ram's throat.

Alexanor reined in as soon as he could see that his trap would be successful. He couldn't really fight, so he watched the opposite ridge and the ground to the south.

On his left, the Scythian girl was methodically dropping arrows into the Aetolians who had tried to rally and skirmish. She loosed five arrows off her hand like a man playing knuckle-bones, rolling the arrows off her bow hand into her reaching arrow hand, shooting with her thumb. In five shafts she hit one man and three horses.

The surviving Aetolians charged her. She was all alone, halfway across the southernmost barley field. It might have been a scene in a comic play – thirty-odd mounted men chasing one single adolescent female.

She sat perfectly still on her little horse – drawing, shooting, drawing, shooting ...

Alexanor couldn't leave her to fight all by herself – just by watching her, he was encouraging his mare to go towards her. He had covered half the ground towards her when he saw the sparkle of a formed body of men; off to the east, a mass of horsemen passed over the crest of the distant ridge.

'Oh, shit,' he muttered.

Most of his Achaeans saw the young girl, alone against the Aetolians, and they were all turning ...

And then, so was she. She turned her lithe little horse and loosed a shaft over its rump. The nearest Aetolian was perhaps ten horse-lengths away; he was at a dead gallop and she started from a stand.

She shot backwards, and the lead Aetolian flipped over the rump of his horse and fell like a deflated wine sack.

In the time it took her horse to accelerate, the next Aetolian made it to perhaps five horse-lengths.

He died.

So did the man behind him.

She sailed over the field's boundary wall at its highest point, and she never even glanced at it. Her whole attention was behind her. She shot from the top of the leap, backwards, into a man forty paces behind, missed him and hit his horse.

The Aetolians were committed too deeply, and Alexanor led a dozen of his own disorganised cavalry in an impromptu counter-charge as the main Aetolian host swept down the eastern ridge. The Aetolians flinched; the men at the back turned tired horses to run, but those at the front were caught. Alexanor got a blow on the crest of his beautiful new helmet and then reached down with his left hand, took a man's boot and flipped him from his seat to the ground. That was the whole of the combat – and Alexanor waved his arm.

'All the way back!' he roared. 'Run! *Run!* **RUN!**'

They ran. They were still half the valley ahead of their pursuers, and the Aetolian advance guard had been crushed.

The Achaeans passed over the far boundary wall and into the shade of the olive trees below the Heraion, and their flight slowed. Men began to pick their way; the horses were tired.

'Keep going!' Alexanor insisted.

Kleander was congratulating the girl, who was beaming.

'Six!' she whooped. 'Maybe eight.'

Kleander laughed. 'I got one,' he admitted.

Theophoros, one of the older Epidaurans, laughed with the release of survival.

'The *archon* said one, I dropped one.'

Their banter pleased Alexanor, who knew what it meant. Victory. Confidence.

They gathered on the grass of the Heraion, and Alexanor ordered them to water their horses. He was looking down at the valley. There were perhaps a thousand cavalry there; most of them were still in the olive groves on the far slope, and the commander was now sending scouts cautiously into the farmstead.

The Aetolians began to form ranks on the far side of the valley.

Another squadron came over the far ridge.

'Apollo's sacred harp,' Alexanor muttered.

He was looking at fifteen hundred Aetolians – fully half their estimate of the enemy raiders. He had a few more than a hundred troopers under his hand.

But the new squadron formed on the rest of them, and the whole force . . .

Sat.

'I didn't get to fight,' Kritias said.

'You did what you were ordered to do – you held open our retreat.'

Alexanor was not paying much attention to his novice. He was fully focused on his next move. He could feel his opponents' caution;

having lost fully a hundred men in a pointless cavalry skirmish, his enemy now wondered how big the force by the Heraion really was.

Confusion reigned.

'Kleander!' he called. 'Take two files and go ... north. Show yourself. Raise dust.'

Kleander waved.

'Kritias,' he said. 'Go south, take two files ...'

Kritias smiled. It was an odd smile – arrogant, and full of meaning. 'Of course.'

He waved at his file, which was composed of two of his aristocratic friends and their three servants.

Alexanor continued to watch the valley from his near-perfect observation post. Dariush brought him more olives; he drank some wine, and complimented the Scythian girl on her skills.

'Tell my mother. Please tell my mother.' She shook her head. 'No one will believe how many, but if you say?'

Alexanor smiled.

One of his men shouted, and the smile was wiped off his face.

A rider burst from the cover at the edge of the Heraion hill, riding east across the barley fields.

It was Kritias.

First Alexanor thought, *What's he doing?*

And then he realised that his novice was riding at a fast canter, straight at their enemy.

In a flash, Alexanor realised that Kritias knew as much as he did himself about their army, their dispositions ...

'Oh, shit,' he muttered.

Kritias cantered past the burnt farmstead and then he turned and reined in. The word 'traitor' was fully formed in Alexanor's heart when Kritias raised his spear and roared a challenge.

'What is he doing?' the girl asked. 'Is this a Greek thing?'

A horseman burst out of the Aetolian ranks. He wasn't any bigger than Kritias but he rode like a Centaur. He rocked his horse back on his haunches purely for show and then shot off in a mad charge across the eastern barley field. He leapt the low wall with heartbreaking grace and rode down on Kritias.

Kritias turned his horse and threw his javelin ...

And missed.

His opponent swung his spear at Kritias at close range, but the shaft passed over Kritias who was suddenly flat on his horse's back. By luck or skill he caught the shaft as it went past and then he had the man's spear. He turned it in his hands even as he turned his horse with his knees.

He threw it. He didn't even seem to put much effort into it, but it went into the other man's back, and the man spread his hands. He rode for a long time like that, and then, slowly he fell.

Kritias turned his horse to face the Aetolians. He called something.

'I like him,' the girl said. 'This was well done. He rides well, you know?'

Alexanor knew. One forgot that Kritias rode well – that in the ambush at the high coastal pass, he'd plucked Alexanor expertly from the snow. He was very rich; of course he rode well.

*I thought he was betraying us.*

A second rider emerged from the Aetolians. He had more armour, and there was a cheer from the whole enemy line. Kritias sat astride his horse with his shoulders a little hunched, as if he regretted the whole thing – as if he'd been seized by dejection.

'Just ride away,' Alexanor said.

'No!' the Scythian girl said. 'It is marvellous. This is how people should fight.'

The Aetolian rode up at an easy trot until he was perhaps a hundred paces from Kritias. He sketched a salute in the air with his spear. Kritias turned his horse and began to ride away. The whole enemy force hooted in derision.

The Aetolian gave a screech and charged him.

Kritias continued to ride away. He wasn't going very fast at first . . . then he accelerated.

At some point he turned slightly, raising a puff of dust. The Aetolian screeched again.

Kritias reached down and plucked his spear from the back of his first victim, who lay in the mud near the edge of a shallow farm pond. He and his mount turned, with his grab at the spear as the axis of the turn, so that he was almost sideways to his horse's back – a beautiful piece of trick riding.

The Scythian girl clapped her hands together.

Now Kritias was riding straight at his opponent, who was clearly surprised by the change. He reined in, turned his mount slightly, and then threw overarm, but the range was too far.

He drew his sword and came on.

Kritias and his horse spun and rode at an angle, forcing the other man to rein in, and for a moment the spearless man was at a stand ...

Kritias' spear caught him in the chest and went right through his bronze.

Before the dying man's horse had stopped, Kritias had dismounted in full view of the enemy.

He urinated, raising the hem of his *chiton* and pissing in the direction of the Aetolians. The Achaeans on the hillside behind him were few, but they were shouting themselves hoarse.

Then he vaulted onto his horse's back and trotted unhurriedly to where the second Aetolian lay choking in his own blood. Kritias took the spear and pulled it free of the dying man's guts. He flourished it, and then turned his horse and began riding towards the League line.

Two men emerged from the Aetolian line; they came from opposite ends, and they were hesitant, each clearly hoping that the other would gallop forward to claim the honours.

Kritias ignored them, and kept riding towards the Heraion.

The Scythian girl clapped her hands again.

To the west, the sun was going down in the sky. Across the valley, the balance of fear had changed; Alexanor's opponent, whoever he was, had hesitated too long.

'Dismount,' Alexanor said. 'We're staying here. Stay close to your horses. If we run, it's over the trails behind us.'

Everyone seemed to understand. Alexanor rode over the rocky ground, ensuring that every man understood the programme. He ended up high on the slope where Kleander sat amid a stand of thousand-year-old pines.

'Under no circumstances will you do what Kritias did,' he said.

Kleander grinned ruefully. 'I waited too long,' he whispered.

'Your turn will come, young hero. Right now, we're standing up to fifteen times our numbers, and nothing – *nothing* – is more important. I not only order this, I request it.'

Kleander frowned. 'Oh, sir,' he said, exasperated. 'Only ...'

Alexanor looked back at the Scythian girl.

'Only you and Dadas and Kritias are locked in a competition for a certain young maiden?' he asked.

Kleander tried to look into the distant sunset and it dyed his face with a ruddy glow.

'Your lust has a noble end in view,' Alexanor admitted. 'She is quite a woman. But the army is more important than the battle of your youthful egos. Do not do it.'

Kleander shook his head. He looked as if he might cry.

'You understand?'

'Sir!'

'You understand me, Kleander? Yes or no.'

'Yes, sir.'

'Good.' Alexanor rode back to his post at the Heraion. Kritias was there, bathing in the praise of the other soldiers, and Alexanor clasped his arm. 'Well done,' he said loudly. 'You bought us half an hour.'

Kritias flushed. 'Thanks, sir,' he said.

'I had to order Kleander not to join you,' Alexanor said.

Kritias nodded.

Alexanor made his face solemn. 'If you had lost ...'

'But I didn't ...'

Alexanor felt a hypocrite, but he rode close. 'This is not the Trojan War. Do I need to explain?'

Kritias thought for a moment.

'No,' he said with new-found wisdom.

As the shadows lengthened, the Aetolians opposite them began to withdraw up the ridge behind them. They left in neat files, and their rearguard stayed on the field to the very edge of darkness and slipped away into the last of the dusk, with an expertise that belied long practice. Alexanor kept up a running commentary on the skill of his adversaries and two dozen of his younger troopers watched and listened. The older men went to sleep.

Just at the edge of darkness, Philopoemen came from the ridge behind the Heraion. His white horse seemed to glow in the last light.

'By the gods!' he said. 'You held them all day! How on earth? Never mind now – we need to go.'

'Go?' Alexanor asked.

'The whole levy of Elis is out – four thousand infantry marching west. They're camped just the other side of this ridge.'

Dinaeos appeared. 'Congratulations,' he said. 'I hear you killed ten thousand Aetolians and held the ridge like Leonidas at Thermopylae.'

'Nothing like,' Alexanor said in deep relief. 'We had one brush, emptied a few saddles and rode away. This Scythian girl killed more of them than all the rest of us combined, although later Kritias rode out and challenged their whole force—'

'We heard,' Philopoemen said. 'Her father watched the whole fight and then came and found me. We trapped another wing of the Aetolian cavalry ... away to the north. It wasn't perfect – most of them broke free, but we took a hundred and killed as many again.

'Kuka,' the Scythian girl said. 'My name, Greeks.'

Philopoemen clasped arms with her. 'Well fought, Kuka.'

Alexanor had a moment of pain that he'd never asked her name.

She grinned. 'And my mother?'

Philopoemen nodded. 'Knows all.'

She whooped, leapt onto the back of her little horse and sped away uphill into the darkness.

'We're withdrawing,' Philopoemen said. 'Take your time. Pick your way over the hill and you'll find the main Elis road at the foot of the next ridge. You are still the rearguard.'

'What happened?' Alexanor asked as he mounted.

Philopoemen was now just a pale shape in the darkness.

'Damned if I know. Our column got too spread out. The Aetolians didn't know we were coming, and the result was ... chaos and confusion and hell come to earth. I might call it a contest of incompetence. I lost contact with you in the first hour. There must have been an Aetolian force between us, because we were attacked from behind ...'

'Gods!' Alexanor said. 'I'm sorry.'

'Don't be! The Thracians caught them in the flank, and then everything was like a maelstrom at sea – a big spinning fight with people entering from every direction. But Aristaenos arrived from the north and won the fight for us.'

'Crap. Philopoemen killed everyone in front of him and the Aetolians were already begging for mercy,' Dinaeos said with a wag of an almost-invisible hand.

'Dinaeos should write plays. It was Aristaenos. Regardless, then it was a different fight, or rather, a set of flights and rearguards and ambushes spread over five valleys. I think we lost almost as many men as they lost, but we won. And now we run before their infantry forces us into an unwinnable fight. Tomorrow afternoon we meet up with our infantry and we have a big battle.' Philopoemen sounded satisfied.

The Eastern cavalry filed off and Alexanor led the way up the steep slope with Kleander and Kritias close behind him.

'You were brilliant,' Kleander said aloud to Kritias.

Alexanor turned, but he couldn't see much beyond the shapes of riders.

Kritias stuttered. And then said, 'Oh ... uh ... thanks. Thanks, Kleander.'

Alexanor put his horse to the slope, and they were moving. He felt as if he had a ball in his throat; he knew it wasn't the dust.

*My troops.*

Morning, and the Achaean horse, unslept but victorious, had broken contact and ridden all night along the only good road in the Peloponnese. Alexanor had that strange feeling that comes with no sleep and combat – a sense of unreality. His losses from the day before had been so light that he didn't have his usual heavy post-combat regrets. They had half a dozen Aetolian prisoners who were closely guarded but not stripped.

By late morning they came up with Aristides, whose fresh cavalry became the rearguard. Just after noon they rode over a low pass and saw the full muster of Achaea drawn up in the valley below them: thousands of infantry in loose phalanxes, most of the men at their ease or even lying full-length on the stony ground.

It took them two hours to arrange themselves on the wings, to water and feed all the horses, and to get food into the men. Most of Alexanor's troopers lay down next to their horses and went to sleep, their cloaks over their eyes. Alexanor had one more look at his dispositions – he was on the right, with Philopoemen and the Agema – and then he lay down himself.

The sun was much lower in the sky when he awoke. Dariush gave him water.

'The *Hipparchos* is asking for you, sir,' he said.

Alexanor mounted his Aetolian mare and rode to the centre, where he found Philopoemen with Kykliadas and most of the officers of the League.

Opposite them, less than two stades away, the Aetolians and Eleans were formed. They had slightly fewer infantry and cavalry, and their line was both thinner and longer.

'Damophantos sent a herald asking for a parley,' Philopoemen said. 'Care to come?'

Alexanor nodded. 'Delighted, I'm sure.'

So he rode across the fields, just barely green with a haze of new wheat sprouting from the soil. There were Kykliadas and Cercidas, Lykortas and Philopoemen, as well as Dinaeos and twenty troopers of the Agema. A middle-aged man with a long beard, wearing a dark red cloak over plain bronze armour, was introduced as Nikeas. Nikeas was a friend and supporter of Kykliadas acting as a second phalanx commander. Alexanor took to him immediately – a big, bluff, no-nonsense sort of man who carried a heavy spear. He didn't ride a horse, but walked along with them, his spear over his shoulder, like any hoplite walking out to a battle.

They halted on a low rise between the armies where a dozen stelae marked the dead of the village off to the south. They didn't wait long; a party emerged from the Aetolian lines, perhaps half again as large as their own.

'Send back for more cavalry?' Dinaeos asked.

'No. Never mind,' Philopoemen said. 'Although it would make for an interesting fight – Damophantos and his best against us.'

Dinaeos laughed. 'You're as mad as the Pythia, but I still like the way you think.'

'That's Damophantos,' Alexanor said.

The huge man was at the front, not cowering amid his companions, and he rode up the hill at a good pace. He reined in by Philopoemen.

'Well,' he said, 'you must be Philopoemen.'

Face to face, the two men might have been brothers. Both of them had magnificent armour; both of them were a head taller than most other men, and rode big horses – Philopoemen's was a pale grey that he called Kineas, and Damophantos' was a dark bay.

'And you must be Damophantos,' Philopoemen said.

Damophantos glanced over the rest of the Achaeans and then he saw Alexanor and his nostrils pinched.

'You,' he said. And then slowly, calmly, 'You killed a good friend of mine.'

Alexanor didn't answer. He just nodded. And then, as Damophantos wouldn't look away, he said, 'It was a fair fight.'

'Fuck that!' Damophantos said. 'No fight is fair. You're riding his horse. When I find you, you're dead.'

Alexanor nodded. 'Someone will be dead.'

'Are we boys?' Philopoemen asked. 'Why the parley, *Strategos*?' He was addressing Damophantos, who turned his horse.

'It's over,' the Aetolian said heavily. 'By no will of mine. We are told we have a thirty-day truce, imposed by the Romans and the Macedonians.'

Kykliadas spoke up. 'Are you the commander for your alliance, Damophantos?'

'Who the fuck are you?' Damophantos asked.

'I am the *Strategos* of the Achaean League.' Kykliadas was annoyed, it was obvious.

Damophantos shrugged. 'Whatever. We'll be back when this foolish truce is over – and we'll rape your little army.'

Kykliadas was not a great warrior, but he was a very able politician and he was used to wordplay and tough speeches.

'I'm sure you Aetolians excel at rough wooing,' he said. 'But given that you never managed to penetrate our outer garments, I can't imagine our virtue is under much threat.'

Men laughed.

Damophantos was stung. 'Only this stupid truce—'

'Save it for your own boys,' Kykliadas said. 'Philopoemen beat you yesterday and if you want to fight today, truce or not, we'll probably beat you again.'

'You tempt me!'

'Bring it,' Dinaeos growled.

Damophantos' hand went to his sword hilt. 'You Achaeans need lessons in manners.'

'Perhaps,' drawled Philopoemen. 'But try as we might, we've never had such lessons from Aetolia.'

Alexanor couldn't stand it any more.

'Are we children?' he asked. 'Can we drop the childish insults? Damophantos, I for one am not proud that I killed your friend. I hate killing. We fought and I bested him. It is war. But I have no pride in it.'

Damophantos shook his head. 'You are a strange man. I wish I'd killed you when you were under my spear, but as you say, that's how war is. Next time.'

He turned his horse and rode away, and his escort clattered away behind him.

'As arrogant as Nabis,' Dinaeos said.

Philopoemen watched him go. 'He is a much, much more dangerous man than Nabis,' he said. 'Let's not kid ourselves. We're lucky to get a tie, and we all know that our phalanx is terrible.'

'You don't know the half of it,' Cercidas said ruefully. 'Thirty days' truce!'

'If Philip makes peace, we'll have saved Achaea,' Kykliadas said.

'If Philip doesn't make peace, we'll have it all to do again,' Philopoemen said. 'And this time, they'll all come at us together.'

# CHAPTER NINE

—◦◦◦—

## Megalopolis and Sparta

HOMOLOIOS (LATE MAY TO LATE JUNE), 209 BCE

On the morning after the battle that didn't happen, Philopoemen had an argument with his fellow commanders. Alexanor missed it, being deep in a dream of darkness and horror: his fellow *epheboi* lying white and cold under a cheerless moon as their parents gathered to mourn them like a chorus of the elderly in an Athenian play. In the dream, each one of them rose in turn to tell him what their lives would have been like if only they had lived.

Dariush awakened him, shaking his shoulder roughly.

'You are crying, master,' the boy said.

Alexanor was weeping uncontrollably, and he lay there in abject misery for several minutes before he could make himself rise.

People depended on him. He had to get up.

Dariush had some cold water and he washed his face and felt better; Dariush had a clean *chiton* for him and he got that on as well. He drank off a cup of watered wine and a cup of herbal tea and he began to feel like a human being, the shadow of the evil dream lifting like the corner of a curtain.

Kritias was putting wax on the reins of a bridle. He looked up.

'Why ...' he began to ask and then changed his mind. 'I hear we're going home.'

'Home?' Alexanor asked.

'The phalanx is already gone,' Theophoros said. 'Useless fucks.'

Theophoros, in his one month of soldiering, had taken on the guise of a hardened veteran.

'*Hipparchos* coming!' called a picket, and men straightened up. Some dice were put away. All the cavalrymen stood and so did their servants and slaves.

Philopoemen's face was red and he was obviously angry.

'*Archon* Alexanor,' he said formally.

Alexanor saluted with his arm. He had no helmet and no weapon and he was not feeling up to formality.

'We are to dismiss our cavalrymen with the thanks of the League,' he said.

Alexanor shook his head. 'But the truce—'

'The council of the League *Synodos* is confident that the truce will become a peace. For political reasons it is apparently essential that we send our forces home.' Philopoemen looked as if he might explode.

Alexanor nodded. 'Yes, sir.'

In fact, he could imagine the immense pressure from the entire propertied class of Achaea for them to go home and get some work done.

'Do they think Machanandas will send his *mercenaries* home?' Philopoemen spat. 'Do the Roman legions go home?'

No one spoke.

'I offered to keep the League Cavalry together at my own expense,' Philopoemen said. 'Demodokos accused me of trying to build a private army.'

Lykortas hurried up. He looked as if he'd slept as badly as Alexanor.

'Wait!' he called.

'What now?' Philopoemen barked.

Lykortas looked around. 'The *Strategos* relented and suggested that you be encouraged to keep the Agema and another squadron for further training.'

Philopoemen looked at him. He shrugged. 'You catch more flies with honey than vinegar, *Hipparchos*.'

Philopoemen allowed himself a quarter of a smile. 'You mean my righteous indignation was misplaced?' he said slowly.

Lykortas shook his head. 'I'll say no more.'

Philopoemen glanced around. 'Very well. I'll go and apologise for my temper.' He glanced back at Alexanor. 'Send the Epidaurans home but ask for volunteers to stay with us.'

An hour later, feeling better, Alexanor found Philopoemen with Cercidas. The treasurer of the League was going over a pair of wax tablets that turned out to hold the whole listing of the herds Philopoemen's cavalry had scooped out of Lacedaemon – and Elis.

'Gods, this is better than I had expected,' Cercidas said. 'The cupboard is bare, I promise you.'

'That's too bad, because we need another thousand horses,' Philopoemen said.

'Somehow I knew you'd say that,' Cercidas allowed. 'Aphrodite's radiant tits, man, I can't just hand you all our money.'

Philopoemen was sitting on an iron camp stool – a folding stool with a cloth seat, a wonder of cunning. He saw Alexanor looking at it.

'Roman,' he said. 'They make wonderful things.'

'Mostly for war,' Cercidas said.

'True for you,' Philopoemen admitted. 'What do you need?'

'I? Nothing. I have a suggestion, though,' Alexanor said.

'Go ahead.'

Philopoemen was making a note on his own tablet, made of ivory, with a golden stylus. His wealth was palpable.

The other man going over the accounts was Nikeas, the assistant *strategos*. For all his size, it was obvious he was an able mathematician, as his tablet was neat and his scorings precise. He nodded to Alexanor. Alexanor nodded back and then turned to Philopoemen.

'We train the cavalry at Epidauros. First, because the temple will pay. Second, because there is actual flat country to train on, and good fodder – your estates bore the whole cavalry for three weeks.'

'Third, you get to see your wife.'

'Perhaps I should have put that first.' Alexanor smiled.

Cercidas raised an eyebrow. 'I admit it would look better in the *Synodos* if the Agema were not sitting around on your estate.'

Nikeas agreed. 'I like it. I like it very much.'

'We have to fight a war and look politically reliable while we do it,' Philopoemen said, pettishly. But then, shaking his head, 'Yes, yes, I get it. It's a splendid idea, Alexanor. What does Aristides say?'

'He liked it too. And Stratos of Hermione says he'll take all his people home for a week and then come and join us.'

'I'm no cavalryman,' Nikeas said. 'But it looks to me like your easterners are your best cavalry already.'

Philopoemen's smile was bitter. 'It's always the ones who don't need the drill who come to drill.' He got up. 'I have a terrible idea.'

'How terrible?' Alexanor asked.

'If we hold the "training" at Epidauros and the Epidaurans are willing, then I don't need to nominate them as the squadron I'm allowed in addition to the Agema.'

Cercidas looked up. 'I suppose not,' he allowed slowly, as if he was suspicious, which he probably was.

'So I can *order* the Argosians to appear,' Philopoemen said.

'The worst cavalry in the League,' Alexanor allowed.

'Best run this past Kykliadas,' Cercidas said. 'He doesn't like a political surprise, and the Argosians are loud.'

'See why I might fancy being tyrant?' Philopoemen asked as they walked away.

'Not funny,' Alexanor said.

The army broke up quickly. The next morning the last men of the phalanx were gone, even those who didn't really *want* to go back to their wives and their farm labour. And the cavalry contingents vanished even faster, like late-spring snow when the sun comes out.

Alexanor suddenly had no responsibilities except Kritias and Dariush. So he followed Philopoemen to Megalopolis – a day's ride, slept for an entire day, ate a huge meal, and then rode into the magnificent *agora* of Megalopolis and found a priest of Zeus at the great temple: the foundation of Zeus *defeater of Titans*, the centre of the Megalopolitian law courts.

'Wait here,' he told Dariush.

He went up the steps, where he gave the sign of his own priesthood.

'How can I help you, brother?' the priest of Zeus asked. 'You're the famous priest from Rhodes, I think.'

Alexanor was struggling with his fame; it seemed ill-earned to him. 'I am a priest of Asklepios.'

'Of course,' the priest of Zeus said. 'I am Therion of Megalopolis. What can we do for you?'

'I want to manumit a slave,' Alexanor said.

'Delightful! I have to charge you thirty drachmae. In silver. My apologies, but it costs that much for the stone carver to carve the charge.'

He led Alexanor along the flank of the temple and together they chose the spot where the manumission would be carved in stone. Alexanor saw the stone carver and they had a brief conversation, and then there were all the tiresome formalities: Alexanor had to write out his intention in three different documents, had to sign a promise that he would care for the released slave in any legal circumstance that should arise, and then paid over two precious gold darics to see that the work was done immediately.

Therion handed another slave copies of the documents for the treasury, and a second slave took one leaf of the fair copy and walked off into the city.

'Can I offer you a cup of wine and a skewer of meat?' the priest asked. 'We sacrificed a lamb this morning.'

Alexanor sat on the portico and exchanged political gossip with his new friend, the priest of Zeus. Before an hour had passed, the second slave returned, bowed, and offered Therion a leather bag.

'I admit that if you weren't a friend of Philopoemen's and a hero in your own right, this would have taken longer,' Therion said. 'Even the slaves leapt to do your bidding.'

He handed over a repoussé copper plate that held the slave's full name and the details of his manumission.

Alexanor knew a request for a bribe when he heard one, and he was delighted with the speed of the operation. He put another gold piece on the table and slid it under the wine *krater*.

'You run a tight ship,' he said. 'Ten thousand thanks.'

'I'd like to meet the lucky new freedman,' the priest said.

'He's waiting with my horses,' Alexanor admitted.

The two priests went down the steps, out of the temple precinct and along to the agora, to a shaded arcade where there were a dozen horses and some donkeys being kept out of the sun. Dariush was leaning against a wall with another boy, sharing a cup of wine, but he sprang to attention and blushed furiously.

Alexanor couldn't resist the opportunity.

'Here I am bragging that I have the perfect slave!' he spat. 'A boy who fights for me, who always brings me wine, water, anything, before I even ask. And now?'

'Oh, master,' Dariush said.

'And now what am I to think? Drinking wine like a free man?'

'Very bad,' the priest of Zeus agreed.

'Here, take this.' Alexanor handed Dariush the copper tablet wrapped in leather and linen. 'And cheap wine! Damn it, boy, buy good wine.'

Dariush began to realise that he was being mocked. So did the other boy, someone else's slave, who began to breathe again.

Alexanor wasn't good at practical jokes; he shook his head.

'Open it, Dariush,' he said.

Dariush only had to see the colour of the copper and he burst into tears; he who had fought like a lion against Aetolians who outweighed him, now wept just to see the plate.

'Oh, master!' he said.

'Well, this has made my day, I must say,' Therion admitted. 'I love manumissions. Best part of my job, except maybe weddings.'

He embraced the new freedman and then Alexanor.

'Will you stay with me?' Alexanor asked the Persian.

'Of course! Gods, what else would I do? Go home?'

'Let's get you a *thorax*, then,' Alexanor said. 'So I don't have to spend as much time fixing you up.'

They returned to Philopoemen's house at the fall of evening and no one came out to greet them, which was odd. Alexanor could hear voices, and a pair of house servants came, both grinning. They tried to hide their grins and then smiled all the more when Dariush, who was almost one of them, burst out with his news.

'What is all the racket?' said a beautiful voice.

And there was Phila.

Alexanor noted that his pulse responded even to a fully dressed Phila.

'We all wondered where you were,' she said. 'Come and help us drink all this wine. I hear we're going to Epidauros.'

'I was arranging for Dariush's manumission.'

He said it as if from a great distance, because her presence was so palpable that he had some difficulty speaking.

'You freed a slave?' Phila asked. 'How lovely. Let me see him.'

She went past, out of the *andron* doorway, and he introduced her.

And later, when she was reclining with Philopoemen, she reached out and took his hand.

'Such a lovely thing to do,' she said.

'You are still committed to ending slavery?' he said.

'First the slave trade. Slavery will not go away in my lifetime. But the trade? Kidnapping women for brothels in Athens and Rome?' She nodded. 'Yes.'

He couldn't tear his eyes from her, and he knew he was being rude; it seemed remarkable to him that Phila could exist in the same world as conflict and death.

'I'm drunk,' he announced.

He went to bed.

A week later, he lay beside his own wife on his own *kline* in his own house, and Philopoemen and Phila were on another. Lykortas lay with Dinaeos, who had already made a joke about how much he missed his wife.

'But, Phila,' Aspasia said, 'surely you think the truce will hold.'

Alexanor was already amazed at the grasp his wife had on the military events and politics around them. She had taken his advice to heart and developed a circle of letter-writers.

Phila rolled over and lay on her side. She was not a tiny woman, but lying full-length against the titanic Philopoemen she looked like a toy woman, a beautiful doll.

'I do not,' Phila said with asperity. 'Philip had a chance – more than a chance. He destroyed the main Aetolian army at Lamia. He won two major battles against the Aetolian *strategos* Pyrrhias despite being outnumbered. Pyrrhias had Roman troops and Pergamene mercenaries and he *still lost.*'

'I thought Damophantos was the Aetolian *strategos*,' Alexanor said.

'Only for the Peloponnese,' Aspasia said, in the voice she would have used to remind her daughter to close the door.

'So why no peace?' Philopoemen asked, looking down at the woman at his side.

'Because it was not the time for a truce. It was time to destroy the Aetolians and drub the Romans. He had them at utter disadvantage, and he squandered it. The Romans do not fight like Greeks. Anything is fair, to them.'

'This is the new manner of making war,' Philopoemen said.

'Well, it's not superior to the old way,' Phila said. 'Philip assumed that by granting a truce, he was dictating the peace. The Romans assumed he was a fool, accepted the truce, and moved their forces out of the threat.'

'To be fair ...' Aspasia nodded to her steward, who began to serve another round of wine. 'To be fair, Philip thought we were in far more trouble than we actually faced.'

Philopoemen nodded. 'Or, to be even more fair, maybe we were in so much trouble. If we *lost* the battle with the Aetolians, I think it would have been the end of the League.'

'We would never have lost,' Alexanor said.

'What a patriotic Achaean you have become,' Philopoemen said with a gentle smile. 'Our infantry is very bad – they are badly armed and unmotivated. Our cavalry is coming along, but man to man in the open field, I don't fancy our odds. All that said though, Damophantos also doesn't fancy his odds, which tells you something. If he really liked the odds—'

'He'd have come at us and pretended he'd never heard of the truce,' Alexanor said. 'I thought the same thing.'

'Who was it who said that war was simple?' Phila asked.

'Not I,' Philopoemen said.

'So what now?' Alexanor asked.

'We'll have a peace conference, probably at Aegio or Lamia.' Phila made a face. 'Philip will discover that the Romans dictate peace, they don't negotiate it. Hannibal has killed anything in them that was ever soft – now they always aim to destroy. They will make outrageous demands and we'll be back at war in twenty days.'

'By Ares!' Alexanor swore.

'Ares will definitely lead the way,' Philopoemen said.

There followed a week of very thorough training: cross-country rides, and repeated drills in breaking a full squadron, flying over rough country, and rallying at a pre-selected point.

'By the Queen of the Gods,' Kritias muttered. 'We did this for real!'

'And now we'll learn to do it better,' Alexanor said, although he had private reservations. He spent a day with Chiron in the infirmary and visiting sick pilgrims in the dreaming hall.

'I can't keep going to war,' he said to his mentor.

'A trade at which you are quite brilliant,' Chiron said. 'By all accounts.'

'I hate it. And if I stay at it, I will become something ...'

The old priest put a hand on his shoulder.

'The other night I had trouble making love to my wife ... She was patient. But gods, Chiron. It is always with me. The dead. The...the feeling.'

Chiron kept a hand on his shoulder. 'To my mind, from the peace of my sanctuary, there are a dozen pairs of hands keeping Greece from the Barbarians this summer. And yours are perhaps the most important. Listen, my son. You will be the master of this sanctuary all too soon. You will go from a battlefield of men and the cutting edge of the sword to the soft gossip of priests and pilgrims, the constant complaints, the backbiting ...'

'Yes,' Alexanor agreed. 'I long for it.'

Chiron smiled. 'I need you to keep the alliance together this summer. I am preparing another five talents of gold of the League treasury.'

'You will save them.'

'I am saving *us*.' Chiron raised an arm so that it seemed to encompass all of Greece. 'Money buys power. Yours will be the loudest voice in the councils of war.'

'What would you have me say?'

Chiron shook his head. 'You have to decide for all of us.'

Alexanor put his hands on the railing. They were standing in the priest's *stoa*, near the theatre, on a perfect summer evening.

'By the god, Master. I do not want this power. I do not want to make war. I am sorry to whine, but none of you seem to be listening to me.'

'I hear you,' the old priest said. 'But I have no one else like you, Alexanor. Nor does the god. We are saving Greece. We may well die in the process. I will die here, in the armour of my priesthood – you may die in a fight with some Roman. If those are our fates, we cannot change them. But we can struggle to save something. So people will remember who we were and what we stood for. Liberty. Education. Perhaps even medicine and philosophy.'

'I have never heard you so ...'

Chiron was looking out too. The sun was setting in the west; the air was perfumed with temple incense and with the smell of good food. The air itself seemed soft.

Chiron shook his head. 'The Romans could land here tomorrow. And burn it all. Or Athens, or Corinth, or Delphi. Perhaps I wrong the Romans. Perhaps it will be the Pergamenes or the Aegyptians.' He sighed. 'Civilisation is fragile, and destruction is so much easier than creation or maintenance.'

When Alexanor got home and Dariush took his lightest, least necessary summer *chlamys* off his shoulders and he was in the cool darkness of his own home, his wife put her arms around him.

'Was it beautiful at the temple?' she asked.

'Yes,' he admitted.

'Did Chiron whisper sweet nothings into your ear?'

'Not exactly.' He put his arms around her and held her.

'Sweet,' she murmured. And after a moment, 'This is a long hug. Do you have ulterior motives?' she whispered.

He kissed her, but it was not a passionate kiss, but rather the kiss of a man for his partner in life.

'I am afraid.'

'Oh, gods, husband, so am I,' she said. 'Also pregnant.'

'Pregnant?' he asked, putting a hand to her belly.

She smiled.

'You know in three days?' he asked.

'I am a priestess of Hygeia,' she said. 'I'm not sure. But I'd wager. It's just like last time, and I knew then, too.'

He kissed her neck, meaning only to show his wonder, his affection. His delight that, despite everything, they had made another child.

She moaned. It was a very slight sound; she was not a wildly demonstrative person.

He was suddenly aroused in a way he had not been the other night, and he gripped her, and her mouth found his.

He lifted her with his war-hard muscles and carried her into the *andron*. The pins seemed to fly out of her long *chiton*. She was laughing, but it was not the laughter of amusement.

On the other side of the *andron* curtain, Alexanor heard Philopoemen.

And then Dariush. 'Ah, *Hipparchos,* you honour us. Master is at the temple and I believe that Mistress is shopping in the agora with her ladies.'

Alexanor and Aspasia were at such a moment that neither interruption nor cessation were very likely.

'My dear Dariush. I wouldn't exactly call you a liar, but your master's horse is right here,' Philopoemen said. 'Listen – I need him on horseback as soon as possible. You too.'

Aspasia wrapped her legs around Alexanor's back and her eyes did something ... wanton and unusual, as if they were not old married people.

'I'll tell him, sir. As soon as he comes back from the temple.'

'I can see why he freed you, Dariush.'

'You flatter me, *Hipparchos*.'

And the sound of Philopoemen's cavalry boots retreating down their front steps.

And later, Aspasia pinned her *chiton* quite calmly, as if this was their usual mid-afternoon habit. She pecked him on the cheek.

'I suspect something bad has happened,' she said lightly. 'So please come back and don't die out there, eh?' She leant close. 'I have a list of things we might do.'

'A list?' he asked.

Aspasia smiled. 'I know a famous courtesan.'


'Machanandas has invaded the League.' Philopoemen had all the League contingents paraded in the agora. 'Four thousand mercenaries.'

'Apollo's spotless diadem,' Lykortas swore. 'We had what, fifteen days of truce?'

No one was particularly surprised. Aristides already had his baggage packed and he had two pack mules and four slaves with him. Alexanor knew that Dariush would have him packed in no time. Kritias had purchased two Thracian boys and had bought further horses for them.

'We can be ready to march in an hour,' Aristides said.

'We will be massively outnumbered,' Philopoemen said.

'Not for long,' Lykortas said. 'I need forty mina of silver and I can change the odds.'

'I have it,' Alexanor said. 'In fact, I already have five talents of gold for the League coffers.'

'Hera's fecund—'

'Keep a civil tongue, Lykortas,' Philopoemen said.

'I can't help it,' Lykortas said. 'That's ... incredible.'

Philopoemen shook his head. 'The gods ...' he began.

Lykortas chuckled. 'I need to take the Spartan spy you allowed to remain in the temple,' he said to Alexanor.

'Be my guest.'

There followed a dramatic hour: slaves and masters ran up and down stairs and up and down the streets of Epidauros; the military camp where the Agema had lived was struck down by the grooms; a pair of *epheboi* went into the temple precincts and seized a pilgrim without a word of complaint from the priests.

'He's the one,' Kritias agreed.

'You traitor!' the Lacedaemonian roared.

'Interesting perspective,' Lykortas said. 'You took his helots?'

'Over there. Dariush has them.'

Lykortas smiled wickedly.

'You enjoy this far too much,' Philopoemen said.

Lykortas nodded. 'Probably.'

Philopoemen turned to Kleander. 'Take your file and ride to Hermione. Tell them that it's a full muster and to meet us at Argos tomorrow.'

To Kleostratos and Kau-Ippa he said, 'Go as far west as you have to, find the Spartans and do not fight them. Just tell me where they are.'

Kau-Ippa nodded, and her smile was much like Lykortas'.

'I've never taken orders well,' she said. 'Maybe some of these Spartans will die.'

'Whatever you do,' Lykortas said quietly, 'do *not* kill any of their Tarentine mercenaries.'

Kleostratos made a face.

'That's an order,' Philopoemen said.

The Thracians and Scythians were gone before the Agema was packed.

The League's cavalry rode west before mid-afternoon and they rode hard, passing along the coast at the Gulf of Nauplion and then riding inland to Argos, which, by dint of some hard riding by a pair of *epheboi*, greeted them with open arms, ready food and fodder, and a muster of her cavalry.

Their local *hipparchos* greeted Philopoemen, took his horse, and embraced him.

'You were right, *Hipparchos*,' he said formally.

Philopoemen was always a gracious victor. He brushed off the apology as unnecessary and praised the men of Argos for their preparedness.

In the morning they were all mounted in the dawn when a very tired-looking Kleander rode up the coast road, covered in dust.

'Aristides has the whole of the Hermione cavalry and he's coming strong. But *Hipparchos*!' Kleander said.

Philopoemen turned his horse.

'Arkas!' Kleander burst out. 'He's come! From Crete!'

Philopoemen's horse fretted; he clamped his thighs and calmed her.

'By all the gods. By Zeus of the rulers.' He looked right and left.

'With men!' Kleander said.

'Now,' Philopoemen said. 'Now we will show the Spartans something.'

They rode west from the plains of Argos into the mountains. Scouts from the Agema scoured the ground ahead; every copse of trees was searched. Philopoemen began to rotate the men of Argos through the advance guards and rearguards.

'He's training them,' Alexanor confided to Kritias. Kritias just shook his head.

'All Philopoemen does is train,' he said.

'Yes. I think that's his Stoic appreciation of a good life – always train.'

Kritias laughed. It was a revealing laugh; it showed him as a man who was learning things.

They camped high up in the mountains; there wasn't enough grass for the horses nor food for the men, despite food taken from Argos. But they were becoming veteran campaigners and in the morning they were up, their donkeys packed, and the whole column was moving half an hour after dawn. They passed through a hamlet at the base of the pass and the peasants came out and cheered them, which brought tears to many an eye, and then they were on the great plain of Mantinea.

A Scythian man, no older than Dariush, rode up during a halt south of Mantinea and handed Philopoemen a scroll. He handed it to one of his growing staff – a young man in an enormous *petasos*.

'Oh, Philopoemen,' Phila said.

Alexanor nearly fell off his horse.

'They've burnt my house again,' Philopoemen said. 'But all my stock had been moved, and most of my valuables. And more important, all my people.'

Phila was reading the scroll.

Dinaeos looked at Alexanor.

'Your house too,' Philopoemen said. 'I'm sorry. Your wife is safe.'

Dinaeos was red in the face.

'I want to go.'

'I want to rest the horses. Our homes will not be less burnt.'

Phila shook her head. 'But otherwise ...' she said enigmatically.

Philopoemen seemed unfazed by the destruction of his home.

'Otherwise we are on schedule,' he said.

At evening, they were at the foot of Mount Athenaios, bivouacked in a series of walled fields and with strong outposts and a third of their force awake at every watch. Before dawn, Dariush woke Alexanor.

'The *Hipparchos* is calling all officers,' he said.

He put a steaming cup of hot lamb broth in his master's hands, and his master muttered some praise and drank it off.

'Apollo,' he grumbled, and got up.

It was cold for the time of year, but Dariush got him into his *thorax* and greaves, and he glittered in the firelight as he stepped up to the command meeting.

'Our Lacedaemonian raiders have chosen to take a scroll from our case and are planning to force a cavalry fight before we're prepared,' Philopoemen said. 'They have no idea how many cavalry we have. In fact, I think we have inadvertently suckered them by moving our training to Epidauros. Apparently their spies didn't know we were keeping our forces together.' He shrugged. 'Regardless, they've sent almost five hundred cavalry to face us – the whole of their regiment of Tarentines and a troop of Spartiate cavalry to watch over them.'

The *Hipparchos* motioned to Lykortas, who was fully armed.

Lykortas nodded. 'We have to be cautious,' he said. 'I cannot answer any questions, but I beg of you to be careful of the Tarentines. If you come across Spartans, fight them. If you find yourself facing Tarentines, avoid them if you can.'

'This is Letos, my trumpeter,' Philopoemen introduced a new man, a small, dark foreigner. Alexanor couldn't tell in the firelight if the man was African. 'He plays well. He's loud. If he sounds his trumpet, it means that you can take on the Tarentines.'

'We're not so bad,' Dinaeos said. 'I think we can take the Tarentines. Don't you trust us?'

Philopoemen slapped his bronze backplate. 'In this case, I trust you to obey orders. That's all. I have the dispositions ready. Alexanor, you have the rearguard with the Epidaurans, Dinaeos, the vanguard with the picked men, Lykortas, the Agema. Everyone ready?'

There was a growl. Many officers had lost homes and flocks already.

They were moving before the sun crested the mountains and they spread out as they hit the next valley floor. Alexanor saw nothing; he was two stades or more behind the action. Just as dawn began to light the landscape, the Agema halted. Alexanor put a post high on the hillside above the road and then took half his troop *back*, just to be sure.

An hour later they halted again. He assumed that the scouts were scouring the valley floor. He rode back again and this time he saw a heavy column rolling down the pass behind him.

He cursed. 'Right. We'll hold the road at that little hollow,' he said. 'Make them take the fight into the fields—'

'Isn't that Aristides?' Kritias asked innocently.

Alexanor blinked and released his breath and his fear.

'Gods, yes, it is.' He turned his horse. 'Kritias, ride ahead. Tell Philopoemen that Aristides will be up with us in half an hour.'

Kritias turned his horse and leant forward and he was gone in a swirl of dust.

The day was warming. Alexanor kept an eye on Aristides and went forward to his main position. His own rear scouts brought in two of Aristides' men; there were embraces all around and then Aristides came up.

'The Agema is halted right there.' Alexanor pointed. 'I'd say go forward until you find them. Do not fight the enemy Tarentines unless you have to. No idea why.'

Aristides shrugged. 'Strange order,' he said. 'The boss's Cretan mercenaries are behind me on the road. Not far behind, either. They're fast.'

'Cretan mercenaries?' Alexanor smiled. 'Ah, Philopoemen. Never a dull moment.'

They remained halted until mid-morning, and a dust cloud appeared in the east. The day was going to be very hot. Alexanor had all his men dismounted, and he had the horses watered on a rotation. Kleander found a barn with grain and Alexanor served it out.

'We're moving,' Kritias said. He had appeared from the front of the column covered in dust, but he hadn't seen anything useful. 'I *think* that the Thracians are skirmishing with the Tarentines. It's all taking too long.'

They began the long climb onto the plateau of Megalopolis. They moved fitfully – a few stades and halt, then another few. The air smelled of smoke, but behind them, peasants were bringing the Megalopolitan flocks down the road and Philopoemen had to order them back into the hills.

'Poor bastards don't know we're a small force,' Dinaeos said an hour later.

It was afternoon and the low hills on either side of the road were a haze of white heat.

'Spartans are retreating,' Lykortas said. 'They're retreating at the very *rumour* that we're coming. That's what Philopoemen has done in one year.'

Despite his confident words, the wily Lykortas was tense and irritable.

Shadows were beginning to lengthen where the tall acacia trees lined a rich farmer's road to the north when the Cretans came up the road. Alexanor rode back to make sure that they were friendly, and his suspicions were exploded by the embrace of Telemnastos, no longer a callow youth but a big, bearded man with a thousand armoured archers at his heels.

'We're not mercenaries,' he said. 'We're the federal troops of the Cretan League, here to support our allies!'

One of his officers, a familiar-looking man of Gortyna, waved from the ranks.

'And the money, of course,' the Cretan called. 'Hello, Alexanor.'

'Like old times,' Telemnastos said. 'What's happening? I hear we're fighting.'

'Not really fighting,' Alexanor said. 'I don't know. Lykortas has hatched some plot – I assume he has a traitor among the Spartans and we're trying to arrange an ambush and failing. I could be utterly wrong.'

Telemnastos grinned. 'It really does sound like old times.'

Alexanor motioned for Dariush. 'Spare horse for our Cretan ally,' he said.

Dariush nodded and vanished.

Alexanor left Kleander in command of the rearguard; no one objected. He took Kritias with him.

They rode forward to the Agema. Lykortas wasn't there; the Spartan spy from Epidauros was gone, and Aristides had taken command.

'Don't ask me,' he said. 'Everyone important went forward half an hour ago. This is insane – are we fighting, or not?'

Alexanor shook his head and rode on forward with Telemnastos and Dariush.

It was the edge of dusk. They weren't making camp, and as Aristides said, the whole thing was insane. Alexanor rode up to Aristaenos, who was temporarily commanding the Argosian contingent of Federal cavalry. Aristaenos looked knowing, but then, he generally did.

'Philopoemen won't thank you for going farther forward,' he said. 'It's complicated.'

'They're torturing the Spartan and they don't want us there?' Alexanor asked.

The thought had occurred to him and he'd dismissed it as unworthy. And he suspected that Aristaenos didn't know any more than he did, and it was just his usual way to pretend to knowledge he didn't have.

'I'm going forward. Philopoemen needs to know that Telemnastos is here.'

Relations between Aristaenos and Telemnastos were ... still difficult, due to an incident years in the past, and Alexanor took the Cretan forward up the long slope before words could be exchanged. They went forward two more stades and the gorge opened out. Alexanor saw a picket of Agema cavalry and he waved. A young man in a beautiful panoply rode down.

'Ah, *Archon*,' he said and saluted.

Alexanor realised it was Dadas, who looked more Greek than Thracian. He introduced the Cretan.

'*Archon*, I am not to let anyone farther forward,' he said.

Alexanor might have expressed annoyance, but in the very last light, Philopoemen could be seen riding down the road. His white horse shone, and they could hear Lykortas laughing. Beside him was their captured Tarentine mercenary, Alexios, who was also laughing. Philopoemen saw Alexanor and Telemnastos and put his horse to a canter.

'Telemnastos!' he called. 'This is better than a month of feast days.'

Lykortas was shaking his head.

'I brought a thousand of the best,' Telemnastos said.

'Of course you did!' Philopoemen said. 'Where's Arkas?'

'Too seasick to march. I'm sure he'll be along soon. He and Thodor have another half-troop of Thracians, too.' Telemnastos laughed.

'Suddenly,' Philopoemen said, 'we have all the cavalry.'

'All the cavalry?' Alexanor asked.

Lykortas flushed.

Alexios nodded gravely. He was an Italian from Magna Greca and he was very dignified.

'My colleagues have not been paid in quite some time,' he said.

'And now we're paying them,' Lykortas said. 'I suppose that technically, they're yours, as the Temples at Epidauros provided the money.' His smile was vulpine.

Later, in the hasty camp, Alexanor shared his canteen of wine with the commander of the Spartan cavalry, whose entire contingent had been captured in the defection of the Tarentines. He was Timolaos, the same man whom Philopoemen had captured earlier.

He drank Alexanor's wine and shook his head.

'I can't go back,' he said. 'Machanandas will have me killed. He will think I arranged the whole thing.'

Alexanor helped the poor Spartan get drunk.

'So,' Alexanor said when he sat on the warm ground next to Philopoemen. 'War is over? Back to the truce?'

'I plan to strike into Lacedaemon,' Philopoemen said. 'I have all the cavalry. Machanandas must be terrified.'

'Don't be smug.'

'I'm not smug. Merely satisfied. Have some wine.'

'I've had plenty. I don't want to burn any Spartan homesteads.' Alexanor looked at his friend in the firelight. 'You've humiliated him. Isn't that enough?'

'Machanandas? No. I intend his destruction and replacement by a democracy.' Philopoemen smiled. 'Humiliation is for the schoolyard. You say you hate this. I agree that despite my love for it, it's a stupid way for men to settle their differences. I want Sparta restored to her former government – no more tyrants. Ephors and kings. Then we can all at least know who we're disagreeing with. Until then, it's war, despite what they say.'

Alexanor shook his head. 'I thought, when I saw the Tarentines, that we might be done.'

'No.'

'May I stay behind then?'

Philopoemen glanced at him. 'I need you.'

'To burn farms and kill women and children in Lacadaemon? Really? You need me?' Alexanor raised an eyebrow.

Philopoemen met his eye. 'Yes.'

Alexanor considered outright revolt. 'Hmm,' he said.

The next morning they crossed the boundary stones into Sparta. All day they passed dead helots and Illyrians – mercenary *peltastoi* caught in the open by the Thracians and the Agema.

'The helots are the most oppressed class in Sparta, yes?' Alexanor asked.

'Technically, there are no longer helots,' Philopoemen said.

Alexanor pointed angrily at a tangle of dead men – perhaps as many as half a dozen who had tried to make a stand and been shot down.

'Who are they, then?'

'Machanandas has "liberated" the lowest classes in Sparta and made them soldiers,' Philopoemen said. 'Timolaos says that he's giving them property from the Spartiates and even wives from the Spartiate class as rewards. So they'll fight for him.'

Alexanor made a face. 'We're killing slaves and peasants.'

'They're trying to kill us,' Dinaeos said.

Alexanor shook his head. 'Are any of these poor men a match for Dadas or Kleander?'

Philopoemen nodded sharply. 'No,' he said. 'And thanks to the gods and our training, we haven't lost a man yet. I have no intention of making this war "fair".'

*

They manoeuvred with Machanandas for two days. The enemy *peltastoi* were expert mountaineers, but the Cretans, with their excellent armour and their heavy bows, were simply better and more effective. Their horn bows outranged the Illyrian javelins by a hundred paces, and they, too, were expert mountaineers.

The sun was high in the sky; a magnificent day, burning hot. The morning's first skirmish had involved a mountain spring that both armies needed. The Achaeans had taken the spring with no loss.

Philopoemen had followed the combats from the road and then, as the Spartan mercenaries began to collapse down the pass, he led the cavalry forward. He took the command group up to the top of the pass that led down into the Vale of Sparta. They stood a hundred paces above the dry stream bed that marked the pass, on a round hill covered in olive trees, most of them wild.

Telemnastos could be seen running up the hill from the direction of Sparta, his long, bronzed legs flashing in the sun. And behind them, to the north, a dust cloud heralded a party of horsemen moving very fast. Philopoemen was pointing south.

'If you look carefully, you can just see the sun shining on the Temple of Artemis,' he said.

'You've been to Sparta?' Alexanor asked.

'My fathers helped negotiate the truces in the war with Cleomenes. Gods, we thought Cleomenes was bad. He was, by comparison with Machanandas, a noble adversary.' Philopoemen turned as the Cretan commander ran up.

'*Hipparchos?*' Telemnastos held out a large rock, partially encrusted with dirt.

Philopoemen laughed. 'For my very own?' he asked. 'I appreciate the thought, but what's the occasion?'

The Cretan laughed too. 'Because all the ground is ours,' he said. 'An hour ago, the Illyrians started to run whenever they saw us. Machanandas' retreat is turning into a rout. Their *psiloi* are beaten. Which is just as well – I'm almost out of arrows.'

Philopoemen turned in his saddle. 'Kleostratos?' he called. 'This should be it. We'll cut loose the cavalry, all but the Agema, as soon as the valley widens, and ...'

There were three horsemen cantering up the hill from the north. Alexanor knew Aristides immediately, as did Philopoemen.

'Aren't you commanding the rearguard?' Philopoemen asked.

'*Hipparchos*, we have a messenger from …' Aristides reined in his horse and the horse stopped, eyes rolling from fatigue. He dismounted. 'By Poseidon, I thought I was going to fall to my death there. *Hipparchos*, the *Strategos* of the League orders our immediate withdrawal.'

Philopoemen blinked. 'What?'

'The peace conference has collapsed. The Romans have moved their entire fleet around to Naupactus – Kykliadas says they will land on our coast—'

Philopoemen looked down the pass. 'See that, Aristides?' he said, pointing south. 'See that pinpoint of light? That's the Temple of Artemis in Sparta.'

'Goddess save us!' Aristides said. 'So close!'

'We are thirty stades from Sparta and Machanandas' army is collapsing.'

Dinaeos spat. 'Ignore the *Strategos*. Let's smack the Spartans while we can.'

'If the Romans sack Aegio,' Philopoemen said, 'stealing some Spartan flocks will not console us.' He shook his head. 'Fuck,' he muttered, one of the few times Alexanor had heard him swear.

'We can do it,' Aristaenos said.

'Not fast enough,' Philopoemen said. 'And never underestimate the tenacity of a cornered animal. We have no heavy infantry and no siege train.'

'Sparta has no walls!' Dinaeos said.

'They have stone buildings and barricades. They stopped Pyrrhus – I'm not going to risk the only standing force in the League.' He looked at Dinaeos. 'But I hear what you are *not* saying. We'll have to come back and do it all again. And now they'll be ready for our Cretans and our cavalry.'

'Bloody Romans,' Dinaeos said.

After three heady days of rapid manoeuvre and advance, the retreat up the mountain passes was silent. The men were despondent, many already worried about the possibility of Roman invasion. Alexanor lived in daily fear that a messenger would arrive to say that Pergamene marines were burning Epidauros.

The messengers came regularly – mostly young men from the north coast cavalry – every one of them bringing a more highly coloured account of the *Strategos* needing them immediately.

'Where's the king of Macedon?' Philopoemen asked the latest.

'At Nemea, at the games,' the young man said. 'People say he goes out every night, dressed as a young man of fashion, and he drinks and fornicates and—'

Philopoemen laughed. 'Fornicates?' He laughed again. The young man looked shocked. Philopoemen shook his head. 'When did young people become such prudes?' he asked. 'It's the Nemean Games. You are supposed to drink all night.'

'Brother, we're from an older, coarser generation,' Alexanor said.

'Too true. Where is Philip's phalanx?'

'At Nemea, *Hipparchos*, as is some of his cavalry.'

Philopoemen rolled his eyes. 'Then why have we been recalled?'

The young man looked frightened. '*Hipparchos*, I have no idea, except that Kyrkidas is afraid that Philip isn't going to help.'

Philopoemen shook his head. 'What a mess. Halt! Gentlemen, have your commands change horses. Grab a bite.'

Alexanor rode back along the column to 'his' cavalrymen. The column was on the switchback of a mountain track that led down into the valley of Megalopolis. Alexanor was struck by how he *didn't even think* of the steepness of the hill, the narrowness of the track, the difficulty of the riding.

Most of his men had already dismounted.

'We'll walk for three stades,' he called out.

They'd all learned from the Tarentines that walking every hour or so kept the horses much fresher. And on a trail this steep, it would hardly slow the column. They remounted when they reached the valley floor and the good road, and before dark most of the little army was billeted in Philopoemen's fields.

Phila had erected three magnificent tents, all linked together, and turned them into something between a palace and a stage set. Her tents were set just a stone's throw from the blackened bones of Philopoemen's house.

'Think of it this way,' she said. 'You can redesign the floors and the heating system.'

Philopoemen laughed.

The next day, he rested the army. There was food and fodder, and naturally, Philopoemen went for a run and Alexanor had to keep up with him.

'I don't think we'd have got soft if we'd slept in,' Alexanor panted, but he admitted that the run was much easier than it had been a few months before. He had no fat on his abdomen, which was starting to have as many muscles as his bronze breastplate.

Philopoemen glanced over at him.

'Listen, brother,' he said softly.

They were running up the long ridge above Philopoemen's farm, under the altar to Zeus.

'All ears,' Alexanor panted.

'How do I handle Philip? I'm worried by what I hear. Why is he cavorting at Nemea instead of stopping the Romans? What happened in the peace talks?'

Alexanor nodded. 'Slow down and I'll do what I can to unravel the knot,' he said, and Philopoemen obligingly slowed his pace.

'Sorry,' he muttered.

'Your legs are a foot longer than mine. Anyway, listen. Even kings have morale. Philip won two solid victories and he had to think the war was over. Right?'

'Yes,' Philopoemen agreed.

'When is a man weakest in battle?'

'When he turns to flee,' Philopoemen said.

'Fine. After that?'

'When he thinks he's done. I see what you are saying. You are saying that Philip is like a warrior in battle who thinks his fighting is over. And then finds that he has to make a desperate fight—'

'Exactly. So he drowns his sorrows and chases flute girls and boys.' Alexanor had seen these behaviours often enough in people who were not kings, but merely tax gatherers and farmers and bankers. 'He's avoiding the world.'

'Allowable enough, unless you are a king,' Philopoemen said.

'What does Phila say?'

'She said about the same, with some details of the king's sex life and the complexities of Macedonian politics. She thinks he's trying to avoid committing his army to a fight in the Peloponnese because then he'll be too far from Macedon to march back, if the Romans sail around.'

Alexanor thought about that. 'Damn.'

'Damn indeed,' Philopoemen said. 'Almost home. Let's sprint.'

'You sprint,' Alexanor said. 'I'll just plod along.'

# CHAPTER TEN

—◦◦◦—

## Megalopolis, Nemea and Aegio

### HOMOLOIOS AND THEILOUTHIOS
### (LATE MAY TO EARLY AUGUST), 209 BCE

The League cavalry marched into the environs of the Nemean Games, and Alexanor felt as if he was reliving his youth. Fifteen years before, the games had saluted the king of Macedon and then Philopoemen, and now, the entire scene was repeated with minor variations. The Ephors of the Nemean Games were ecstatic to be hosting the mighty king of Macedon, who had a magnificent box of gilded leather and wood painted like marble in the middle of the stadium. But they were, if anything, even more delighted to arrange for the League Cavalry to be cheered.

Alexanor led a selection of the men of Epidauros and Aristides led a selection of the men of Hermione. The small contingents allowed them to manoeuvre better in the confines of the stadium and gave them an excuse to leave the many awkward sods who might have fallen off their horses or couldn't be bothered to polish their bronze. The Agema came in two squadrons, looking like polished bronze statues, and only a handful of senior officers knew that fully a third of the polished and expert horsemen were the Tarentine mercenaries.

The result was the public appearance of a magnificent professional cavalry force, the kind of force that Aegypt or Macedon or the Seleucids might boast of, but that small states like Achaea never possessed. The crowd roared themselves hoarse, but Alexanor watched the royal box,

193

and Philip of Macedon watched the cavalry with an odd expression – part admiration, part annoyance. He was certainly unimpressed with the enthusiasm of the crowd's reception of the League cavalry, and when Philopoemen entered, looking like a war god on his fine white Nemean stallion, the waves of 'Achilles! Achilles!' shook the ground and left Philip with a very wry look indeed.

'Watch out for him,' Alexanor said, when they could be heard. 'He doesn't like all this adulation going to someone else.'

Philopoemen smiled. Alexanor was disappointed to see that his friend's nostrils were widened and his pupils dilated; he was elated by the roars of approbation.

'Do not, I pray, let this go to your head,' Alexanor snapped.

Philopoemen's eyes were sparkling. 'Go to my head?' he asked absently.

He made his horse rear, and twenty thousand men roared their approval.


'I'm not sure that the League needs me at all.'

Philip said it with a brilliant smile – he was a very handsome man. But the comment bore a sting.

Kykliadas shook his head vehemently. 'Your Grace, with the Romans just across the narrow sea, I promise you that our cavalry, no matter how beautiful, cannot guarantee us peace.'

Philip glanced at Philopoemen. They were inside the precinct of the Temple of Zeus, standing under the ancient trees of the sacred grove of cypresses. The trees were a thousand years old and towered above them, providing a deep and comfortable shade better than a palace.

'And you, Philopoemen,' the king said. 'What do you think? Will you need my humble troops to face the Romans?'

He looked tired; his eyes were rimmed in red, and despite his excellent physique, he walked like a man with too little sleep.

Philopoemen laughed softly. 'Your Grace is pleased to be humorous. The Achaean phalanx can no more face a Roman legion than they can grow wings and fly. But ... Your Grace, do we really think that the Romans will attack us?'

'Yes,' Lykortas said. 'Pardon, gentlemen ... Your Grace. We have reliable reports that Galba is loading supplies for a descent on our northern coast.'

Philip shook his head. 'Reliable how? Gentlemen, I applaud you for your efforts, but Achaeans have a habit of saying that the sky is falling when in fact the sun is shining. We are about to enter into the second round of talks and the Aetolians—'

Lykortas bowed. 'Pardon, Your Grace, but the Aetolians, according to my source, are about to change their demands.'

Philip made a sound of disgust.

'Because the Romans are covering them. They are bold,' Lykortas said.

Philopoemen asked quietly, 'What's your source?'

Lykortas whispered, 'Phila.'

Philopoemen nodded.

Philip raised an eyebrow. 'You believe this?'

'The source has been very reliable for us in the past,' Philopoemen said in a level voice that Alexanor admired.

Philip glanced at his own officers. 'Alert the phalanx and the *peltastoi* to be ready to march,' he said. 'We will, in the meantime, hear what the Aetolian delegates have to say for themselves.'

It took them two days to reach Aegio – the League capital and scene of the negotiations. If Philip was sorry to leave the Nemean Games, he didn't mention it, but each night on the road he and his retinue had all the lamps lit in their tents until the early hours of the morning.

The next morning, Alexanor was summoned to the king's tent by a very arrogant young Macedonian cavalry officer who hadn't even buckled on his *thorax*.

'The king wants you,' the young man said.

'Sorry, sir,' Dariush said. 'He shoved me out of the way.'

'The king of Macedon wants you,' the young man said again. 'Get a move on.'

Alexanor was not at his best when rudely awakened, and he was not used to being ordered around.

'Hmm,' he managed.

'Foreigner!' the Macedonian ordered. 'Get your arse out of those blankets and follow me.'

Alexanor kicked his cavalry cloak off his pallet and stood up. He was naked, and his mood was sour. He took a drink from his canteen.

'Are you an officer?' he asked.

'What?' the young man demanded. 'Get moving.'

'Are you, in fact, an *archon*? A *dekarch*? A *phylarch*?' Alexanor was warming to his anger.

The younger man's eyebrows narrowed. 'Listen—'

Alexanor stepped very close to the younger man. 'No, you listen. I'm an officer of the League – in fact, I'm an *archon* of League cavalry. You, as far as I can tell, are a well-born galloper. Go back to your king and tell him to send someone with more courtesy.'

'Don't be a fuckwit. I'm a Macedonian. You're a Greek. Get your worthless arse in motion—'

Alexanor dropped him. He was relatively nice; he swept the man's legs and put him on his own bedroll.

'Don't make me hurt you,' he said. 'Out. Now.'

'The king needs you! He's pissing blood!' the man shouted.

Alexanor froze. 'Ah,' he said. 'Now I hear this? You really are a fool.'

He pulled a *chlamys* over his shoulders to cover his nudity and grabbed his medical bag, a fine leather bag that Aspasia had ordered for him – a beautiful bag with hundreds of pockets. He sprinted for the royal tent, which was only a hundred paces or so away in a stand of sea pines. Their scent was glorious in the early morning sun.

Alexanor nodded and the sentry let him pass, and he went inside. Philip was lying on a camp bed not much fancier than Alexanor's own. The man was pale.

'My lord?' Alexanor asked.

'Alexanor,' Philip called. 'Thank the gods you are here.'

'You passed blood ...?'

'I feel like death. I can't seem to breathe correctly and I'm ...'

Alexanor took his pulse. 'You drink far too much,' he said. 'What did you eat last night?'

The king's body slave was called for – a Persian man, as Alexanor had expected. He listed an impressive string of sweets and delicacies.

'What was the main dish?' Alexanor asked.

'Tuna,' the slave said.

'Any left?'

'How is this going to help me?' Philip asked.

'Patience, Your Grace.'

In fact, he was very much enjoying both his ascendancy over his patient and the feeling of practising medicine instead of killing people. He was almost sure what he was looking at; he'd seen it a dozen times.

He walked to the king's field kitchen, where a dozen cavalry troopers were guiltily hiding food under their cloaks. Alexanor was not interested in the corruption of the royal cooks.

'Any of the tuna left?' he asked.

The two cooks, both free men, looked very guilty indeed.

'All gone?' he asked.

The cooks squirmed. One of the cavalry troopers began to shuffle away from the cook fire.

'Don't go anywhere,' Alexanor said. 'The king is very sick – I need to look at the tuna. If you lot are eating it, I may need to look at you.'

'Oh gods,' one of the troopers moaned.

''Ere,' said the smallest. 'I ain't had mine yet.'

Alexanor took the cold tuna. It was a dark wine red, the way fresh, raw tuna looked, but when he prodded it with his finger, it was firm and well cooked.

'You coloured it?' he asked the cooks.

'Aye,' said the paler of the two. 'Aye. His nibs likes it coloured.'

'What did you use to colour the fish?'

'Beetroot,' the darker cook said. 'It'll colour anything, doc.'

'Yes, it will,' Alexanor said, suppressing a smile. 'Don't say anything about this.'

When the column was mounted, Alexanor trotted his charger over to Philopoemen.

'You are looking at a hardened criminal, false to his oaths,' he said.

'I am?' Philopoemen asked. 'You really do not have the look.'

Before he could say more, Philip rode up. They both saluted. He nodded politely to Philopoemen.

To Alexanor he said, 'I thank you from the bottom of my heart. I feel much better. You're certain …?'

'Absolutely certain,' Alexanor said with a clear conscience. 'You need to abstain from wine for a week, and lower your consumption to perhaps a single amphora a day.'

The king bowed as if Alexanor, and not he, were king.

'I will do so. No wonder my uncle spoke so highly of you.'

He rode away surrounded by his officers and some guilty-looking troopers of his household cavalry, several of whom looked at Alexanor and then looked away. Philopoemen raised an eyebrow.

Alexanor smiled. 'A life of crime,' he said.

'How so?'

'The king ate too much beetroot and his piss turned blood-red. Absolutely harmless. But I told him the wine was getting into his bloodstream.' He smiled.

Philopoemen laughed. 'That's your idea of crime?'

'If I just told him to cut back on his drinking, what do you think he'd do? But now I'm a charlatan.'

'We use such deceptions in war and people call us heroes,' Philopoemen said.

'Do they, though?' Alexanor asked.

In the grove of oak trees at Aegio, the representatives of a dozen sovereign nations were gathered. Alexanor was pleased to see a pair of Rhodians he knew: Solon, a patrician from Kos, white-haired and hale, and Apollion, a fellow native of Kos. He introduced himself and heard the news of Rhodes and Kos while Philopoemen canvassed the representatives of Athens, Boeotia and Elis. There was an officer from Aegypt as an observer, and Telemnastos produced a scroll to be included as the accredited representative of the Cretan Federal League.

Philopoemen came back to Alexanor with Lykortas by his side.

The two Rhodians, both former magistrates, were cautious in meeting Philopoemen, but he swept away their concerns.

'I have nothing but respect for Rhodes and for the Rhodian government.'

'We are allies of Rome,' said the elder of the two, the white-bearded former admiral, Solon. His *himation* was spotless; he looked like the kind of man who ran most Greek cities – old, stable and cautious.

'We can still find common ground,' Philopoemen said. 'For example, we all hate piracy like we hate disease and earthquakes.'

'More,' Solon said. 'Well said.'

His partner, Apollion, vouchsafed a small smile.

'Nonetheless,' Philopoemen said, 'I'm going to predict that we'll be back to war in an hour or so.'

The Rhodians drew back as if Philopoemen had uttered a blasphemy.

The *Hipparchos* of the League shrugged. 'I'm sorry. But the Romans aren't here, the Pergamenes aren't here, and the Aetolians are late. I assume they are only coming to make some extreme demand.'

Solon looked at his colleague. 'No,' he said. 'We were not consulted, and we have counselled peace since the battles at Lamia. Earlier. This war helps only the pirates – it's the death of commerce.'

His colleague nodded solemnly. He had less white in his beard and he seemed hesitant even to speak, but finally he opened his mouth …

'The Aetolian League commissioners,' announced a herald.

'And no one from Sparta,' Alexanor noted.

'Even Spartans might hesitate to violate a truce and then send delegates to a peace conference,' Philopoemen said.

The herald raised his staff. 'The delegates for the Aetolian League wish to address this assembly,' he said.

The leader of the Aetolian delegates was none other than Damophantos.

'Here we go,' Philopoemen said.

Damophantos towered over the other delegates, and his smile was more predatory than conciliatory.

'Gentlemen,' he said. 'Aetolia and her allies, Rome and Pergamum, are prepared to make peace.'

'Told you,' whispered Solon.

'In consultation with our allies, these are our conditions,' Damophantos said. 'First, Macedon is required to return to the Messenians the city of Pylos which it holds illegally.' He looked around and the wolfish smile broadened. 'The king of Macedon is required to return Atintania and her environs to Rome and surrender any territory he has taken to the northern tribes. To make full restitution to Aetolia for any harm he has caused.'

Everyone looked at Philip. He was seated, surrounded by courtiers, and he didn't return any reaction at all.

'In addition,' Damophantos said, 'the League of the Achaeans must repay Sparta an indemnity for her depredations there equal to fifty talents of gold, and must promise not to maintain a cavalry force greater than a hundred men. There are a few other conditions,' he said over the rising and indignant murmurs, 'but if these are met, we will have the basis of a lasting peace.'

He smiled when he said the last words; no one doubted that the peace described would not last long.

'How on earth would we pay fifty talents of gold?' Kykliadas shouted.

'Stop paying all that expensive cavalry,' Damophantos said. 'I care nothing for how. Those are our terms.'

Philip of Macedon rose to his feet. He'd been seated on an ivory stool – the only seated man in the whole sacred enclosure. Damophantos seemed a trifle surprised to see him.

Philip walked to the bema, the speaking stone.

'Are you done?' he asked politely.

Damophantos stepped away without a word.

Philip smiled slightly. He was sober, dignified – far more like the youth that Alexanor remembered.

'I came here in good faith to find the basis of peace,' he said. 'I call all of you to witness that after repeated victories, I allowed the enemy from under my foot in hopes that we might find some path to end this war. And instead, the very men I have defeated use these talks as a time to rearm and a pretext for further attacks.' He turned to Damophantos. 'When your temples are burned and your gods thrown down to the earth, do not tax me with desiring war. You have brought this on yourselves.'

Damophantos seemed surprised by the king's vehemence, but he recovered quickly.

'You will not even consider our terms?' he asked, mockingly. 'It seems it is you who wants war.'

'Your terms are a mockery of a peace conference,' Philip said. 'Look at your own allies. Look at the Rhodians or the Athenians and read in their faces what they think of your foolish demands. Very well. War. I will bring it to you, Aetolia.'

He stepped down from the bema.

Every taverna, brothel and hostelry in Aegio was packed with men – richer men than Alexanor would ever be – and when he had served at the temple and made sacrifice to Apollo, he had pitched his tent in the military encampment behind the town. They only had a single squadron of the Achaean Agema with them, so as not to overtax the resources of the town. The rest of the League cavalry lay a day's march away nearer Corinth.

Alexanor was surprised to find Philopoemen in the military camp.

'You have a beautiful house here,' he said accusingly.

'I used to,' Philopoemen said. 'I sold it. But you're right – I have another, and I rented it. I wanted to be here with the cavalry. I have a feeling. It's Damophantos. And the Romans. Something here is rotten. The demands were outrageous – they are a cover for something.'

Alexanor poured his friend a cup of wine, cut half and half with water.

'You are terrifying me.' He frowned. 'You said they'd be outrageous.'

'I thought they'd be unacceptable to Philip. Those demands were so extreme that I assume they were some deliberate plot. I had a cup of wine with your Solon – a fine man. He was outraged that Rhodes hadn't been consulted and the Aetolians, whom he describes as "pirates and bandits", dictated the policy.'

Alexanor nodded. 'Rome is a difficult ally. I've heard that almost all my life.'

'I'm probably just scaring myself,' Philopoemen admitted.

Dariush laid a wool carpet by the fire and both men sat on it. Kritias was heating something that smelled delicious.

'What's that?' Alexanor asked.

'Wine and cheese and barley,' Kritias said. 'The farm wife ... showed me how to make it. It's called *kykeon*, and—'

'Kritias cooking?' Philopoemen said. 'The world is ending.'

Kritias was not pleased. 'I can cook,' he muttered.

Alexanor chuckled. 'Anyone can make *kykeon*, Kritias.'

'Not like this,' the young man said, and indeed, the smell was delicious.

Philopoemen suddenly sat up.

'Hoof beats,' he said.

'Damn it, it's just night patrol.'

Alexanor knew there was a night patrol; he'd met it himself when he came back from his devotions.

'Too fast.' Philopoemen rolled to his feet. 'Dariush, get Arkas and our armour.'

'Yes, sir.'

The Persian ran off.

'Philopoemen!' called a voice.

'Here!' roared the *Hipparchos*.

Lykortas rode up to their fire. His horse didn't like the fire and fretted, but Lykortas had always been a fine horseman and he stayed in charge of his mount.

'Philopoemen, the Romans are going to land all along the coast. Phila says they mean to capture the delegates – to take Philip and end the war.'

Philopoemen was silent.

Alexanor grabbed Kritias by the wrist. 'Get my *hyperetes* and Philopoemen's. Tell anyone you meet to get armed.'

Kritias handed his mug to Alexanor.

'You drink this, then,' he said. But he smiled. 'I'm on it.'

He dashed off into the darkness beyond the firelight.

'How many Romans?' Philopoemen asked.

'All their marines – maybe four thousand,' Lykortas said. 'Their whole fleet is crossing in the darkness.'

'Right. Messenger to Kykliadas – everyone out of Aegio. We'll cover their withdrawal. Send someone to Dinaeos – better yet, Alexanor, go yourself.'

'Right.'

'Bring up all the League cavalry. No. Stop. First we go to the king.'

'Because ...?'

'Maybe Dinaeos will come up with the Macedonians. Four thousand Romans will take a lot of handling.'

For once, Philopoemen acted without dignity. He ran along the top of the ridge to the Macedonian camp. The camp was alert, and had sentries out, but no night patrol.

'I need the officer of the night,' he said.

'That's me,' said a cheerful, short, bandy-legged veteran with a terrible Macedonian accent.

'The Romans are landing all along the coast to take the king,' Philopoemen said.

'Fuck me!' the officer said.

'Wake the king.'

'I'm *that* sure he's awake,' the Macedonian said.

'Take me to him, please.'

'The problem is, he's awake between some pretty thighs, and he ain't here.'

Philopoemen nodded. 'There's no time for that. He's in his tent?'

'No,' the officer said. 'That's what I'm sayin'. He passed out o' the camp two hours ago, bent on some mischief.'

'Aphrodite!' Lykortas swore.

'Just so. An' I can't just stop the king o' Macedon,' the officer said.

'Does he have an ... escort?'

'Only if you like the kind that plays the kithara and maybe the flute. Fuck. I don't e'en know where to look.'

Alexanor glanced back at the league cavalry. 'I'll find him,' he said. 'Send Kritias—'

'No,' Philopoemen said. 'Lykortas. Go to Dinaeos and tell him to come as fast as he can. If he can convince the Macedonians to move, more power to him.'

Lykortas didn't wait to salute; he was running for his horse.

Alexanor followed him. He got into his breastplate and greaves, and then swung up onto his charger's back with the ease of a summer's practice, no spear required. Dariush mounted beside him. Alexanor leant down to Kleander.

'Get their reins in their hands and wait for Philopoemen,' he said.

'Yes, sir.'

'I'll be back,' Alexanor said, and together with his servant he cantered down the ridge to the city.

As he'd expected, it was far too late for most houses to be lit; there were perhaps a dozen with oil lamps burning, and the loudest was a big taverna right on the beach. Alexanor listened to the town for ten long breaths, trying to hear the sounds of chaos that would herald an attack by Romans. He didn't hear anything, nor could he see ships on the moonlit sea, but he could only see a very narrow slice of the sea.

He came down the street to the beach, his horse's unshod hooves wooden on the paving stones, and he tossed his reins to Dariush.

'Stay ready to ride,' he said, and went in through the beaded curtain.

There were a hundred men of ten races packed in under the awnings; the whole place stank of urine and cheap wine. Alexanor looked over the patrons with the practiced eye of a professional, and he found what he sought – a Macedonian. In fact, it was the young man who'd come to his tent. He went over. The young man was not eager to see him.

'Where's the king?' he barked.

The young man quailed. 'King?'

'Is the king here?' Alexanor asked. 'It is life and death. Don't fuck around.'

The young man gathered his wine-soaked wits.

'Fuck,' he said. 'He *might* be.'

'Might be?' Alexanor snapped. 'Be quick.'

'Fuck.'

A slave appeared. 'Wine, sir?'

'I'm looking for a Macedonian, middle height, blond hair. Sound familiar?' Alexanor asked.

The slave smiled – an utterly false smile. 'They all look like that.'

'Damn it!' Alexanor showed a gold coin. 'Yours if you find him.'

'What's his name?' the slave asked.

'Philip. He's the king of Macedon.'

'Sure he is,' the slave said. 'I'll see what I can do.'

'Are there rooms upstairs?' Alexanor asked.

'Only for paying—'

'If he's here, that's where he is,' the young Macedonian said. 'He's all off drinking. He said he'd just fuck his way to …' He looked at Alexanor. 'Sorry, sir.'

Alexanor wondered when he'd passed from ignorant foreigner to 'sir'.

'Go upstairs, knock on every door, and tell the customers you are looking for the king of Macedon with a message from Philopoemen of Achaea,' Alexanor said. 'Quickly now.' He turned to see Dariush pushing through the crowd. 'What now?'

'The bay is full of warships,' Dariush shouted. 'I can see their oars flashing in the moonlight.'

'Ares' dick!' Alexanor swore.

He ran out of the tavern. Men shouted after him, demanding an explanation. He ran to the sea wall, climbed to the small shrine to Poseidon and looked out to sea. The moon was bright, and the stars were clear.

He saw them at once; Dariush had sharp eyes, but the Roman ships were obvious enough coming in under oars. The wet blades flashed in the moonlight at the top of every stroke, making the ships look like water insects in the darkness.

The young Macedonian was with him, and a dishevelled older man in a wine-stained *chiton*. Alexanor realised that he was the older of the Rhodian delegates, Solon.

'I see four ships,' the Rhodian said.

'My informant says they are landing all along the coast – probably four for Aegio and the peace conference. The rest are probably going for the fortresses.'

Alexanor glanced at the Rhodian in the moonlight. Solon was looking out to sea.

'They're not very good seamen,' he said. 'The Romans. They're not as bad as some people say, but they don't have the sea-keeping skills that a Rhodian would have. I'm going to guess that their *navarch* can't decide whether to try and run in while it's dark, or hang off the coast and wait for dawn.'

Alexanor rubbed his beard. Then he glanced at the Rhodian.

'I'll help them decide,' he said. 'Dariush, run to the citadel – the acropolis. All the way to the top. Run all the way. Tell the commander to sound the alarm. Go!'

He went back to the tavern.

'Come with me! Bring torches!'

Solon grabbed his arm. 'You can't be serious? You think you can stop the Romans with a rabble of drunkards?'

Alexanor nodded. 'I certainly hope so.'

The arrogant Macedonian youth was shoving men out into the narrow street. Many of them had grabbed the taverna's torches and some oil-lit lanterns – expensive items that the taverna owner would regret losing.

'Follow me!' Alexanor roared in his deep-sea and high-wind voice.

At least sixty men stumbled off up the beach with him, and then up onto the sea wall.

Above him in the citadel, a dozen small bells began to ring: pottery bells with clappers, making a rattle and a ratchet and a clang – the sound of an enemy attack that every man and woman in Greece knew and dreaded. Men rose from sleep to grasp a spear and a shield; naked, most of them rushed into the streets.

More importantly, the sound carried out over the town and over the water as well.

Alexanor stood on the sea wall of the Temple of Poseidon and watched for the flash of oars. One great galley, a *penteres* or five-er, had a stern lantern lit, and she turned. She was only two stades off the port itself, where the stone breakwater and jetty enclosed part of the sloping beach, protecting the larger ships that couldn't be beached and turtled.

Alexanor could imagine her, with her upper deck packed with soldiers, and hence she'd be hard to balance and murder to row. He'd been a marine; he knew how fragile even the largest galleys were.

The drunkards stood and swayed in the torchlight, and the alarm went on. Above them in the town, shouts and the sounds of pounding feet and sandals slapping told Alexanor that the whole town was awake and the citadel was manned. He slipped away from the men he'd dragged out to the beach and walked briskly back to the taverna.

'I found him,' the slave said. 'He don't look like no king to me.'

'Take me to him,' Alexanor said.

'He's busy ...'

Alexanor walked into the upper hallway. There were curtains – twenty curtains, each for a room the width of a couch and no more. Alexanor had been in brothels before, and this one was as bad as most. The smell was spectacular: sweat and old perfume, red ochre and the indefinable musk of sex. It occurred to him, not for the first time, that humans probably emitted scents like other animals, and that this was worth study if he ever got to stop killing people and return to his real duties.

And he smiled to think of taking Phila's pulse.

'An interesting subject to study,' he murmured to himself.

'This one,' the slave said.

Men and girls and boys were coming out of most of the curtains in various stages of undress. The sound of the alarm was clear in the air and no one, no matter how lost to purchased passion, could have missed it.

'Your Grace!' Alexanor called.

'Go away!' Philip replied. 'What the fuck are you, my nursemaid?'

'The Romans are attacking the town,' Alexanor said in his doctor's voice, devoid of emotion. 'Philopoemen thought you'd prefer not to be captured, but I can leave if you wish.'

Philip's blond curls appeared through the curtain.

'Damn, don't be an arse. No, I'm the one being an arse. Romans? Fuck.'

His head vanished and the king of Macedon came through the curtain, naked, trailing a *chlamys* and with a ball of wool in one fist and a sword belt in the other.

Alexanor, with the imperious authority of the medical professional, said, 'You have money? Give this slave two gold pieces.'

Philip opened the purse on his sword belt and handed over two gold pieces without complaint. Then he pulled his *chiton* over his head and did the shoulder buttons one-handed.

Alexanor paused at the head of the narrow steps. At the bottom of the brothel steps there were three men with clubs, demanding money from the fleeing patrons.

'I left my boots at the door,' Philip said.

The three bruisers shared a look; it was obvious they knew or guessed who their customer was. Suborned by a Roman spy? But the look alerted Alexanor, and he drew the *xiphos* he had under his arm, faster than any of the three big men could react.

'Don't,' he said.

The man on the left, who was so big and so well muscled that his head, neck and shoulders seemed all built together, looked at the sword.

Philip had his in hand as well. He had a handful of gold in his other hand.

'Pick a hand,' he said brightly.

'I'll take the gold,' said the rightmost man.

The leftmost nodded sharply. 'Gold.'

Philip tossed it in the air and the two of them darted clear while the three collected the gold from the floor. Out in the narrow street there was quite a crowd, but Dariush had moved the horses up the street and they got mounted. The annoying Macedonian youth of the day before was with Dariush and had the king's horse.

'I'm not always like this,' Philip said.

Alexanor said nothing.

He rode with the king all the way through the darkened, noisy town and then up the ridge behind the town to the camp, where the same officer was waiting with the royal escort, all hardened veterans of the Royal Agema, all mounted and ready to ride.

'Have you sent for Prince Alexander?' Philip asked his officer.

'No, Your Grace. Weren't my place.'

Philip sighed. 'Right. Amyntas! You're the youngest and you have a good horse. Ride to the prince and tell him to bring all the regular cavalry out, and have the *peltastoi* advance to Aegio. Tell them to march all night if they have to. And messengers to all our fortresses to be alert.

'Cavalry immediately, *peltastoi* as fast as they can march, messages to fortresses.'

Amyntas was apparently the name of the annoying young Macedonian, who was suddenly sober with responsibility.

'Don't fuck this up the way you did my last message.'

Philip slapped the boy on the back. And then winked at Alexanor.

'Philopoemen has already notified Dinaeos,' Alexanor said.

'Who's Dinaeos?' Philip asked.

'He has all the Achaean horse at Nemea.'

'Oh, the Achaeans. Noble men, I'm sure, but these are Romans.' The king glanced over at his escort – just fifty men. 'Aegio has a garrison and a militia. Let's just ride along the coast and see if we can annoy the Romans as they are landing.'

'I'm going back to my command,' Alexanor said.

'You have a command?' Philip asked. 'Aren't you a doctor?'

Alexanor sighed and made no answer. Philip's lack of interest in his allies was chilling, but of a piece with his other behaviours.

Alexanor rode along the ridge, but the Achaean camp was empty. However, there was Eupolis, one of the *epheboi* from their winter march to Corinth.

'Here, sir!' he called. 'Kleander told me to wait for you.'

He followed Eupolis down the ridge and south, away from the Macedonians. In minutes they were riding through pines in almost total darkness and Alexanor got a branch full in the face that almost unseated him, to Dariush's obvious amusement. They rode along through the woods and then started up a long, steep hill. A long steep hill in the dark would, just a few months before, have been a nightmare for Alexanor, but tonight he was thinking of Philip's lack of thanks, his arrogance ...

Up and up. They suddenly emerged from the trees into the relative brightness of the coast road within sight of the sea, well below them. There was another cavalryman waiting for them at the road. He pointed out over the sea, and they could see a long way; they were on the headland between Aegio and the next deep bay. The sky was just beginning to lighten; to the east, there was just a hint of pink.

Out in the Gulf of Corinth, at least a dozen warships could be seen. And as if the appearance of the sun over the rim of the world was the signal, the stern lantern on the great *penteres* flared, and all of the ships began to row for the coast of the Peloponnese.

'Come with me,' the young man said.

They trotted down the road, heading east. Before they'd reached the base of the hill the sun was high enough to bring colour to the world, and Alexanor thought he could hear the sounds of the rowers out on the water.

'This way,' said their guide.

They turned down a gravel slope. Alexanor's horse picked its way carefully and then stopped and neighed, and a dozen horses answered.

'Please tell me you found Philip.'

'I did.'

'He was in a brothel?'

'Splendid guess. I was tempted to leave him for the Romans.' Alexanor snorted.

Philopoemen put a hand on his shoulder. 'Well done. We really can't lose him.'

'Can't we?'

'No. If the Romans took him, he'd trade us ... our freedom, at least. To Sparta and the Aetolians.' Philopoemen nodded. 'Now we just have to make trouble until the army comes.'

'Philip thinks that it's a joke that you sent for the Achaean army.' Alexanor realised that he was quite angry at Philip.

Philopoemen smiled, his teeth flashing in the first rays of sunlight.

'Try and remember that it *was* a joke until recently. And we're still not that good.'

'Better than anyone we've face so far,' Alexanor said.

'What a patriot you've become, by the gods! Tell me how good we are in an hour.'

The day passed in an ugly haze of fighting, and Alexanor couldn't remember most of it. He'd charge a dozen Romans, and they'd form a little knot and fight back; some were overcome, and some fought clear. They were incredibly stubborn, and no one had ever told them that scattered infantry were no match for well-led cavalry; he had to prove it again and again.

Across fifty stades and three beaches, he and Philopoemen and their hundred troopers disputed every homestead, and every hamlet – road junctions, hillside trails, and farmyards. Often there was no clash of weapons – just a long ride on a tired horse, and then the sight of a dozen Romans running for cover.

As the sun crept towards directly overhead, Alexanor found Philopoemen resting most of the Agema in an olive grove high on the ridge behind the beach at Longos, ten stades from Aegio. He dismounted to give his weary horse a rest and sat on a fallen tree. Dariush appeared with watered wine and a hat full of figs.

'Oh, gods,' Alexanor said. 'I think I love you.'

Dariush blushed.

Philopoemen laughed. 'I have some nice garlic sausage.'

Alexanor ate. He had blood on his hands. All his men were dismounting; Kritias was seeing to the horses, a stunning moment all of its own.

'Where's Eupolis?' Alexanor asked.

'Dead. Spear in his gut,' Kleander said woodenly.

Alexanor shook his head. 'They must know that they've missed the delegates,' he said, disgusted.

'They don't have any way of calling it off,' Philopoemen said. 'Or that's what I guess. But I agree that there's no point in our doing any more fighting.'

'I agree that the Romans are very different,' Alexanor said.

'And these are their second-class infantry.'

'No, I captured two. These are marines.'

'Romans put their second-class troops on ships.'

To Alexanor, from Rhodes, this was a remarkably stupid approach to war. 'What?'

'I suppose they do most of their fighting by land,' Philopoemen said.

'I find it remarkable. And more remarkable still that they're just *thureophoroi*, but they'll stand and fight ... anything.'

Philopoemen smiled. 'Perhaps no one is "just" *thureophoroi*,' he said. 'Consider the Athenian and Boeotian mercenaries we had on

Crete. Consider the possibility that it is the man and not the weapon that defines—'

Alexanor shrugged. 'I'm fully occupied trying to imagine how the human body works. I suggest you study war and I'll go back to medicine.'

He had never been so wearied with strife and killing. He'd scarcely known Eupolis as a man, and yet the youth's death upset him.

Philopoemen smiled, but the smile conveyed some hurt. Alexanor shook his head to clear it. He felt his spirits depressed; he felt physically weak, as he always did after fighting, and he had fought, hand to hand, more times that day than he could remember.

'Messenger!' Kleander called.

It was Lykortas.

'They have the king,' he called.

'What?'

Philopoemen had been lying on the soft pine needles. Only now did Alexanor see that he had a long sword cut along his right thigh – despite which, he leapt to his feet with his usual amazing athleticism.

'Philip was harrying one of the Roman detachments and fell into an ambush.'

'Gods. How far?'

'The other side of Aegio!' Lykortas yelled.

Men were mounting. No one needed an order.

'Dinaeos?' Philopoemen asked.

'On his way. Prince Alexander as well – no troubles there.'

'How far?'

'Aristides is perhaps half an hour behind me – then Dinaeos, then the rest. Macedonians were fast off the mark. They might beat Dinaeos in the race.'

'They are very professional. Pity their king is not.'

It was one of the few catty remarks that Alexanor had ever heard Philopoemen make. Then he turned and waved his riding whip.

'Follow me!' he roared, his full Titan battle call, and they were off – first single file along the ridge, and then down, far down, into a deep gully. Alexanor had no idea where they were; they were on shepherds' trails that ran high above the road.

Training told. They rode single file at a breakneck pace, and no one fell. Up a long ridge, and then immediately down the other side, through a magnificent volcanic caldera with a huge whale's jaw of rock riding out of the vent, and then across a bare rock face and through another grove of wild olive.

The horses were flagging.

'Halt,' Philopoemen said.

They stood, bridles in their hands, for ten minutes. Alexanor thought that Philopoemen was beyond human; he walked around, talking to every man, relaxed as if he was giving morning instructions to his farmhands. He smiled at Alexanor. Close up, it was obvious that it was all a lie; his eyes told of his worries.

'We have to rest the horses,' he said very quietly. 'I'm trying to beat the Romans to their ships. But I may not be correct about where they are.'

And then he walked past, mocking some quip of Kleander's, and then he joined his *hyperetes* in throwing stones at the trunk of a dead olive tree.

And then, without a word, they mounted again. Philopoemen had only to walk to his horse, moving with purpose, and every man was mounted.

'Pray we are in time,' the *Hipparchos* said, and led them over the ridge top.

They came down a steep hill and crossed the road. Alexanor could just see the Temple of Zeus in Aegio off to his left, which meant that they were close to the western beaches of the town, and the little hamlet of Nikolalika. In the small bay straight ahead of them, two Roman warships floated – *quadraremes*, heavy two-deckers with big crews.

Philopoemen smiled.

'This is good?'

'It means that if they took Philip over the headland, there, they have to bring him back to their ships here,' Philopoemen said. 'If Tyche and Fortuna are with us, we're ahead of them.'

On the road they formed quickly into a column of fours like metal filling a mould. As soon as the last dozen men were falling into their places, Philopoemen ordered his column to form a line to the right – a tricky manoeuvre on horseback – but they did it in heartbeats. Philopoemen led them down the slope towards the ships.

Men were shouting in both Greek and Latin below them.

Alexanor was watching the beach. There were a hundred men formed on the beach in good armour – chest plates and bronze helmets, tarnished from long usage at sea.

'Wheel to the left!' Philopoemen roared.

The Achaean cavalry, four deep and thirty long, was a compact mass. They turned like the spokes of a wheel towards the east, despite the slope and the sand and gravel under their horses' hooves.

'Forward!' Philopoemen ordered.

They were moving almost parallel to the beach, leaving the formed Romans behind them. As the Romans had no bows, they couldn't do anything to stop the cavalry.

There was the sparkle of polished bronze in the trees above them on the headland, and the sheen of weapons, and shouting in Latin. A horn sounded on the beach.

'Let's go!' Philopoemen roared.

The Achaean cavalry went to the trot, passing over a corner of the beach and then starting up the hill on the far side, their line still well formed, now heading back towards Aegio, invisible beyond the intervening headland.

Above them, the slope was *swarming* with Romans – hundreds of them, some with loot, some just hurrying to their ships.

Horns sounded – first two, and then more. Horns from the ships . . .

Orders in Latin. And the long line of skirmishers began to coalesce.

'Ready!' Philopoemen said.

The Agema gathered their horses; men who still had a spear after a day's fighting readied them.

'*Cave! Cave! Inimicus! Equites!*' called some bronze-lunged officer.

Twenty paces out, on a slope littered with loose rock and cluttered with stands of cypress and pine – the worst cavalry terrain Alexanor could imagine.

Philopoemen did not seem to agree.

'At them!' he roared.

The Achaean line burst out of the screen of trees. Some of the Romans had seen them for more than a minute; others caught their first glimpse of their peril only in the last seconds.

The Roman response was incredible; the whole line seemed to draw together as if linked by chains of adamant. Only a handful of men ran, or froze.

Officers roared and bullied. The lines began to thicken ...

The Achaean cavalry slammed home. There was no shower of javelins to break up the charge, and the Romans did not quite get formed close enough that a brave or foolish young Achaean couldn't thread between the files and slam his *falcis* down on a Roman's head. The big horses, so laboriously purchased far to the east, did their work with their jaws and forefeet, and the Roman line broke up as the Achaeans blew through it.

Alexanor thrust his spear down at an officer in a magnificent helmet, with a white sash around his waist. The man was as old as Solon; he was also quite expert in managing his shield, and Alexanor couldn't get to him. The flow of the combat pulled them apart, and Alexanor broke out of the back of the loosely formed Romans, looking for his *hyperetes*. There was Philopoemen, calling for his men to rally.

Alexanor looked back. Kleander was just turning, dragging his spear free of a falling Roman.

'Gods!' Alexanor swore.

Despite having been ridden through by a hundred cavalry, the Romans were reforming. In fact, now they were rallying faster than the Achaeans. Some of them had clearly just lain down. They were getting up.

'They are very good,' Philopoemen said. 'Luckily, I don't think we have to fight them again.'

He pointed up the hill, where a dozen Romans had formed a small clump around a man with curly blond hair.

The Achaean cavalry rode farther up the hill, despite the derision and the angry shouts of the Romans behind them. They surrounded and captured the dozen Romans, almost all officers, in twenty beats of a nervous man's heart. Kleander pulled the king of Macedon up to ride double. The Agema took most of the Romans prisoner in the same manner; two chose to fight and died for it. Nor did the marines lower on the hill choose to charge the Achaean cavalry to rescue their friends.

The Roman second line was coming along rapidly, so that the Achaeans were threatened with being caught between them. One Roman scrambled up on a rock and stood with a javelin poised, facing Philopoemen.

'Kaeso!' Alexanor called. He put a hand on Kritias' arm. 'Surrender!'

Kaeso shook his head. 'No, thanks. I'd rather you killed me.'

Philopoemen shook his head. 'Very Roman, I'm sure. Leave him,' he called.

The Achaean cavalry flowed around Kaeso's rock and rode away uphill as the Roman second line came forward. But the officer commanding the second line was too slow. Probably, he hadn't yet figured out what had happened: a long day, tired men, and cavalry riding around a steep hillside studded with trees – not part of his usual experience.

The cavalry flowed up the hill, a handful of riderless horses moving with the Achaeans and showing where they'd taken losses in rescuing the king.

'Take me to my cavalry,' Philip ordered.

Alexanor bit down on the retort that came to him.

'Immediately, Your Grace,' Philopoemen said with an easy smile.

# CHAPTER ELEVEN

※

## Corinth, Megalopolis and Elis

THEILOUTHIOS (LATE JUNE TO EARLY AUGUST), 209 BCE

'And doubtless King Philip was deeply thankful for his rescue,' Phila said.

She was lying against Philopoemen, wearing a magnificent necklace of gold and enamelwork that was worth the ransom of a city.

'You know he was not,' Alexanor said.

She laughed and waved a wine cup at him in a toast.

'Here's to arrogance,' she said. 'May it benefit us in the end.'

Draco, the Athenian ambassador to the peace conference, was lying with his friend Hephaestion.

'Did you hurt the Romans much?'

'Aren't you Athenians allied with Rome?' Philopoemen asked.

'We Athenians, as you put it, are definitely at war with Philip of Macedon,' Phila said. 'We just spent a fortune putting artillery towers on all the gates. I know – I gave a talent of gold.'

'What Phila is trying to say,' Draco put in, 'is that while we are allies of the Aetolians, we are not really all that fond of Rome.'

'Hannibal and his warmongers have changed Rome,' Phila said. 'The longer they fight Carthage, the more like Carthage they become. Rapacious and unreliable.' She rolled on her back so that she could see Philopoemen's face. 'Besides, I'm not inclined to love them when they sliced your leg.'

Philopoemen leant back, drank some wine, and put it down on the side table.

'We beat them badly by the end of the day.'

He didn't seem inclined to say any more and Phila glanced at Alexanor.

'My lover is too modest to tell me.'

Alexanor tried not to writhe at the phrase 'my lover' from Phila. And he was mildly inclined to resent the suggestion that he was less modest than Philopoemen.

'Really . . .' he began. And stopped.

They were in the house of Nicanor and Penelope, friends of Philopoemen's from childhood: radicals in politics, and also very rich – an uncommon combination. The couple owned no slaves and all their servants were free; they owned their goods in common, and Penelope ran a school for girls.

While it was their house, it was clearly Phila's party, and she had invited an eclectic group as she often did – delegates from the conference and soldiers too. Kleostratos lay with Thodor, newly returned from recruiting in Thrake, and Lykortas with Solon, the Rhodian. Phila had invited Kritias, son of Corinth's richest slaver, and he shared Alexanor's *kline*, and now he spoke, despite being the youngest.

'We harried them all day,' he said, sitting up to speak.

He glanced at Alexanor for permission, and Alexanor was happy to relinquish the description. He was still recovering, inside his head; he was sick of war.

'In the morning,' Kritias said, 'we surprised them for a while. But they were incredibly tough – they scarcely ever surrender. Around noon, I guess, they trapped the king and took him and scattered his bodyguard. I heard from one of their Agema that a javelin killed the king's horse and he was pinned under it. The officer who commanded the escort was killed trying to rescue him.'

He had perfect silence; even Kleostratos was silent.

'Philopoemen led us by shepherds' paths to cut in between the Romans and their ships and we cut him loose. And then Dinaeos came up with our Agema and we charged again, and almost cleared the beach. Philopoemen and Alexanor scattered Galba's bodyguard but he escaped.'

Alexanor smiled.

'Prince Alexander led the king's Agema and some of their mercenary cavalry into the hills and surprised another landing. The Romans had come in on four different beaches and they had no communication with each other.' He sat back. 'By sunset we had two hundred prisoners and the Romans were all off the beaches and rowing away.'

Philopoemen sat up. 'Well spoken, Kritias. Let me add that if it had been anyone but these Romans, we'd have wiped out their marines and taken the ships.'

Solon laughed. 'I can't agree. If they'd been Rhodians, we'd have had signal flags and trumpets, and once your cavalry appeared we'd have vanished like mist on a sunny day.'

Philopoemen shrugged. 'Certainly. As it was, the day was terrible and confusing and we only won because our chaos was slightly less devastating than theirs.'

Phila raised her cup. 'A victory is a victory. And your cavalry won it.'

'Don't tell that to Philip,' Alexanor put in.

'Now what?' Draco asked.

Philopoemen lay back. 'I'm afraid that's for the *Strategos* of the League to decide, in consultation with our ally Philip of Macedon.'

'Meaning you aren't saying?' Draco asked.

'Although we share a symposium,' Philopoemen said, 'we are technically enemies.'

'Do you say that to Phila, I wonder?' Draco asked, grinning wickedly. 'We are allies of Pergamum. King Attalos has guaranteed that he will not touch the Greek cities.'

'Except Aegina,' Alexanor said, with some heat. 'Which he and the Romans destroyed and looted.'

'Aegina has always been a thorn in the side of Athens,' Draco said.

'This is why we can't have nice things,' Phila said. 'Because any two Greeks can and will find something to fight about. I brought you all here to try and save something from the wreck of the peace conference. This war is poison for the suppression of piracy or the changes in slavery that we all desire.'

'We can't face Philip without Pergamum, and Pergamum is allied to Rome,' Draco said.

'We can't face Aetolia and Rome and Sparta and Pergamum without Macedon,' Philopoemen said. 'If we could …'

Draco leant forward. 'If we could?'

Philopoemen shrugged. 'It's a dream. If we could, by luck or military effort, break up the ring of enemies, we might be in a position to—'

'To what?' Draco pressed.

Philopoemen glanced at Alexanor, and then down at Phila.

'Let's just say I'm as tired of Macedon as you may be of Rome.'

Later, at the door, Solon took Alexanor by the arm.

'Rhodes needs Rome,' he said. 'I would not tolerate any defection from Rome. But individual Romans can be greedy fools, or just fools – I dislike the Aetolian alliance.'

'What are you saying?'

Alexanor hadn't had so much wine, but the older man didn't seem to be making sense.

'If Achaea ever wanted ... to explore ... different relations with Rome,' Solon said, 'send someone to me. I'll say no more.'

'But you said yourself that they are barbarians.'

'They can be better than that. And when they are not directly threatened, they can be both stable and fair.' Solon shrugged. 'And they don't have an adolescent whoremaster as a king.'

Alexanor smiled, and the two men clasped hands.

Alexanor could still taste the cardamom of the fabulous spiced olives from Phila's symposium when the messenger from Megalopolis rode into Nicanor's courtyard as if the legions of Tartaros were hard on his heels.

It was Arkas, who Alexanor hadn't seen in some time; he'd apparently been left behind with a detachment.

'The Spartans are across the boundary,' he said, still mounted. 'Rumour is that Elis and the Aetolians are already in motion.'

'I told you that they'd come at us together this time,' Philopoemen said. 'Right. Order Dinaeos to concentrate the cavalry at Tegea. Where is the *Strategos*? I must go to him. But I'm sure he'll move for Tegea. Go! Tell Dinaeos. He should have the cavalry ready to march.'

'Ready to march?' Alexanor asked.

'Why do you think he wasn't with us last night?' Philopoemen smiled.

*

Tegea sits at the centre of the flat plain amid the mountains of Arkadia: a perennial battlefield for contesting armies, and a massive drill field for the contestants. The wheat and barley stood tall, not the full gold of harvest but getting there – a terrible time of year for a farmer to have cavalry ride over his crop. The sun was hot, and the horses required more water than ever, and wearing a bronze breastplate over a wool *chiton* led to a particular smell. Sweat corroded the bronze, and stained the *chiton* green, and insects and the salt of sweat both tended to get into every abrasion.

Summer, and war in the Peloponnese.

Aristides had the cavalry of the coastal towns in hand. Dinaeos had the Agema. Aristaenos led the cavalry of the central plains: the Argosians, the Tegeans themselves, and the men of Messene and Megalopolis – the worst of the League cavalry, but far better than they had been. Alexios of Crotona led five hundred Tarantines; Thodor of Thrake led almost three hundred Thracian cavalry.

Altogether, despite two campaigns already fought, the League could muster almost three thousand cavalry of real quality, and another thousand full-time professionals – more cavalry than all their opponents combined.

Across the plain, the hoplites and *thureophoroi* of the League were slowly mustering at Mantinea. Food in the central plain's agoras was already selling for a premium, and the infantry had not yet received its allowances for the last campaign against the Spartans and Aetolians.

'They didn't fight anybody,' Kritias said.

'They still had to eat,' Dinaeos said. 'They aren't the best infantry in the world, but they eat just as much as good infantry, and you can't expect farmers to pay these food prices and not get angry.'

They had just attended an impromptu assembly where a council of hoplites had threatened to take the infantry back home if the food prices weren't reduced. Kykliadas had heard them out in dignified silence and then begged them to hold on until he could raise money.

'We will not last out the summer if you go home,' he said. Now he turned to the cavalry officers. 'Can you do something?' he asked Philopoemen. 'I know – you've performed so many miracles this summer that I expect them now. Philip of Macedon is on his way – with his phalanx. I need a week.' He shrugged. 'I can't wait until I'm out of this office, which mostly seems to involve begging my political foes while punishing my friends.'

Philopoemen gave the *Strategos* a crooked smile. 'You do it well.'

'Is that a compliment?' Kykliadas asked.

'You often find a way to conciliate when I would be very tempted to tell men what I really think.'

'Ares' balls, Philopoemen, don't you think I'm tempted?'

'And that's why you are a good *Strategos*.'

'You'll be better,' Kykliadas said.

Philopoemen shrugged. 'Maybe. In the meantime, I can leave you two thousand good cavalry and still have enough to annoy the Spartans. I'll leave ...' He looked back.

'I'll stay,' Aristaenos said.

'Of course you will,' Dinaeos said.

Alexanor had the feeling that relations between the overtly political Aristaenos and the far more military Dinaeos were deteriorating.

'Excellent,' Philopoemen said, as if there was no context to the exchange. 'Aristides can take half the Argolid cavalry; the men of the northern Peloponnese; and Alexanor can command the coastal cavalry.'

'I'd like to beg to be excused,' Alexanor said.

Philopoemen met his eye. 'No,' he said. 'I need you until the end of this campaign.'

'Damn it!' Alexanor spat. Every head turned. 'I'm a priest, not a soldier!'

'In fact, you are one of my best officers, and I need you,' Philopoemen said. 'Get me through the end of the summer and I promise you that you can retire to your temple covered in laurels.'

'I don't want the laurels!'

Kykliadas turned. 'I will happily join Philopoemen in begging you to stay, Alexanor. You and Epidauros are keeping us in this war. I will, if you like, clasp your knees and recite some Homer.'

Alexanor was embarrassed. 'Philopoemen ...' he began, then he shrugged.

He reached out to Dariush, who was behind him on his own horse, and took his new helmet, a magnificent thing made in far-off Chalcedon and covered in figures of Apollo. He put it on.

'Very well,' he said. 'This is the last time.'

Philopoemen turned to Kykliadas. 'Alexanor has reasons, excellent reasons, of his own – but the manpower problem will become acute. We're using men who have no experience of war, and using them beyond their limits. Some of the boys in my Agema have now seen more combat than most veterans. We cannot go on like this.'

Kykliadas met his stare. 'Do you imagine I don't know this?'

Philopoemen nodded. 'Right then. Ready to move west in one hour.'

Philopoemen marched west, and Alexanor ate dust. The roads were bone dry and the sun beat down on them like the hammer of Hephaestos on his anvil of bronze.

It all had the feeling of a dream – of repeating something they'd lived before. They crested the same hills, and encountered Spartan skirmishers in the same places; homesteads burned, and the choking reek of smoke was added to the extreme heat.

This time, the Spartans retreated swiftly, but Philopoemen played a different game. He separated his cavalry into detachments and manoeuvred, with strong bands of Telemnastos' Cretan archers in the hills above them, linking the cavalry columns. It was hot work, and called for stamina from the cavalry. In the heat, they had to dismount and walk their animals more and more often, and the whole campaign became a war for watercourses and wells. Twice the Achaean cavalry caught Spartan helots in the open. They took them prisoner or butchered them if they fought – ugly skirmishes with desperate men.

Alexanor hated it, but he had to admit to the efficiency of his friend's manoeuvres and his vision of war.

He'd spent all day tracking a detachment of enemy *psiloi*, whom he'd trapped in a gully. This band had surrendered; he hadn't had to kill anyone, and he was in a good mood. He also thought he understood the way Philopoemen intended to make war. His troops rolled into camp and began to picket their horses. Kleander found him and told him that Philopoemen was summoning all the officers as they came back from patrols.

He was the first patrol back, so when he'd seen to his horses and his armour, he made his way to Philopoemen's fire.

Philopoemen was lying with his head on his bronze *thorax*, enjoying a cup of wine in the firelight. Arkas was no longer his body servant, but had become a cavalry officer, so that he and Dadas and Kritias had become almost inseparable. Philopoemen had a new servant, an Aegyptian man provided by Phila. His name was Wewa, and his Greek was excellent and educated; he was also immensely strong.

Now he handed Alexanor a cup of wine.

'Cavalry?' Philopoemen asked.

'You worked this all out on Crete, didn't you?' he asked. 'How to use the cavalry as a mobile defence.'

Philopoemen smiled. 'Yes. Hoplites and phalangites are all very well for the day of battle but they're useless for stopping ...' He looked away. 'Raiders,' he said in an altered voice.

'And now that we have all the cavalry ...'

'That was always part of my strategy,' Philopoemen said after a sip of wine. 'Buying the enemy's troops is a perfectly legitimate tactic. Next we have to face the Aetolians. Machanandas is trying to retreat towards Damophantos. I'm trying to stay between them and still drive the Spartans south.'

'Where is Damophantos?' Alexanor asked, alarmed.

'About seventy stades farther west. The Thracians and Scythians are tracking him.

Alexanor sat down; Wewa had laid a sheepskin on the stony ground and waved an inviting hand. Alexanor smiled his thanks and got a brilliant smile in return. The man's face fairly radiated intelligence and Alexanor glanced at him again.

'Ares! How bad is it?'

Philopoemen smiled. 'At the risk of offending the gods with my *hubris*,' he said, 'I'd say it is all going very much according to plan.'

Alexanor all but snorted his wine. 'What?'

Philopoemen drank off his wine. 'We'll see tomorrow,' he admitted. 'I may not be as brilliant as I think I am. But look, we have no infantry, right?'

Alexanor shrugged.

Lykortas came and Wewa brought a sheepskin.

'How many of those do you have?' Alexanor asked.

Wewa smiled. 'Greece seems to have shortages of many things,' he said, 'but sheep are not one of them.'

Aristides, who had just appeared in the firelight like one of the shades addressing Odysseus in Homer, laughed.

'Is this a command council or an impromptu symposium?'

'The *Hipparchos* is explaining his strategy,' Alexanor said.

Dinaeos was covered in dust and looked even more like a shade from the underworld than Aristides had done.

'Strategy?' he spat.

'Wine for Dinaeos,' Philopoemen said.

'Water first,' Dinaeos said. 'I can barely spit, and when I do, it tastes like horse sweat.'

'That's you,' Lykortas said.

They all laughed, even Philopoemen.

'Will you all laugh when Philopoemen tells you that Damophantos is just a day's march away with all the Aetolians? Trying to link up with the Spartans?'

'I have an idea.' Dinaeos drank deep from a canteen handed him by Wewa.

'Silence for Dinaeos and his idea,' Aristides said.

'We let them link up, and then we leave them all to find water and starve in these valleys.'

Philopoemen laughed. 'That is a fine plan,' he said. 'I'm glad to hear you think that way. Because one of the major limiting factors in this war is food and water, and most generals tend to forget that.'

Aristides looked as if it was a new idea to him.

'Philopoemen was just explaining his plan,' Alexanor repeated.

He wanted to hear it. He wanted to believe that the rest of his life was not going to be an endless, hellish pursuit of broken men through dusty mountains.

'Here it is, then,' Philopoemen said. 'We have no infantry. The Spartans have no cavalry but very dependable infantry. I'm dangling us as bait to Damophantos, to try and lure him to make a dash with all his cavalry to join his Spartan allies. If he were to succeed, we'd be cut off, facing the Spartans with Damophantos to the south and the Aetolians and Romans to the west.'

'Romans?' Dinaeos had developed a healthy respect for the Romans.

'The Romans landed troops at Elis.'

'And your plan?'

'Catch Damophantos before he links with the Spartans and smash his cavalry.' Philopoemen smiled. 'You see, then we will really have *all* the cavalry, and we can dictate the pace of operations.'

Alexanor admired the plan the way he admired the workings of the human body – elegant and efficient.

'And then we can do to the Aetolians and the men of Elis the same as to the Spartans.'

He didn't say it with much enthusiasm. It was a brutal kind of war. There was no contest to it.

'Exactly. We'll always out-scout them and outmanoeuvre them. They won't be able to forage except high on hillsides, and then, Dinaeos' humorous notion will become fact. They'll have to retreat or die of starvation and lack of water.'

'Ares' nut-brown staff!' Lykortas said. 'It's beautiful.'

'However, that's why we won't be getting any sleep tonight, gentlemen. We will move north and west, in moonlight – the guides are already moving out. You get four hours of sleep. Don't waste them.'

The sun was high in the Peloponnesian sky; the sweat had soaked Alexanor's *chiton* under his backplate. The cheek plates of his helmet were biting into his chin despite the padding of his summer-old beard, and the weight of the helmet's crest could be felt in his shoulders and all the way to the top of his hips.

He was standing by his warhorse – the horse he'd taken in combat in the stone barn so many weeks before. Rain. It had once rained . . .

The Arkadian mountains were like a steep desert. Everything was bronze and brown, and the rock reflected the sun like a lethal enemy.

And there were no Aetolians. The sun climbed higher and Alexanor watched the lizards at his feet, gave his canteen to his horse, and waited, the sweat pouring down his face to trickle down his back.

When the sun was high in the sky, a trio of riders appeared on the Elis road, and their dust helped make obvious how alone they were. In moments, Philopoemen was mounted, and he rode down the shallow hill he'd chosen for his cavalry charge to meet Thodor, who rode with Kau-Ippa and another Thracian.

Letos, Philopoemen's trumpeter, blew the 'rally' and Wewa, carrying the small hanging banner that Philopoemen now affected, waved it. The waiting men mounted and began to form by squadron, all along the ridge. Alexanor handed over command to Kritias and cantered easily down the hill to Philopoemen.

'No battle today,' the Titan said cheerfully. 'That's the problem with plans. Things happen.'

'Where's Damophantos?'

'Dozens of stades east of us and marching hard.' Philopoemen shrugged. 'While I was fooling Machanandas, Philip has been fooling Damophantos. And Kykliadas, but that's because Philip thinks we're worthless.'

Alexanor was too hot to make sense of this. He untied his cheek flaps and let the springs fold them up against the bowl of his helmet.

'So now what?'

'Philip is at Dyme, launching an invasion of Elis. The Romans have been caught off guard – their fleet is somewhere in the south – and Damophantos has to march north to face Philip.'

'And we?'

'We follow Damophantos,' Philopoemen said. 'If we allow him to reach the men of Elis and the Romans before we reach Philip, Philip will be badly outnumbered, especially in cavalry.'

'He didn't want us,' muttered Thodor. 'We could let him—'

'If Philip is defeated, we're done,' Philopoemen said. 'We need to beat Damophantos in a race to Dyme. The only good part is that by marching here to attack him, we cut his first day's lead in half. He has to think we're down by Megalopolis.'

'So we follow him?' Dinaeos asked.

'Not precisely follow,' Philopoemen said.

Thodor pointed almost straight north. 'I have a way. Some hard country.'

'And the Spartans?' Alexanor asked.

'Aristaenos craves an independent command,' he said. 'And Machanandas is already retreating.'

'Food?' Dinaeos asked.

'Lykortas is going ahead with the Thracians,' Philopoemen said. He looked around. 'Three days' ride for Damophantos on the plains of Elis. But to make it to the plains, he will take a long detour east. We'll go straight north.' He turned his horse. 'Any questions?'

'Where's Pegasus when you want him?' Dinaeos asked.

The country they crossed, the very heart of the mountains, was sparsely inhabited and almost empty. The men who lived in High Arkadia were mountaineers – hardy men and tough women who had little time for politics. Food was scarce and forage hard to find; the tiny valleys of the high mountains were never big enough to support five thousand horses for even a single night.

They had to move quickly because of the shortage of fodder. In the large valleys – at Koumanis, for example – they could feed the whole force. Otherwise, they went hungry. The horses got the minimum of food, and they were visibly thinner as they were walked, exhausted, down the last ridges at Mito and down into the plains of Dyme.

But there, on the afternoon of the third day, they found food, wine and fodder waiting: carts of food; donkey-loads of wine sacks; fields of grass and bags of grain. Lykortas looked tolerably smug.

As Alexanor fell asleep that night, all he could hear was the sound of five thousand horses chewing.

In the morning, the Achaean cavalry marched north and west. They hadn't lost a man or a horse moving through the mountains, and now they were moving across a vast green and gold plain, into a land of plenty. They rode along the Parapilos river for fifteen stades, and before the heat of the day was oppressive they were marching into the Macedonian camp south of the city of Dyme, whose acropolis was as ancient as Mycenae or Pylos.

The ease of their passage wasn't the only surprise. The Macedonian pickets were courteous; the Macedonian phalangites in camp cheered them as they rode along the dusty, orderly camp streets, and the king himself mounted and rode out to meet Philopoemen.

'When my scouts told me that your cavalry was coming out of the mountains, I stopped and made sacrifice to Herakles,' Philip said. 'By all the gods, Philopoemen – men will long remember that march. You are a loyal ally.'

Later, in camp, Philopoemen permitted himself to say, 'It might have been easier if the king had simply admitted that he planned to stay on the coast, and told us so.'

Alexanor ate a third sausage.

After a full day's rest, Philip ordered his cavalry to cross the boundaries into Elis. At his command meeting on the city walls of the acropolis of Dyme, he waved at the flat coastal land and the distant river which marked the boundary.

'This will be a tough nut to crack,' he said. 'My guiding principle, gentlemen, is to fight this war on my enemy's territory and not in my own. We have, among us –' and he smiled at Philopoemen – 'managed to convince the Romans to send their fleet south to support the Spartans.' He glanced around. 'The numbers are nearly even, and we'll be attacking. If we can get across the river, I will wager my crown we can defeat Damophantos before the Romans can land their army.'

He sent the Macedonian cavalry north, right along the coast, and the Achaeans south, to cross the Larissa river at the main ford, well south of the city, at Petrachori.

But the Achaeans were not even fully clear of the camp before Thodor and Dadas were reporting that the whole cavalry of Elis was holding the ford. Philopoemen sent the scouts back to Philip and continued.

But within the hour he had orders from Philip to slow his march and wait for the Macedonian cavalry under Prince Alexander. There was more than a little anger at this; Dinaeos spat.

'Elean cavalry?' he asked the sky. 'We don't need any help.'

Philopoemen shrugged. 'I believe that for once I can join with Alexanor in saying that waiting for our allies will make for an easier victory and fewer casualties. And Damophantos cannot be far away.'

Alexanor smiled. He knew perfectly well that Philopoemen had sent all the Thracians south, and was waiting for Thodor, Dadas or Kau-Ippa to report.

An hour passed.

Dadas came in with half a dozen tattooed Thracians. Alexanor was chatting to Philopoemen about Stoic philosophy, and both men were watching a huge anthill and debating how it was ruled. Dadas' stallion stepped on it and crushed the top. An army of ants boiled out, running, leaderless, in every direction, and Philopoemen laughed.

'Confusion is the kin to fear,' he said. 'However they are governed, it is now every ant for itself.'

Alexanor laughed.

Dadas raised his hand. 'My uncle has found a small ford south of the main ford, unguarded,' he said. 'And Kau-Ippa says that there are two fords north of the road ford, but that determined men could swim the river anywhere – the banks slope, the stream bed is gravel.'

'Macedonians are coming!' shouted a voice from the rear of the Agema.

'Excellent.' Philopoemen seemed to grow. He turned to Alexanor. 'Would you prefer to swim the river or ford it?'

'Swim, please.' Alexanor wasn't sure he'd ever been so hot.

'Very well. Let Dinaeos pass in front of you here and give him ten minutes' head start.' Philopoemen smiled. 'See you on the other side of the river.'

Alexanor saluted and rode to the head of the *taxeis* of eastern cavalry.

'Ready to move,' he said. 'You have time to piss.'

Some men laughed, but other men hurried off into the brush and rocks of the ridge.

Alexanor watched Dinaeos ride away at the head of the Agema and the mercenary horse. They moved fast, but he waited more than ten minutes, until they were almost out of sight.

His squadrons, the cavalry of the cities of the east coast, were all still dismounted; the officers had ordered the horses watered in shifts. Alexanor could still see the ribs on some horses, but two days of good grain and abundant grass had largely restored their condition.

The time seemed not to pass. A scorpion sunned itself on a rock and then was gone, and Dinaeos was still in sight.

When the sun had crept a little farther across the sky, Prince Alexander appeared with his staff. He had Philopoemen with him, and Philopoemen was watching Dinaeos' dust.

Alexanor nodded to Dariush. 'No trumpet,' he said. 'Column of fours. When we cross the ford we'll form either to the front or to the left, depending on the terrain and what faces us. Understand? We may have to swim.'

Aristides and the Epidauran *Hipparchos*, Lycurgos, both nodded.

'Swim sounds good,' Lycurgos said.

'Right,' Alexanor said, pulling down his cheek plates. 'Follow me.'

He led the way, with Aristides commanding the right half of the *taxeis* and Lycurgos of Epidauros the other half. Alexanor had the oddest feeling. His hands did not shake; there was no emptiness in the pit of his stomach. Either he had made so much war in one summer that he no longer feared death, or he was too tired to care. And yet, at the same time that he observed his own lack of fear, he also observed the bizarre alteration in the passage of time. It seemed as if he'd watched the scorpion on the rock for half of eternity, and yet now, as he followed two of Dadas' guides down the long slope of farmland to the river, time seemed to run faster and faster, accelerating away like a horse pushing from the walk to the gallop. Suddenly Alexanor was across, wet to his waist and with no memory of his horse swimming the river.

His mount scrambled up the gravel bank and through a line of scrubby bushes, mostly jasmine long past its flowering and so dry it seemed impossible that it had ever bloomed, yet there was just the hint of the scent as he pushed his horse through the reaching tendrils.

A farm field, bordered in an ancient, low stone wall.

Empty.

He turned to Dadas. 'Find me the enemy,' he said, and turned his horse to form his column, always watching to the south.

Just west of the river was the farmhouse and yard and two stone barns. He sent the first forty men across, the *epilektoi*, or picked men, all young and all good riders, into the farmyard to watch his flank under a *dekarch* called Nestor. Then he sat in agonised indecision as his amateur cavalry swam their horses across with all the hesitancy that he had shown himself. They seemed to take *forever* and he noted that time had changed again; the river of time was as sluggish as the Larissa itself.

He had fewer than three hundred across when Dadas galloped up.

'A thousand cavalry or more, formed behind the ford – they're behind the slope of the riverbank. The Macedonians are forming on our side of the river now.'

'Which side is our side?' Alexanor asked.

Dadas smiled. 'The side we started from. Prince Alexander is forming to charge through the ford.'

'Were you seen?'

Dadas' smile widened. 'I doubt it.'

'Philopoemen? Dinaeos?'

'No idea,' Dadas said. 'They're late.'

'At least we're not late,' Alexanor said.

In that moment he decided that if he hated war, and fighting, he hated commanding even more. And yet he felt the joy of it, the way he felt when a patient began to mend – when a bound wound began to heal without mortification.

'And the ground between here and the ford?'

'Once you clear the riverbank, it's farm fields,' Dadas said.

Alexanor looked at his cavalry. They had dismounted without an order and they were in four neat ranks. He rode over and waved.

'We're going into the flank of the cavalry of Elis,' he said. 'We're going to break them, and if we can, end this endless war.'

That got a cheer, and he turned his horse. Time was moving faster again. There were suddenly almost five hundred cavalrymen waiting for his command and Lycurgos, bringing up the rear of the *taxeis*, was waving from the ford.

Forty of his best men were holding the farmyard, and it was obvious they weren't needed. He had a minute . . .

He turned to Dariush. 'Fetch Nestor and the *epilektoi* from the farm.' Suddenly he changed his mind. 'No, get me Kritias.'

Kritias rode up and saluted. 'Fetch Nestor from the farm, but stay on that line. I'm guessing there's a road parallel to the river. Stay on it, and stay in sight of me.'

Kritias saluted smartly and rode west.

Alexanor trotted to the front of his line of cavalry.

'We'll incline to the right,' he said.

This was a very tricky manoeuvre for cavalry, whereby they kept their line facing forward but rode at an oblique angle. It required good discipline and good riding skills and earlier in the summer he'd never have tried it.

It didn't go particularly well, and both halves of his *taxeis* were in a state of chaos after they crossed the first farm wall, even though it was merely a line of boundary stones no higher than a hump in the road. He cursed and watched the ground ahead and to the right for enemies. Half a squadron of well-led mercenary horse would have routed his entire command, had they appeared.

But as they moved forward into the second set of fields parallel to the river, the whole *taxeis* began to sort themselves out, so that by the time they crossed their third boundary wall, they were in something like order, and most of the riders flowed over the walls as if they'd jumped on horseback all their lives.

They could now hear the sounds of fighting, and the line began to move faster without an order, and the lines began to expand.

Alexanor leant forward, put his horse to a canter, and rode along the front.

'Close up!' he roared. 'Close up!'

Dariush had the little square pennon of their *taxeis*, just a piece of azure linen. Someone had put the lyre of Apollo on it since last he'd looked at it, and he smiled – a good omen.

And he had made no sacrifice.

But he could hear the fighting, and he could see, at the top of the next low rise, Dadas waving.

'Close up!' he roared one more time.

They responded well; the front rank was in close order. He looked west, and there, perhaps a stade away, was Kritias. The man was waving his helmet. Alexanor read his body language. Something was wrong.

'Halt!' he roared. 'Dress your lines! Look sharp!' He cantered along the line to Aristides. 'Put the right half in front of the left half.'

'Why?' Aristides asked.

Alexanor shook his head. 'Just do it.'

He turned his horse on its haunches and urged him to a gallop. At speed, Kritias was less than a minute away. It seemed to take a very long time.

'There!' Kritias pointed. 'That can't be Philopoemen.'

Alexanor watched the body of cavalry with a feeling in the pit of his stomach, as if he had to vomit. His throat was tight.

'Aetolians,' he said.

Damophantos had been, if not faster than the Achaeans, at least no slower, and was coming up behind his allies.

He couldn't count them, but it was a big body of cavalry. Two thousand? Three thousand? Damophantos had had three thousand a month before.

'Form a line on the road facing west,' Alexanor snapped.

He turned and galloped back towards his command. Everything took time; time was flowing away like blood spurting from a wound in great gouts. And where was Philopoemen?

He came up to Lycurgos and Aristides together.

'Aristides!' he said. 'Straight forward to Dadas! And then down into the flank of the enemy.'

'Why did we halt?' Aristides asked.

Alexanor was watching the end of the manoeuvre by which the right half of the *taxeis* had advanced and the left half had ridden in behind them, so that the whole force was now eight deep.

'Damophantos is on our flank,' he said. 'Just go. I'll cover you.'

Aristides looked at him, blinked, and his mouth opened. But training told.

'Yes, sir.'

He rode to the head of his squadron, and if he had doubts, they didn't show. He held his javelin point up.

'Now is the day and the hour, men of Hermione! Men of Corinth!'

They cheered, and the whole block started forward. Alexanor had to bellow for the second squadron to stay halted. It took a long minute to sort out the men of the southern towns, who'd assumed they were to follow Aristides. Lycurgos rode in and pushed men back into the ranks; unwilling horses balked or shied, and for an interval of precious time it seemed that they would never be formed.

The road to the right was still held by Kritias' handful.

'Squadron will wheel to the right!' Alexanor roared.

Wheeling – the pivoting of an entire line on one end like the opening of a door – was perhaps the weakest area of manoeuvring in the Achaean tactical lexicon. But without coaching, Lycurgos rode out in front of the line and Alexanor joined him, and they kept the wheel moving. When the centre began to fall away they physically pushed men with their spears. A man in the centre was suddenly crushed out of the rank by the press of his fellows and he fell, and there was chaos …

Alexanor looked over his shoulder, but the road was still held by Kritias and his beautiful helmet, which flashed reassuringly in the sun.

The wheel was ugly, and another man fell, but they had changed their front; now they were parallel to the road, and Alexanor called for them to reform.

'Dress the line!' he called, and rode along.

The man who had fallen had remounted, and he caused more chaos by pushing into the ranks, but such things were common with volunteers. Alexanor left Lycurgos to force them back into formation. He had to know; he rode west to the road and looked down the gradual slope to the green barley fields.

The Aetolians were moving – but they were going straight forward to the ford. There were thousands of them.

He looked back.

Lycurgos had the second squadron together.

233

'We're about to pretend to be a lot of men,' he said to Kritias.

'I've always enjoyed deceiving people.' Kritias smiled.

'Go down along their flank. No, listen. Don't be a hothead. Through those olive groves. Let them see you but not close – move fast and make dust.' Alexanor pointed, and Kritias nodded.

He turned away while Kritias began calling orders. The young man had a high voice, for a man, but he seemed to sing his orders rather than shouting, and they carried very clearly. He was singing something about trees. Alexanor rode away; that die was cast.

'Ready!' he called.

Lycurgos waved his spear.

Alexanor turned his horse. 'Forward!' he called.

His throat hurt.

The second squadron was in excellent order now, and they came to the road all together, and crossed the boundary wall without a hitch.

Alexanor rode to the south end of their line and tried to figure out what was happening to his left, where the fight at the ford was. In the distance, at the crest of the next fold of earth, where there were neatly terraced olive groves, he saw the blinding sparkle of bronze or gold.

Suddenly, his heart pounded, and time seemed to stop.

Even two stades away or more, the man on the white horse with the huge plumes was clearly Philopoemen. He was deeper behind the ford than Alexanor, almost certainly manoeuvring against the flank of the Aetolians.

Alexanor released a breath he hadn't been aware of holding.

'Halt!' he called.

To his front, Kritias' *epilektoi* were riding down the slope. They raised an incredible amount of dust, and only then did Alexanor realise what his novice had been shouting – they were dragging branches of acacia and cypress. Alexanor could see the limbless trees standing by the road, white scars where their bark had been stripped and their branches ripped away.

'Double your front,' he said to Lycurgos.

The Epidauran *Hipparchos* nodded. 'Yes, sir.' His posture suggested that he had no idea why Alexanor had ordered it.

The two rear ranks turned in place, no easy feat on a narrow road, and moved off to the right, extending the front of the half-*taxeis* until it was only two deep but a hundred men wide.

The sounds of fighting from the ford rose; there was the sound of a trumpet . . .

The lead Aetolian squadron was forming in a front. They were less than a stade from Alexanor, to his left front, and it was clear from their hesitancy in forming that they'd just spotted Alexanor's cavalry.

They shuffled. Alexanor had seen the same in other fights; he'd seen pirates shuffle like that when they had had enough of a close fight.

The Aetolian cavalry hesitated, and then there were men and horses going past them, emerging from the broad gully that led to the ford. And then more, and then . . .

Like a dam bursting, the Elean cavalry, still invisible to Alexanor, broke. They had Macedonians to their front and Aristides had fallen on their flank. They'd held as long as they could, but now they gave way, and men began pouring out of the gully and past the Aetolians. And then the routers from the fight by the ford were too many, and they crumpled the front of the hesitant Aetolians, and the whole body was swept away, their horses turning to run with the Elean horses.

'Stay right here!' Alexanor called and rode off to his left, looking for Aristides.

The Achaean cavalry were completely intermixed with their defeated adversaries, and pressing too close to be rallied. Alexanor couldn't find Aristides. He gave it up and rode back as the flood of routers and pursuers passed the position that Lycurgos held. He rode up to the long, thin line of Epidaurans and Argosians.

'Everything depends on our looking like a full squadron!' he called. 'Keep that line!' He reached the centre. 'Walk! March!'

The line had to immediately negotiate the roadside wall and the fringe of tall cypress trees that bordered the road, but they did so well enough, and began to move into the sun-beaten fields of barley.

As they emerged from the line of trees, there were shouts from the Aetolians. The very shallow valley to Alexanor's left, where the main road ran from the contested ford to the city of Elis some hundred stades away, was a disturbed hive of fleeing Eleans and paralysed Aetolians. Upwards of three thousand horses milled in confusion and the Aetolians were attempting to unfold their column into a line facing the Macedonian onslaught.

But now they saw Alexanor hanging off their flank. There were trumpet calls, and Alexanor could see a square of scarlet moving across their front, but it moved slowly, as the enemy commander fought his way through the rout of the Eleans and the press of his own cavalry column collapsed back on him.

The Achaean cavalry with Alexanor pressed forward slowly, their line well formed. Farther west, Kritias raised more dust than Alexanor was doing.

Very slowly, Alexanor appeared to be turning the Aetolian flank.

'Walk!' he growled. 'No faster!'

The thin Achaean line, slow as it was, was slightly faster than the collapsing Aetolian column, the routing Eleans and their Macedonian pursuers. They began to pull ahead as some of the Eleans rallied and attempted to hold the road.

The lead *taxeis* of cavalry in the Aetolian column was poorly formed, but they charged anyway, gallantly sacrificing themselves so that the column could have room to manoeuvre. Some of the Eleans joined them, and together they cut deeply into the Macedonian pursuers, who'd lost all pretence of order.

But Prince Alexander was an old and canny fox, and he had his own reserve, well formed. The Aetolians were successful only until they reached the Macedonian household cavalry.

Alexanor knew none of this, but he trusted that the Macedonians, masters of war, knew their business, and he pressed on. To his immediate left, Aristides, his white and red plumes now visible, emerged from the shadow of the hillside and his squadron fell on the flanks of the Aetolians even as they faced the Macedonian reserve.

But the enemy commander had used his respite brilliantly. More than half the Aetolian column wheeled by sections to the left, so that the back half of the Aetolian line was suddenly facing Kritias.

Alexanor smiled. 'Halt!' he called. He looked at his thin line. 'Double your files!'

Men cursed him as they turned their horses and went back to the files from which they'd started, but they did it quickly, and well.

A man muttered, 'Make up your mind.'

Alexanor ignored him.

In less time than it would take a priest of Asklepios to cut a decaying limb from a patient, they were formed four deep.

The Aetolians went forward at the dust raised by Kritias.

Over to Alexanor's far left, Philopoemen's helmet flashed, and Alexanor heard his trumpeter sound.

Closer in, the front squadron of Aetolian cavalry broke under the pressure of the Macedonian household cavalry and the Achaeans on their flank.

Alexanor could see the entire drama playing out at his feet. The shallow valley in which the Elean road ran was only a stade wide – and the Aetolian commander had turned to face the wrong threat.

Now the Achaean Agema charged. They came down the shallow slope unopposed, into the flank of the front half of the Aetolian force, a column already penetrated by the fleeing Eleans. Now, even as they struggled to turn to face the new threat, the routed remnants of their own front squadron blew into them and the unravelling was complete. Individual men tried to ride free ...

The Achaean cavalry, perfectly formed, charged home. The impact was audible, like a butcher's cleaver falling on a haunch of beef, repeated a thousand times, and in that charge, almost every man in the Agema's front rank felled his opponent.

'Walk!' Alexanor called.

Lycurgos' squadron started forward again, now more compact. Straight ahead of them, half the Aetolian cavalry were charging a handful of *epilektoi*, who dropped their branches and fled.

Alexanor was attacking twice his own numbers, but he knew that the day was won and he had felt that fine balance shift. His men glowed like gods, and the Aetolians ahead of them, looking over their shoulders in fear, were already near panic, fooled and fooled again.

*Confusion is the kin to fear.*

The squadron nearest Alexanor broke without being contacted, the men fleeing west along the line of their comrades – most of whom were trying to rally – having charged nothing but dust.

Alexanor raised his spear, and waved to his trumpeter.

'Charge!' he roared and the trumpet's call pierced the air.

Alexanor's horse seemed to fly.

He unhorsed a man in no armour, a rear-ranker caught by the changing front. Alexanor simply slammed his spear shaft into the man's head, and then he was in the midst of dozens of Aetolians. Men surrendered, slipping from their horses, and other men tried to ride clear, and he had the odd experience of failing to find an opponent in the dust of what *seemed* like a melee. He rode west, but the chaos was complete, and he turned south, lost in the column of dust and iron and horseflesh, looking for his own men.

Dariush stayed with him, and a handful of his Epidaurans. He emerged from the dust to find that he was deep in the valley, less than half a stade from the Elean road, and there was another massive dust cloud ahead of him.

Aristides rode up from the east, leading a dozen troopers.

'Well met,' Alexanor said.

'What's happening?'

'No idea.'

'Prince Alexander is rallying all his cavalry,' Aristides said. 'Somewhere back there.' He pointed a thumb over his shoulder.

'Philopoemen charged—'

'I saw it.'

More Achaeans were coming out of the dust to the north and the east. It seemed like a miracle – or the will of Hermes, messenger of the gods – but cavalry troopers were gathering from three directions, as if a rally point had been appointed an hour before. In as long as it took to sing the *Paean*, Alexanor had two hundred troopers, and then two hundred and fifty.

They were tired, thirsty men on blown horses, and they'd survived battle; none of them had any further urge for glory.

Neither did Alexanor. But his friend was somewhere to the south, and the battle was not over.

He rode through the dust to the front of his command, such as it was.

'Listen up!' he called.

He spat, took a swig of water, and turned his horse. Dariush dismounted, caught his horse's head, and poured water into its mouth. Alexanor looked at them, and they stared dully back.

'It's not done!' he called. 'Philopoemen's over there, facing three times his number of Aetolians. You can stay here if you're tired. I'm going there.' He had lost his javelin – odd, in that he couldn't remember fighting anyone. He drew his sword. 'Anyone coming?'

He started to ride south, towards where he'd last seen Philopoemen.

They growled, and for a moment he thought no one was coming, but of course they were all coming. A handful had dismounted, or were caught drinking water. They weren't in any kind of order, but the whole mass began to flow down the shallow slope towards the Elean road.

They hit the edge of the massive dust cloud. There were flashes of bronze and steel like metallic lightning in the cloud – the very rage of Ares itself, the dreaded battle haze. Alexanor was tempted to flinch, but he threw his *chlamys* over his mouth and clamped his knees on his mount's back, leaning forward when the horse balked.

Only then did he realise that he and his men were actually *behind* the melee. He was coming up on the back of the Aetolians, and he felt foolish.

'Charge!' he croaked, and then 'Charge!' louder and stronger.

He leant forward, and his tired horse managed something like a heavy canter, and Dariush and Aristides were there, and he had the feeling of being at the point of a massive spear.

His 'charge' had no impetus but it was a total surprise and was the last straw for the embattled Aetolians, who fled the moment they knew that there were enemies behind them. Alexanor had the pleasure of taking an Aetolian officer merely by tapping him with the butt of his spear; the man dropped a gold-mounted *xiphos* into the dust and raised his hands.

'Take him!' Alexanor spat to Dariush and rode on.

His horse's gait was bad. He knew that his people were now at their end, but victory had its own power, and the Aetolians flowed away, although some of them, on horses that had made a longer march than the Achaeans, simply foundered.

Alexanor emerged from the Aetolian ranks. There was less dust here, and to his right, a formed Aetolian body, magnificent in fancy metal, were still fighting, and he turned that way.

The Aetolians glittered with purple and gold. He rode forward, his fine horse skittish, and he went sword to spear with a man, covered the spear and there, ten men away in the dust, was Damophantos.

Alexanor wished he had a spear, but he didn't. His tired horse carried him into Damophantos' bodyguard, with Aristides at one side of him and Lycurgos at the other. He managed to cover a spear thrust from a man in a magnificent Gorgon's head breastplate. His horse carried him in close, and he got an arm locked around the man's left, and thrust his *xiphos* in under the other, raised arm – a killing stroke. He felt the man's spirit go, but the weapon was stuck in his chest, and Alexanor suddenly had no weapon. He let the man fall, took a spear-blow on the crest of his helmet, and got a hand up, his desperate hand closing on the shaft of the spear. Then he'd pulled the man right off his horse; he had the spear and he killed the man on the ground, a single stroke to the back of the head. His horse backed at his weight shift, and he turned to see Aristides unhorsed. He threw the spear overhand into Aristides' opponent's armoured back and the head went through his bronze like an awl through parchment.

He rode over to Aristides. His friend had a bad cut on his thigh, a common wound in cavalry fights.

'Up! Alexanor called.

He extended a hand, and Aristides grabbed his wrist. Alexanor moved his horse and Aristides got to his feet and then, clumsy with pain, was up behind Alexanor, and his charger grunted.

Alexanor turned them to leave the melee and there was Damophantos.

He seemed inhumanly big.

Alexanor didn't have time to be afraid. He just backed his loyal horse, and the charger responded, slipping back, and back.

Damophantos came forward like a cat stalking a cornered mouse. He had a long spear, almost a *kontos*, but when he'd followed a few paces, he threw it.

It took Alexanor's horse in the head, a perfect throw, and killed the animal immediately. Aristides fell, and Alexanor fell back over him. He scrambled to his feet, looking for a weapon in the dust. He stumbled, fell to one knee, and rose.

'There. You made me kill the horse you stole,' Damophantos said. 'You're a priest. Say your prayers.'

Alexanor didn't have to feign fear or fatigue; he was enough of a priest of Asklepios to know how closely twinned they were.

Damophantos was tired of stalking, or perhaps, aware of the rout of his army. He was in a hurry. He leant forward and his horse burst into motion.

Alexanor stood his ground, swayed, and threw the handful of sand he'd grabbed when he knelt into the horse's face as he slipped to the left, raising his arms to cover his face.

The horse reared, lashing with its hooves, but Alexanor wasn't there.

Damophantos managed to cut his arm, but the two men were close, and it wasn't the sharp edge that hit Alexanor but the part closer to the hilt. The blow broke his arm but didn't sever it as might have happened. He tried nonetheless to close his hands on the sword arm, for a grapple and a throw, but his right hand simply wouldn't function from the pain, and he missed. His one opportunity was gone, and he turned, ready to die.

Damophantos wasted the time it took Alexanor to take two deep breaths turning his mount. Alexanor had that time to think of his wife, his child and the child to come, and of the calm of a morning in Epidauros – the sun rising, the smell of flowers in the air, and the moment of the immanence of his god. He had that long.

'My turn,' Philopoemen said, cheerfully.

He came out of the dust like a Centaur; he glittered in the dusty sun, and his horse was wild-eyed and yet perfectly in hand.

Damophantos roared. They were too close to charge each other. Both horses were war-trained, and so as they came together, both reared, their hooves lashing like equine maces, their teeth tearing.

Alexanor knelt in the sandy dirt, his left hand finding a spent javelin. The pain in his right arm was incredible, and it hung wrongly.

Damophantos struck, his sword hand so fast that Alexanor couldn't follow it.

Philopoemen's horse was on two feet; Damophantos' horse was back on its haunches, getting the worst of the horse fight. But Philopoemen was still in control of his mount and it stepped forward as if the horse's legs were Philopoemen's legs, so that he went into Damophantos' blow. His left hand caught the Titan's sword arm, thumb down, and he cut with his own long *falcis* – the first blow into his opponent's sword wrist, severing it, the back stroke into his neck, killing him. He didn't quite sever the head, and the body flopped, slid back and fell into the dust. The Titan's horse screamed and backed, and Philopoemen turned his horse as if looking for another opponent.

Alexanor wanted to applaud, or shout something. He seemed to be very far away, watching an Olympic event – cavalry fighting. It seemed very natural, and there were cheers, and he wanted to add his.

And then it was black.

# CHAPTER TWELVE

———ↄ৶৶ↄ———

## Epidauros, Aegio and Megalopolis

### HIPPODROMIOS TO HERMAIOS
### (LATE AUGUST 209 TO MARCH 208 BCE)

Alexanor missed the rest of the summer campaign. He took a fever and they moved him to Dyme, and then it was all gone. Later, he heard that the Romans landed and burnt all the farms around Dyme and even broke into the city; it was sacked, burnt to the ground, and the Romans took its whole population and sold them as slaves. By then, the Macedonians had put all the wounded in wagons and were marching east. Macedon itself had been invaded by Dardanians and Illyrians and Thracians, and Philip abandoned his campaign in the Peloponnese and moved by forced marches to the Isthmus, where he left his wounded and his baggage at the Acrocorinth.

Alexanor heard about it all later. The only part he remembered was a nightmarish moment on the climb to the Acrocorinth, when he could look out from his wagon and he felt as if he'd fall into the sea and drown, or die in the fall. He had dreams ...

And woke in the Sanctuary of Epidauros with Chiron sitting by him, and Aspasia standing with a cloth in her hand.

'Hello,' he said.

Aspasia burst into tears. But she smiled, and threw her arms around him, and squeezed him so hard he thought he might suffocate.

And later, Chiron gave him a compound of medicines.

'You were so far gone when you got here,' the old man said, 'I am amazed ... amazed that you came all the way back.'

Alexanor didn't recover quickly. He'd lost a month to his wounds and to fever, and now he lost another in slow recovery. He caught a cold and suffered, and Chiron feared a relapse; he tried physical exercise too early and exhausted himself. But as Theilouthios gave way to Hippodromios, and the shadows of evening came earlier, and the heat of the air began to abate a little, Alexanor finally returned to himself. He played with his child and made rounds of the other sick. He enjoyed the baths and recorded his dreams in the sleeping hall of the god. He served at the altars, made sacrifices and led them, and the inner wounds began to heal as the outer ones had done.

The sack of Dyme was a scandal and a horror – it shook the League to the core. It could have been any coastal community; it sharpened the fears of every Achaean about the reach, the ferocity and the barbarity of the Romans. The *hippeis* of Dyme were said to have sworn a death pact, as the only free men of their city, and the district was being devastated by the Aetolians, like vultures on a corpse.

Alexanor heard men mutter that Philip of Macedon had deserted them, and that he was to blame. He refused to take part in such conversations; he eventually stopped listening.

By the middle of Hippodromios, he was ready to move back to his home. He began to put on weight and, determined to avoid the censure of his wife, he stripped every other morning and ran – first around the headland and back, but by the end of Hippodromios, all the way over the ridge to the sanctuary and back, sometimes stopping to check a critical patient.

Aspasia was heavily pregnant, but pregnancy seemed to fill her with energy and she moved rapidly about the house, mending, repairing, ordering ...

The pilgrims brought word of the war. After the cavalry battle, the Eleans had been utterly broken; Philip and Philopoemen had pillaged Elis, hitherto inviolate, all the way to the city walls. There had been a fight there, and Philip had actually been captured by the Romans for almost an hour, and again rescued. And then the news of the attack in Macedon had come, and Philip had retreated, leaving the north coast of Achaea unguarded, as Kykliadas had sent Philopoemen south against the Spartans. Dyme had fallen; the Romans had made an attempt on Corinth, but failed.

At the end of Hippodromios, Lycurgos returned with the cavalry. He'd marched away with a hundred troopers and he returned with only eighty – a very high casualty rate for the richest young men in a Greek town. There was outrage, which Lycurgos discouraged.

Alexanor invited him to dinner, with Kleander and Nestor and other men he knew. At his door, Lycurgos embraced him.

'We all heard you were dead,' he said. 'Philopoemen will be so happy! He poured ashes on his head when he heard, and wouldn't bathe—'

Alexanor was appalled. 'Who said I was dead?'

'Aristaenos heard it in Corinth and told us when he returned from the early *Synodos*.'

'Aristaenos would say anything to hurt Philopoemen,' Aspasia said. The men looked at her. She shrugged. 'He does a great deal to undermine the *Hipparchos* behind his back. I assumed you all knew that.'

Lycurgos frowned. 'I did not know that. Aristaenos can be difficult, but I think . . .'

He paused.

Kleander nodded. 'I've certainly heard him boast that he, not Philopoemen, did all the work on Crete.'

Lycurgos flushed. 'I've never heard him say that.'

'I have,' Nestor said.

'How is it that Philopoemen can spare you, his best cavalry?' Alexanor asked.

Lycurgos sat back on his *kline* and shook his head. He'd brought his wife, Glykera – an act of great daring in conservative Epidauros – and she was still trying to decide what to do with her old-fashioned *peplos* while lying on a couch.

'My dear, would you like a seat?' Aspasia asked her.

'I'm just not used to lying on a bed to eat,' Glykera said.

Aspasia sent for a chair, and then moved to sit by her.

'You know we had another battle?' Lycurgos asked.

Alexanor shook his head. 'I'm not surprised. It was only a week ago. The Eleans and the Aetolians tried again – they came over the mountains by Megalopolis. Kykliadas had been training the phalanx all summer, and we beat them. The phalanx is still not very good, but the Eleans—'

'They broke before we could envelop them,' Kleander said, proud of his extensive military vocabulary. 'Philopoemen led all our mercenaries in a charge, right at the outset. He broke their cavalry, and we were manoeuvring against their flanks, and then they all ran.'

'It was mere butchery,' Lycurgos said, and Alexanor liked him still better for his disgust. 'We followed them for hours, killing their stragglers. We hadn't even fought in the battle.'

All the men were silent.

'And the war is over?' Alexanor asked.

'The Eleans have asked for a truce. It is an Olympic year next year and they are asking to invoke the ancient law – Olympic truce.' Lycurgos looked at Alexanor. 'How would the temple feel about that, Alexanor?'

It was an odd moment for Alexanor – the moment in which he realised that he had become a man of consequence. Lycurgos wasn't just a man used to obeying Alexanor in the field; he was the leading magnate of a rich town, and he still saw Alexanor as a voice of authority.

Alexanor sat up. 'I will have to speak to Chiron,' he said. 'But I would guess that any true peace between Greeks would be acceptable to the temple.'

Kleander spoke up. 'That's almost exactly what Philopoemen said. Alexanor, if I get married, may I bring my wife to your house for dinner?'

'Of course you can.'

'Only her father says it's immoral to lie with your wife at dinner.'

'Her father is a famous moralist, is he?'

Kleander flushed, and then laughed. 'He chases his slaves, and forces himself on them when he catches them.'

'And you love his daughter anyway?' Aspasia asked.

'Yes.'

Aspasia smiled bitterly. 'Men like to keep women out of dinner parties. That way they can have sex with slaves and *porne* and pretend it never happened.'

'Say what you will about the Romans,' Nestor said, 'they have close families. Kaeso says—'

'Kaeso?' Alexanor asked.

'Old Galba sent him to us to ask for the truce. He's on the old bastard's staff. He unhorsed Aristaenos in the fighting last week, but very courteously didn't kill him.'

'How's Aristides?' Alexanor asked.

'Also wounded. He's at Megalopolis. They're talking about taking off his hand.'

'Gods!' Alexanor said, half rising. 'Which hand?'

'The left – he tried to cover a sword cut with his bridle hand.'

'Ouch.'

The next morning, despite the protests of his wife, he was on horseback, his old medical bag on his horse's rump. He rode along the seaside to Argos and then across the hills to Megalopolis, with no company but Dariush.

He rode into Philopoemen's yard and was again greeted, as in past years, by a forest of scaffolding and fifty workers.

'Where's Philopoemen?' he asked a workman.

He found him at the back of the house, laying a chalk line along one of his underground conduits and making notes on a wax tablet.

When Philopoemen looked at Alexanor, he was shaken for a moment. And then he endeavoured to render Alexanor as dead as he had thought him by the expedient of crushing him in his great arms.

'By all the gods!'

'Aristaenos must have got it wrong,' Alexanor said.

'By the gods!' Philopoemen was crying.

Alexanor was stunned at the man's happiness – amazed. Secretly delighted, as he was, in his heart, always amazed that a man so like the gods was his friend.

And later, he sat in Kykliadas' house in Megalopolis, watching over Aristides.

'Can you save him?' the politician, and now victorious *strategos*, asked him.

Alexanor wanted to tell the man, regardless of his importance, to bugger off, but instead he smelt the wound and worked the hand a little.

The cut had gone to the bone – indeed, it had chipped the bone between the elbow and the wrist. The muscles were ruined; several vital tendons were cut and the wound was too old to even think of finding them, much less attaching them.

But the fingers of the hand were not dead; there was blood flow and little mortification.

'Who cleaned the wound?' he asked.

'Your friend Kritias,' Kykliadas said. 'If we survive this summer he'll be a force to be reckoned with – war hero, rich boy, and friend of Epidauros. He'll be *Strategos* someday.'

'A better man than his father expected,' Alexanor said, somewhat absently.

'He's worth ten of his slave-selling father.'

Alexanor looked over the wound carefully, feeling for the edges of the muscle damage, and his patient writhed and tried to stifle a scream. But when his eyes fluttered open, he smiled.

'Is this a dream?' he asked. 'I thought you were dead.'

'I'm not,' Alexanor said. 'And I'm going to save your hand.'

Aristides smiled. 'I knew you would,' he said with complete confidence, and went to sleep.

It took more than a month to get the skin to heal and in the end Alexanor had to find the bone chip and remove it – a process made easier by the body, which had pushed it closer to the surface. But Aristides was strong, middle-aged and in perfect physical shape. He weathered the storm of infection and Alexanor had the satisfaction of watching the muscles begin to recover – not, of course, where they were totally severed, but all the other ones – so that although the hand was very stiff and slow, Aristides could still open and close it.

Alexanor lived with Philopoemen for that month, and shared his house with Phila, newly come from Athens, and Wewa, whom he discovered to have a fund of Aegyptian medical knowledge, so that the time was pleasant and passed quickly.

On his last evening, when Aristides was well enough to travel back to Epidauros and eventually home to Hermione, they had a symposium in Philopoemen's rebuilt dining room. The floor was heated, which was wonderful as autumn had set in outside, and had a magnificent mosaic of the gods gathered at a dinner party. Arkas was a guest; now

Wewa directed the servants, most of whom were cavalry troopers wintering over on Philopoemen's farms.

'You no longer have slaves?' Phila asked.

'I'd like to say no,' Philopoemen said. 'But in truth, I have a dozen old slaves. I mean, I've freed them, but they are my dependents, and I won't "free" them to starve on the frozen roads.'

Phila applauded him nonetheless.

Alexanor looked at them both, and he could see age in Phila's face, and lines around Philopoemen's eyes. And yet they were like the gods on the mosaic floor – he like Zeus, and she like Aphrodite. Alexanor watched them, and tears came to his eyes, because he loved them both; because his life was so much better than he had ever imagined when he was young and alone on the deck of a stricken ship; and because he held himself blessed to have such friends.

Phila caught his eye. As if she could read what he was thinking, she smiled, and raised her cup.

'We have an announcement,' she said.

Philopoemen smiled. 'Indeed. We're going to marry.'

Alexanor sat up, crossed the room, and embraced them both. In truth, he had a touch of jealousy; he could clearly remember Phila declining his invitation to marry, but that had been ten years before. She pressed his hand, again as if she read his thoughts.

'All the fashionable old hetaerae are doing it,' she said. 'And my face is going. My breasts will sag and I'll run to fat. Time to marry.'

'I want you for your beautiful spy service and your enticing mind,' Philopoemen said.

'I know,' Phila smiled. And it was still utterly brilliant, that smile – captivating and godlike. 'I know. That's why I'm so fond of you.'

And later, after salmon and venison and a hundred side dishes, Aristides asked, 'Is the war over?'

Philopoemen grinned and rolled over so that he could put an arm around Phila.

'That is the question of the hour. I sent Kaeso back to Galba with some thoughts; and I sent a letter to your friend Solon in the name of the League and with Kykliadas and Nikeas in agreement.'

'Nikeas?'

'Commanded the left of the phalanx this summer. Big, plain-spoken man. I'm guessing he'll be *Strategos* in the spring.'

'Not you?'

Philopoemen shrugged. 'Not me. I think that most of the magnates think the war is over and they can have one of their own as *Strategos*.'

Phila made a noise.

Alexanor took a barley roll from the stack and made a bread pill, which he threw at Philopoemen.

'Answer the question!' he said.

Philopoemen threw a whole roll back, and Phila sat up, her hands raised.

'Stop!' she said. 'This is not some Spartan mess. If I am to be lady of this house, there will be no bread fights.' She looked at Alexanor. 'Shame on you. I'll tell Aspasia.'

Alexanor couldn't tell if she was joking or serious; Philopoemen was immediately contrite.

'Well?' she asked. 'Come, prophesy for us. Will there be war?'

'Yes,' Philopoemen said. 'The Romans want Philip humbled, and we're just a sideshow for them. They can put two legions here and not even miss them. But Elis is out of the war, and that changes a great deal for us. We don't have to watch our longest frontier – in fact, we only have the north coast and the Spartans. We know how to handle the Spartans. And curiously, the Romans are the most dangerous, but given their current numbers, they can inflict the least damage. It takes manpower, time and dedication to ravage a district – naval landings by a hundred marines won't do it. So while I expect the war to continue ...' He shrugged. 'With a little *fortuna*, it will not reach the white-hot epic that was this summer.'

Alexanor escorted Aristides back across the mountains in beautiful autumn weather; the fields of Tegea were golden with ripe wheat, and the winds were pleasant.

As they wound their way down into the valley of the temple complex, the patchwork of fields was laid out like the glory of Demeter – each plot ripe and undamaged: a fine year for farmers.

'I suppose ...' Aristides said, and then stopped.

He reined in his horse and the three men, Alexanor, Aristides and Dariush, sat on their horses, drinking in the beauty of the evening.

'I suppose,' he began again, ' that this is what we're fighting for. So these people in these fields can grow their crops in peace.'

'In that case, we did well,' Alexanor admitted.

He had suffered from some darkness the last week: pain from his wound; an ugly tinge of jealousy that his best friend would marry Phila; guilt about that very jealousy; worry for his wife's pregnancy; and the overwhelming reality of the war that Philopoemen said was not yet over.

But looking down into the Vale of Epidauros, he couldn't be sad.

'May war never come here,' he said quietly.

'Amen,' Aristides said, and they rode on.

A month later, sated with exercise and food and long evenings watching the stars with his wife, Alexanor sailed north in a coastal merchant bound for Corinth. At Corinth he attended the annual horse fair with Kleostratos. Together they purchased two hundred horses for Philopoemen's farms and another sixty for Alexanor and Lycurgos, who had pooled their resources to buy an abandoned farm in the Epidauros valley where they would raise cavalry horses for the League.

Alexanor also purchased two cavalry chargers for himself and another for Dariush, who was so happy that he went and slept in a city stable with his new mount.

Alexanor sent the whole herd south with Kleostratos and rode west to Aegio with Dariush, arriving in time to attend the opening of the *Synodos*. This time he was invited to be the sacrificing priest, which surprised him, and he was more surprised to find that he was elected to the *Boule*, the inner council of one hundred, on the first vote. Philopoemen, Kykliadas, Cercidas, Aristaenos and Lykortas were all elected, as were Dinaeos and Nikeas; almost every officer appointed for the former year by Philopoemen was elected, and the resulting *Boule* was surprisingly united. The opposition centred on Cronan of Corinth, who led a strong party of oligarchs – strong, but not strong enough to prevent the passing of sweeping taxation measures on the richest classes.

Kykliadas could not run again for *Strategos*, as the office was limited by the constitution; no man could hold the office twice in succession. But he was by far the most popular man at the *Synodos*, and he pressed for the election of Nikeas, who had commanded the left wing of the phalanx all summer and in battle at Messene in the autumn.

'Have they forgotten Philopoemen?' Alexanor asked Lykortas.

'No. It's not easy to explain, but many … imponderables … are against him.'

Alexanor shrugged. 'What's imponderable? He saved Achaea.'

'Well,' Lykortas said. 'First, Kykliadas saved Achaea. He was *Strategos*, and Philopoemen hasn't gone against Kykliadas – nor should he. Second, he's a cavalryman, and, believe it or not, there's a prejudice in the voting against the cavalry. It's the hoplites who are viewed as essential—'

'Not last year!'

Lykortas chuckled. 'Do you think that the farmers of the Tegean plains have kept up with the latest evolution in tactics?' He shook his head. 'It's farmer-hoplites who run the League, not cavalrymen.' He looked around. 'Also, Philopoemen has the unique honour of being the only man I know who is simultaneously viewed by most of our citizens as an oligarch – a very rich man – *and* a radical. He's blamed for both sets of politics at the same time. Someone, somewhere, is whispering against him very effectively.'

'Cronan?' Alexanor asked.

'Certainly, but then, he dislikes us all.'

'Aristaenos?'

Lykortas' eyes narrowed and he looked at Alexanor under his lashes. 'Why do you say that?'

'My wife says he's been whispering against Philopoemen,' Alexanor said. 'She's become very active in collecting … gossip. Accurate gossip.'

'Taking lessons from Phila?' Lykortas asked. 'Zeus, I hadn't thought of Aristaenos. Ungrateful arse.' He nodded. 'I'll be down your way in spring – I'm your cavalry inspector this year. I look forward to hearing all this from Aspasia. And by the way, congratulations on being appointed to the *Boule*. Your name was selected almost unanimously. You should consider a career in politics.'

'No thanks, my friend. I am needed at Epidauros.'

'Anything you are not good at? Medicine, war, politics …'

'I can't sing,' Alexanor said.

'Good. You're human.'

\*

The *Boule* had the disadvantage of meeting all year; they were the council who made most of the actual decisions about the treasury and the allocation of taxes and funds. The first meeting that Alexanor attended drove him to a remarkable combination of feelings: a strong sense of boredom and a desire to sleep, cunningly combined with frustration, anger and outrage.

'How do they get anything done?' he asked Lykortas.

'Mostly they don't,' Philopoemen said. 'However, this year there are so many of us on the *Boule* that I suspect if we spoke up we could run the thing.'

He smiled, and Lykortas smiled back.

Later that afternoon, over wine with Kykliadas and Cercidas, Alexanor heard Philopoemen and Kykliadas agree that Nikeas would be *Strategos* and Philopoemen would again be *Hipparchos*, with Kykliadas taking the treasury.

The next day the assembly elected them; Demodokos mounted the bema and was shouted down. The *Synodos* voted to prosecute the war, and voted in the new taxes on the oligarchs.

The next day, at the *Boule*, Lykortas rose to his feet during a long discussion of the effect of the new taxes. Apparently there were no limits on debate in the *Boule*, and the oligarchs, secure in their political power in the upper house, were protracting the debates.

'Vote!' Lykortas roared.

Dozens of voices took up the cry.

The man at the speaker's desk turned and shouted back 'Sit down!'.

'Vote!' roared Lykortas in his battlefield voice.

The speaker attempted to ignore him, but no one could be heard over the roars and shouts.

Eventually the speaker, Telemon of Dyme, sat, and Lykortas walked to the speaker's desk. Another oligarch tried to get in his way and Lykortas gave him an undignified shove.

He smiled. 'I move we vote on the new taxes.'

In minutes, the vote was tallied and carried.

Afterwards, Cronan approached Lykortas where he stood with Philopoemen and Alexanor.

'When you've been in the *Boule* a while,' Cronan said with a smile on his lips, 'you'll appreciate how we do business. We don't shove our colleagues and we don't hurry speeches.'

'We do,' Lykortas said. 'And we are the majority. I'm sorry, Cronan, but I have an agenda of one hundred and seventy-five items on which we intend to vote, and I plan to have them done in three days.'

Cronan paled. 'This is mere democracy. The tyranny of the many. The *Boule* is not for demagogues, but for responsible gentlemen who—'

'Save it for a speech,' Lykortas said.

'And did you carry all one hundred and seventy-five motions?' Aspasia asked.

She was lying on a *kline* of her own, because she was as broad as two women, or so she had joked. Alexanor was rubbing her feet and her back.

'No. In fact, we didn't even win all of the motions we moved. But we got through more than a hundred, and we passed the cavalry farm bill and the budget. And the taxes. And Nikeas took his seat.'

'How did that go?' she asked. 'Why do I have to be pregnant to get my feet rubbed, I wonder?'

'Nikeas is a very likeable man ...'

'I sense a "but".'

'It was odd. He was seated as *Strategos* and he ...' Alexanor shook his head.

'He became suddenly very autocratic?'

'Yes,' Alexanor admitted.

She shrugged. 'Men should pay more attention to the world of women. I've seen the same happen when young girls become wives. From powerlessness to command of a house and twenty slaves, they become little tyrants. For a while.' She shrugged again. 'Give him time. He'll adjust.'

'I hope so. He was rude to Cronan, which is just foolish – the man's an arse, but he's powerful. And then he was rude to Philopoemen and Kykliadas in a speech, suggesting that he, and not they, won last year's battles.' Alexanor shrugged.

'Gods,' she murmured. 'Please don't stop.' She was silent for a moment. 'And Aristaenos?'

'Very quiet.'

'He would be,' she said. 'He's trying to have himself made *Strategos*.'

'How can you know that and Lykortas doesn't?'

She smiled. She was lying sideways, her head on a little pillow, playing with the tassels. But now her eyes met his.

'His wife writes letters she shouldn't.'

The winter came on, and Alexanor ran, rode, drilled with the cavalry and twice rode over to Hermione to train there, because Aristides couldn't handle his reins well.

'I need you to be well.' Alexanor wasn't joking.

Aristides made a face. 'It hurts all the time. It's like ... like a sprain. But all the time.'

'Because the tendon is severed, all the other muscles are having to work overtime.' Alexanor looked at the hand and shrugged.

'He's going to make you command, isn't he?'

Alexanor shrugged, but he knew it to be true. And his dream of spending the summer at the temple instead of in the field grew smaller every day.

Panamos drew on; there was snow in the Arkadians to the west, and Alexanor was taking an increasing role in the day-to-day running of the great temple complex. Chiron was growing infirm.

'Soon, I will have to ask you to take control,' the old priest said.

'I am in no hurry, sir,' Alexanor said. 'And I expect I will have to spend the summer fighting.'

'Once you are high priest, you should not fight. You have become even more important to the League than I imagined you would. Here – I have a letter from Leon. Your little temple is prospering, as is Crete.'

Alexanor read the letter with delight and hurried home to tell Aspasia. Her baby was due any day. Their daughter was making dolls, assuming the new baby would be a girl. Their son was covered in mud and his nurse was rolling her eyes, and Alexanor laughed.

He'd brought Kleopatra from the temple, and she was living in the house; a fine woman with excellent training who had performed many of the sacrifices with both of them, a family friend who happened to be a midwife. She was good company, and Alexanor discussed politics freely with her and still had time to go with Lycurgos to their farm.

'Imagine us, farmers!'

Lycurgos was a merchant with six ships; he had olives all over the hills, but a horse farm was not something for any but the fantastically rich.

Together they spent hours making sure that their precious horseflesh was well guarded, warm and well fed. Increasingly, though, Dariush took charge; he'd brought in two other Persian boys. The third time Alexanor visited the farm he was stunned to find Kuka, the Scythian warrior maiden, riding one of his mares with Dariush and another Persian watching. Theophoros, one of the Epidauran cavalrymen, was sitting on the wall, chewing on a stem of wheat with his friend, Antigonos.

'I didn't know you were here,' Alexanor said to Kuka. He bowed.

She laughed. 'I'm not here to visit you. Just your horses. My mother sent me to visit all the new horse farms. Yours is clean and Dariush is better with these than any of you Greeks.'

Lycurgos frowned. 'I am doing what I can ...'

She smiled and looked at Dariush. 'Just do whatever he says. He knows horses, almost like a real person.'

She leant over and kissed the Persian boy on the cheek and he flushed.

'Come and have dinner,' Alexanor said.

She smiled. 'No, I can't. Perhaps next time I come through.'

'My regards to your mother, and everyone at Megalopolis.'

She smiled.

Theodoros came down off his wall.

'What a woman,' he said. 'Remember when she killed all those Aetolians. I asked her to marry me. She just mocked my riding.'

Alexanor nodded. 'I've been turned down once or twice,' he admitted, thinking of Phila and feeling a twinge of real guilt. His wife was days from giving birth ...

The middle-aged cavalryman shrugged. 'It's no dishonour, being turned down by the best.'

He was a very plain-spoken man, small, compact, heavily bearded like the ancients or a Spartan Ephor. Alexanor had a twinge of embarrassment; he'd commanded the man for an entire summer and this was the closest they'd come to a conversation. He knew Antigonos and had marked him for file-leader or more; the big blond man was reliable, and had the size to survive close combat.

'Well, back to work,' Theodoros said.

'What do you do?'

Alexanor only knew the man as a competent cavalryman, no more.

'I have a dozen farms,' the man said. 'I think I'll buy a new one with Antigonos here and raise horses,' he went on. 'I like the inspection system.'

They all laughed.

Two days later, Aspasia gave birth to a baby girl, who was named Theodora. She was round and perfect. Her labour took very little time; Kleopatra declared that it was the most delightful delivery of her career and Aspasia was up and about in six hours.

'I'm getting good at this,' she said.

Kleopatra winked. When she was gone, Aspasia pointed at the letter from Leon.

'She read it,' Aspasia said.

'Oh?'

Alexanor was looking at a bill for lead ropes for his horses and he was working on outrage.

'Kleopatra fancies our Leon.'

'That's nice,' Alexanor muttered, or some other platitude.

'Sometimes I suspect you are not listening to me.'

'Of course, my dear.'

'So I thought I'd run naked through the streets and perhaps revile the gods.'

'Of course ...'

There was a pause.

'I wasn't listening,' he admitted.

'I know,' Aspasia said.

Alexanor lost more than a week to being a new father; even with house servants and slaves and a temple to run, he couldn't get enough of his daughter. And his son delighted him by leaving his mud puddles to love his little sister. Every day was more delightful than the last, at least until Theodora woke them in the middle of the night or every hour ...

And then they all settled down to a routine. The number of pilgrims dwindled away almost to nothing. Evenings grew long, and work days short. It took more and more effort of will to go out and run in cold rain, and the same seemed to apply to the cavalry, who had to be forced out to drill. Victorious and well drilled, they seemed to feel that they had nothing left to learn, but a dozen young men were just joining them and had to be taught their duty. Alexanor purchased three Thracians and a Persian man who knew horses, manumitted them all and made them into cavalrymen. If he had to go back to war, he was taking his own escort; he had a great deal to live for. And the horse farm needed workers.

At first, Dariush and the new man, Xartes, quarrelled constantly, but the Thracians proved tractable and the horses looked healthy, and Alexanor lost himself in the temple and his family. Chiron lost none of his imperious intelligence, but every day he seemed to be more fragile, and Alexanor was afraid he wouldn't make it through the winter. He met with all of the priests often. Chiron insisted on making every meeting, walking carefully through driving rain or early snow.

Winter came, and Alexanor lost track of the world beyond the walls. More than two dozen pilgrims, all very rich men and women, some from as far away as Alexandria and Antioch, had elected to winter at Epidauros. Every one of them had made a major donation, and in return they seemed to think that his temple of healing was a taverna for a select audience.

The petty crises rolled on: claims that a temple slave stole jewellery; claims that there were bad smells in the apartments and the dream house and the baths; the discovery that there was, in fact, an ugly mould in the baths, a creeping black tide that set in to one corner and began to spread like one of the god's deadly plagues.

The mould in the baths took up his every waking hour for many days. The side-effects were positive; he spent a great deal of time with Sostratos, his first friend and mentor, and he rediscovered his early love for the mixtures of earths and various minor powers – acids and bases.

Together, like two guiltless schoolboys, they played with vinegar and lemon juice and burned sulphur. Kritias, who was taking a greater role in the temple and had begun to show signs of learning to work, persevered with his own theories, which involved incessantly scraping away at the mould on the stone of the baths. It amused Alexanor to see him work so hard – an amusement which he did his very best to hide.

At the same time, Leon's letter suggested that he was still having trouble with the youths he'd been sent. Alexanor was considering sending Kritias to Leon; his conversion from arrogant rebel to mature priest was as remarkable as any of the alchemical reactions that might turn lead to gold.

But he wasn't ready to part with the young man yet.

In the end, after a week's work, they triumphed, although it was difficult to say whether Kritias' abrasive sand or Alexanor's lemon juice was responsible.

'You there!' called an old Macedonian courtier. 'You!'

The last stain of the creeping black was gone; even the stone seemed cleaner. Alexanor and Sostratos were examining their efforts and Kritias was lying on the mosaic floor, trying to see into the join where the floor met the wall.

'I mean you, *pais*!' shouted the courtier.

Alexanor was wearing the brown *chiton* of a workman or temple slave.

'Yes?' he asked politely.

'I hate the smell of lemons. See to it.'

The man waved his hand at Alexanor. Alexanor turned away to hide his anger.

'Are you sure you want to be hierophant?' Sostratos asked.

'No one's ever asked me that before,' Alexanor laughed. 'But yes. I wonder why you are not to be hierophant, though.'

'I'm not from the right family. Nah, don't take it that way. I'm not bitter. You people have connections. You know Philip of Macedon and Philopoemen and you know the hierophant on Kos and the whole *Boule*. You are the sort of man to run this place. I'll help you run it – I know where most of the bodies are buried.'

'I would stand aside for you,' Alexanor said.

'Would you, though?' Sostratos asked, cocking his head to one side. 'I'll gloat over that another time. But if I was hierophant, I'd make you do half the work. You'd be going to the *Boule* for me, to Cronan of Corinth, who just made a massive donation—'

'What?'

'Kritias is to be elevated. It's common for parents to make a donation. Cronan has to be seen to be richer than anyone else.'

Alexanor walked back to the main *stoa*. He was curious, and he looked over the older man's shoulder at the list of beneficiaries and the contents of the treasury.

'We are very rich,' he said.

'Yes,' Sostratos said. 'With the donations from our winter symposiasts –' he made a face – 'we've more than recouped the donations we made to the League treasury. Indeed, we could afford as much again.'

'Perhaps I'll eradicate the smell of lemon in the baths after all,' Alexanor said with a smile.

'What kind of man doesn't like the smell of lemon?'

Sostratos went out to change for a sacrifice and left Alexanor with the scrolls of accounts, the tally sticks and the physical reality of the riches the temple held. He'd never realised the extent of the temple holdings, and he was pondering whether it might be worth his while to move some of the treasury to other places so that, in the event of a disaster, like a Roman landing ...

'I don't like to interrupt ...' Philopoemen said.

He was standing very quietly in the doorway. Alexanor leapt up and the two men embraced.

'Sostratos tells me you are to be the hierophant,' Philopoemen said.

'Yes,' Alexanor admitted.

'I'm going to Chiron to ask him to hold on for the summer. I'm sorry, brother. I need you.' He even had the grace to look sorry.

Alexanor took his friend by the hand and led him out to the railing of the second storey of the great *stoa*. It was a cold winter evening, but the Vale of Epidauros was as beautiful as ever, and the temple and the great theatre were magnificent in the winter light.

'This is my world,' Alexanor said quietly. 'I almost forgot it last summer. Listen, brother. I killed a dozen men last summer – perhaps more. I killed more men than I saved with my knowledge.'

Philopoemen was silent.

'Tell me that you don't have another cavalry officer who can fill the role. Perhaps one who rides better and doesn't have three children and a temple complex to manage. This is my life. War is not my life, it is yours.' Alexanor was calm; he did not plead.

Philopoemen nodded slowly. 'You and Dinaeos are the best. Aristides is competent. Lycurgos will serve well if well led.'

'Kleander. I might even mention Kritias.'

'Young, and immortal. They'll be killed, or get others killed. We have no margin of error at all, Alexanor. I can't afford a single loss – not in a skirmish, not a raid, much less a battle.'

'You said that with the Eleans out of the war—'

'It will be easier. But we still face Sparta and Rome and the whole of the Aetolian League. Perhaps Carthage or Aegypt could invade—'

'You are making this up.'

'I am. Alexanor, I can't make this better. You can say no. But none of my other officers would have made the decisions you did on the Larissa river – to pretend to be so many men, to send Kritias to threaten the Aetolian flank, to send Aristides into the melee. These little decisions are everything. I know you'll make them.'

'I hate it!'

But Alexanor was flattered. He noted, with the clinical detachment that he had for most things, that Philopoemen's praise elevated him. He suspected his pulse ran faster; perhaps the flush on his cheeks ...

'Which is odd, as I love it. Nonetheless.' Philopoemen smiled.

Alexanor shrugged. 'I don't know why I'm arguing. I have already told Aspasia that I'm going.'

'Thank the gods,' Philopoemen said.

'Is that why you are here?'

'No,' Philopoemen said. 'I came with Lykortas. I'm doing what I did last winter – watching the reviews and the drills. And I came to see you, you ingrate. Can't I just—'

Alexanor laughed. 'Of course.'


Dinner: a feast, really. Aspasia had the slightly mocking triumphant look of a woman who has, in an afternoon, created a magnificent dinner and a clean house out of chaos, and received no help from her husband.

There was chicken in spices and red snapper done in parchment and fresh greens, the first of the new spring, and a barley soup, and three types of bread, and jars of fragrant olive oil, and brilliant wine. Philopoemen had brought wine from Athens, and Phila had brought wine from Boeotia, and Lykortas had brought an amphora of a rich red from Lesvos, and they all drank too much, feasted their servants, and encouraged Dariush and Wewa to drink too much.

Drunk, Aspasia rolled over on her couch and said, 'You're taking my husband!'

And Philopoemen smiled. 'Yes,' he admitted.

It was the only sour moment in a delightful evening.

'Bring him back to me alive,' she said.

'I give you my word.'

And later, when they'd drunk more, Lykortas asked Aspasia to talk about Aristaenos.

'Windbag,' she said. 'You know that he's talking to Pausanias at Messene.'

'Pausanias?' Alexanor asked. The world was starting to spin.

Aspasia kicked her heels like a child. 'Really? You exiled him, love. From Crete.'

'Ah, *that* Pausanias.'

'He's talking to Aristaenos?' Philopoemen didn't seem very drunk, suddenly.

Aspasia sat up and adjusted some clothing.

'Darling,' she said to Philopoemen, her voice taking on the same tone she used with a difficult child, 'there's a whole pack of these dogs. The current charge is that you are using the cavalry remount bill to mask your own accumulation of wealth and that all the horse farms are money-laundering fronts.'

She barely slurred her words, although her eyes were very bright and she'd never called Philopoemen 'darling' before.

Phila rose from her own couch and dropped a curtsy.

'Bless you,' she said. 'I think you've surpassed me.'

Aspasia smiled. 'I had a great teacher. And that other thing you said, about the appearance of casual wantonness being the key to men's—'

'Darling,' Phila said.

Aspasia laughed. 'I am drink. Drunk.'

Phila lay down by Aspasia. 'It suits you, a little,' she said. 'But let's stick to political secrets.'

'I see what you mean,' Aspasia said. 'So ... Where was I?'

'Horse farms.'

'Only your friends have them, and so they are a front for crime.

Really.' Aspasia laughed. 'They'd do it if they were in office, so they assume you do it.'

'Forewarned is forearmed,' Philopoemen said.

'But I only have two arms,' Alexanor said. 'Four arms is anatomically impossible.'

Aspasia slapped him. 'That's not even funny to a drunk.' She smiled at Phila. 'Fatherhood seems to inflict on them the very worst sense of humour.'

The magnificent helmet that Aspasia had purchased for him last year was already like an old enemy; it smelt of last year's wars, and sweat, and fear, and he put it on with a tiny shudder of revulsion.

And wearing a heavy bronze helmet with a magnificent horsehair crest while your head pounds from the worst hangover of a lifetime of good parties is like penance for all your sins. The loud clangs of spears thrown at a bronze-covered shield were enough to drive him mad, but Alexanor stayed on his horse and led the Epidaurans through wheels and inclines and filings off to the right and left until Lykortas laughed.

'I'm not sure the precious Agema can do all these things.'

'They practise every week,' Lycurgos said proudly.

'They are very good, but this year, most of them are veterans.'

Alexanor turned bloodshot eyes on his friend. 'You know Phodor? The boat builder?' Philopoemen shook his head. 'He killed his wife. With his sword.'

'Terrible.'

Alexanor nodded. 'Then he killed himself.'

There was a long silence, punctuated by the sound of men throwing javelins at the carcass of a pig, hanging from a tree limb.

'You are saying this is my fault?' Philopoemen asked cautiously.

'Don't be an arse. I'm saying that Phodor was not a violent man before we took him to war.'

'Blame the Spartans and the Romans ...'

Alexanor shook his head. 'No, it's not that simple. We are all to blame. We use war like a drug ... and not everyone can handle it.'

Philopoemen sighed. 'I know you are trying to tell me something important. But I can't see beyond defeating ... no. I can't see defeating anyone. Survival. Another year of survival, waiting for Philip to win a major victory, or perhaps for Machanandas to die, or the Aetolians ...'

Alexanor had never heard the superhuman Philopoemen sound so defeated.

'I thought—'

'I'm tired too,' Philopoemen said. 'And all I can see is summer after summer, facing them all, until I go down, or you do, or Dinaeos, or all of us in one day. Better that way – then I don't have to face your wife and Dinaeos'. I'm not joking, my friend. I know what your wife was saying last night. She blames me—'

'No,' Alexanor said.

'Yes. She knows that if I were not there, you'd sit this out.' He shrugged. 'I am ruthless to my friends. And whatever Chiron fears, the truth is that neither the Aetolians nor the Romans will sack this sanctuary. You are safe here. You could just sit and wait.'

He looked away.

'But I won't,' Alexanor said.

'I'll do whatever it takes to wring every advantage I can before we fight, and that includes you and Dinaeos.' He looked away. 'And then we'll die. All of us.'

Alexanor smiled through the hangover, which was less, anyway, as if emotion was a relief.

'I'm a doctor,' he said. 'We'll all die.'

'We may all die this spring,' Philopoemen said.

Alexanor grunted a bit of a laugh. 'I find this an interesting role reversal, but listen, brother. We're fighting for all these small farmers and all the men and women who live in these mountains and the valleys between. Is that not noble?'

'It won't make us less dead.'

'Odd. I've always assumed you didn't have doubts like this.' He shrugged. 'I'm mostly past them. It's like a surgery. If it must be done, let it be done well and quickly.'

Philopoemen turned and met his eyes. 'Alexanor.' His voice was gently chiding. 'When you first came to my farm, my best plan was to drink myself to death. And you don't think I have doubts? It was you who brought me out of a wine-soaked, ignoble death, and showed me a path to be ... I don't know. The mechanism of the salvation of Achaea? Something like that.'

Alexanor writhed.

'But the wine-sotted despair isn't all that far away,' Philopoemen said. 'I'm just a good actor.'

'A very good actor.'

Philopoemen yelled 'Fine throw!' and pumped his fist in the air, watching Kleander.

'Oh, yes,' he said. 'A very good actor.'

# CHAPTER THIRTEEN

————✦————

## Epidauros and Tegea

HERMAIOS TO HOMOLOIOS (MARCH TO JUNE), 208 BCE

Alexanor had four more weeks at home and he used them well: linger-
ing over wine with his wife, or chatting with Kleopatra and Aspasia
while the two women carded wool or spun yarn; playing with his
children; standing with Chiron and watching the magnificence of an
Epidauran morning; riding out with Theodoros and Dariush on his
new horse, listening to the cocks crow and watching the sun drench
the hills with new life, or running, feeling the age fall away from his
limbs as he crested another hill and started the glorious run down
through the roses and jasmine of a Peloponnesian spring.

It was not that he had some premonition of death. It was simply
that this year, he was prepared to admit to himself all that he was
going to lose when he died. And increasingly it seemed to him that
another year of desperate effort would probably kill one of them. He
could see it in Philopoemen's eye, and he wished that he could pass
some of his understanding to Kritias and Dariush, who remained utterly unaware of mortality.

But the day came, and he collected his things. This year, he had the
best of everything, thanks to the loot of Elis. His helmet and *thorax*
had always been fine, but now his cloak was all but stiff with Aspasia's
embroidery, a last-minute gift in the courtyard with many tears.

Aspasia came down with a pitcher of wine and washed his new, light Tarentine-style cavalry shield, and gave him her blessing and the blessing of all the household gods. Despite her tears, she smiled, and gave him his new cloak, and a kiss. He mounted Pegasus, his magnificent pale-grey charger, and looked back at three pack mules carrying all his kit, and wondered what had happened to the former Rhodian marine with a broken sword.

He had his own bodyguards this year – three Thracians and Xartes – and they were under Dariush. He'd armed them himself. Their horses had breastplates of bronze, as the old *Hipparchos* Xenophon himself suggested; all of them wore shirts of scale, brought from Thrake, and all of them had the new, Antigonid-style bronze gauntlets on their bridle hands.

*What money and training can do, I've done*, Alexanor thought. And he spared a moment for Philopoemen who was, of course, doing the same on a much larger scale.

*I'm not leaving Dariush safe at home, am I?* he thought.

He kissed his wife. 'Last time.'

'Sure.' She didn't believe him.

'The children ...'

'It's all those horses I'm worried about,' she said, with a false laugh and now-dry eyes rimmed in red.

She and a dozen other women were to be the caretakers of a horse farm. The general levy of the Achaeans was stripping every town of men. There was a rumour that Machanandas had received a thousand gold talents from Aegypt and that he'd spent it all on mercenaries.

He met her eyes and they said *Don't make me cry again.*

And he left her.


The main army formed under Nikeas at Tegea.

Alexanor was more than a little surprised to learn that he would not be serving with the main army. Philopoemen looked more puzzled than angry.

'Nikeas is keeping Aristaenos to command his cavalry,' he said. 'You and I are ordered to Dyme, to cover the north coast against the Romans and the Aetolians.'

'That's—'

'That's what we've been ordered to do,' Philopoemen said. 'I'm going to have a word with Kykliadas.'

'May I come?'

'Of course.'

The two of them rode easily through the camp, which was a much more professional camp than the year before, although the hoplite class was still not good at digging latrines or using them. They found Kykliadas sitting with a circle of young men, explaining the basics of camp cooking. He grinned when he saw Philopoemen.

'Our hero,' he said.

The two cavalrymen dismounted and sat with him while the young men looked on with more than a little hero-worship.

'You want to know why you are being sent to face the Aetolians,' Kykliadas asked.

'I do,' Alexanor said.

Kykliadas shrugged. 'Nikeas thinks that you are too important, and need to be taken down a peg.' The former *Strategos* shrugged. 'I confess I hadn't expected this behaviour, but he's well within his rights. He's the *Strategos*.'

Philopoemen nodded. 'Yes,' he said. 'But Aristaenos ...'

'Has as much experience as you do yourself – and Philopoemen, I know what you will say, so *listen*. You left him with us last year when you raced north. He did a fine job, and he and Nikeas get along.' He shrugged again. 'That's politics.'

'Aristaenos isn't half the cavalry officer that Philopoemen is,' Alexanor said.

Kykliadas nodded. 'Perhaps. But we'll do what we're ordered to do, and frankly, you two and Dinaeos may have the harder role.'

'Aristaenos will keep the Agema, though,' Philopoemen said. 'Which I have raised and trained—'

'It is not yours,' Kykliadas said. 'It is the League's.'

Philopoemen looked away.

'I know,' Kykliadas said. 'Listen, Philopoemen. I *know*. I tried to talk him out of this. But he's sure.'

'Because if I win another battle, I'll be *Strategos* next year,' Philopoemen said.

'Yes,' Kykliadas admitted.

'Whereas this way, it's Aristaenos.'

'Yes.'

Philopoemen nodded slowly. 'Interesting. Very well. I will, of course, obey.'

Kykliadas looked relieved. 'Listen …'

Philopoemen had turned away with a swirl of his cloak. Now he stopped.

'Just …' Kykliadas looked around as if afraid to be overheard. 'Don't go so far you can't hurry back.'

'I'm going to Dyme!' Philopoemen said. 'That's as far from Tegea as you can get in and be within the bounds of the League.'

'I'm only saying …'

Philopoemen nodded. 'You're asking me another impossible thing.'

'You are so good at them,' Kykliadas said. 'You know what is the only thing worse than being the *Strategos*?'

'What?'

'The former *Strategos*. Everyone tells me everything.'

Philopoemen smiled. 'I'll do what I can.'

'You always do.'

Alexanor was already mounted. Philopoemen came back, and looked up at him.

'I wish …'

'Interesting,' said Nikeas. He was standing in his plain armour, about six paces away. He must have walked up with his staff while Alexanor was listening to Kykliadas. 'Discussing whether to obey my orders, *Hipparchos*? Am I just too amateurish for you?'

Philopoemen swung onto his horse's back. 'I suppose I would have liked to be consulted,' he said carefully.

'There is no requirement for the *Strategos* to consult his *Hipparchos* on matters of strategy, that I know of,' Nikeas said. 'Or do you dis-agree?'

Philopoemen made an odd face, as if he was deeply puzzled by something.

'None that I know of.'

'Good. So glad we've had a chat. Now please obey. And while you are at it, the treasurer would like a look at all the accounts to do with your horse farms.'

Philopoemen smiled. 'He should go to my house and ask my steward, then.' He rode closer to the *strategos*. 'Just for the sake of saving time,' he said quietly, 'you realise I've never taken a drachma from the state for my horse farms, right? Which the treasurer could confirm for you. And Cercidas will support me.'

Nikeas looked as if he'd been struck by one of the thunderbolts of Zeus.

'Just to clear the air,' Philopoemen said, 'I purchased all my horses with my own funds.'

*Thank you, Aspasia,* Alexanor thought, and the two of them rode away.

The campaign opened with a naval raid by the Macedonians against the coast of Aetolia – a true case of the biter bit. Alexanor watched Lykortas, who was the League *Navarch* for the year, lead six Achaean warships to join the Macedonian fleet. By launching their attacks in early spring, they managed to hit the Aetolians on the north coast of the Gulf of Corinth before the Roman fleet had raised its rowers and put to sea.

Alexanor lay on a sun-drenched rock on the Achaean side of the gulf, watching the smoke rise over Aetolia. He and Kritias had just used an ancient altar-stone on the hillside for their dawn sacrifices, and Dariush was roasting skewers of meat from the sacrifice on a small fire.

'Is this the end of the war?' Kritias asked. They could see a warship crawling across the shining surface of the gulf, oars flashing in a perfect rhythm. 'Can we rejoice?'

'Should we rejoice that Aetolian farms are burnt and Aetolian women raped and made slaves?' Alexanor asked.

'Better theirs than ours.'

'Practically, yes. Philosophically, no.'

Alexanor turned his back, his delight at the beautiful day ruined by his imagination of what each rising column of smoke meant.

They were on picket duty. Philopoemen had turned most of his cavalry into watch teams with beacons, spread all along the coast; Alexanor and Lykortas had designed a signal system. Alexanor should have been too senior to actually stand a watch, but he found that the long, lonely hours high on a mountain hillside were perfect for prayer and contemplation. He thought carefully about the course of the war, his life with his children, and ways of minimising the danger of interference with a body – surgery.

Prostaterios became Agrionios; Philopoemen held a review of the whole cavalry force, and led the sacrifices, and held cavalry games.

Four days later, Telemnastos marched into Aegio with his Cretan archers. Philopoemen assigned them to the watch posts along the coast from Dyme to Corinth, each post being in sight of those on either side, and having not only a signal fire but a half-file of cavalrymen as messengers.

The raid on Aetolia was over, and Lykortas was back. The Achaean warships had been taken to the Isthmus and then moved ashore because the Romans were at sea.

'Now they'll come,' Lykortas said.

'So the raids did nothing?' Alexanor asked.

Lykortas shrugged.

Philopoemen nodded. 'It's always better to fight the war on your opponent's ground.'

Lykortas pointed at the mountains of Aetolia. 'The herds we took will feed us this summer and lower the cost of the war.'

Alexanor couldn't help himself. 'How glorious,' he said bitterly.

Philopoemen nodded. 'This isn't the Trojan War.'

Lykortas shook his head. 'You think that Trojan War wasn't just like this?' he asked. 'Eleven years of cattle raids?'

They watched the Roman fleet sail into Naupactus; the signal system worked. And the next morning, when a dozen Roman warships rowed across the mirror-flat sea towards Achaea, the beacons warned the army, and messengers arrived to identify each landing. The cavalry responded.

And the next day, again.

And again.

After a week, Alexanor was having trouble mounting his horse. He was so tired that everything tempted him to instant anger.

'Are we winning?' he asked Philopoemen.

The *Hipparchos* was riding along the coast, reviewing all the stations.

'The Romans land, burn a farm, see the cavalry and run for their ships,' Philopoemen said. 'We haven't had a fight yet.'

'We're always late,' Alexanor said.

'We always show up. These pinpricks won't accomplish anything for them.'

'My people are exhausted.'

Philopoemen looked out over the gulf. 'Imagine how their rowers feel.'

The pace of the Roman raids slowed. Alexanor slept for an entire day, and a messenger summoned him to the meeting of the *Boule*. Philopoemen gave him leave.

'I can't go,' he said. 'You go, and take Lykortas.'

As it proved, it was not a particularly discordant meeting; there were ambassadors from Elis at the opening ceremony.

After an invocation, the Eleans asked to speak, and their leader, a short, powerful older man with a terrible scar across his face and neck, walked to the bema. He was charismatic; despite the scar, or because of it, men leant forward to listen. Alexanor didn't know him, but Memnon, one of the Argosian officers, said he was Troilos.

Eleans always commanded respect. As the city which sponsored and administered the Olympic Games, Elis had a special – almost religious – status with all the other states in Greece. No Achaean actually liked to make war on the Eleans, but since the opening of the war, Elis had been allied with the rapacious Aetolians and the Spartans too.

Now Troilos raised an arm in rhetorical greeting.

'Men of Achaea!' he said. 'We have not come to make bombastic speeches, to threaten, to demand repayment for injury – nor to beg forgiveness. We are strong men, and so are you. We do not desire war. We desire that you honour the ancient obligation to a truce from to-morrow until the end of the games, and then for forty days thereafter.'

There was scarcely a murmur; although the man spoke well, what he was saying was known to every member of the council.

'In keeping with our place as the keepers of sacred Olympia,' Troilos said, 'we would have you know, neighbours, that we have refused to allow the Aetolian Federation to land soldiers in our lands. We refused also the Spartans. Specious arguments were offered to our councils, that we could refuse to participate and still keep the truce while Aetolians and Spartans crossed our land to attack you. Neighbours! We declined such sophistry. Our borders will remain inviolate. All we ask of you is to recognise the truce, that our farmers may gather the grain that feeds the sacred athletes.'

Lykortas rose for the League. 'Troilos, and men of Sacred Elis, as long as no force enters Achaea from Elis, we will uphold the truce. Indeed, I believe that we will send more than twenty athletes to the games.'

The Elean ambassadors bowed and withdrew.

'That was exciting,' Alexanor said.

'My first speech,' Lykortas smiled. 'Listen – now we get to fight through the tax allocations.'

Lykortas was correct. It took four days to allocate the federal contributions; each district in the League claimed that it was overtaxed, and that all its farmers were already with the army. The clamour went on and on, and the federalism that joined thirty different cities in the League had never seemed so fragile to Alexanor.

He was also astounded at how often his opinion was solicited. At first he offered no comment whatsoever, but by the third day, at Lykortas' urging, he said what he thought.

'This war runs on money,' he said baldly to a delegation of Argosians who came to him. 'We must all pay. If we do not pay with our treasure today, we'll pay with our lives and our freedom later.'

Lykortas made him write that down, and later, he rose in the *Boule* and put Alexanor's words into a speech.

There was another day of negotiations, but Lykortas' speech broke the back of the opposition, and the financial arrangements were passed. The date of the next *Synodos* was set, and the *Boule* dissolved.

'There it is,' Lykortas said. 'Federal government in all its glory.'

'I got five good nights of sleep,' Alexanor said.

'And the food was excellent. Now back to smelling horses.'

'You're the *Navarch*!' Alexanor said.

'My fleet is on rollers above the tide line at Corinth. Two of the hulls have so much worm I was afraid to take them across the gulf on a perfect day. It's an office without much to say for it. Come on.'

'I miss your fanciful swearing,' Alexanor joked.

Lykortas shrugged. 'I'm a politician now.'

After the meeting of the *Boule* they had a week of peace; rumours from the south that the Spartans were marching. Philopoemen sketched it in the sand of a beach a few stades west of Aegio.

'Machanandas apparently thought that he could force the Eleans to let him cross their passes to come at us from the west,' he said with grim satisfaction. 'Instead, they turned out their phalanx and he had to march all the way back to Sparta to come at us. A third of the campaign season wasted. I hope – I truly hope – Nikeas is sending ambassadors to treat with the Eleans. They have behaved honourably.'

'They don't dare make peace,' Lykortas said. 'If they did, the Aetolians would attack *them*.'

'I wonder if they would join the League?' Alexanor asked.

'Interesting,' Philopoemen said.

After the feast of Demeter, the Aetolians landed in force. Dyme was their target because, after the Roman sack of the year before, it was lightly defended.

The Aetolians landed almost four thousand men, but two days later they were rowing away with the tails between their legs, leaving more than a hundred men as prisoners and twice that number dead. The signals system had functioned smoothly and the Roman fleet was gone; the war had switched to the Aegean and Achaea had returned to being a sideshow.

'Are we winning now?' Alexanor asked.

He was sharing dinner with Philopoemen and his command staff in the ruins of a burnt farm. Wewa and Arkas had half a dozen rabbits and two women were making flatbreads on hot stones, while Wewa kept up a running commentary that had one woman laughing so hard she could scarcely punch the dough into shape.

'We're not losing. That's the best we can do in a contest like this.' Philopoemen's frustration was beginning to show. 'We're dependent, as I keep saying, on Philip to win. Or lose. If he could penetrate into the Aetolian heartland ... If he'd let us send him troops ...'

'If he'd treat us like an ally and not like an ugly stepsister ...' Lykortas spat. 'Damn, this bread is good.'

'Ask the good sisters. Wewa found them hiding in the hills – now they're family. All I know is that they make bread.'

Alexanor watched the two women mixing olive oil with their dough. They gave no appearance that being in an army camp cooking bread was anything but normal. They laughed easily and quickly, but as he watched, Lycurgos passed their fire and both women moved suddenly closer to Wewa.

Philopoemen was watching them too. But he waved towards Macedon.

'Exactly. But he doesn't see us as a real ally, and, in a way, that defines all his failings and perhaps our own. He imagines he's the king of Achaea. We think of him as a distant evil.' He shrugged. 'I mislike the silence from Nikeas.'

'As do I,' Lykortas agreed.

Alexanor looked back and forth at the two. 'Silence?'

'Two weeks ago we heard that Machanandas was moving north towards the boundary after his little problem with Elis,' Lykortas said.

'And that's the last we've heard,' Philopoemen said.

Alexanor suddenly sat up. 'Where's Kleostratos? Where's Kau-Ippa?'

Philopoemen glanced at Lykortas. 'I sent them down the mountains.'

'The mountains we rode through last year,' Lykortas said.

'You're spying on Nikeas?'

Lykortas looked embarrassed. Wewa brought a pile of flatbreads and some olive oil and salt, and they all began to eat.

Philopoemen made a face. 'I'm not convinced that military strategy is Nikeas' strong suit.'

'Gods!' Alexanor took some bread and salt. 'Damn, that's good bread.'

The next day the Aetolians landed just west of Corinth, at the other end of the vulnerable coastline. It was clearly done on purpose; the intention was to overstretch the Achaeans, but the Cretan archers resisted the landings and the cavalry was there three hours later. While the Aetolians could cross the gulf in two hours, their ships were visible the moment they left their coastline.

Alexanor was in the fighting, which was brief and brutal. The Aetolians he faced were desperate and disheartened, but they fought with the courage of abandonment because they'd been left by their ships, and because Kritias charged them before Alexanor could stop him.

And just like that, men were dead. Kritias was wounded; but his friend Kleophanes was dead in his arms, and two other young men who were his friends.

Kritias wept. And then he joined Alexanor in tending to the

wounded of both sides. His tears weren't yet dry when Philopoemen came up with his bodyguard.

'We have to move,' he said.

'I'm doing my best to save some lives,' Alexanor said.

'We're forming up right now,' Philopoemen said, but he dismounted.

Alexanor's patient was an Aetolian. His right arm was so badly broken that it hung at an impossible angle. Alexanor set it before Philopoemen could walk over, and with Dariush's help he put splints on either side. The Persian took a small axe from his belt, found a broken spear shaft, split it with a single blow of his little axe and Alexanor bound the results to the arm, stabilising it.

'I'll be another hour ...'

Philopoemen put a hand on his shoulder. 'I'm very sorry about your men.'

Alexanor turned his head away.

'Machanandas crossed the boundary three days ago, fooled Nikeas, and some traitor opened the gates of Tegea.'

'Tegea!' The word penetrated Alexanor's grief and the blankness that accompanied it. 'God? What?'

'Tegea has fallen,' Philopoemen said quietly.

Tegea was one of the principal cities of the League. In fact, it dominated the central plain of the Argolid, one of the richest parts of the Federation.

'I'm sending Lykortas to Philip,' Philopoemen said. 'And we're marching. Right now.'

Alexanor realised that the *Hipparchos* of the League was taking precious minutes to talk to him. And that he was speaking very quietly, as if to an invalid.

'I'm sorry,' he said.

'I'm also sorry. All these men deserve better than this. But we have to ride. If Nikeas risks a battle ...'

Alexanor looked over the wounded men. 'I have to finish here. No ... I'm not possessed or mad. Leave me two files and I'll follow the moment I'm done. Please. This is what I owe the shades of my people.'

Philopoemen nodded. 'Very well. Lycurgos!' he called out. 'Ready to march!'

Alexanor went to the next victim, another Aetolian. A spear had passed through him. He was young, and handsome, and he would die. Alexanor made himself focus and did what he could. Farmers and their women from the area were coming into the hasty cavalry camp; he sent to Corinth for another healer-priest.

He rode into the camp at Nemea so late that he was challenged by pickets and then taken by a patrol of Argolid cavalrymen who knew him, but not well enough to ignore their orders. He was hauled to Philopoemen, who dismissed the overeager troopers.

'Everyone is on edge,' he said. 'Wewa made you up a pallet. Go to sleep.'

'How bad is it?' Alexanor asked.

'As bad as it can be. I was hoping that the loss of the city was exaggerated, but there are already refugees here. The Spartans took Tegea the way they took Megalopolis in my youth – some citizen opened a gate for them and they were in the citadel in less time than it takes to slit a ram's throat. Machanandas needed money. He's already sold the whole populace as slaves and looted the houses and temples. No matter what we do, it will be a generation before we get Tegea back as a functional part of the polity.'

'Not to mention the people whose lives are ruined ...'

Philopoemen looked at him. 'Yes.' The tone of his response suggested that he had, indeed, had that thought all by himself. 'Yes. All our little victories gone. And Nikeas will try and force a battle.'

'Of course,' Alexanor said.

'No "of course" about it,' Philopoemen said. 'The horse is gone. Too late to close the barn door. The Spartan phalanx is better than ours and most of our cavalry is with me. But Nikeas has just lost his political career unless he does something spectacular, and Aristaenos—'

'Oh, gods,' Alexanor said.

Philopoemen was looking at his armour on its stand. 'Well, I may be wrong. Let's get some sleep.'

'Gods!' Alexanor said.

In the morning, the cavalry was formed in the darkness. Before they marched, Philopoemen wheeled the column into line, formed it eight deep, and rode to the front.

'Brothers,' he said. 'Today will be another long day in a war of long days. And we must do our duty regardless – regardless of our losses, regardless of our fatigue or our anger or even the rising darkness around us. Look to your left and your right – these are the men on whom you depend.'

The sun began to cast a pale pink into the darkness to the east, and the outlines of the Arkadian mountains began to take form as he spoke.

'Stay together! Look for your leaders! And do not lose heart! The Achaean League is *you*. As long as you are in the field, fighting, there is a League. You are not the men of Argos or Epidauros now. You are the living, fighting body of the Federation. Never let it go.'

There was a cheer. It wasn't a hearty cheer – more the growl of tired workmen willing to finish a job.

'Sections will wheel to the left! March!' Philopoemen called out.

And they were away. There were still stars in the sky to the west.

Philopoemen's guides turned them south into the Argolid, through a narrow gorge that was as defensible as the famed Gates of Fire and past the looming citadel of Mycenae. They went in three long files, walking their horses to save their energy, and as they entered the sun-drenched Argolid plain, Philopoemen ordered a halt. A dozen carts rolled out with honey cakes from the villages, arranged by the guides, and huge clay jars of water.

And then they were moving again: riding an hour and then walking, making almost twenty stades an hour over ground. Before the sun was in the middle of the heavens, they were marching under the looming citadel of Argos itself, and then due south along the beach to Kiveri before turning into the mountains. Philopoemen had another rest there, with water and garlic sausage, and then they were climbing away from the sweltering plain and the endless barley fields and into the pass of Achladakampos – up and up and up. From the height of the pass they could see the haze of the central plateau and the ancient city of Pelagos; Tegea was hidden by a spur of the mountains.

Alexanor was leading the Eastern cavalry that day and he was riding with Lycurgos, while Dariush carried his banner. So he was not immediately aware that messengers had come in until Wewa rode down the column. He was waiting by a small, stone-built house with an extensive sheepfold and a series of walls. The column had slowed to a crawl and he was thinking of changing horses.

'The *Hipparchos* requests that you come to him,' he said.

In the narrow defile, it took Alexanor almost half an hour to negotiate his way forward. By the time he reached the front, the column was beginning to form sections on flatter ground. Philopoemen was off to the left, standing by his charger, with Kleostratos and Kau-Ippa. As soon as Alexanor came up, he pointed.

'Nikeas committed to battle this morning,' he said. 'They'll be fighting by now.'

'Where?' Alexanor.

Kleostratos waved his spear. 'Dmiros,' he said. 'It's a town so small the sheep can't lie down.'

'We're an hour away,' Philopoemen said.

'And you're forming a battle line,' Alexanor said.

'I have to assume we've already lost.'

Alexanor's mouth was dry.

Very quietly, Philopoemen said, 'If Nikeas has been defeated, we are all that stands between the Spartans and the death of the League.'

Alexanor took a swig from his canteen. 'You're not holding back to make sure that you win the battle, and not Nikeas?'

Philopoemen raised an eyebrow. 'Lykortas might. I would not.'

Alexanor put a hand on his friend's bridle arm. 'I'm sorry.'

'No,' Philopoemen said. 'I fear to become that man. I'd just as soon my friends were watching me.'

As soon as the lead squadrons were formed they moved forward. The Thracians and the Tarantine mercenaries were in front, and Philopoemen took them straight down the road, leaving Alexanor to bring the federal cavalry as they formed.

'Wait for the Cretans,' he said. 'Don't leave Telemnastos alone on the plain or we'll lose them all.'

'What's our plan?'

'Find out what's happening, then do our best.' Philopoemen curbed his charger, but the horse had caught his eagerness to go forward. 'I'll send messages.'

'See you do!' Alexanor called, and his friend was gone.

The dust of Philopoemen's wing was still hanging in the air and Alexanor's anxiety began to peak.

He bit down on it. To Lycurgos he said, 'Here we go again.'

'Sir?'

'I'm going to lose touch with Philopoemen and then we'll have to make things up.' He shook his head.

The Argosian cavalry, once the worst in the League, was now formed in four neat ranks; perhaps passing under the walls of their own homes had put them on their mettle. Behind them, the squadrons from Epidauros and Corinth and Hermione formed.

'Ride back to the men of Hermione,' Alexanor ordered Lycurgos. 'Tell them that if Aristides were here he'd be yelling himself silly. And then stay with them until they are formed. You are my reserve. Stay on the road and follow me.'

Lycurgos' face registered the fear of failure that Alexanor felt, and hoped he was not radiating to all about him.

'Bring the banner,' he called to Dariush. 'Sound the advance.'

His *hyperetes* raised his bronze trumpet.

He had perhaps seven hundred cavalrymen under his hand and another two hundred coming up behind. He missed Aristides. He called for Nestor. The young man was too young for complexity; Alexanor looked along the ranks. Kritias was too hot-headed ...

'Theodoros!' he called.

Theodoros was not the army's finest trooper. He lacked some sort of passion – or perhaps he was too intelligent to both curry his horse perfectly and polish all his armour. He was never awarded a prize as the best man in his cavalry troop.

Nonetheless ...

'Take command of the *epilektoi*,' he ordered.

'Yes, sir.' Theodoros seemed unsurprised; was that a good sign?

The ground to the right was steep and rocky – the last of the mountains. To the left, the plains of Tegea opened.

'Cover my right – stay in touch.'

He rode back to Telemnastos. The Cretans had kept up easily while the cavalry walked their horses, but now ...

'I need two hundred of your best,' he said.

Telemnastos smiled. 'I remember when you were just a priest.'

Alexanor smiled. 'I remember when you were just a green boy. If you give me two hundred men, I'll put them up behind my Epidaurans and maybe—'

'Done,' Telemnastos said.

They mounted double on the horses of the Epidaurans and some

279

Corinthians, and Alexanor thanked Poseidon that Philopoemen had ordered them to walk so much. The horses weren't fresh, but they weren't jaded, and the column of squadrons moved off at a fast walk with the young *epilektoi* off to the south.

They hadn't gone three stades when Dadas rode up.

'It's a mess,' he said. 'One of the flanks has already collapsed. The *Hipparchos* says to come forward, moving to the left. Look, I'll lead you.'

They rode up what appeared to be a low hill. But that was a trick of the ground, and as Alexanor crested the hill, he realised that he was at the top of a long, low ridge running from north to south. The battle was laid out below him as if it was a play in the great theatre of Epidauros.

And the play was a tragedy.

He was perhaps three stades behind the Achaean position; the Achaean phalanx took up most of the battle line, twelve thousand men packed into a thousand paces of frontage. They were being pushed steadily back by the red-cloaked Spartans and their mercenaries – indeed, on the far flank, the right, the phalanx was breaking up like an old wicker basket that's been dropped too many times.

Alexanor looked at the ground. Halfway down the ridge was a farm with an olive grove and a rocky stream bed running through what appeared to be a gully; he had to guess that there might be a gully from the visible weeds and cypress trees.

He turned to Andronicos, the commander of his Corinthians.

'Take all the double-mounted men, and put the Cretans into those woods. And the gully. See it?'

'Yes, sir.'

'Go,' Alexanor said.

He motioned to the Epidaurans and they moved forward. He could see the Hermione contingent a stade behind, and the dust of the marching Cretans.

Before he had reached the farmstead, horsemen appeared – first a few, and then a dozen.

They were the federal cavalry of the central plains.

'Halt!' he called, but they rode on, the men as panicked as their horses. He stole a glance off to the right. He was pretty certain that he could see Philopoemen on the main road, which was choked with fleeing men.

'Let them go,' he told his cavalry.

Xartes quivered with excitement. Dariush sat patiently, his small blue standard hanging like an icon from its crossbar. The day was windless and hot, and Alexanor was covered in sweat, but Pegasus was still fresh.

'Watch your order,' snapped Lycurgos behind him.

Another stade. Suddenly a hundred cavalrymen, all together, galloping flat out – and leading them, Aristaenos.

'About time!' he called. He reined in. Most of his troopers rode on. 'Follow me!'

Alexanor pointed to the farmstead. 'Stay with our plan, gentlemen,' he said to his officers.

Aristaenos rode over, his horse covered in lather.

'Now!' he called. 'I need all of you to—'

Alexanor rode up close. 'Talk to me. Don't give orders to my troops.'

'If you'd come earlier none of this would have happened!' Aristaenos said. 'We can't face the Spartans!'

Alexanor's captains continued to move forward.

'Perhaps with this many cavalry I can.'

The Epidaurans and the Corinthians were halted, shedding their second riders. The Cretans ran into the trees and broken ground, more like a swarm than like drilled soldiers, and vanished except for the occasional sparkle of bronze or steel.

'Form a line!' Alexanor called.

'No!' Aristaenos said. 'Form a rhomboid and—'

'You are not in command here,' Alexanor said. 'There is Philopoemen. Go to him and ask for orders.'

'You are a priest playing soldier,' Aristaenos said. 'I am your officer and but for a political error I'd be the fucking *Hipparchos*. Philopoemen will do whatever he thinks is best for Philopoemen. We can still win this battle and you *will* obey me.'

Alexanor made no answer. He simply pointed with his heavy spear at the centre of the phalanx giving way. It was like watching a huge wave break over a wall of sand. A hundred farmers died as they turned to run, the Spartans butchering the fleeing men. Alexanor could see the spears rise and fall as the rear ranks killed the wounded men lying on the ground.

He ignored the emptiness, the hollow of his gut, and he ignored Aristaenos as well. He was in a race with the collapse of the phalanx and he watched his two squadrons form four-deep behind the abandoned farm. To his right front, the rear ranks of the phalanx were running. More immediately, the mercenary cavalry serving the Spartans was riding easily over the barley fields, sweeping wide of the wreck of the Achaean phalanx to fall on the routers like wolves on fleeing sheep.

'Steady!' Alexanor called. The anxiety was gone.

'Listen to me!' Aristaenos called.

Alexanor used his horse to cut the other man off. He felt the rumble of hooves to his right and saw Philopoemen charge at the head of the Tarentines. Alexanor understood that they were committed to save the phalanx if any of them could be saved. He could see it in his head – and he knew what his role had to be.

'Silence, now,' he said.

'I will arrest every one of you and haul you before the Assembly on charges of treason,' Aristaenos said.

Lycurgos looked at Alexanor, and then pursed his lips and looked away.

'Steady,' he said to his troopers.

Antigonos pretended not to hear.

Alexanor turned to Aristaenos. 'You might collect your men. We could use them.'

'Fuck you!' Aristaenos said, his rage boiling over.

His anger calmed Alexanor. It was difficult to explain, but it was as if all his decisions were made and he knew exactly what he was up against. He looked back at Telemnastos, and then at the sun, and then at the hills behind him.

Telemnastos was just a stade behind him, and his men were sprinting into a loose skirmish line as they came. They were very visible – a long line of infantrymen without big shields and apparently without supporting cavalry.

With a whoop, the enemy mercenary cavalry turned to overrun the skirmishers they could now see beyond the farm. Because of the ground and Alexanor's cunning and some luck with dust, they couldn't see Alexanor's cavalry behind the farm and they'd missed the Cretans in the gully and olive grove.

Alexanor never drew his sword or wetted his spear. But the

mercenaries came on, took a volley of powerful arrows from the two hundred Cretans in the olive grove, veered suddenly to the north and the Argosians charged into their disordered flank and wrecked them.

Then the much-reviled Argosians lost their collective wits and pursued the broken mercenaries back towards the Spartan lines. Alexanor watched, too far away to stop them, and wanted to cry.

Instead he turned to Dadas. 'I beg you, run them down and stop them.'

'I'll try!' Dadas said cheerfully, and he was off like an equine arrow.

'No!' Aristaenos roared. 'Follow me! We'll—'

Alexanor reached out with his spear and tipped Aristaenos onto the ground.

'Hold your ground!' he roared at his Epidaurans.

They didn't look disposed to follow Aristaenos anywhere.

The first infantry began to pass Alexanor's position. They were rear-rankers, unarmoured men who could run well, free of greaves or maille or bronze; also the first to die in close fighting, and often the poorest farmers.

Alexanor stopped them by the simple expedient of moving the Epidaurans into their path. He ordered Lycurgos to collect them and give them water and he moved to the right, where he asked Telemnastos to take command of the farm and its yard and orchard.

His front was stable, at least for the moment.

'I'm going to Philopoemen,' he said. 'Telemnastos, you are in command.'

'Sure.' The Cretan mounted his horse and looked off to the west. 'Cavalry coming.'

'No amount of Spartan cavalry can make it past this farm unless they go way out to the south to get around you.'

'Agreed.'

'Keep your retreat open. I'll be back in a minute.'

Telemnastos saluted.

Alexanor rode north, along the slope of the low ridge, and his horse leapt a stone wall and flowed along with it, his whole attention on the wave front of broken men coming at them. He slipped into a swirl of rallying cavalrymen – like a training day, except for the number of wounded men still in the saddle. He realised he was looking at Kleander and the men of the Agema.

'Philopoemen!' he called.

'Here!' roared the Titan.

He pushed through the haze, and reined in. Philopoemen was covered in dust, his right arm was bloody to the elbow, and the spear ...

'You held the left. I saw it.'

'What now?' Alexanor asked.

'Now the hard part. We need to break off and slap them in the face so they don't pursue us.' Philopoemen tossed his lance to Wewa, who began to wipe it down. 'Let them attack you – as soon as you stop them, attack. Then break off and get clear. That's all I can say.'

His attention was entirely on the Agema.

'I need to know which way you intend to retreat.'

Philopoemen turned; he had a slight smile on his face, and a kind of resolution that Alexanor never felt. The smile was genuine, as if he was enjoying their conversation.

'Back up the Argive road,' Philopoemen said. 'I have to get this done. I'll follow you.'

'Got it!' Alexanor shouted.

'One more time!' Philopoemen roared. 'Every heartbeat you rest your horse, ten more farmers die. Are you ready?'

'What do I do with Aristaenos?' Alexanor called.

Philopoemen ignored him as the Agema began to cheer.

Alexanor rode clear and then dashed south, ignoring the desperate men his horse had to dodge. Now the survivors of the front ranks were coming, and intermixed with them, their pursuers: some of the Spartiates, but mostly professionals – *sarissa*-armed Greek and Macedonian mercenaries. Off to his left he could see well-armed *thorakatoi*. Alexanor thought, *Machanandas must have spent gold like a drunk man in a wine shop.*

Roman gold. Aegyptian gold. Alexanor shook his head; none of that mattered for the moment.

He galloped up to Telemnastos. Pegasus was the best horse he'd ever had – calm, yet full of spirit – and now his head was up, his nostrils drinking in air, the very spirit of a horse.

Alexanor pointed at the Argive road. 'We're retreating the way we came,' he said.

He watched Philopoemen's charge. He went into the flank of the pursuing Spartiates. Ordinarily, pike-armed infantry were immune to the best efforts of cavalry, but the pursuers had lost their order and they were too busy killing the fleeing Achaeans to see the threat.

But Philopoemen lacked the numbers and the energy to affect the outcome of the battle. The Agema had lost dozens – if not hundreds – of men, and their horses were blown, and the 'charge' was made on jaded horses. Beyond Philopoemen, a rising pillar of dust was gilded by the sun and marked where Alexios' Tarantines were buying Philopoemen time. Immediately in front of Alexanor, he could see the man himself, his arm like the thunderbolt of Zeus.

He went deeper and deeper into the ranks of the Spartiates. Alexanor could see Simmias close by him, and Polyainos, a horse-length behind. But it was Philopoemen who blazed like the sun, and seemed to cut a road.

Alexanor closed his eyes. *Blessed Apollo, do not let him die today.*

A handful of tired men followed him into the bloody lane they'd carved. Far behind him, the remains of the Agema struggled to urge their desperate horses forward, to match their commander.

'Lycurgos,' Alexanor said. He thought of giving the order.

And then he thought, *Apollo, I offer myself. Asklepios, let me save my friend.*

'On me!' he roared. 'Men of Epidauros! Achilles needs his Myrmidons!'

Lycurgos smiled.

'Telemnastos! Hold here!' He leant over. 'Ignore Aristaenos. Cover the phalanx. If I fall, cover the phalanx.'

'Yes, Alexanor.'

Alexanor raised his spear. 'Half wheel to the right!'

The Epidaurans moved crisply, faces set. He knew every one of them: his friends and neighbours; men he liked to drink wine with; men he wouldn't trust with an investment.

None of that mattered now.

'Rhomboid!' he called.

He'd done this before – but he'd never been the apex, the point of the spear of men and horses. He had Xartes at his left shoulder and Dariush at his right.

'March!' he ordered.

The *taxeis* started forward.

Philopoemen was still up; that invincible arm rose and fell. He was turning his horse, which was trampling the *peltastoi* who were all around him.

Fifty paces.

A hundred paces.

'Ready!' he called.

Unbidden, Pegasus began to trot; he had leant forward. The whole formation sped up.

Fleeing men turned. Forty feet away, a Spartiate set himself, ready to fight, but a mercenary threw down his shield and ran.

He held up his spear. *Apollo, I offer myself.*

*Aspasia, I am sorry.*

The wedge of Epidaurans shook the earth.

And then, like the bow of a ship parting the waves, the enemy split. The one lone Spartiate stood his ground and vanished, his corpse pounded into the dry earth by a hundred horses. But for the rest, there was no fight. The pursuers became the pursued; the victorious Spartans turned from their prey and ran, and were cut down in turn. A swirl of fighting to his left...

'*Halt!*' roared Philopoemen.

As obedient as if they were drilling in the fields below the temple, the Epidaurans reined in. They were no longer an oblong, but rather a mass – but they were together.

And Alexanor was unhurt – unsacrificed. He felt odd ...

He'd been so certain.

'Are you hit?' Philopoemen flashed a grin. 'That was brilliant. Let's get the hell out of here.'

Alexanor blinked. But his senses were returning. For a moment ...

He blinked again. 'Send the Agema first,' he said. 'They're exhausted. The Corinthians are still fresh.'

It was a fine plan, but the Spartans showed no interest in pursuit. Alexanor's care was wasted on a hot afternoon and the reaction that set in the moment they had broken clear.

By the time Philopoemen judged them safe, they were halfway up the pass. It was then that Alexanor realized that Kritias was gone. He looked for the young man, but other Epidaurans thought he'd taken a wound in the fighting with the Spartiates.

A litter of exhausted men lay where they had fallen, or sat, their heads in their hands, or nursed small wounds, and too many had deeper cuts or worse. The heaviness of defeat and loss lay over them all like a miasma.

Alexanor abandoned his search for Kritias and gave his horse to Dariush. At some point he'd stripped his helmet and his armour. His fine *chiton*, embroidered by Aspasia, was sweat-soaked and added blood and other bodily fluids as he went to work on the wounded like a man enduring a penalty for crime. The army had other doctors, but none so well trained.

He was aware, dully, that Lycurgos and Theodoros were still mounted; Antigonos, now a phylarch, had dismounted to help him. He was also aware that the Corinthians, who had not fought, were the only rearguard that the survivors had. He was aware that Kritias must be dead. He ignored all that to concentrate on being a doctor.

He was trying to decide if he should remove a wounded soldier's helmet, the blood and the crushed bronze making him wonder if the man had any chance of survival. He was too tired to make a good decision, and he kept wiping at the neck-guard with a canteen-damped cloth, trying to imagine what the flow of blood meant.

The man's eyes were open. 'Am I dead?' he asked.

Alexanor forced a smile. 'Not a bit of it.'

The man was lying by the road.

'Did you walk here?'

Alexanor held out the pad of damp, bloody cloth to Dariush, but the young man wasn't there. Philopoemen was.

He took the pad. 'I need to talk to you.'

'I need to get this done,' Alexanor asked.

'I walked most of the way,' the man said. 'Then a mate helped me.'

Alexanor put a hand under the man's neck and massaged the muscle. His neck didn't seem damaged. Alexanor had seldom felt so helpless.

'What hit you?' Alexanor asked.

'Fucked if I know,' the man said. 'I was blind for a little.'

*Apollo. Blessed Apollo, lord of healers. Asklepios, god of medicine. I want to save this one.*

*I want to save them all.*

*I will never hold a sword again. I swear it. Help me save this one.*

'What do you want me to do?' Philopoemen asked.

'I need to get the helmet off his head,' Alexanor said.

Philopoemen reached one of his big hands towards the helmet.

'His head is injured. I can't afford to dislodge bone ...' Alexanor said.

Philopoemen nodded. 'Hold his shoulders.'

Alexanor started to stop his friend, but Philopoemen said, 'My hands are very strong.'

He took hold of the cheek plates and folded them back. And then he bent the metal at the temples with his bare hands, peeling the helmet back from the wound as if it was made of leather.

'What's your name?' Alexanor asked the man.

'Gods! Hermes! Fuck!' The man's eyes unfocused. 'Apollion.'

That was like a bolt of lightning. *Apollion: man of Apollo.*

'Well, Apollion, you may be the only wounded man in the army to have the *Hipparchos* as a doctor.'

Alexanor could hear the falseness in his tone, and he expected to see the sudden burst of bright brain-blood that would kill the man, but Philopoemen continued to peel the bronze back until he reached the crushed section.

For a moment, Alexanor thought he was looking at the wounded man's brain. Then he realised that the straw liner was soaked with blood and hair.

'Sharpest,' he said.

Dariush put a flint knife in his hand. He cut, and the volcanic stone went through the bloody mess and it fell away.

The head under it was whole; there was a massive contusion, but ...

'Oh, gods,' the man moaned. His eyes fluttered.

Alexanor put a hand under his head.

'Can I talk to you now?' Philopoemen said.

Alexanor nodded. 'Water, here.'

Dariush leant over and, at a motion, poured canteen water over the wound. Alexanor reached out a hand and Dariush put another pad of linen into it. Alexanor wiped at the wound.

'Honey,' he said. He smeared some on. 'Now,' he said to his friend.

'We have a problem,' Philopoemen said.

Alexanor took a deep breath. 'I am no longer a soldier.'

Philopoemen nodded, as if he'd expected this. 'This is not just a military problem,' he said. 'Listen, and advise me. *There is no water in this pass.* And in the morning, Machanandas will recover his wits and come after us. Can these men make it across the pass to Argos? I ask you as a priest of Asklepios.'

'Many of the wounded will die,' Alexanor said.

'And those who are merely exhausted?'

Alexanor closed his eyes. 'It is only forty stades.' He made a face.

'If I let them stop, I think many will never rise again, and once night falls ...'

Alexanor nodded. 'All the choices are bad for men like this. Is there no other way?'

'Yes, there's another choice. All choices have risk.' Philopoemen looked at the sun; the shadows were already long. 'Nikeas died in the front rank. Kykliadas is badly wounded and needs you. Cercidas is dead. The Agema ...'

Philopoemen's voice cracked. Alexanor put out a hand. Philopoemen went on, his voice back to normal.

'The next day will decide everything.' He turned to his own escort. 'I want this man to survive,' he said. 'Make a litter and take him to Argos.'

Kleander, who looked like an old man, nodded. 'Yes, *Hipparchos.*'

'Someone get me Kleostratos,' he said.

Alexanor hesitated. 'Where's Dinaeos?'

'Dead or taken,' Philopoemen said.

'Gods!' Alexanor said.

It was Kau-Ippa who rode up. She was on a small pony, and she didn't dismount.

'How far down the pass do my stragglers go?' Philopoemen asked her.

She frowned. 'Many, and then many,' she admitted. 'All the way.'

'Hundreds?' Philopoemen asked.

'At least hundreds.'

He shook his head.

'Right.'

In the morning, the Spartan advance guard found the pass held by Cretans, where the stone-built farm with its stades of stone walls filled the saddle. The Cretans were on the hillsides and a strongly posted cavalry force waited in the saddle of the pass behind the house. The first *peltastoi* to test the hillsides were shot at and then chased off by cavalry who didn't seem to know that steep hills were no place for horses.

Machanandas deployed his whole army into the saddle, and made his phalanx double depth. This took time, and it was clear that even the elite Spartiates were tired. His cavalry was hesitant to engage. When Alexanor emerged from an amputation to breathe clean air, he could see the Spartan tyrant himself, and see his anger as he turned his golden horse and roared at his timid cavalry. He was only a few hundred paces away.

Alexanor was too tired to care. He went back to his god's work.

The Thracians, Scythians and Epidaurans were all on fresh horses. And each time Machanandas attempted to push into the position, Philopoemen showed the Tarentines, waiting with their horses, and the Cretans would close in on the flanks of the enemy advance, and catch the Spartans and their mercenaries in a murderous crossfire.

Machanandas would try to get higher on the hillsides than the Cretans, but by early afternoon, it was clear that his *psiloi* were simply unwilling to take any casualties. And because the Cretans were higher on the hillside, they held the key.

Machanandas was seen to lose his temper, and he cut down one of the men who led his skirmishers, killing him with his own spear.

Alexanor had seen the worst of the wounded in the farmhouse and the outbuildings. He'd been awake for two days, and he was running on training and will. Several times he saw Kritias working with him, and he knew the boy was dead, but the image of Kritias kneeling by men, washing wounds ...

He kept being there.

He wasn't the only dead man present – merely the most persistent.

Wewa worked with him, and Dariush, and Antigonos the horse farmer, blond hair black with sweat and other men's blood, and ten other men besides. And they saved a few, but mostly they watched men die as the sun climbed higher.

Finally, in early afternoon, Alexanor went outside the house for a second time. The place smelled of blood and excrement and death, and he stood in the sun, watching the birds of prey circling. They weren't omens today – merely carrion birds waiting for his dead.

Philopoemen was sitting on his charger, perhaps fifty paces away, watching the ground below the house, to the west. Alexanor walked over to him like a moth drawn to the flame of a lamp. As he walked up, there was a murmur from the Tarentines by the house. Philopoemen glanced at Alexanor.

'Now or never,' he said softly.

Alexanor looked down. There was the Spartan phalanx, which appeared to fill the pass from side to side. They were two stades away, but in the clear mountain air it appeared that Alexanor could reach out and touch them.

'Now or never?' he asked.

He didn't care much, but it seemed good to talk to another human being.

'Machanandas has just killed one of his own officers,' Philopoemen said. 'Now he either orders a general assault up the valley, or he doesn't.'

'Can we hold?'

'No,' Philopoemen said.

What the Spartans could not see was the chaos behind the stone house. All night tired cavalrymen had laboured to bring water from the other end of the valley, and where, from the dawn, the surviving leadership of the Federation had cajoled, begged and forced the survivors of the defeat to rise from the cold ground and make their way down the pass towards the safety of the walls of Argos. The whole pass was choked with the remnant of the phalanx, and there was nothing that could make them move any faster. Nor could any of the fresh cavalry make their way to the rearguard.

'I'm out of troops,' Philopoemen said wearily. 'And Telemnastos is out of arrows.'

'I could challenge someone to single combat?' Kleander asked.

Philopoemen nodded. 'You …'

Whatever he was going to say was lost.

The enemy *peltastoi* began to fan out across the pass.

But the phalanx began to retire.

# BOOK TWO

# STRATEGOS

# CHAPTER ONE

—⟨ℴℴ⟩—

## Argos, Megalopolis and the Olympic Games

HOMOLOIOS TO PANAMOS (JUNE TO SEPTEMBER),
208 BCE

In the night, Philopoemen abandoned the defence of the pass and retreated to Argos to rebuild his shattered army. He did it under a thunderstorm of protests from Aristaenos, who berated him for abandoning a defensible position and exposing the Achaean heartland on the plain of Argos to the Spartans.

Philopoemen only engaged with Aristaenos once. He was organising the movement of the wounded with Alexanor, and so Alexanor heard all the pettiness, and all the insults, employed.

'If you retreat, your career is over. I will see to it that the *Boule* never offers you another command!' Aristaenos spat. 'Are you a coward? This position is impregnable!'

Philopoemen offered neither frown nor smile. He merely turned his head.

'Water. Arrows,' he said. 'Alexanor, I have found twenty-four carts, or rather, Kleander has.'

'Make arrows!' Aristaenos shouted. 'Send the Cretans out to collect them!'

Alexanor was facing the gut-wrenching decision about who he'd take and who he'd abandon. The men left would almost certainly be killed by the Spartans, and for some of them, that would only be a mercy.

'Ask for a truce then!' Aristaenos said.

Philopoemen finally snapped. He turned, his eyes afire, and he seemed to grow.

'You ask for a truce,' he said. 'You forced a battle with a superior force, and you *lost*.'

'Oh, very nice. You abandoned us, left us to die …'

Philopoemen looked at Aristaenos with something very like hate. 'If you take these lies to the Assembly, you could kill the League. You cannot possibly believe these things.'

'I'm not losing my career for your comfort. Always the great Philopoemen, always the calm, godlike leader. Where were you?'

Alexanor stepped between them. The moment he did, Philopoemen turned away, the light in his eyes fading. Aristaenos opened his mouth to speak and Alexanor seized his arm with his blood-sticky hands.

'We were where you and Nikeas sent us,' Alexanor hissed. 'In the north, facing the Romans. Now get out of my hospital before I make you a patient.'

Perhaps he seemed insane. Or perhaps, covered in the blood of the wounded, standing among them, wild from three sleepless days, he carried more authority even than Philopoemen.

Aristaenos turned, and left.

Just forty stades to Argos – but they lost another hundred men. Some of them had seemed to be recovering, and some, it appeared, simply lay down and died.

The men they lost were not mercenary infantry. They were Achaean citizens: fishermen from Hermione, or leather-workers from Argos, or Corinthian shipwrights, or Dymian farmers.

It was better in Argos: better because the citizenry rallied to the army, and better because food and water were the best medicine Alexanor had ever found. Dozens of his wounded, the ones free of Apollo's arrows of infection, began to recover the moment they'd had twenty hours of sleep and two meals.

Alexanor slept through an entire day and night. And he rose to find his messages and prayers answered, and ten priests from Epidauros present with a dozen servitors and slaves, led by the aristocratic Erenida. And Apollion was still alive.

Alexanor went to the precinct of the Temple of Apollo Lykeios, the wolf god. The wounded were being cared for on the temple grounds, where there was a fine spring and a beautiful grove.

Out on the plain below the city, the Spartan army began to burn the farms on the plain. They also moved detachments to cover the city's roads, opening the siege. Machanandas sent a herald, and after an exchange, he came himself to the western gate of the city.

He was tall, although not as tall as Philopoemen. He rode a magnificent golden bay horse, and he had a leopard skin as a saddlecloth.

Philopoemen mounted his own grey charger and rode down under the ancient gate, and Alexanor rode at his side, unarmoured, wearing the white robes of a priest of Apollo.

He thought that he was used to the language of diplomacy; he was unprepared for what he heard.

'Ah, *Hipparchos*. What a pest you are, and what a pity you are still alive to watch the end of your League.' The Spartan was jocular – even vulgar. 'If you'd arrived an hour later the other day, we wouldn't have to waste time on sieges. Just surrender, there's a good boy. The longer you wait, the worse it will be.'

Philopoemen nodded gravely. 'This is not the usual language of gentlemen.'

'Fuck off!' the Spartan spat. 'I don't have time for all that. I'm making a new Sparta, and we'll be rid of all that time-wasting, old-fashioned crap. Now bend the knee and get it done.'

Philopoemen managed a half smile. 'You are so very persuasive.'

'Do I have to lay this out for you?' Machanandas asked. 'Everyone wants a piece of the League, now that I've put a sword in its guts. If you surrender to me, I'll do my best to protect your little people from the Aetolians and the Romans.'

'You, the Tyrant of Sparta, would just take the whole of Achaea?'

'It's all Greater Sparta, laddie. All these towns owe their allegiance to us. Always have.'

Memnon, the *Hipparchos* of Argos, shook his head vehemently.

'Argos has never owed *shit* to Sparta.'

'I hear a dog yapping,' Machanandas said. 'Look, feel free. Stay here and hold out. The Romans will rape their way through the north and I'll loot every house in the east. I hear the treasury of Epidauros is full, which will be so helpful, because my own is empty.' He smiled. 'I'll give you a day or two.'

Philopoemen nodded.

The Spartan nodded back. 'You, at least, I'd think would know how *thorough* my burning will be,' he said, with a nasty imitation of a smile.

Philopoemen was looking at the tyrant's escort. He went white at the tip of his nose, a sign Alexanor had seen before, but his voice was inhumanly calm.

'Is that Nabis you have there?' He turned back to Machanandas. 'Perhaps you should ask him what happens now.'

'Now?'

Philopoemen nodded. 'We have heard your threats.'

'What do you mean "now"?' Machanandas asked.

Philopoemen smiled at Nabis. 'You'll see. I don't like threats. I will utter none. Let us see what the next few days bring, shall we?' He backed his horse. 'I will ask, formally, if you have prisoners to exchange.'

'I have nothing but slaves,' Machanandas said. 'Some new helots that fell into my hands.'

Philopoemen nodded. 'Well, then. You are dismissed.'

'Dismissed?' the Spartan spat. 'I summoned you to this parley and I'll decide—'

Philopoemen held up his hand. 'You are standing where my Cretans can hit you, and you have no archers of your own, and I say, Tyrant, you are dismissed.'

'You are a dead man,' the tyrant swore.

'Run away, little man,' Philopoemen said. 'Or stay and die, and see how long your little state lasts in the squabble over your corpse.'

'You fucking bastard!' Machanandas said. 'I'm glad I killed your wife.'

He turned his horse and clattered away down the road, his escort closing in behind him. Alexanor was surprised to find that Philopoemen, who had seemed so calm, was shaking.

'I hate him so much,' the hero admitted.

'He's very easy to hate,' Alexanor agreed. 'By contrast, Nabis is almost human.'

'I was thinking the same thing. I was wondering how a man like

Nabis – a Spartiate, a man of honour, despite his ... How Nabis tolerates that ...'

Alexanor took a cup of wine from Wewa and handed it to him.

'I've sworn off for the duration of the contest,' Philopoemen said.

'What?'

'I'm afraid that if I start, I'll never stop.'

'Gods,' Alexanor said. 'And all your tough talk ...?'

'Real enough, brother. Look around. Do you see Kleander? Or Kleostratos? Or Kau-Ippa?'

Alexanor had had one day of sleep in five and he blinked.

Philopoemen pointed out over the plain. 'All our cavalry is out there. And I suspect that the Spartans are about to find the Argive Plain a very, very difficult place.'

That night, Alexanor was called away from his wounded by Wewa.

He went to the walls and looked out.

The Spartan camp to the east was afire.

Philopoemen was farther along the wall, watching, and he walked along the wall to his friend.

'Kau-Ippa,' Philopoemen said. 'The best light-cavalry officer I've ever met. I told her there were no longer any rules.'

Alexanor looked at his friend. 'That's not like you.'

'We are down to the last coins, the last throw.' Philopoemen glanced at Alexanor, his face cast in firelight. 'When he withdraws, I will pursue. Will you come?'

'I will never bear a sword again,' Alexanor said. 'I have sworn.'

Philopoemen looked out at the fires. 'The man we saved ...'

'Apollion?'

'How is he?'

'Alive. Recovering rapidly by the altar of his god.'

Philopoemen nodded. 'Call me superstitious, but that man is Achaea.'

Alexanor nodded. 'I would come to help the wounded, or give counsel. But I will neither command nor fight.'

'I accept,' Philopoemen said.

Over the next days, as the wounded recovered or died, and Alexanor got to know the citadel of Argos, and the priests of the sanctuary, a terrible kind of war was waged on the plains below them. Any Achaean cavalryman taken was tortured and his broken body displayed in front of the Spartan camp. But Kau-Ippa was both cruel and inventive. She sent men back alive: blinded or emasculated or both; hamstrung in just one leg; or with a hand cut away.

The effect on the Spartan's mercenaries was immediate; before two days were out, their entire hired body of *peltastoi* marched away. They had been doing the foraging and skirmishing, and now they simply melted away.

In the meantime, Philopoemen was drilling what remained of the Achaean phalanx in the citadel.

After a week, Machanandas had to march away. His force was penned inside its fortified camp, and even foraging for food was hard, and a plague was ravaging his men. The priests of Apollo were both fearful and delighted.

Philopoemen collected the Cretans, left a hundred to bolster the garrison, and then marched out with a thousand Achaean hoplites, rearmed as *peltastoi* in light armour, with small shields and javelins. Most of them had thrown away their *thureophoroi* shields to run faster, and their spears, so the *peltastoi* equipment was an inspiration born of desperation.

Alexanor rode with the baggage. He wore only his robes, and he had with him four other priests of Apollo and a dozen servants. He kept his personal escort, however, and Dariush wore his armour.

Alexanor missed command – he couldn't hide it from himself – and he watched Kleander and Theodoros and Lycurgos and Antigonos struggle with details and tried not to interfere. Men came to him with questions, and he often knew the answers.

He maintained a pleasant reserve as best he could.

Philopoemen collected his cavalry under the walls and then followed the Spartans towards Kiveri with the Thracians, who killed every enemy straggler. The Spartans retreated along the same road that both the Achaeans and Spartans had used: south along the beach to Kiveri, then over the long pass to Achladakampos and so to Tegea on the central plains.

Kau-Ippa stayed on the Spartans, and she had a Cretan archer up behind every rider and a hundred spare horses.

Philopoemen doubled back to the north, marching on the main

road to Skinon and then into the mountains towards Lykeios, the 'Wolf Town' of the hills, where there was a pilgrimage shrine to Apollo the wolf. The trip through the mountains was longer, but there was forage all the way and a better road and they moved at a dizzying speed, and the former hoplites seemed willing to run all the way. Alexanor got to know them in camps; they were mostly young, and fit, and as the army moved they got fitter. A few fell by the side of the track, but the rest were leaner and faster every day.

'You can't hope to fight the Spartans?' Alexanor asked. 'Not even with a thousand revenge-mad, athletic *epheboi.*'

'Oh, no,' Philopoemen said. 'But Machanandas has made a mistake and I'm going to make him pay. With a little luck. Get any sleep you can. This isn't going to be fun.'

They rose in darkness and the moon was still shining when they marched onto the central plain; twisted ankles and broken toes were the result of passing down the mountains in the dark. But now they came down on Tegea from the north, and the stars winked at their rapid progress over the plains. They had won the race, and they were at Tegea before Machanandas.

It almost killed Alexanor to watch, to be a spectator, as Philopoemen made his final arrangements. And Alexanor stayed back, so that he would not have to watch from the ditch under the ramparts.

But an hour later, as the sun rose above the mountains towards Epidauros, Kleander rode back.

'We did it!' he shouted, and the whole army cheered.

Alexanor began to breathe again.

What they had done was to retake Tegea in a single assault, with the gate opened by citizens. No one in Tegea had any love for the Spartans, and Machanandas hadn't left enough garrison to cow them.

'What could be better than an arrogant opponent?' Philopoemen asked the gods.

That afternoon, the Spartan army discovered that their supply depot had fallen to the enemy and that the plains of Tegea were as perilous as the plains of Argos.

Machanandas hesitated for a day, contemplating an assault on Tegea, but Philopoemen had put the thousand *peltastoi* inside with half his Cretans. He drew his cavalry up under the walls and taunted the Spartans to come forward.

That night, Kau-Ippa scooped most of the horse herd of the enemy mercenary cavalry.

In the morning, the Spartans retreated south. They entered the mountains thirty stades south of Tegea, in the very same ground that last year's campaign had covered, and Telemnastos pursued them for a day while the cavalry rested.

'And now?' Alexanor asked.

'There are only three valleys that lead from Sparta into the Federation,' Philopoemen said. 'And we took his entire supply convoy and his logistics base. He has to go all the way back to Sparta, or starve. Even as it is, he'll lose men and animals.'

'The ones we haven't already taken,' Kau-Ippa said. She smiled, and her teeth, many filed to points, glinted.

Kleostratos grinned proudly. 'We have never owned so many horses.'

'And oxen,' she reminded him.

Alexanor shook his head. 'And that's it? War over?'

Philopoemen was looking west, to the battlefield of a week ago. Most of the Achaeans and even the Tarentines were burying the dead. Philopoemen had not ordered it. He'd asked them to bury the dead, and endure the stink and the horror, and they had gone, despite marching all night.

'To remember,' he had said.

Now he watched them working.

'War is more like a craft than an art,' he said. 'It requires practice, and attention to detail – technique and patience.'

Kau-Ippa nodded.

'Most men have no patience,' she said.

'Exactly. Nikeas, for political reasons, fought and lost an unnecessary battle, because he didn't understand what makes war work.'

'Money?'

'Food and water. And certainly, money. And camp security, and health, and luck, and ten thousand details. But first and foremost, food, forage and water for man and beast.' Philopoemen was still watching his burial parties. 'I think I will go and bury the dead,' he said suddenly.

Alexanor nodded. 'That much I will share, and willingly.'

And so it was that he found Kritias. He was under a pile of Achaean dead – mostly the wreckage of the Agema, where they had fought desperately to penetrate the Spartan phalanx, hopelessly trying to do the impossible. Kritias' body was bloated with the gas of decomposition and his jaw had been ripped off his face by the pike-blow that brought him down. Alexanor, from a great emotional distance, was almost happy to see a second pike thrust through the young man's neck. He hadn't lain here for two days without a jaw, dying. He'd been killed in the full heat of youth. If that was better. And Alexanor thought perhaps it was. All Kritias' beauty was gone, robbed by death and replaced with decay and horror, but Alexanor kissed his face anyway, and Kleander came, and Dadas, and then Philopoemen, and the Scythian girl, Kuka.

She made a face, drew her knife, and thrust it in under the dead man's breastplate, so that all the gas in his abdomen came out in a stench. But his distended gut was gone, and she put a helmet on his head that hid his missing jaw, and Kleander, fearless, washed his face.

Dadas threw a handful of barley seeds onto his corpse after they had put it on the pyre to burn.

'Be immortal, hero,' he said. 'Once you were dung to me, but you fell like a man of old. Go fast.'

Kuka threw an arrow on the pyre.

'Hunt well,' she said. 'Find me on the dark plain.'

Dariush produced a handful of myrrh.

'I hated you,' he said simply. 'And then you grew up.'

Alexanor found that he had nothing to say. But when he could control his voice, he raised it, and they sang the *paean*. And the song rose, wild and free, and the priests lit torches.

The torches lit the fires – ten pyres for a hundred other youths of the Agema.

Alexanor sang, and three thousand other voices and the smoke of the burning bodies of the youth of Achaea rose to the heavens like a sacrifice.

And the next morning, the cavalry of the Achaean League started north, to face the Romans.

\*

The *Boule* met. The *tholos* enclosure in the sanctuary was curiously empty, and legalists asked aloud if any finding of the inner council was valid, as fewer than half the members were present – or even alive. The collapse of the Achaean phalanx had not just hurt the army. The polity of the Achaeans was crippled.

Aristaenos was hard at work, rallying support.

Philopoemen left him to it, and marched east to face the Aetolians, who had landed at Dyme for a second time.

Alexanor left Philopoemen. He attended the *Boule*, and set himself to counter Aristaenos. It was a difficult form of war, and it reminded him of his time at Kos – where a smart boy judged the interest and ambition of every other boy before he said anything.

Or like the temples, where men would do almost anything to undercut a rival and promote their careers.

Alexanor had always tried to stay aloof from such manoeuvres, but he knew how they were performed. And he found Aristaenos to be weaker than he had expected – angry, and all too aware of his own position.

Alexanor's role was simple. Each time Aristaenos rose to blacken Philopoemen's reputation, he would rise after. He would point east.

'Where, gentlemen, is Philopoemen now?' he would ask. And into the silence, he would say, 'And where is Aristaenos?'

The first time, it made men think.

Repeated daily, it drove Aristaenos to anger. Eventually he cornered Alexanor in the sanctuary.

'You need to walk softly,' he said. 'When I come to power …'

Alexanor turned to walk away.

'I have friends, and your man has none,' Aristaenos said. 'And I will see to it—'

Alexanor turned. 'Listen, Aristaenos. I have known you since you were a boy. And your capability for self-delusion is amazing. Let me explain a few things—'

'No one talks to me this way.'

'Perhaps the most foolish thing is that you threaten me,' Alexanor went on. 'Right now, the temple contributions to the treasury of the League are the only funds keeping an army in the field. You cannot survive without me, and I have come to represent all the temples.'

Aristaenos shook his head. 'There are many rich men—'

'Certainly, you can create some solution that will allow you to continue to pretend you are master of the situation. Or you can face the reality. You bear the blame for Tegea, and you, and only you, are the problem. And if you try to hurt me, I will see what the power of twenty talents of gold can do to rid Achaea of your meddling.'

'You must be mad.'

'One of us must be,' Alexanor said.

The next day Aristaenos rose and proclaimed that the meeting of the *Boule* was illegal as it did not have enough attendees, and proposed immediate adjournment.

Alexanor rose. 'Gentlemen, we have had a disaster, and we are still on our feet, like a *pankrationist* who takes a heavy blow and does not go down in the dust.' He looked around, and had the feeling that they were, for the most part, with him. 'We are all the government that the League has just now – with the *Hipparchos* as our acting head. I suspect that Achaea needs us now more than ever, and that our dissolving would be seen as a sign of dissolution.'

There was a heavy silence, and Alexanor spoke into it.

'We lost three thousand citizens at Tegea.' He did not need to pretend emotion, and his voice thickened as the base of his throat swelled and his vision blurred. 'We burned their bodies,' he said. 'Are they a sacrifice to the gods for our democracy? Or are their deaths wasted?'

He stood facing them, and they made no sound.

Aristaenos flushed, and then the man rose without a speech and left the assembly.

The motion was not just defeated, but stricken.

The next day, Lykortas returned from Macedon.

'Not Macedon, Elatea,' Lykortas corrected when Alexanor greeted him. 'How bad is it?'

'I think we're past the most desperate hours,' Alexanor said. 'He's very silent these days, but the Aetolians withdrew last week. Unless the Roman fleet returns to the gulf, we should make it through the autumn.'

'Philip is coming,' Lykortas said. 'But don't ask me when.'

'We need to prepare for a very contentious *Synodos*,' Alexanor said.

Lykortas slapped him on the back. 'That's not what I hear. I hear you are the greatest orator since Demosthenes. Are you running for League office?'

'Never.' Alexanor frowned. 'What's at Elatea?'

'Another peace conference. This time the Rhodians and the Athenians led the way, and Philip was, and is, perfectly willing to make peace with both of them. He's undercutting the Romans, mostly because they continue to not send a representative. Phila says that Hannibal just handed the Romans another massive defeat and killed one of their consuls.'

'Will it end the war?'

Lykortas shrugged. The two men were walking on the beach, un-attended; Lykortas' habit of secrecy extended even to not keeping a slave or body servant.

'Phila says no. I wonder how many times this Hannibal can crush their armies and they can rebound.'

'Philopoemen says that their manpower reserves are deep.'

'How many times can anyone lose ten thousand citizens?' Lykortas asked.

Alexanor looked at the *tholos* across the sanctuary. 'For us? Not even once. Three thousand and we're crippled.'

Lykortas nodded. 'Dinaeos?'

'Dead or captured.'

'That's what we heard at the conference.' Lykortas shook his head. 'Philip is angry. Just so you know. The defeat at Tegea … He said, publicly, that Greeks were all useless cowards and they should know better than to try and fight a battle.'

'I'm not surprised,' Alexanor said, but he saw the mangled body of Kritias.

'It was bad?' Lykortas asked, in a more human voice.

'You can't imagine …'

'I'm not sorry I missed it. You all look like you paid a visit to the underworld.'

A week later, the army, which now consisted of nothing but cavalry and Cretans, was camped on the new-cut barley fields of Aegio. No Roman fleet had appeared. Alexanor, whose grasp on geography was better than most, struggled to understand how close Italy really was. The Romans had laid siege to Locri; he'd had a teacher from Locri. It was no farther than Rhodes, perhaps closer, and the rumour was that the Roman fleet had left the Aegean and sailed for Locri.

Philopoemen came and addressed the *Boule*, but he would not take the stone seat of the *Strategos*. Instead he stood, and the *Boule* voted to ask the *Hipparchos* to remain cautious. Memnon, the *Hipparchos* of Argos, actually mentioned the Roman dictator Fabius in his speech, praising the barbarian magnate for his caution and care.

Philopoemen nodded and made no complaint.

'We have only light troops,' he said. 'We cannot make a stand in the field. However, unless the Spartans choose to make another incursion, or the Roman fleet returns, I believe we are safe. I think we must risk putting our little fleet in the water to cover the coast.'

Lykortas sighed. 'So much for the joys of the fleshpots of Corinth.'

The days began to grow shorter, and the possibility that the League would stagger through the finish line of the campaign year became a probability. Most of the citizens praised Hannibal, whose defeat of the Romans near Locri had paralysed the enemy high command; a few praised Philopoemen.

Alexanor wrote letters to his wife and then prepared to go home. Philopoemen had released half of the federal cavalry to see to their affairs. The citizen army was in a crisis even without heavy losses, as men struggled to run their businesses or assure themselves that their farms were being well handled. The cavalry troopers of the League included some of the richest men in the Peloponnese and they clamoured for release.

Philopoemen was rebuilding the Agema; Alexanor knew all about it from a dozen evenings spent listening. But without the volunteers, he would only have the Tarantines, a thousand men under Alexios, and the Cretans, now just eight hundred under Telemnastos. Disease had taken a toll on the Cretans, as had the endless rapid marches.

Philopoemen moved a remnant of the army back to Argos, where Alexanor was going to leave him.

He invited Erinida and another senior priest to dinner the last night they were to be together, with Philopoemen, Lycurgos, Aristides and Alexios, the taciturn Italiote who commanded the Tarantines. Aristides was recently arrived from Hermione with twenty young cavalrymen.

'And your wrist?' Alexanor asked.

Aristides shrugged. He had a heavy leather bracer to support the wrist.

'If I wear this contraption, I can manage the reins most of a day,' he said. 'After I heard of the fight at Tegea, I couldn't stay home.'

Erinida was good company – a true aristocrat, well educated and well spoken – and he and Philopoemen got on well, discussing Stoic philosophy and the new Epicureanism that had become popular.

'The people have no idea what Epicuros was saying,' Erinida complained. 'They imagine he's in favour of unbridled excess.'

'These are dark times,' Alexanor said.

Erinida nodded. 'Sometimes I wonder if there will be anything left of our world, when the dust settles and the rage of Ares is slaked.'

Philopoemen nodded. 'I agree. But perhaps this is a moment when we can break free of the tyranny of old ways. Surely the generation after this one, from Rome to Aegypt, will detest war and look for new ways to avoid it.'

Erinida smiled bitterly. 'Sir, you are a gentleman and a radical, together – you have the hope of one and the desire of the second. I am an old conservative. I think that two generations of war will drive people to fear and seclusion – hatred breeds hatred. Education is failing. The standards of my generation are all but gone. Look at the behaviour of Machanandas! The Spartans of even fifty years ago would never have allowed him to finish the *agoge*, much less to direct the state.'

Philopoemen nodded and waved at Wewa to keep the wine circulating.

Alexios rarely spoke, but he did now.

'I know the Romans better than any of you,' he said. 'If they survive the Carthaginians, they will never rest until they destroy all their rivals.'

'More war?' Philopoemen shook his head. 'Listen, friends—'

But anything he might have said was interrupted by Dadas.

'I'm sorry, *Hipparchos*,' he said formally. 'There is a … man. From Elis.'

'Elis?' Philopoemen asked.

They had all consumed enough wine that a gentle fog obscured everything, at least to Alexanor. Philopoemen was sharing his *kline* with Kleander.

A cloaked man in riding boots came in. He was short, very powerful, and Alexanor struggled to remember his name. Philopoemen stood and took the stranger's hand.

'Troilos, I believe?'

Wewa extended a cup of wine, which the Elean drank off.

'The Spartans have attacked us,' he said.

Alexanor blinked, and even Philopoemen looked shocked, as if someone they liked had just repudiated his wife, or been accused of incest.

'What?' Erinida asked. 'In an Olympic year? Impossible. No Spartan would submit to such impiety!'

'Nonetheless,' Troilos said, 'the games begin in five days and a Spartan army is marching across our boundaries as of yesterday. I went to your home at Megalopolis. Your steward sent me here.'

Philopoemen looked at Alexanor.

'I feel honour-bound to remind you that the *Boule* requested that you take no risks,' he said.

Philopoemen glanced at Troilos, and then at Kleander.

'Tell the Agema we ride in one hour. Alexios?'

The Italiote smiled. He rose. 'I have had a nice rest. My lads would like a bonus for the night marches.'

'Double pay for a month,' Philopoemen said.

'This is what a mercenary calls a great leader,' Alexios joked. He picked up his cloak.

Alexanor was still trying to make it out.

'Philopoemen,' he said, putting a hand on the arm of the *Hipparchos*.

Philopoemen took his hand. 'We cannot sit on our hands. If the Spartans take Elis, our whole western border is at risk, and like it or not, all the riches of Elis are at the disposal of the tyrant. Including the treasury of the Olympics, I assume.'

'More than forty gold talents,' Troilos said. 'Although we are moving it.'

Philopoemen nodded. 'We must march. Will you come?'

'Is everything we do a last desperate gamble?' Alexanor asked.

'Yes,' Philopoemen said.

'We have no infantry!' Alexanor said.

Philopoemen said, 'So we'll move faster.'

The next day and the two years of planning began to pay off in ways none of them had anticipated. The march over the mountains to Tegea and on to Megalopolis was made as rapidly as human flesh could endure. Philopoemen stripped Tegea to the bone and took five hundred citizen *peltastoi*, as well as half the Cretans and all the cavalry he had. At Megalopolis, the horse farms had enough fresh horses to furnish the Agema with remounts and the Cretans with mounts, although a third of them were on mules or even donkeys.

Phila greeted them on the steps of what was now her house, and led Philopoemen and his immediate staff to dinner: Alexanor, Simmias, Polyainos, Lycurgos.

'We will not be staying,' Philopoemen said. 'Even now the army is marching west.'

'You have to eat,' she said. 'And you will find a dozen mules and twenty horses, already loaded with food, meeting your people west of the city.'

'You know I love you.'

'You only love me for my organisational skills,' she said with a moue.

'Yes,' Philopoemen said, with a look that suggested that this was anything but the truth.

'Please,' she said. 'I'm an old woman. Alexanor, your wife must miss you. I know I do. Sit by me, wolf your food and pretend to listen to my prattle.'

Alexanor smiled at her without jealousy. 'Indeed, my friend, I'd prefer to stay and listen to your wisdom. I do not like this movement to Elis.'

Phila handed him a beautiful bowl of olives with the head of a god raised in the base.

'Well, you are wrong,' she said cheerfully. 'We have no other choice. If Machanandas takes the treasury of the Olympics, I predict that not only will we lose the war, but Philip will lose as well.'

'Gods!' Alexanor spat.

'Pass the olives,' Simmias said. 'Phila, have you seen *my* wife?'

'She's at Argos,' she said. 'We're moving the families back to Argos, or even north.'

'That bad?' Alexanor asked.

'Yes. We need the gods. It is a bold move – the move of an atheist and a cynic. But in this I must almost admire Machanandas. He has few roads to victory, but this is one.'

'No one will ever trust him again!' Alexanor said.

Phila leant close to him, and his breath caught.

'May I tell you a political reality?' she said softly. 'If he wins, every-one will love him. This is the awful truth of politics and war.'

'It is high time I returned to my temple,' Alexanor said.

'Help us save Greece first,' Phila said. 'Aspasia would say the same – I'm sure of it. In fact, I've just had a letter from her.'

Alexanor smiled, reassured.

And two hours later, he was riding west with Philopoemen.

'I need your bodyguard,' Philopoemen said.

'Take them,' Alexanor said.

'Thanks. Dariush, take your file and report to Simmias and tell him you are to be a file leader.'

'Great Lord. I am not even a citizen.'

Philopoemen laughed grimly. 'None of that matters now. Any man who rides by my knee tonight is a citizen of Achaea forever.'

'Can we win this race?' Alexios asked.

'It depends on a thousand things,' Philopoemen said. 'But thanks to Phila we don't have to forage food, and thanks to the *Boule* we have remounts, and we actually have the shorter route because the Spartans are running up the coast by Neochori, or that's what I guess. They'll come onto the plains of Olympia from the south.'

'Ah,' Alexanor said.

'And for all that, really it depends on how early Troilos was informed, and how long the Spartans had already been marching.' Philopoemen shook his head. 'We've been night marching for two years. There is one positive aspect to a mountain pass – you really can't get lost. Pray for a bright moon and no clouds.'

In an hour they were climbing. Near midnight, in the still air of the high Arkades that even summer could not make warm, Alexanor pulled his cloak close at the halt, and every rider who had a spare switched horses.

Philopoemen turned to Kau-Ippa, Thodor and Kleostratos.

'Go,' he said. 'Win the race if you can.'

'We will race with the mountain goats,' Kau-Ippa said. 'See you tomorrow.'

'Perhaps we'll have some Spartan heads,' the girl, Kuka, called out.

Kleostratos was last, after Dadas and Thodor.

'Don't dawdle, just because we can do all the fighting,' he said.

Their hooves were loud on the stony ground for a few minutes and then, despite the bright moonlight, they were gone. They were moving at a trot, faster than Alexanor could imagine going on the rocky track.

'Troilos had one piece of very good news,' Philopoemen said. The big man was very quiet, and always seemed to enjoy coming up on Alexanor.

'I would love a piece of good news,' Alexanor said.

'Dinaeos is alive. The Eleans located him – they want to trade him for some of our prisoners. The Spartans refused, and there were difficulties. But Troilos swears he'll get him for us.'

'Alive!' Alexanor grinned.

'Exactly,' Philopoemen said. 'We ride in ten minutes.'

The ride over the Arkades might have been legendary if the Achaean cavalry hadn't made movement through mountains so routine. As it was, the *epilektoi* of the Agema went down into the plains of Olympia just after the ruddy glow of the sun reached the mountain peaks. Alexanor had the curious experience of riding from a midnight snowfall to a furnace-like day in the plain.

There was a pair of Thracians at Furos, the first town in the valley, and as the valley broadened they encountered another pair, guiding them through a tangle of farm roads to the west and a little south. As the sun rose, Olympia became clear across the valley and they needed no guide.

Just south of Pisa, one of the principal towns of the Elean state, they met Thodor, who turned them south, away from the massive fields of participants, spectators and vendors that lay along the river for stades, and towards the pass that led south to the Messenian road and the ports.

'Too late,' Philopoemen said with satisfaction as they turned south.

'Too late?'

'Not us, brother. Machanandas had lost the race and his gamble.'

'But in battle ...'

Philopoemen nodded. 'I am going to guess that there will be no battle. Ah, look, a welcoming committee.' He turned. 'Troilos!'

The short man rode up on a tired bay.

'The *archons* of the games,' he said. 'I confess—'

'Best tell me now.'

Philopoemen eyed the deputation of men in long *himations* waiting by the road.

'Not everyone was in agreement about ... you.'

Philopoemen nodded. 'Interesting.'

He rode forward to the Elean deputation, but ten paces distant he dismounted. He went forward on foot, his head bent.

'Fathers,' he said.

'*Hipparchos*,' said one of the Eleans with great formality.

'I come only to protect the games,' Philopoemen said. 'I swear on the altars of my fathers and before Olympian Zeus that as soon as the Spartans turn away, I will leave with my army.'

'The Spartans are at Krestena. We *cannot* have a battle here. It is sacrilege.'

Troilos dismounted. 'Councillors, it is not the Achaeans who commit the sacrilege.'

And Philopoemen nodded. 'Regardless, Fathers, if you allow me, I will see to it that no Spartan reaches the plains, unless as an athlete.'

The Olympic Fathers stepped aside to confer.

'Where is your cavalry?' Alexanor asked Troilos.

'In the north, watching the coast,' he admitted. 'The Aetolians threatened to do the same as the Spartans. We have bad allies. Our enemies are better friends.'

'Remember that next spring,' Philopoemen said. 'I cannot wait for your council to confer.'

'Give me a moment,' Alexanor said.

He was dressed in the robes of his priesthood. He slipped from his horse, and approached the council, a priest among priests.

'I am Alexanor of Epidauros,' he said.

All of them inclined their heads; one man made the sign of the priesthood of Apollo.

'I swear on my priesthood that we mean you no harm. Indeed, I would do almost anything to prevent sacrilege, and I will not allow the Spartans to spill blood on the sacred plain if I can help it.'

The leader of the Elean council turned aside. He was clearly angry, and angry men make mistakes. He was a big man, even in old age, heavily muscled, and Alexanor realised that he'd heard that the head of the Elean *Boule* had been an Olympic wrestler. Alexanor guessed that he was enraged by Troilos' imposition of a solution without discussion. He suspected that Troilos was the very model of the rich oligarchs, like Cronan of Corinth, that they were dedicated to fighting.

'Councillor,' Alexanor said formally, 'our only motive is to try and win the friendship of the men of Elis. There must be no blood. I swear to you that Achaea is tired of war. Let us do this to prove our good intent.'

The man turned, and his eyes met Alexanor's.

'Your words are godlike in their wisdom,' he said. 'You see to the root of my problem.'

'Whatever Troilos' intent, in this case, his solution will give you a dustless victory.'

The man smiled hesitantly. 'That was well said.' He nodded. 'Please proceed with our thanks.'

'Good day,' Alexanor said.

Mounting in the robes of a priest was annoying – one of the reasons women seldom rode horses. Long garments make riding difficult. But Alexanor had sworn an oath that he would dress only as a priest until he was allowed to return to his temple.

Philopoemen had stood to one side, sensitive to the fact that Alexanor could sway men in ways where he might only irritate. Now he sprang onto his charger's back as if he was twenty-five and had slept well that night.

Alexanor forced his eyelids to stay open, and followed him, leaving the Olympic officials standing, as the *Hipparchos* rode away from them.

They rode across the plains south of Olympia and then up again, into the southern pass. All the horses were flagging; the men were asleep in the saddles.

But as the sun passed across the sky and the shadows began to lengthen, clouds gathered in the north. They passed the last farms and entered the bareness that marked the untillable lands at the edge of the rich valleys. There were reports of fighting, and the pace quickened. Exhausted men sat up; even horses raised their ears.

Telemnastos dismounted all his Cretans and they ran forward like fresh men.

Philopoemen formed the Agema in the narrow space on either side of the road and pressed forward, leaving Aristides to bring up the laggards and the mercenaries at the back of the column. Alexanor left Lycurgos urging the last men forward. He followed Philopoemen, carrying the staff of his office like a javelin.

Kau-Ippa was at the top of the pass. Her horse had an arrow in the withers, broken off, with a trail of blood running down over the white of his hair. He was a piebald stallion of no particular breeding and seemed untroubled by his wound.

Kau-Ippa was also wounded – a long slash down her right thigh. She had another on her left arm. She waved her *akinakes* at him as he came up and went on.

'... halfway up the pass, and we charged them and scattered them. We took some heads, and Thodor pushed through, up to here.' She shrugged. 'We could have killed more. But Kleostratos said "the top of the pass" and here we are.'

Alexanor dismounted. Dariush rode out from the waiting Agema and handed him his shoulder bag.

'Sponge, canteen.' Alexanor began cleaning Kau-Ippa's thigh.

'Great *fucking* sky god that hurts!' Kau-Ippa closed her eyes.

Her horse didn't move, a tribute to her control.

Around them, and above them in the rocks, the Cretans were settling into positions.

'Will you dismount?' Alexanor asked Kau-Ippa.

'No. If I do, I could have trouble mounting. Do it, whatever you have to.'

He shook his head. 'I can't do anything until you stop using the leg.' He put a loose bandage over it. 'I won't even say keep it clean. Just come to me as soon as we're ... done.'

'You are a good man,' Kau-Ippa said.

Dariush grinned.

'What are you smiling at, young man?'

'You are a good man,' Dariush said. 'Listen, may I ask a question?'

'Anything.'

Alexanor was watching the Spartans. Their formed infantry was well down the other side of the pass, but there was both cavalry and infantry moving on the flanks, some quite close.

'What is a "dustless" victory?'

'You heard that? What good ears you young people have. Listen – he was a wrestler, yes?'

'Sure,' Dariush said.

Just beyond the young Persian, Philopoemen had stopped to listen. He was smiling.

'In wrestling, dustless is when you throw or defeat your opponent and you don't have to go down in the dust yourself. You don't even have to get dirty. Sometimes an opponent refuses to come out. Sometimes he is disqualified. Sometimes the wrestler gets a lucky throw right away and the contest is over.'

'I get it. No rolling in the dirt.'

'Exactly.'

Philopoemen's smile widened.

Alexanor walked forward to where he could watch the Spartans at the bend in the road far below. He could see Machanandas; he knew the man and his horse. And his anger – the man seemed to wear anger all the time. He had a vision – a waking vision; a true dream.

He went back to Philopoemen, who was issuing orders to his officers. Alexanor waited.

'I want to address the Spartans,' he said.

Philopoemen thought for a moment. 'Very well. But brother, I have to tell you that a man who will invade Elis during the Olympic truce might shoot a priest under a flag of truce.'

Alexanor smiled. He was afraid of Machanandas, but he was in the hands of his god; he knew what he had to do, as clearly as if the god had whispered in his ear.

He didn't ride. He walked down the pass in his white robes, carrying a staff, as if he was going out on a spring morning at Epidauros to make the sacrifices.

He was alone. It was a very odd feeling, and he heard men shouting in the Laconian dialect, and he kept walking, his sandals crunching along on the summer gravel of the mountain road. Off to the west, an eagle circled. To the north, the sky was growing darker – rain over the gulf, perhaps, or more. Summer storms were not unknown in the high Arkades.

Alexanor kept his eyes on the sky and tried not to look at the two helots tracking him with arrows, nor at the javelin men who were gathering behind him.

An officer trotted up on a tired horse. As Alexanor expected, it was Nabis.

'Priest, you are like a shrewish wife – you are always there when I don't want you to be.'

'Nabis,' Alexanor said, with a polite inclination of his head.

'Come to beg a truce?'

'I have come in the name of the gods to beg you to end this impiety and go back to Sparta.'

'You mean you've come from the Achaean League. Never heard them referred to as gods before.'

Alexanor shook his head. 'Nabis, you are a Spartan. I want to look you in the eye and have you tell me that your gut does not roil in disgust at the idea of attacking the Olympic Games during the truce.'

Nabis blinked, and looked away.

Softly, he said, 'You know that it roils, priest. You know that it disgusts me.'

'Even if this act brought you victory,' Alexanor said softly, 'what would you tell your ancestors?'

'Nothing,' Nabis admitted.

'He has the pass above you filled with archers.' Alexanor didn't name 'he'. 'He has all the League cavalry. Even if you somehow fight through the pass—'

Nabis' eyes narrowed. 'You waste your breath, priest. I've told Machanandas these things myself.'

Alexanor shook his head. 'Take me to him.'

'I'd rather not compound our impiety by watching him kill you. Truly. You and I are not friends, but I know a true priest when I see one. Go back.'

'No,' Alexanor said. 'I call on you to go back. I speak for Achaea and for Elis and I promise you, I speak for the gods. Go back, or pay the price.'

The wind was picking up. His heavy *himation* began to flap about, and his cloak blew straight out and then settled.

'On your head be it, priest,' Nabis called.

He turned his horse, and Alexanor followed him.

He felt alone. He was walking down through the skirmish line of the enemy *peltastoi* – small men with crescent-shaped shields and heavy spears. Most of them had already thrown their javelins. They didn't meet his eye; some shuffled.

A few drops of rain began to spatter the ground.

Machanandas did not await him, but rode up, his beautiful pale horse shining in the increasingly grey light.

'I told him to go back. He insisted on speaking to you directly.'

Nabis saluted. His scarlet cloak blew around his armoured shoulders like blood-coloured wings. Machanandas didn't bother with a courtesy or a salute.

'What brings you here, priest?'

'I have come—'

'Let me tell you, priest, if you interfere in any way, I'll rip down every fucking stone at Epidauros. Your interference has reached a level that demands revenge.'

Machanandas was mounted; he sat above Alexanor, and he was not a small man. Alexanor walked forward, past the warhorse's vicious head, to the man's booted foot.

'Turn around and march away.' Alexanor was a trained orator with a summer of practice, and his voice carried over the wind.

'Shut him up ...'

Alexanor ignored the tyrant. 'March away or take the consequence. Machanandas, you have offended the gods with the impiety—'

'Take him!'

'*I speak for the gods!*'

By luck, or the will of Olympus, off to the right, a fork of lightning flashed. Every head turned, and there was the sharp crack of a thunderbolt. Machanandas' horse shied, and he had to circle to control his stallion, and Alexanor spoke out.

'Go back, or pay the price!' he roared into the wind.

The lightning flashed again – three distinct strikes – and the resounding thunder echoed up the pass.

The Spartiates closest to him didn't meet his eye.

Alexanor turned on his heel and began to trudge up the pass away from them. A gust of wind hit his face, and his long, white cloak blew out behind him, the fabric tearing slightly on the heavy pin that held it and threatening to choke him. He had to lean into the sudden wind.

But no arrow reached out for him; no peltast sprang to do the tyrant's bidding and kill him. He walked up the pass, and the rain began – big, cold drops. It was coming at him like a curtain; Alexanor had a moment of divine clarity, when he saw the curtain of rain as the symbol of the future, cutting him off from the present.

He turned to look at the Spartans, who were only a hundred paces away. Their ranks were stirring as if they had suffered heavy casualties.

A fork of lightning split the sky, and the curtain of rain swept over him and the Spartans were gone, washed away. There was a massive crash of thunder, close at hand.

He was soaked to the skin in seconds, the heavy wool clinging to him like a cold, wet enemy. He trudged up the rocky road, feet squelching inside his sandals, until he reached the top.

Philopoemen, his helmet under his arm, somehow contrived to look like a god even under a torrent of rain; his horse's head was up. Telemnastos stood by him, gesturing angrily.

'All our bowstrings are soaked!' he yelled. 'We can't face their *peltastoi* without bows.'

Philopoemen nodded. 'Withdraw!' He smiled at Alexanor. 'I thought—!' He had to shout.

There was another ripple of lightning that lit the whole sky and a massive concussion, as if the thunderbolt had struck the very hillside above them. The water began to run down the road as if it was a stream bed, and the Cretans came back with it. The citizen *peltastoi* took their places in the rocks, and the Cretans retreated, grumbling.

And then it was done. The water ran down the hillside in every gully, and the rocks of the sides of the pass gleamed in the new sun, and the ground smelt marvellously of rain and growth.

Above Alexanor in the wet rocks, a pair of young citizen *peltastoi* gripped their javelins and looked at each other nervously.

After another quarter of an hour, the sun was going down and men were cold and wet. But the ground was already drying; isolated puddles were the only sign of the gushing streams that had tumbled down the hillside minutes before.

Kleostratos took a dozen Thracians forward over the pass. He whooped when he reached the first turn in the road and they heard him, and again as he turned and came back.

'They're marching away!' he called.

Philopoemen raised his arm and looked at Alexanor – the salute to an Olympic victor.

'Dustless!' he shouted.

All around him, the citizen *peltastoi* who had not had to face the Spartiates and die began to cheer.

'Achilles!' they called, and others yelled 'Dustless!'
'Dustless!' shouted Dariush. He was smiling.
'But damp,' Alexanor said. 'Very, very damp.'

# CHAPTER TWO

—◦◦◦—

## Epidauros, Megalopolis and the Olympic Games

PANAMOS TO PROSTATERIOS
(SEPTEMBER 208 TO APRIL 207 BCE)

The autumn meeting of the *Boule* corresponded with the meetings of the whole Assembly of the Federation, the General *Synodos*, and the celebration of the autumn feast of Artemis and Apollo at Aegio.

The world seemed a different place from the last time Alexanor had taken his seat in the *Boule*. He was hollow-eyed from lack of sleep, but not from any desperate cause. Most of his closest friends were in Aegio, and the night before, they had celebrated the return of Dinaeos from captivity with a symposium that had greeted each of the Seven Sisters as they became visible in the night sky. In a matter of days they would be gone for the winter, and it was Phila's notion that they should drink a cup of wine to each as they rose.

Alexanor had left his wife face down in a tangle of sheets, unable to face the day and muttering imprecations, and had brought his hangover to face Philip of Macedon.

Philip had left his army at Corinth, but his presence was just as palpable, and he sat on an ivory stool as if he was their king. He sat in the place of the *Hegemon* or president of the League – an honorary position which Doson had ignored and Philip had tended to view as a form of absolute monarchy.

The seat of the *Strategos* was empty.

Philopoemen stood by the pillar, where by tradition the *Hipparchos* stood and served wine and water to the *Strategos* to show his subordination. He wore his armour, which was a remarkable departure from tradition. No other man in the great round *tholos* of the Achaeans was armed.

Almost a third of the seats in the Assembly were empty; disease and a summer of battles had winnowed the men of Achaea, so that more than a hundred representatives were dead, or so incapacitated by wounds that they could not attend. Even among the men sitting patiently, there were bandages, staffs and slings.

Philopoemen was a priest of Zeus, and he opened the *Synodos* with the sacrifice of a ram, and the smell of burning fat filled the hall with a healthy scent. He wiped the sacrificial knife on a clean cloth, and handed it to another priest. He raised his arms.

'Companions!' he called.

He used the military word: *hetaeroi*. It was the word that kings used for their bodyguards, but it had a literal meaning: war-friends.

'Companions!' he called again.

He had them.

'We meet in the midst of the storm,' he said. 'All around us, our enemies gather like carrion birds around a dying man.'

He paused, and looked out over the hall. The altar was before him, with a fire, and the smoke of the sacrifices rose around him as if he was some sacred being.

'But we are not dead!' he proclaimed. 'We took the best our enemies could offer, and we have not fallen!' He looked around again. 'I come before you today in armour, because we are not yet in a place where we can take off our panoply and rest. Now is the time when we must train every man – when every eye must be on the mark, every hand must be heavy.'

He spoke with his back to the king of Macedon, which had the peculiar effect of making it seem as if Philopoemen was ignoring him.

'Today, I ask you to elect me as *Strategos* of the League,' he said. 'I ask this because I am best fitted to train the phalanx as it must be trained to face the Spartans, the Aetolians and the Romans. I offer you no bed of ease, Achaeans! Our ancestors warred down Troy. We stood against the Medes. We marched away into the east with great Alexander.' He looked out at them like some great eagle on a perch, and his eye seemed to meet the eye of every man in the hall. 'I will

322

make our phalanx into the Myrmidons of Achilles, and with it I will find us peace. *We* do not seek to rule others. *We* do not seek foreign conquest! *We* seek the peaceful enjoyment of our farms and ships – yet he who wishes for peace must gird for war.'

He lowered his arms. 'I invite any of you to stand against me in this election – come forward and speak.'

Lycurgos nudged Alexanor. 'Watch this.'

Aristaenos walked to the altar. He raised his arms.

'Brothers!' he called. 'I come not for myself, but to shout, "Philopoemen!"'

Men cheered.

Alexanor turned to Lycurgos, stunned through his hangover.

'Aristaenos is no fool,' Lycurgos said. 'No one can defeat Philopoemen this year. Listen.'

Lysipos, a magnate of no particular party, walked to the altar. He bowed deeply, and then raised his arms.

'Philopoemen saved the League,' he said into the cheers. 'Give him the command.'

Memnon of Argos rose. He raised his arms.

'I am no ally of Philopoemen,' he said. 'But I know who I want to hold the spear.'

As Lycurgos said later, that was the day's best speech.

But when they had had their say, Philip of Macedon rose.

'I will not tell you who to choose as your *Strategos*,' he said with a smile. 'But I will say that I am well pleased with your choice. I will only add that if the League will raise eight thousand heavy infantry and arm them, I will return to the League the border fortresses which I hold. And I will contribute a thousand full bronze panoplies.'

He held out a hand to the cheers.

'Wait,' he said. 'I have heard it said that I abandoned you last year, and that because of me, Dyme fell to the Romans.' He held up his head, and looked out over the *Synodos*. 'I have ransomed the entire population of Dyme. I will rebuild their city with my own silver. The men and women of Dyme will be returned this winter.'

The roar was titanic.

The voting was anticlimactic, and Philopoemen was elected without opposition.

Kykliadas rose after the vote; as a former *Strategos*, he was always eligible to speak. He went to the altar, prayed, and then announced Philopoemen's victory.

The Assembly cheered.

He turned. 'It is traditional for the *Strategos* to take his seat in the spring, at the rising of the Pleiades,' he said. 'But Nikeas lies under the mound at Tegea. I move that Philopoemen take his seat today.'

The motion was carried by acclamation.

Philopoemen could not help himself. He grinned like a small boy, transported by their evident delight. He took the seat by Philip, who said something to him.

Philopoemen's grin vanished.

Kykliadas was still at the altar.

'Does this mean that the phalanx has a drill day tomorrow?' he asked.

The roar of laughter was the sincerest tribute.

That night, Philopoemen hosted a victory dinner that included Dinaeos and Alexanor, Phila and Aspasia, both looking a little pale, and Lycorgas with his wife, and Lykortas on the same *kline* as Aristaenos; Kykliadas lay with Cronan of Corinth, Memnon of Argos with Aristides of Hermione. Alexios the Italian lay with Kleostratos, and Simmias lay with his brother Polyainos. The soldiers ate and drank well but were silent because it was obviously a political dinner. It was a sharp contrast to the evening before, because the dinner was all business. The food was excellent, but the conversation was deeply practical, and there were no drinking games.

'I am naming Dinaeos as *Hipparchos*,' Philopoemen said. 'Aristaenos, I mean no insult and your turn will come, but Dinaeos is the best cavalry officer in Greece.'

Dinaeos rolled his eyes. 'The pickings must be slim,' he said.

They shouted him down.

'I'll have Kykliadas to share the phalanx. Aristaenos, would you support Dinaeos?'

Aristaenos had no choice but to accept; but he did so with a good grace.

'Lykortas will have the fleet, such as it is. Lysipos will have the treasury. Will that satisfy? I mean to prosecute the war as efficiently as possible – what we did for the cavalry we will now do for the phalanx.'

Lykortas raised a wine bowl. 'Which you started at Argos,' he said.

Philopoemen nodded. 'Anyone who accepts any office this year must be prepared to travel. We will retrain the phalanx all winter. Will the temples contribute again?' he asked Alexanor.

'Yes,' Alexanor said.

'Then we will hire the very mercenaries that Philip is releasing – three thousand veterans. I admit they've had years in garrison to get soft, but in a world at war, we're lucky to get any professional heavy infantry at all.' Philopoemen was standing. 'And if we don't buy them, Machanandas will.'

'Where does the bastard's money come from?'

'There's a powerful pro-Spartan faction in Rome,' Lykortas said. 'And there are Spartan factors on Crete and in Aegypt that provide a steady flow of funds.' He glanced around. 'And the Romans know that every cavalryman that Sparta buys out of Italy is one more that Hannibal can't hire.'

'The moment is coming when we need to send a delegation to Rome,' Philopoemen said. 'We need to approach the Senate and look for a road to peace.'

Phila spoke up. 'You would abandon Macedon?'

Philopoemen smiled down at the woman he would soon make his wife.

'Philip is hard-pressed and needs peace as much as we do ourselves,' he said. 'He is not turning over his border fortresses—'

'Which we call the "Fetters of Greece"!' Lykortas yelled.

'Just so,' Phila grinned.

'... from general benevolence,' Philopoemen continued. 'Or boyish enthusiasm for our liberties. He cannot afford to maintain those men any longer. He needs the money at home, to raise more phalangites from the fields around Pella. He's as much as said he won't make war on Athens this summer.'

'So he's getting us to pay for our own defence, and he's ceding us some increased autonomy.' Alexanor shook his head. 'Can we abandon him?'

Philopoemen was sitting on the edge of his couch, and he took a drink of the wine and handed it to Wewa.

'Abandon? No.' He glanced around. 'But if we can last another year, we might be in a position to broker a peace – relief from a war that no one wants any more. Rome is like a boxer that's taken too many punches – Macedon too. You know what happens in a fight like that.'

Alexanor nodded.

Aristaenos sat up. 'Can we make it through this summer?' he asked.

Philopoemen looked around. 'Brothers,' he said, 'you know how close we came to the end this summer.'

Everyone nodded.

'Listen, then. Find me twenty-five talents of gold, and we will live through this summer. I mean no *hubris*, but I have outmarched Machanandas twice. He will have a very good army. But he will not have Elis and he will not have Rome.'

Lykortas shook his head. 'He may have Elis. The Aetolians are openly saying that they will seize Elis if the Eleans won't live up to their oaths of allegiance.'

Philopoemen raised an eyebrow. 'That's hard news to hear. But not unexpected. My guess is that if the Roman fleet stays in home waters, we have even odds. If the Romans come here, we have one army to face three opponents, and the support of their fleet will make them faster to move and faster to react.'

Phila smiled at Aspasia. 'What women can do by persuasion and bribery has been done to keep the Roman fleet at home.'

Aspasia waved her hands. 'Don't look at me! She's the one who knows everyone.'

'Who wrote a letter to Galba through Kaeso?' Phila asked.

'Shameless!' Aspasia laughed.

Philopoemen made a gesture – a flick of his wrist, like a man playing with bones.

'The bones are cast,' he said. 'What can be done will be done. Pray for a long winter and a late spring.'

'Pray that Hannibal moves early in Italy,' Phila said.

'Pray that our horses come from Thrake,' Kleostratos said.

Alexanor rose with the wine bowl. 'Friends, we are in the hands of the gods.'

The *Synodos* broke up after voting the tax measures to support the army. Philopoemen and the Temple of Epidauros each offered to purchase five hundred bronze panoplies for hoplites, and Philip of

Macedon donated another thousand. From Corinth to Tegea, every bronze smith in the Peloponnese was hammering out greaves; slaves and apprentices beat the metal thin, and the masters cut the shapes. And Corinth imported more, from Athens and Rhodes and Aegypt, because sometime enemies still sought profits.

The cavalry was busy guarding convoys of bullion – temple treasures donated to keep the League in the war for one more year. Alexanor rode from Corinth to Aegio. He visited Philopoemen at Megalopolis, went to the Temple of Poseidon at Tegea, to Argos, and finally to Epidauros, raising money.

The temples were no longer donating surplus. The magnificent treasury at Epidauros was stripped of silver; only six silver lamps hung in the sanctuary of the god, and the last gold lamps were melted down.

Philopoemen sold his ships, and every house or farm he owned outside his home at Megalopolis.

'So much for riches,' he said.

Cronon of Corinth handed the League treasurer three gold talents. He put a statue of his son, wearing a horseman's cloak, on the steps of the Temple of Aphrodite in Corinth. When he met Alexanor at midwinter, he embraced him.

'I know my son loved you,' he said.

Alexanor couldn't think what to say.

'Dinaeos of Megalopolis says that you know where his bones are,' Cronan said.

'I do,' Alexanor said. 'I saw to his funeral rites myself.'

Cronan looked down. And then at Alexanor.

'I never expected him to make himself a hero. Or to die before me.' He was suddenly weeping.

'He surprised me,' Alexanor admitted. He found that Cronan's collapse made the man pitiable, despite his dislike. 'He was remarkable. Did he tell you of his riding out to fight the Aetolian champions?'

'Other men have told me the story. But I would hear it from you.'

Alexanor told him that story, and others; and despite their differences, they ended as two middle-aged men weeping together.

'I hear he loved some barbarian chit?' Cronan said. 'I would ... have that child, if I might.'

Alexanor had not heard any such thing, and he bridled at the word 'barbarian' from a man who bought and sold children.

'Kuka?' he asked.

'I don't know,' Cronan said, with his arrogance returning. 'Some camp follower.'

Alexanor nodded slowly. 'I will ask.'

In Damatios after the Feast of the Sun, Alexanor returned home to Epidauros. He had quartered the Peloponnese begging funds for the League from the temples, and he had broken his own vow twenty times to teach young citizens enough Rhodian drill to perhaps keep them alive in combat.

He confessed as much to Sostratos on his first night home, to a noisy welcome from his children and a long embrace from his wife.

'I can't just watch them,' he said. 'I spent my youth as a marine.'

Sostratos laughed and drank wine. 'Listen, priest. It is the best form of medicine – preventative medicine. We tell an old man to get exercise, so he will loosen his muscles and avoid fat. So, teaching the young to fight prevents wounds.'

Aspasia gave him a wry smile. 'I detect the faintest scent of sophistry.'

Sostratos leant back, spat out a chicken bone, and smiled.

'Perhaps you do, lady. But I'm an old soldier too, and I have been drilling the levy here. Every day they practise, I think perhaps more of them will come home.'

Aspasia blinked. 'May your words go to the gods. But I want Alexanor to come home.'

When their guest was gone, Alexanor attempted to take her in his arms.

'I'll come home,' he said.

'Will you, though?' she said. 'I have to wait here, to see if you are dead. Try it some time, husband. Try sitting in the dark, waiting for your love to be dead. We have three children and a life here. We could be on Rhodes, or Kos, or Crete, and out from under the shadow of this war.'

Alexanor took her hands. 'Aspasia ...'

'Alexanor!' she shouted. 'How many times will you leave and then return? Every time you leave, it is the last time. Did you have to force yourself to drill those young men, or do you just love war like *he* does?'

Alexanor bridled. 'I do *not* love war.'

'You spend a great deal of your time on it. Here's what war is to women, Alexanor. We dream of the thousand ways you die, and then some ugly bastard burns our town, kills our children and makes us slaves. In between these events, we wait, and try not to weep too much.'

Alexanor had no words.

'And if you imagine that sitting here alone with some wine and three children is somehow relaxing ...' she went on.

'Aspasia,' he said. 'You married me. Must we?'

'No!' She pointed at him, face flushed. 'No. I will not be silent. You put everything before us: your family, temple, League, war. I married the priest of a sanctuary on Crete, not the lynchpin of the League of Achaean Cities.'

Alexanor was silent; he had no rebuttal.

Aspasia walked away into the house. He heard her slam the door to their room.

The next morning, her smile was brittle, and Alexanor felt like a stranger in his own house. He went out early to the sanctuary, and spoke to Chiron; the old hierophant was very fragile, and repeated himself.

Alexanor found himself repeating the fight with his wife.

When he was done, the old man seemed to be asleep, and Alexanor prepared to leave him in the warmth of two braziers.

'Well, well,' Chiron said.

Alexanor froze.

'It is, I suppose, the penalty of being a great man.' The old priest coughed.

'A great man?'

'Are you not, now, a great man? Every temple in the Peloponnese listens to you. No one here will dispute your appointment to preside when I am gone.' Chiron raised a hand which shook slightly. 'Don't dispute with me, there's a dear boy. You do too much. And your wife has the essential element correctly. You love it. You were born to be yoked with Philopoemen. You are two horses on one chariot, like Achilles and Patrokles.'

Alexanor moved to protest and then his hands fell by his sides.

'Exactly,' the old man said. 'Admit it. You hate the taking of life – that is noble. Otherwise, you revel in all of it – political debate, financial committees, battlefield strategies. Diplomacy – your forte. Every man in Greece knows that you walked up to the Tyrant of Sparta and ordered him to retreat from his impiety, and that he went like a whipped cur.'

'That's not exactly what happened—'

'No one cares what happened!' the old priest shouted. 'Men live by myths. Most men. And you and Philopoemen are giving Greece one last myth.' He smiled, and then coughed. 'Listen to me. I am so close to death that I talk to him every day. I have never been married, but I know some things. Go home to your wife and apologise. There is nothing else you can do.'

Alexanor bowed, and then kissed the old man on the brow.

'You have always given me excellent advice.'

'You have usually ignored it. And now you are the most famous priest in Greece.'

Alexanor went home, took his wife's hands, and led her to a *kline* in the tiled room.

'My love, I am here to apologise,' he said. 'It is true – I love the life of command, of politics. I thought, all the way back, of promising you to leave it. I will, if you demand it. But first let me offer something else.'

She put her head on his shoulder. 'I could just apologise and return to my wifely duties,' she said. 'I lost my temper last night ...'

'Don't retreat now,' he said. 'I've thought this through. Leave the children with their nurse and come with me. We'll have the winter together, and in the spring, come to the *Synodos* and then to Megalopolis. Phila will want you for the wedding feast anyway.'

She kissed him. 'Sometimes you say the nicest things. 'Although that last "anyway" implied that perhaps I wasn't much use.'

'Ouch,' Alexanor said.

'You married me,' she said in exactly his tone.


It seemed at first like a cautious peace, but the winter was one of the happiest of Alexanor's life, and while the *hippeis* rode and the phalanx drilled, he played with children, hosted dinners, and served his full rota at the sanctuary.

He was amused, and a little sorry, to find that his peers now viewed him with a semi-religious awe.

Philopoemen came twice; passed on the date of the wedding, which was set, with no coincidence, for the same day as the general muster of the federal army, at the rising of the Pleiades. Alexanor heard of him, criss-crossing the Federation, drilling both cavalry and infantry, but Alexanor stayed home. He drilled the men of his district, and the great Temple of Epidauros freed forty young slaves and sent them to join the *taxeis* in good *spoles* of tawed leather and bronze helmets made by local smiths. The town gave them a feast and enrolled them as citizens.

Alexanor performed another duty that winter; he began training a travelling unit of priests, novices and freedmen for the medical needs of the army. He intended to lead it himself, and he stocked it with the best of the younger priests, and led them on long rides and walks, gathering wild plants and learning to live rough.

He returned from one such ride to find Leon sitting in his tiled room, sharing a *kline* and a brazier with Aspasia. The two men embraced for so long that Aspasia said, 'Don't make me jealous, you two!'

'Who's making the decisions at Lentas?' Alexanor asked.

'Omphalion,' Leon said. 'With able support from Lysistrata of Athens. All is well. Gortyna sends you a hundred greetings.' He grinned. 'And the Federation of Cities is sending Telemnastos another thousand men.'

'By the gods!' Alexanor said.

'By the gods,' Leon said. 'I was beginning to forget you. But I heard a rumour of a travelling hospital. I decided that I could hear the voice of Apollo in the waves and that you needed me.'

'How did you hear that?' Alexanor asked, looking at Aspasia.

She smiled. 'Not me. I write to Leon, but about other things.'

Chiron seemed unsurprised to see Leon, and he led the first celebration of spring at the temple with Leon and Alexanor as his principal celebrants. Leon lived with them, and dined every night, and as the weather warmed and the passes opened, and the pilgrims came, Alexanor's house became an open lodge. Aristides came and went, and Lykortas, and Philopoemen, who pronounced the men of Epidauros to be fit.

'Perhaps the best,' he admitted.

Lycurgos grinned, and Aristides frowned.

'Or perhaps the men of Hermione,' Philopoemen said. 'We're as ready as we can be.'

'See you at the *Boule*,' Alexanor said in the morning, when his friend was mounting.

'We are having the Assembly at Megalopolis,' Philopoemen said. 'We have to be ready if the ground thaws early.'

Alexanor nodded. 'Chiron is dying,' he said.

Philopoemen shook his head. 'He is a great man.'

'Yes. If he dies, I may not come.'

Philopoemen looked as if he might protest. And then his shoulders settled.

'Of course,' he said.

A week passed and the flowers burst out on the hillsides and the whole of the valley was scented with jasmine and broom. By the coast, the pale yellow flowers gave their sweet-salt-spice scent to the air, and anxious swains dared an early death to climb the cliff sides and fetch some for their loves. It seemed that every woman in Greece wore a sprig of pale yellow flowers in her hair, including Aspasia. Persephone blessed the earth, and Alexanor led the procession and the choir at the first great rite of spring.

That night, Aspasia and Alexanor held a party for their friends and neighbours, and their whole courtyard was full of people, and in emulation of Philopoemen, they purchased a whole tuna and served it. Erenida pronounced it the 'besht party I've ever attended ...' and stumbled away, the last visitor. Alexanor took his wife to bed and left the washing-up for morning.

Despite the night, he rose early and ran out along the beach, stretching unused muscles, and he returned home feeling better than he had in weeks – tired and hale.

He paused in the entry hall of his house, having heard movement; he turned and peered through the curtain into the tiled room, and found himself looking at Kleopatra. She was pretending to be admiring the mosaic floor, which was quite beautiful, but as the sun was only just fully over the mountains, it seemed early for a visit.

And she was wearing the same saffron dress she'd worn at the party ...

He kissed her on the forehead. 'Stay for breakfast,' he said. 'Or I never saw you. Your choice.'

She laughed. 'I knew you weren't a prig. I'll stay and help clean up.'

'Is Leon behind the curtains?' Alexanor asked.

She smiled. 'Still asleep. I thought I'd leave and save us all embarrassment.'

He thought that she had a shadow across her face when she said that.

He made a face. 'Let's collect cups,' he said.

The house slaves were just up; Alexanor was still stripped for running. They made short work of fifty cups and all the house ceramics. An hour later, Aspasia appeared and dug in, drinking a little watered wine. If she was surprised to see Kleopatra, she didn't give a hint.

Kleopatra grew increasingly silent.

Aspasia gave her husband a long look, and he collected more wooden platters.

Leon came down from the guest room looking as if he'd been hit by the ram of a ship, but he went out, poured water over his head, and Alexanor could hear him talking to one of the slaves in the yard.

'Now I should go,' Kleopatra said.

'You were staying for breakfast,' Alexanor said.

'I have duties at the temple.'

Leon came back in. 'Morning didn't used to be so ...' He paused as he came through the hallway. 'Kleopatra!'

'I thought I'd help clean up,' she said.

Leon walked over, took one of her hands, and kissed it.

Kleopatra blushed.

'Please stay to breakfast,' Aspasia said smartly.

After breakfast, Alexanor walked to the temple with Kleopatra.

'Don't you want to ask?' she said at the top of the ridge.

'No,' he said.

She smiled. 'You are a nice man. We started exchanging letters. And then ...'

They looked out over the valley. Everywhere there were blooms. Alexanor noticed as she turned her head that she had a sprig of yellow flowers in her hair.

He smiled.

And an hour later Chiron took his hand.

'Go.' His voice quavered, but his grip was strong. 'I have served the gods since I was a boy. They can keep me alive for one summer. Go and do what must be done. And then hurry back. I have reached the point where life is more of a burden than death.'

Alexanor bowed.

'And send Leon in,' the hierophant said. 'No doubt he's asking permission to marry.'

Alexanor started as if he'd been stung.

The old priest smiled his old smile of knowledge. 'Oh, I still know a thing or two.'

In the morning, the *taxeis* of Epidauros marched away from the agora, and the *hippeis* followed them to the cheers of the town and the weeping of many young women.

Aspasia and Kleopatra were not weeping. They were mounted on horses from Alexanor's farm. They were waiting with their baggage animals a little apart, in the great open court of the sanctuary, where Alexanor was forming the baggage and material for his mobile hospital.

Chiron came down in white robes, and Sostratos too, and blessed them – a dozen young priests and the best of the novices standing in neat ranks like soldiers. There were twenty donkeys loaded with medicines and bedding.

Alexanor had to pause for a moment, because as he turned to call out to Leon, the world seemed to freeze, and it was fifteen years earlier, and Philopoemen was face down over one of those horses, and Chiron was face to face with Nabis, and the courtyard of the temple was full of danger.

Alexanor shook his head to clear it.

Old Bion, now the chief steward, nodded.

'Long time, eh, sir?'

'I was just thinking of the day—'

'When the Spartans came?' Bion said. 'As was I, sir.' He smiled. 'Let's hope this is better times, eh?' He leant over. 'Not my place, maybe. But the Old Man needs you back.'

'I hear you, Bion.'

'Good. Sir.'

Not for the first time, Alexanor felt that Bion had perfected the art of speaking respectfully while giving orders. He smiled and went to Chiron, and the hierophant wrapped him in a white wool embrace.

'I will not see you again as a living man,' the old priest said. 'No tears! I have had a fine life. Do what must be done and come back. There is more to Greece than war.'

Chiron said something to Leon as well; the two of them were both fighting tears as they mounted.

Alexanor kissed his wife.

'What's wrong?' she asked.

'It will never be the same,' he said. 'The same as it was in my youth. The world is changing, and nothing will be the same.'

'You are crying.'

'Chiron is my true father, and soon he will die, and I am riding to a war. I should be here!'

She looked at him, leant over and kissed his lips.

'Well,' she said, 'I didn't want revenge. But this is how I feel, every time you ride away.'

They rode through the spectacular flowers of spring in the Vale of Epidauros, and it was as if the sprites and nymphs of the valley wanted them to know what they missed: every flower was fully in bloom; bees buzzed; the sun covered all in a golden radiance with the perfect light that old men remember from youth.

'Damn,' Leon said, as they came to the top of the first pass.

He was looking back at the valley – the temple and theatre gleaming in the perfect sun.

Alexanor nodded. They sat there with Aspasia and Kleopatra for as long as the priest might make his invocation to the gods.

And then Alexanor turned his horse's head and led them away to war.

# CHAPTER THREE

—◦◦◦—

## Megalopolis and Mantinea

PROSTATERIOS TO HOMOLOIOS (APRIL TO JULY), 207 BCE

The Army of the League of Achaea gathered in the west country, around Megalopolis. Philopoemen wanted the cavalry to have the benefit of the pasturage for a last week of training. Alexanor watched the horses growing shinier on oats and good grass while he and Leon tended to the sprains and broken bones that resulted from hard training in the fields around Megalopolis.

It was odd to live in a tent, in an army camp, with his wife; but it was very pleasurable to have her warmth against him on a cold Arkadian night, and the women of the camp made it feel very different. Simmias' wife, Heraklea, and Alethea, wife of Dinaeos, were much younger than Phila, Aspasia or Kleopatra, but what they lacked in wisdom they made up in fire and enthusiasm. The army cheered them when they rode by in short *chitons* and broad-brimmed hats, and was respectfully silent when the women took their accustomed roles in sacrifices and celebrations. Achaean armies were not usually accompanied by women to wash and provide other services – not because Achaeans were any different in their needs, but because circumstances forced them to fight so close to their homes. But this season was different; the four thousand mercenaries that the League had inherited from Philip were like a marching nation, with women and children of their own from all over Greece and Italy. The Tarentines had mostly taken Achaean wives who followed the army, and the camp at Megalopolis attracted hundreds more to see the army, to live for a few days with a husband or father – to have an adventure denied to most respectable women.

Phila had brought her tents out of retirement and they rose like a canvas and silk palace in the centre of the camp, and there, every day, dozens of women were welcomed, fed, and sat in circles, gossiping and embroidering Phila's wedding clothes.

Older Achaeans were scandalised that Philopoemen should wed at all, in the midst of a campaign – much less to marry a notorious woman, a courtesan. Philopoemen, as was his wont, made no comment at all. He ignored adverse comments and made his preparations, which were to hold his wedding in the army camp in front of the whole of Achaea.

The night before the wedding feast, he had a small party in his own tent – a thin fiction, as everyone knew where he slept. But the party was only for men. Alexanor, as a married man, was aware that there was a similar party in Phila's palace.

Philopoemen's party was subdued and bore a strong resemblance to an extended staff meeting. There was some talk of philosophy over the second wine bowl, and Polyainos attempted to start some salacious humour about brides and grooms.

Philopoemen smiled. 'That sort of thing is more suited to a younger man,' he said. 'I am fairly sure I know every inch of my wife's body – and what it's all for. I could explain, if you wish.'

Alexanor splorted his wine, and Dinaeos slapped young Polyainos on the back. But after making the attempts, Dinaeos rolled over and waved.

'You want to talk strategy,' he said. 'Be my guest, as long as I can keep drinking.'

Philopoemen sat back, relaxed but sober.

'I do,' he admitted.

'Strategy is a form of learning, and hence perfectly proper for a party,' Simmias called out. Someone threw a barley roll at him.

'Gentlemen ...' Philopoemen said.

Calm settled on them, like the hand of a tutor on so many guilty schoolboys.

'So – there is good news and bad news. The good news – the Romans are concentrating on Hannibal. There is no fleet for Greece this year.'

Alexanor found himself applauding with the rest.

'The bad news – the Spartan faction in the Roman Senate sent money instead of a fleet. Lykortas?'

Lykortas nodded. 'Machanandas has restored his cavalry. He'll have four thousand mercenary horse and another five thousand foot, in addition to his Spartiates and his helots.'

'Perhaps twenty-one thousand men,' Philopoemen said.

The officers were silent, as if they'd been struck.

'Almost a quarter larger again than our best effort,' Lykortas said.

Simmias groaned. 'How can Machanandas afford this?'

'The Romans. The Aegyptians.' Philopoemen spread his hands. 'The oligarchs on Crete, trying to defeat Philip in a long game to regain power at home.'

They looked at each other. Wewa was gone; he'd been invited to join the novitiate at Epidauros. Philopoemen had cavalry troopers to serve, and one of them came forward and poured unwatered wine into Alexanor's cup. The young man was clearly drunk himself.

'On the other hand,' Philopoemen said, 'Philip is invading the heartland of the Aetolians. Without the Romans to back them, he thinks he can knock them out of the war.'

'So he's on the north coast of the Gulf of Corinth,' Alexanor said.

'You see it!' Philopoemen said.

The two men shared the ability to visualise the movements of armies over ground. Alexanor could hold the image in the eye of his mind – the gulf as he would see it from the top of the Acrocorinth, and Philip's army passing Delphi and his ships ...

'Philip is assuming we can defend ourselves,' he said.

'Can we?' Telemnastos asked.

'He has no idea how many men Sparta has this year. But yes, we're on our own. And listen, my friends. We have only Sparta! Elis is out of the war. Aetolia must face Philip. Rome is fighting Hannibal. It is true that we are on our last throw – but it is a throw for everything. If we can defeat Sparta, we can end the war.'

'Defeat Sparta?' Dinaeos asked. 'In battle?'

'By ourselves?' Kykliadas asked.

'Yes,' said Philopoemen. 'When we parade the army the day after tomorrow you will see. We have eight thousand phalangites, two thousand of them in full armour. We will fight sixteen deep, and the first three ranks and the whole of the back rank will be in armour. Wait until you see our phalanx.' He smiled. 'And we have a second phalanx – four thousand mercenaries in the Macedonian manner. Twelve thousand solid infantry, and another two thousand *peltastoi* and Cretans, and almost five thousand horse.'

Alexanor was cheered. 'We've come a long way.'

'We'd be better off with a summer to train,' Dinaeos said.

Philopoemen nodded. 'I intend to train the phalanx for at least a month.'

'How?' Lykortas asked. 'Machanandas won't just sit in his fortified camp and let us move about!'

'Not when he has as many cavalrymen as we do,' Dinaeos said.

Philopoemen nodded. 'I hope to trap him into a war of manoeuvre. Nothing trains a phalanx like marching.'

'Gods!' Kykliadas said. 'Marching ...'

'Every day, until our feet fall off,' Philopoemen said.

Alexios laughed grimly, but Menes, the commander of the mercenary phalanx, shook his head.

'My boys don't like marching. And they don't like drill.'

'Do they like money?' Philopoemen asked.

Everyone laughed except Menes.

'Listen, friends,' Philopoemen said. 'As soon as Philip invaded Aetolia, my original strategy – indeed, the very reason to hold the muster here – was eliminated. We're here so we can invade Elis if we must, to stop the Aetolians from using it as a base. That was a terrible worst case, and now we're free from the two-army threat. So let us rejoice in facing one single army.'

'Twenty thousand on a side,' Dinaeos said. 'That's a real battle. When was the last time there was a battle this size between Greeks, and not just barbarians?'

'Galba calls us the last Greeks,' Philopoemen said. 'The Romans say that all honour and glory have left Greece. I think he means the Aetolians.'

'And the Spartans,' Simmias said. 'Attacking the Olympic Games! What impiety!'

'Regardless,' Philopoemen said, 'we know what the Romans think.

We know all too well in what regard Philip and Macedon hold us. I think they're wrong. I think that we still live in a country that is "glorious and free", as the poet Timotheos would have it. Let us be worthy sons of our fathers.'

'By marching,' Dinaeos said.

'All summer,' Kykliadas said.

They were laughing when suddenly there were hands over Alexanor's eyes. His head was seized, and a blade was put against his throat. He couldn't see; his blood pressure spiked.

A voice in his ear said, 'You will kiss me until I tell you to stop.'

Aspasia tasted of wine and garlic, and couldn't stop giggling no matter how hard he kissed her. Men throughout the tent were laughing as wives or companions spilled in.

'We were bored,' Phila said.

She was dressed, for the occasion, in armour. Alexanor had seen it before; Phila excelled at dancing the Athenian military dances in armour, and the short *chiton* and breastplate left a great deal of her to admire. His wife was in a riding *chiton*, so short that he could see her hips. Dinaeos' wife wore a *chlamys* and had a spear and very little else. Kleopatra was dressed like Artemis and was very striking.

Philopoemen eyed them all with a raised eyebrow.

'I am aware that I have put the phalanx in Macedonian equipment,' he said. 'But I am now threatened with a Macedonian party.'

'We have captured you all in a surprise attack, and you are our slaves!' Phila shouted.

It was a very good party indeed.

The wedding of Phila and Philopoemen was performed by a dozen priests, and they sacrificed so many sheep and bulls that the whole army was fed a feast of meat. Wine flowed like water, and after the ceremonies ended, Phila led the women of the army in dances. Alexanor watched, already a little drunk, as his beautiful wife and Philopoemen's wife danced, garlanded in spring flowers, and hundreds of women joined them in the ring, every woman wearing a crown of flowers and dancing with her hands raised, joined. And eventually men joined in an outer circle, and the two circles swayed and danced – one of the Achaean dances that almost everyone knew, and that could be learned in a dozen circles and yet might take a lifetime to master.

They danced, and drank, and danced, and drank; ate lamb, drank and danced again.

But when he found himself dancing with Kau-Ippa, Alexanor took the plunge for his newly made alliance with the Corinthian magnate, Cronan.

'How is your daughter?' he asked.

'Ask her yourself!' Kau-Ippa laughed.

She pointed; there was the Sakje girl, with Kleander on one side of her and Dadas on the other.

'I have a difficult question,' Alexanor admitted.

Kau-Ippa drank some wine. 'What can you not ask me? We are war-friends.'

'Did your daughter love Kritias?' he asked.

Kau-Ippa smiled. 'She put four Spartan heads on his grave,' she said proudly. 'When she got her adult name, she dedicated her kills to his shade.'

'Ah,' Alexanor said.

'And she bore his child. At least, I think it is hers – girls her age don't have to be too particular.'

Kau-Ippa winked. Alexanor had to remember that the Sakje were matrilineal; their women had different rules.

'Kritias' father—'

'Bah. An arse.'

'He wants to know if there's a baby,' he said. 'He is very rich.'

'My daughter's son is even now safe with our people.'

She smiled, and her sharpened teeth showed, and Alexanor knew it was time to change the subject.

But she danced with him willingly and left him with a smile, whirling away with Thodor and Kleostratos. Alexanor found himself dancing, first with the bride, and then with his wife, who was bright-eyed in the darkness.

'I have an idea,' he said.

Alexanor made love with his wife twice that night: once in a giggling, sudden embrace on the grass outside the firelight, and again, hours later, in the privacy of their tent.

'If I'm pregnant again, I may have to cut your throat,' Aspasia whispered.

'Oh! Mistress!' Alexanor cringed in mock terror.

'We need more parties,' she admitted. 'I feel sometimes as if I never lived at all until I found you again.'

'You say the sweetest things.'

'Will you fight?' she asked suddenly.

He wriggled, not wishing to be serious.

'Phila is terrified he will die. Rather than lose, he will die.'

Alexanor nodded at the darkness. 'Yes,' he said.

'You have my permission to fight,' Aspasia said. 'I owe that to Phila. To save him, you may fight.'

Alexanor looked at the roof of his tent for a little while.

'If we drink water now, we'll feel better in the morning,' he said.

She sighed. 'I know.'

He brought her water and she drank it. He went outside, came back and drank more water.

'I think I'd like to risk another pregnancy.'

He could just see her smile in the gloom.

'Mistress, I am an old man ...' he whined.

'Hmm,' she said. 'Let's see what we can do.'

The day after the wedding, with hard heads and a lot of muttering, the whole army of Achaea mustered in the fields east of Megalopolis.

Alexanor, free of hangover and feeling like a god, rode along behind Philopoemen as he shepherded his army into its ranks and inspected them. The army stood at open ranks so that officers could pass through, but the files were closed. The frontage of the phalanx at close order was five hundred brilliantly armoured men; sixteen deep, they caught the eye from any direction. Every bronze helmet was polished and caught the sun, and every man from richest to poorest wore a deep red *chiton*, the expensive red that could only be dyed with the 'grains' of northern Anatolia far to the east. The red and gold of the Achaean phalanx were themselves imposing, and the standard of drill was remarkable as soon as they were ordered to close their ranks, which they did with a snap and a scarlet unison that Alexanor found moving, like beautiful dance.

Riding along their ranks, from the golden invulnerability of the front to the simple red *chitons* of the rear ranks, Alexanor was struck with the faces of the young men who filled the files.

They reined in, with Philopoemen's escort closed up behind

him. Dinaeos, Simmias, Polyainos and a dozen brilliantly accoutred cavalrymen of the Agema waited as the phalanx closed up, raised their pikes – long *sarissae* in the Macedonian style – and then lowered them in fighting formation.

'We are not the "last Greeks",' Alexanor said. 'Look at them. They are a new generation.'

Philopoemen watched his phalanx with pride. 'Lykortas would tell you that they cost too much,' he said. 'And Phila would note that a third of them are freedmen and *neodamodeis* – new-made freedmen.'

'And Greeks for all that,' Alexanor said.

'You and I think so, certainly.'

On the left, the mercenary phalanx seemed sullen by comparison, and they performed their drill slowly and with no particular beauty. The cavalry of the left wing included the Tarentines, now fifteen hundred strong; two years of Achaean service had invested them in the League, and they had new horses provided by Achaean horse farms. Lightly armoured, they managed their big shields on horseback and demonstrated javelin throwing with an expertise that even the Agema might have admired.

To their left were the federal cavalry of the central plains: Argosians under Memnon, and Tegeans, Mantineans, and the contingent from Megalopolis. They were no longer the laughing stock of the League, and Memnon saluted proudly and Aristaenos led his *Strategos* on his inspection. The horses gleamed, as did the armour. The ability of the cavalry to wheel to right and left, and to change front at the trot, was demonstrated.

'Can you imagine?' Alexanor laughed.

Dinaeos shook his head. 'Three years.'

Philopoemen spoke over his shoulder. 'It's easy. That is, if the citizens trust in their government and are motivated to the work, then training an army is easy.'

Dinaeos nodded, unconvinced.

'Speak,' Philopoemen said.

Dinaeos shrugged, his armour flashing in the sun.

'Achilles,' he said, 'Great Alexander, Leonidas, Aristides of Athens, Arimnestos of Plataea, Lysimachos, Seleucus, Antigonus, Pyrrhus, Ptolemy. Men fight for men, not for political ideals. These men are here for you.'

343

Philopoemen's eyes narrowed. 'If that is true,' he said, 'all the more reason why the men who lead must remember what they fight for.'

After the left they rode off to the right, crossing the front of the whole army, which seemed huge to Alexanor. The citizen *peltastoi* stood in neat ranks, and wore the same scarlet *chitons* as the phalangites; veterans of the last campaign, they had a confidence that made them appear noble. They had plain helmets with no plumes or even cheek guards, small round shields and a pair of javelins. But behind them were donkeys with bundles of javelins – a new innovation.

Beyond the *peltastoi* were Telemnastos and his Cretans. They greeted Philopoemen with a roar, and represented an asset that the Spartans couldn't match – armoured archers, dominant in the deadly contest of the skirmish and the *psiloi*.

And then the cavalry of the right wing, under Dinaeos: Aristides with the cavalry of the coast, the *hippeis* of Epidauros and Hermione and Corinth and all the towns between; Lykortas with the Agema. The Agema and all the federal cavalry wore the scarlet *chitons*, but in the Agema, every man had his embroidered – some in black, some in gold. Dariush wore plain bronze armour, provided by Alexanor, but Kleander looked like a scarlet peacock, with plumes and Gorgons' heads on every surface. All of the file leaders had breastplates for their horses and most had armour on their horses' heads; some looked like monsters out of myth.

The Agema had suffered terribly at Tegea, but they could still muster five hundred, in two well-drilled squadrons and the best horses, in the best armour. The coastal cavalry was not nearly as resplendent, but they could still muster more than a thousand troopers in three heavy squadrons.

And finally, to the right, two hundred young *epilektoi* under Theodoros, with no armour at all, and the Thracian mercenaries – Rhesidae and Getae and Sakje. There were three hundred of them. Alexanor could see the handful of Sakje and Getae women – the girl, Kuka, now with her adult name Jaxarta. She was on a tall horse and wore a shirt of scales that glittered like stars.

She was pointing at Kau-Ippa, who was shaking her head.

Philopoemen rode up to the White Mare.

'What have I done wrong?'

'You know we all think these displays are silly,' Kau-Ippa said. 'And hot. My daughter says we should just ride away. I said a war leader needs to count his host.'

Philopoemen nodded.

Kleostratos was trying to stifle laughter. Thodor pretended to be interested in the silver decorations on his reins. Dadas was shaking his head.

'She is not even a little civilised,' he said.

'Perhaps that is why she takes so many heads,' her mother said.

The Achaean army sent the *epilektoi* and the Thracians south into Lacedaemon and scouts west to the borders of Elis, just to be sure. Lykortas went north to see to the fleet and the coastal alarms, because the Romans could always return, and with so much at stake, no one wanted to make simple mistakes.

The phalanx drilled.

Messengers flowed from the valleys of Sparta; Kleostratos and Kau-Ippa rode all the way around the Lacedaemonian capital and then came back north by the valleys that led to Tegea, past the battlefield of Sellasia, and outrode every attempt the Spartans made to intercept them.

The *epilektoi* tangled with the enemy's Tarentines and honours were even, but Agrionios was passing. The festivals of Demeter were celebrated, and the Spartans were still occupied inside their own borders.

But after the celebration of the Hyacinthia, their principal holiday, their army marched north. They emerged from their camp and marched again on Tegea.

Philopoemen had left a healthy garrison in Tegea – most of his mercenary foot. He sent the federal cavalry under Dinaeos south into Lacedaemon from Megalopolis.

The Spartans turned and moved to Skyritida to cover their farms.

Dinaeos retired, and the phalanx of Achaea marched east with the Agema to cover Tegea.

Now Kau-Ippa took a raid down the very route that the Spartans had planned to use for their invasion. By good fortune she caught one of the Spartan supply caravans in the valley of Petra, south of Megalopolis, on her retreat and carried it away – a hundred donkeys and mules, oxen, carts and horses.

The Achaean phalanx marched back to Megalopolis.

And then back to Tegea.

Lykortas returned from Corinth, with word that Philip, not the Romans, had ships in the gulf and the north coast was as safe as was likely in wartime.

'The rumour is that Philip is already burning his way into central Aetolia,' he crowed. 'You can see the smoke from Aegio.'

Philopoemen nodded. He looked around at the gathered officers.

'Kykliadas?'

The former *Strategos* was a trimmer, fitter man than Alexanor had ever seen him.

'You mean summer camp is over?' he asked.

'The north coast is safe. Troilos of Elis guarantees the truce with the Eleans. The phalanx is ready.'

Alexanor met his friend's eye. 'Last year, you told me that Nikeas had no reason to risk a battle,' he said. 'And I believe that I have heard you praise Fabius, the Roman.'

Philopoemen took a cup of wine from Polyainos. Following his lead, most of the rich men of the army had freed their slaves and paid for their armour, so that the phalanx was larger and everyone had to pour their own wine.

'You think I want a battle from *hubris*, brother?' he asked.

Alexanor smiled. 'It is my role to ask these questions.'

Philopoemen nodded. He spilled a libation to the gods, and then raised it.

'Here's to you, brother,' he said. 'Nikeas was facing the possibility of three enemy armies – Aetolia, Sparta, Rome. He needed to keep the army in being, even if that meant trading ground for time. And his infantry was—'

'Careful there,' Kykliadas said.

'Brittle,' Philopoemen said.

Dinaeos frowned. 'And badly outnumbered. No blame to the hoplites. They lasted longer than any of us expected.'

'Damned with faint praise,' Kykliadas said.

Philopoemen shook his head. 'Let's not do this. What is done is done. Alexanor asks, why now and not last year, and I answer, everything is different. If we lose, Tegea is garrisoned, although I will take most of the mercenaries out and put Cretans in. Argos is well walled.

Mantinea is strong. And it is already midsummer. If we lose, we will still end Machanandas' campaign for the summer. He can't take casualties any more than we can.'

'You do not say, "and if we win".'

'I should, though,' Philopoemen swirled the wine in his cup. 'Any victory has an effect. But last summer, had Nikeas won, Machanandas would have purchased a new army. This summer, everyone is at full stretch. If we win ... I believe we will *win*.'

'Where do we fight? At Tegea?'

'No. I want this to be as bad for the Spartans as it can be. Machanandas is arrogant. I will show weakness, and he will respond appropriately. Let's bleed him a little.'

Even Alexanor heard the rumours of disaffection from the League mercenaries. Lykortas marched away with five talents of gold and eight hundred Cretans, and after a laborious negotiation, he enticed the League's mercenaries out of Tegea and inserted the Cretans. Rumours of the disaffection of the League's mercenaries were everywhere, and it was said that Lykortas had to pay them an enormous bribe just to leave the walls.

Sparta struck.

The League's mercenaries retreated from the walls of Tegea, and Philopoemen ordered the army to collapse on Mantinea, on the north side of the League's central plain. He appeared to be abandoning Tegea to the Spartans and they moved quickly, but so did the Achaeans. The phalanx and the Agema marched by the Vangos Pass and then, staying to the mountains and carefully prepared supply depots, under the great mountain at Kardaras and down into the plains at Mantinea itself.

But the federal cavalry flooded onto the plain at the southern passes at Makri, linked up with the Thracians, and began the kind of deadly, no-holds-barred partisan warfare that had cost the Spartans their victory the year before.

Machanandas spent two days before Tegea, attempting to suborn the garrison of Cretans or to buy a way in among the citizens. He found no takers, and his foragers were terrified of the White Mare.

But he had learnt from his mistakes of the year before, or he had stronger advisors. His army formed a huge square and marched across the plain towards Mantinea, leaving Tegea unbeaten in his rear.

It transformed from a besieged city to a haven for raiders; the Cretans covered the gates and went out with the Thracians, the *epilektoi*, and the federal cavalry of the plains. Every night, fires burned in the Spartan camp – vicious skirmishes for water sources or horse lines. The Spartans had to fortify their camps, and the Achaeans, by the campaign's fifth day, owned the night. Spartan foraging parties required hundreds of cavalrymen to cover them.

That night, Philopoemen stood on the walls of Mantinea with Dinaeos, Simmias, Lykortas, Kykliadas and Alexanor.

'If we fortify our camp,' Dinaeos said, 'we can grind him to paste.'

Simmias growled. He wanted a battle.

'Tempting,' Philopoemen said.

'I hear a "but",' Alexanor said.

'It is only a feeling,' Philopoemen said. 'Listen. I will heed your advice, all of you. But to me, we have the best army Achaea has had in thirty years – but we have taxed our people to the point of exhaustion. The Romans are concentrating on Italy. Will that happen next year? The Aetolians are down. They never stay down.' He looked around at them in the firelit darkness. 'The time is now. Let the Spartans force the battle. If we play Fabius, he may just march away. And we will have to do it all again.'

'He is an arrogant swine,' Kykliadas conceded. 'He might just stay too long ...'

'You think we can win a straight-up battle?' Alexanor asked.

'Yes,' Philopoemen said.

Alexanor nodded. 'I trust you, *Strategos*. And if we could end this here ...'

'Our people could go home and farm,' Philopoemen agreed. 'You could go back to Chiron. And next year might just be better.'

When the others were going to bed, Philopoemen kept Lykortas and Alexanor by putting his hands on their shoulders.

'Will you fight?' he asked Alexanor.

'Aspasia told me I should fight, but only to keep you alive. My hospital is my first duty.'

'Wear armour and ride with me,' Philopoemen said. 'Lykortas, I need you with the phalanx.'

'Of course.'

'Then sleep well. It may be tomorrow.'

An hour after dawn, after a lengthy cavalry skirmish with no clear victor over by the Spartan camp, the Achaean army formed with the mercenaries on the left, and the Achaean phalanx and Agema on the right.

Philopoemen sent Cretans and his Thracians to force the cavalry skirmish to break up. But the effect was to drive the enemy's mercenary cavalry into their fortified camp. The Thracians were overeager, the Cretan arrows too fearsome a hail, and the Spartans stood to arms inside the palisade walls of their camp.

The day passed. Philopoemen withdrew his skirmishers.

Machanandas scented a trap and stayed in his camp.

'Try again tomorrow,' Philopoemen said.

When he was gone, Dinaeos glanced at Alexanor. He smiled.

'Now I feel better about this. I guess I'm afraid of the Spartans.'

'Who isn't? Simmias asked.

'Kau-Ippa,' Alexanor said. 'And now you know they are afraid of us.'

The next morning, restrained by strict orders, Achaean cavalry formed under the walls of the city and did nothing more. The Spartan-led cavalry issued onto the plain to gather forage at dawn and were unmolested.

The day dawned bright and clear; the mountains around them were stark in the dawn sky, like watching gods in an amphitheatre built for war.

And the Spartans began to form in front of their camp. Their Spartiate phalanx formed first, on their right, which faced the Achaean left. Red-cloaked and well-armoured, the most famous infantry in the world filed into place silently facing the Achaean mercenary foot. Next to the Spartiates was a mercenary phalanx that had much the same look as Achaea's: five thousand strong, in a mixture of armours and helmets and clothes, steady and professional. They faced the Achaean phalanx, brilliant in new scarlet and gold, led by Kykliadas.

In front of the phalanxes there were thousands of skirmishers – mostly freed helots and newly enfranchised men – but there were mercenary Cretans and Rhodians and Arkadian javelin-men. They faced Telemnastos' Cretans and the Achaean citizen *peltastoi*.

On the Spartan flanks were their cavalry. On the Spartan right – the Achaean left – were the Spartan cavalry, probably led by Nabis, and a brilliant squadron of fully armoured mercenary Italians, and some Tarentines. They faced the Achaean Tarentines and the League's federal cavalry from Argos and the plains – Tegeans and Mantineans and the men of Megalopolis, in nearly even numbers, under Aristaenos.

On the far flank, the Spartans had more cavalry: three thousand or more, mercenaries from all over the Mediterranean world. They faced the Achaean Agema, the Thracians, and the federal cavalry of the east under Dinaeos.

While the armies formed, Philopoemen was everywhere: up and down the line; sometimes in the midst of the ranks of his phalanx, sorting men out, and sometimes out on the wings; chatting with Menes, the mercenary, or praising the drill of the Agema.

'They have perhaps a thousand more cavalry and as many more infantry. If that.' He nodded with satisfaction. 'I will make my sacrifices.'

Alexanor was in armour for the first time in a year. 'Shall I come?'

'Of course!' Philopoemen smiled. 'The gods love you, brother. Gentlemen, change horses. We've had a busy morning – get a fresh charger for the fight.'

Then, as if they had no cares, Alexanor and Philopoemen walked to the low rise behind the centre of the army, where the camp began, and Leon brought them two white rams.

Alexanor embraced his friend.

Leon smiled. 'The hospital is running very well,' he said. 'In case you were wondering.'

Alexanor was chagrined.

'Never fuss,' Leon said. 'Kleopatra and I have it. Be a soldier one last time. But promise me this.'

'Anything,' Alexanor said.

'Don't die. I'm going to marry Kleopatra. You need to hold my hand.'

Alexanor nodded. 'I'll do my best.'

He turned to the rising sun.

'Ready, brother?' Philopoemen asked.

Alexanor drew his sword. 'Ready.'

They began a song, an invocation to Zeus, older than the ruins of the little temple to their right. Alexanor turned and saw Philopoemen as the sun caught him – godlike in stature, glowing in the new light. His arm went up, and together, the two men killed their animals and the clean blood flowed.

Philopoemen opened his first. He pointed his bloody *xiphos* at the liver.

'Victory,' he said. 'And the fall of a great man. Look at that.'

There was indeed, a white spot on the ram's liver, surrounded by a deadly black ring.

Philopoemen's smile never faltered. 'I will trade my life for this victory,' he said quietly.

Alexanor opened his animal. There was no such spot on his victim; it was perfectly formed, and the lobes indicated victory. He too lifted his arms to the sun, and the phalanx below them roared.

Alexanor turned to his friend. 'I have a better idea,' he said. 'Let's live to enjoy old age, and win anyway.'

Philopoemen smiled. 'I agree that would be better. I am a poor Stoic. I love the world.' He glanced at Alexanor. 'But I will make the sacrifice if I must.'

The day opened with a clash of the skirmishers. Alexanor, in front of the phalanx in the centre, had the feeling he was watching a play or a festival; except for the deaths of men, it was like a game.

The enemy *psiloi* came forward, hesitantly or boldly depending on their temperament. The Arkadian skirmishers were spear to spear with the citizen *peltastoi* and were bested by the apparently endless supply of javelins the *peltastoi* had. The arrows of the Cretans buzzed and flicked through the high grass of the fields in the centre of the line, reaping lives.

The skirmish lines were as long as the battle lines – almost twenty stades. The Spartan line filled the valley of Mantinea from side to side, and the position of their camp indicated their professionalism; someone had counted off their men and chosen his ground well. No Achaean cavalry would slip around the Spartan flanks.

But as the sun rose, the Achaean skirmishers began to force the Spartan skirmishers back. In some places, this had no effect, but in the Achaean left, the Cretans began to loose arrows into the Spartan cavalry. Like the sun on a foggy morning, the Achaean skirmishers were burning through to touch the waiting enemy line.

Like an ants' nest kicked by boys, the Spartan army sprang to life.

'The Spartan right is going to attack,' Simmias said.

Alexanor was looking at a thin haze of dust behind the main Spartan phalanx. He used his knees to get his Pegasus to sidle up to Philopoemen's great grey, Kineas.

'Are you seeing that?' he asked.

Philopoemen nodded. 'I didn't see it until a moment ago,' he admitted.

He looked to his right, and then to the left. To the left, the phalanx of Spartiates was going forward. The mercenaries echeloned on them, lagging perhaps fifty paces. There was an explosion of dust on the far left. Philopoemen looked to the right and back to the left.

'Steady,' he said to his horse, or perhaps the Achaean phalanx. He trotted forward a dozen horse paces. 'Damn,' he said very quietly. He turned and raised his spear.

'*Achaeans!*' he called.

They made no noise – not a single cheer. That's the way he'd trained them: silent, attentive to orders.

Off to their left, the whole of the Spartan left flank cavalry was delivering a massive blow against Aristaenos. Visibility across the plain was diminishing with every beat of Alexanor's heart.

'Forward!' Philopoemen said to Kykliadas. 'I need you to go into those mercenaries and beat them.'

Kykliadas raised a spear.

Philopoemen's charger danced sideways across the front of the phalanx.

'*Achaeans!*' he roared. '*Remember Tegea!*'

'March!' roared Kykliadas and Lykortas together, the rightmost and leftmost men in the front rank.

As crisp as if drilling at Megalopolis, the phalanx of Achaean stepped forward. Philopoemen let them go. Alexanor had expected that his friend might dismount and lead them himself. But he didn't.

'On me!' he called.

He led his escort past the flank of the phalanx, up the low mound that they'd sacrificed on. From the top, they could see shapes moving in the thick dust clouds.

'Aristaenos is attacking,' Philopoemen said.

He watched for perhaps fifty heartbeats. Simmias put one knee on his horse's back and balanced.

'There are more Spartan cavalry ...'

'Machanandas has done a brilliant thing,' Philopoemen said calmly. 'And proven that he is not the only one who is arrogant. Look – he's moved a third of his left flank cavalry all the way to the right. I never saw it. Aristaenos is badly outnumbered.'

And yet he sat on his horse and watched. Time passed; Alexanor was afraid even to speak.

And then the Achaean mercenary phalanx burst apart.

Because of the dust, Alexanor and the men on the little mound couldn't actually see the fighting lines. Only the men at the back of formations were visible like shapes in a sun-bright fog, and then usually only as a metallic glare.

But the mercenary phalanx broke and men ran out of the dust, throwing away their spears and their shields as they ran.

Simmias took Philopoemen's bridle. 'We must withdraw.'

Philopoemen watched the wreck of their hopes, and gave a slight smile.

'Too late for that, friends.'

He pointed due south, where the magnificent phalanx of the Achaeans had slammed into the enemy mercenaries with the sound of summer thunder on the plains.

'We wanted a battle,' Philopoemen said. 'And battles are in the hands of Tyche.'

The federal cavalry of the left was brave, and well led.

But they were not enough.

Philopoemen looked to the right.

Then at the Achaean phalanx.

Then back where the young men of Argos and Tegea were dying under the onslaught of thousands of enemy cavalrymen – so many that when a squadron fell back, another took its place.

The Achaeans had no second line.

The Tarentines went first. They knew the mercenary phalanx was gone, and they were, after all, professionals. And they were fighting their own – Italian against Italian in the dust.

They broke, and the whole cavalry wing began to unravel from the inside to the flank under the mountains, where a huge drainage ditch at the base of the hills guarded the flanks of both armies.

'I'm going to warn the camp,' Alexanor said.

Philopoemen nodded. 'Meet me with the Agema,' he said suddenly. 'On the right.'

'Surely we should help the left!' Simmias shouted.

Philopoemen shook his head. 'We are not done yet. Do you know your history?'

It seemed an odd question in the middle of a disaster.

'Yes?'

Alexanor was astonished at his friend's calm. And he could see that the waiting was done; Philopoemen had made a decision.

'Think of the Battle of Mantinea in the Peloponnesian War,' Philopoemen said. 'Now ride.'

Alexanor touched his heels to Pegasus and leant forward, and his mount felt as if he was flying. He tore down the mound, across the intervening ground to the camp, and straight up to the hospital.

'Into the walls!' he shouted. 'Leon! The left is beaten. Philopoemen isn't done. But the enemy will be here in ten minutes.'

'Got it!' Leon said.

Alexanor collected his horse under him and saw his wife, Phila and Kleopatra, all looking east.

'We've lost our left!' Alexanor called. 'Get into the city!'

All three turned.

Aspasia caught his bridle. 'Don't worry about us!' She kissed his hand. 'Go win!'

He wanted to say *Win? We've already lost.*

But Philopoemen had prepared for defeat. Most of the baggage and camp followers were already lining the walls of the city, with two hundred Cretans he'd left to maintain one open gate. The hospital had stayed out on the plain for obvious reasons, but before Alexanor turned for the battle line, he saw them moving – an orderly flight, with Leon on horseback, the last man in the column as the first refugees from the collapse of the cavalry tore up to the gate.

Alexanor turned Pegasus and galloped to the right. He had a god-like view of the back of the battle.

On the left, dust, and broken men fleeing, and the first flood of pursuing Spartan cavalry. Closer to the centre, the glitter of pike points where the Spartiates were coming forward through the human wreckage of the Achaeans' mercenaries. To their right, the back of the Achaean phalanx, head to head with the enemy mercenaries.

As he galloped for the head of the Agema, he had time to wonder what had happened at the Battle of Mantinea. *Surely this is the Battle of Mantinea?*

He had the slimmest memory of a battle at Mantinea in Thucydides.

Pegasus flew across the smooth ground. The battle lines were long, but the distance from the hospital to Dinaeos was fifteen hundred paces or less; and yet he was too late.

Before he caught the rear ranks of the Agema, they started forward, with the cavalry of the coast on their left. Their hooves shook the earth, and the dust they raised obscured *everything.*

He almost followed them into the dust, when he saw the *epilektoi* waiting, dismounted, to his right, and the Thracians with Kau-Ippa, and Philopoemen and the hundred men of his own guards – the troop he'd raised with his own funds, from his neighbours – and Polyainos with his standard.

To his front, the Spartan's mercenary cavalry counter-charged into the attack of the Agema.

The two lines met, their dust following them, joining in lazy spirals like rival forest fires on a summer day in the mountains.

Alexanor reined in by Philopoemen, who was watching the Agema. 'Welcome back,' he said.

Alexanor turned his horse and looked back. The Spartiates were almost clear of the dust cloud of their combat. Beyond them, the whole of the far flank's Spartan cavalry was in pursuit of the broken Achaean cavalry, right up to the city walls.

But the Spartiates seemed ignorant of the Achaean phalanx which they had passed in the dust, almost shoulder to shoulder.

'Pray, if you have a mind to,' Philopoemen said.

Alexanor rode in close to Philopoemen. 'I will not allow you to ...' He shook his head. 'Die to no purpose.'

Philopoemen was like an excited hound who scented a deer.

'I have no such intention,' he said. '*Ready!*' he roared in his super-human voice.

Alexanor also saw it – the moment when the Agema won their cavalry battle. Well armed and well led, and aware they were the last throw, they had smashed into the enemy mercenaries with numbers and better horses.

'When Machanandas stripped this flank ...' Philopoemen said, and then paused.

Dinaeos emerged from the battle haze five hundred paces to Alexanor's front. He was waving his spear, and before his eyes, Alexanor watched a miracle: the left squadron of the Agema, on a battlefield, after vanquishing their opponents, rallied and immediately wheeled to the left. Alexanor found that he was moving his hips, try-ing to make the Agema wheel faster, like a spectator cheering a race.

'He was betting that he'd win the battle before I did,' Philopoemen finished his thought, as he always did, regardless of delays. He looked back at his *Hetaeroi*. 'On me!' he called. 'Walk!'

The Thracians, *epilektoi*, and Philopoemen's *Hetaeroi* started for-ward. They were fresh – the army's best; most of them had stood by their horses until the last moment.

Now they started forward across the plain.

'Don't tire your horses,' Philopoemen said. 'Alexanor, come with me. Simmias, bring them along. Into the gap and wheel to the left.'

He waved to Kau-Ippa and Thodor as he passed, and Alexanor leant forward as they went straight to a gallop.

Dinaeos was roaring at his Agema. The wheel had not been perfect. There was confusion: men dismounting to get a fresh spear; riderless horses.

But from here, Alexanor was looking into the left-rear of the enemy mercenary phalanx.

'Doesn't have to be pretty,' Philopoemen said. 'Just get it done.'

Dinaeos smiled. 'This is what we came for.'

Philopoemen rode close. 'This is what we came back from Crete for,' he said. '*One more time, Agema! For Greece!*'

They cheered from parched throats and tired horses.

Dinaeos ordered, 'Forward at a walk!'

Off to their right, the rest of the Agema and the whole federal cavalry of the coast were lost in the haze of dust and sun. The temptation to pursue a beaten opponent was almost overwhelming. Alexanor knew that the rally of the Agema had been a miracle.

'Come on!' Philopoemen said.

He was obviously tearing himself away. He wanted to charge with the Agema.

Instead, he rode clear as the Agema rose to a trot, and the two men cantered back. Alexanor had a remarkable view of the fight between the Achaean phalanx and the mercenaries. Even through the dust, because their flanks were stripped, he could see the chaos at the centre of the fight where the pikes had crossed – the scarlet and gold figures on the left, the drabber mercenaries on the right.

The Achaeans were winning. The mercenaries were going back, step by step.

Alexanor saw the Agema charge. The horses changed gait; the men lowered their heads.

The rear ranks of the mercenaries never saw their doom. But the moment that the Achaean cavalry struck them, their phalanx burst apart. The distance from the file closer at the back of a sixteen-man file to the front is only fifty feet. The shock of the Achaean charge was communicated straight through, and any mercenary clear of the immediate catastrophe turned and ran.

All that in the time it took for a man to draw breath.

Philopoemen spotted Kykliadas by his crest and plumes, and rode for him. The politician was a capable spear fighter. He carried an old-fashioned hoplite spear with a long blade, and was on the far right, closest to Philopoemen.

The *Strategos* rode up, right to the very ranks of his Achaeans, clamped his knees and rose.

'*Achaeans! Halt!*'

The beaten mercenaries were turning to run.

The Achaean phalanx stumbled forward, the pressure on their front utterly released; somewhere in the middle of the front rank, men actually fell down. Already, even through the dust, Alexanor could see daylight between the routing mercenaries and the chaotic front of the Achaeans.

'*Halt! Halt!*'

Philopoemen's greater-than-human voice had never been so strong. Boldly, he put his horse into the widening gap between the phalanxes, roaring his commands.

Alexanor followed him closely. It seemed insane, riding down the alley between the two bodies; the ground was littered with dead and dying men, and a single spear thrust ...

'*Halt! Rally!*'

Men were standing up. Men with broken pike-hafts stooped to fetch a fallen weapon. Men pushed into their proper spots, and the gaps left by the dead were filled.

It was like watching a spell cast by a sorceress like Circe – not men into pigs, but men into automata. The chaos became order faster than a painter could paint the scene.

Philopoemen stopped at the centre of the front of the phalanx, and his big horse reared back, and he hung there in the dust and sun.

'*Look at me!*' he roared. He waited until he had their attention. '*The phalanx of Achaea will perform the Spartan change of front!*'

Not for the first time, Alexanor couldn't believe that human lungs could produce so much sound.

'Give them a moment to think it over,' Philopoemen said conversationally, as if they were on a drill field and trying something difficult.

'Gods,' Alexanor grunted.

'*Ready!*'

The ranks shivered.

'*March!*'

The entire front rank faced to the right about, so that every file leader was looking down the whole file that had been behind him. The second man pushed past his leader's left shoulder and turned in behind him, angling his shield to take up as little room as possible.

The third passed them both ...

The fourth ...

Alexanor had seen it done, on a sunny afternoon amid wild flowers. But here, the youth of Achaea did it on a stricken field with their dead friends at their feet and their unbeaten foes within two hundred paces.

The fifth and the sixth and the seventh ...

The half-file-leaders, pushing, shouting ...

It was like watching water fill a bucket, or like salt forming on a hot day on the salt flats of Alexanor's home. At first it seemed slow, but sixteen men were only walking fifty feet.

Philopoemen rode clear, and Alexanor followed him, and they

walked their tired horses up next to Lykortas, who was now on the right of the line.

'By all the names of all the fucking gods!' Lykortas said, his cheek flaps up. 'We did it.'

The Achaean phalanx had reversed direction. Now it looked back towards Mantinea, cocked at a slight angle because no manoeuvre is ever perfect. But the angle tilted their line towards the Spartan phalanx, which had become aware of their peril and was now performing the same manoeuvre.

Philopoemen walked his horse down the front rank. He had not yet fought; he was unwounded, and his spear was unbloodied. He pointed it at the Spartiates.

'There, companions, are the Spartans. In ten minutes, you will be the best hoplites in the world, and they will be second best. You are fighting for your homes, your wives, and your lives. They are impious invaders fighting for a tyrant. They are the terror of Greece.' He swept his spear through the air like one of the thunderbolts of Zeus. '*You are the better men!*' He seemed to grow. 'Charge home! Get it done, so we can go back to our homes!'

Despite their training, someone called 'Achilles!'

And then hundreds of voices, and then thousands. Men slammed their spears against their shields, and the sound was the lungs of Ares and the voice of doom, and it carried across the trampled grass.

'*Achilles! Achilles for Achaea!*'

The Spartans were just completing their manoeuvre. It was neither better nor worse than the Achaeans had done.

Philopoemen pointed at Lykortas.

'Forward!' Lykortas called.

In the Achaean phalanx, every left foot went forward.

Philopoemen rode across the front. They were still cheering, and he reined in by Alexanor.

'All done but the fighting.' He wore a brilliant smile.

'You are so sure our boys can win?'

Philopoemen's smile was the doom of three thousand men. 'It doesn't matter.'

'Doesn't matter?' Alexanor all but shouted.

Philopoemen pointed to their right, where the Thracians, the *epilektoi* and his own *Hetaeroi* were just trotting into line.

'Our cavalry is rallying,' he said. 'Theirs is not. The Spartan phalanx dies here.'

Simmias leant forward. 'I can get on their flank ...'

Philopoemen watched the Achaeans go forward.

'Give them a little liberty,' he said. 'They trained all winter for this contest.'

'You think the youth of Achaea can beat the Spartans?' Alexanor asked.

'I think freedom can defeat tyranny,' Philopoemen said. 'Watch.'

To their front, the phalanx of Achaea went forward. The Spartans chose to receive their advance at the halt.

Sometimes, when phalanxes closed, they only closed to a range of a few feet. Men hesitated, and then the pikes crossed, and the spears licked out, and the fight slowed to a crawl.

The Spartans tended to wait for their opponents to slow or stop, and then launch a sudden, vicious attack – a few paces, slamming their shields into the enemy front, breaking their order, starting the pushing contest in their own favour. It took tremendous discipline. It was based on that moment of hesitation that the Spartans' opponents always showed.

The Achaeans never slowed.

And there was *no* hesitation.

The Spartans of old – the men who had died with Leonidas at Thermopylae or stood with Pausanias at Plataea – might have known how to defeat the disciplined rush of the Achaeans. But those men were dead and so was the *agoge*, the training regimen that had produced generations of disciplined killers.

The Achaean pikes went straight home into the front ranks and the Achaeans went forward over their own dead and the Spartan dead. The Spartan phalanx staggered back five paces at the impact. And then back. And then back again.

'There we go,' Philopoemen said. 'You know, I don't think we're going to lose after all.'

He looked to his left. The battle had reversed; the left was now west, where the Agema had started.

Three hundred paces away in the dust, Alexanor could see cavalry.

'Aristides!' Alexanor shouted.

'Let's finish this,' Philopoemen said. 'Eyes front.'

Alexanor had seen Philopoemen fight, both for his life and on the sands of the *palaestra*; he'd seen how bold he could be, and yet how economical. And now, on a vast battlefield for the fate of nations, he saw that same economy.

Philopoemen and his five hundred trotted forward, and when they were well past the flank of the Spartan phalanx, he turned to Theodoros.

'Their shieldless flank,' he said. 'Break them.'

Theodoros and the *epilektoi* wheeled out of the cavalry line. They were lightly armed cavalry – no shields, no armour, a few javelins and a sword.

In the flank of a decaying phalanx, they were Titans armed with thunderbolts. They rode in close, but they didn't charge.

Not yet.

They cantered up and threw their javelins into men trapped with their shields in front of them, pressing forward, trying to stop the push of the Achaean phalanx. The Spartan files were locked up, disciplined even in defeat, grimly pushing back.

Until the javelins, thrown from a few feet away with the force of man and horse, began to kill them the way fishermen kill tuna running in the straits of Byzantium.

Alexanor lost the thread of the fight then, because the *Hetaeroi* and the Thracians pressed forward up the plain towards the city. The Spartan cavalry was reforming in the Achaean camp.

They were too late. Alexanor could feel it – the excitement of victory.

He looked back.

The Spartiates were not breaking. They were just dying. The Achaean citizen *peltastoi* and the Cretans had rallied behind the red and gold Achaeans and were now sweeping around the dying phalanx like wolves stalking a herd of sheep. Their arrows and spears flicked out and the Spartiates died.

And Aristides, if it was he, was marching the Achaean federal cavalry of the right across to fall in behind the *Hetaeroi*. Alexanor saw Lykurgos for a moment through the dust, shouting an order as the men of Epidauros wheeled by sections and their column became a line, sealing the doom of the Spartan army.

The Spartan cavalry was coming forward. But aside from the

Spartan *Hippeis*, the rest were mercenaries. They, like the Achaean Tarentines, knew a lost fight when they saw one.

Just in front of Alexanor, a squadron of Italian cavalry simply dismounted.

And then Machanandas burst out of the dust.

'There we go!'

Philopoemen sounded exactly like a hunter when the deer bursts from cover; even more, when the stag bursts from the trees exactly where the huntsman expected.

'Forward!' he called.

They went to a fast trot, the Thracians spreading a little, the *Hetaeroi* well closed up, their armoured horses still fresh. Alexanor tucked in by Kleander; off to his right he could see Dariush, and Polyainos, and a dozen other men he knew like brothers.

Machanandas saw them and paused.

'At him!' Philopoemen called. '*At him!*'

He leant forward over his horse's neck, and his grey charger lengthened his stride and began to pull ahead. Pegasus was fast, but Philopoemen's Kineas was faster.

Machanandas turned. He had two dozen riders with him, and he led them east, angling away from Philopoemen, abandoning his army. Behind him the Spartan *Hippeis* charged, trying to buy him time to get clear.

'Take them!' Philopoemen shouted at Simmias. He pointed with his spear.

Philopoemen had his eyes on his prey, and he left the Spartan *Hippeis* to the Thracians. Alexanor had time to see Kuka-Jaxarta rise on her horse and shoot, her bow almost touching a Spartan's breast-plate as she turned and vanished into the dust.

And then Alexanor had to concentrate on staying with Philopoemen. Kineas raced on, as if they had not already quartered the battlefield at a gallop, and he had to hope that Pegasus' heart was the equal of Kineas'.

He lost Philopoemen as they went through the dust that still hung in the windless summer air from the initial clash of the Achaean left and the Spartan cavalry, thick as snow in the mountains. He let his Pegasus have his head, and the horse shied from something and ran off to the left.

They came out of the dust as suddenly as fog parts in the mountains; a glimmer of light, and then Alexanor could see.

A dozen of Machanandas' escort had turned.

Philopoemen was killing them.

One man should not be able to defeat three – much less ten. But as Alexanor drove his horse to a stumbling gallop, Philopoemen put his spear into a man, passed under his arm and stripped the second man from his horse, turning the throw to a grapple on the man's helmeted head, breaking his neck as he fell. He left his spear in the third man and was on to the fourth, taking his sword wrist in both hands, reaching through the key so that the man's shoulder was dislocated. His arm was forced back and then he was ripped from his horse.

Alexanor was low on his horse's neck, spear reaching ...

The fifth man cut Philopoemen. Kineas stumbled, or Philopoemen missed his grip, and the sword cut into his left hand and arm, and blood spurted. But his left arm went around the man's head even as the blood poured out. Kineas, in perfect control, danced under his master. Philopoemen dragged his victim off his horse, stripped his sword with his right hand, and dropped his victim after cutting his throat.

Alexanor rode in like a spear throw – the fastest man in the melee – and his spear swept a man from his mount. He thrust at a second, who panicked, eyes wide, and tried to turn the thrust with his hand. The man screamed as the spear went right through his hand. Alexanor flipped him into the dirt, ripped the spear free and almost lost his seat as Pegasus slammed to a stop. He gone all the way through the fight the way his spear had penetrated the man's hand, and now he had to turn his horse. Only then did he see that Pegasus had saved him from falling into the ditch, which was wide and deep and had sheer sides.

Pegasus backed a few steps and turned on his hind legs. The charger was covered in sweat; Alexanor knew that he was in the danger zone where a man could kill a horse by riding too long.

Right in front of him, a panicked man rode straight over the side of the ditch and fell in a horrible tangle with his horse, who screamed, broken and still alive, at the bottom.

Alexanor still had his spear, and he rode towards the fight, but there was no more fight.

Philopoemen was riding north along the ditch. Blood poured from his maimed left hand and down the side of his pale grey horse.

Alexanor pressed the sides of Pegasus with his knees and leant forward. A trot was all his grey could give him. He trotted after Philopoemen, who was single-handedly pursuing Machanandas and a dozen other men.

'Stop!' he called.

Philopoemen looked back. Shook his head.

Alexanor whispered to his horse. He loved Pegasus. He loved Philopoemen more.

'Come on, my love. For me.'

She gave him a burst – perhaps fifty strides – and he caught Kineas and reached for his reins.

'You will bleed out,' he said.

Philopoemen met his eye. '*I was born for this!*'

Perhaps three hundred paces behind them, Polyainos and Simmias burst out of the dust and hallooed like hunters.

'Wait for your companions!' Alexanor begged.

Ahead of them, Machanandas was looking for a place to cross the ditch. Alexanor could see him, head down, looking over the side.

Philopoemen followed – one man stalking ten.

Machanandas shouted an order to his companions. Men turned.

But none of them charged Philopoemen.

Two of them turned north and put their horses to a gallop. The others milled around the tyrant. He was still looking down into the ditch.

One of the *Hetaeroi* still had a powerful, fresh horse, and he plunged forward, closing the distance rapidly, even as Alexanor and Philopoemen began to close in on the huddle of men around the tyrant. Kleander cantered up, his roan still lively despite the weight of her armour.

'This time, you can't stop me!' he called.

Alexanor knew, then, that there was no going back. He made a prayer to Apollo, asking forgiveness.

As a doctor, then, he made a strange decision.

'Let's charge them,' he said. He released Philopoemen's bridle.

Kleander whooped.

Philopoemen smiled. 'Thank you,' he said simply.

And in those last moments, Pegasus was perfectly willing.

The tyrant's guards were less willing. Perhaps it was clear to them that there were no further benefits to be had; perhaps they had little love for him.

Alexanor killed his man, stabbing once into his reins hand, scoring, and then rifling his spear into the man's uncovered throat – one, and two, as he had practised a hundred times. He had never fought so well.

Kleander burst through the remaining guards, scattering those who stood. His big mare knocked a horse down and Kleander threw a second rider, passing his spear around the man's neck, strangling him. He dropped the corpse, swung his spear like an axe, and another Spartan, bolder or better, came up behind him. The Spartan officer caught Kleander's foot and threw him to the ground; his hand went back, spear raised for the kill ...

Alexanor was too late, and too far ...

The arrow seemed to fall from the clear blue sky. It passed between Philopoemen and Alexanor on converging courses, both too late for Kleander, and plucked his would-be killer from the horse's back, clutching the arrow in his chest.

Kuka-Jaxarta blew through the melee on a small dapple grey. She'd stripped her kaftan off her right shoulder so her right breast was bare; a gold comb flashed in her hair. Her small horse seemed part of her, so that when she leant out for her second shot, rolling the arrows off her bow hand, her horse leant under her, and she loosed into a second Spartan like a trick rider performing for a crowd. She turned in pursuit of the other two.

Alexanor leant down and plucked Kleander from the sand, and the armoured man stood, looking for his horse.

Philopoemen had left his sword in his last victim, through the man's horsehair crest and his helmet and his skull. He had no weapon.

He continued to pace Machanandas – the patient hunter.

The Spartan tyrant turned and saw him.

Alexanor left Kleander and rode for Philopoemen. They were only a few paces apart. The grey's side was covered in blood as if dyed red. Alexanor, too far to save his friend, caught his eye and tossed his spear.

Philopoemen saw it, and Kineas turned, both forefeet off the ground, and Philopoemen plucked the spear out of the air. He turned it, end over end, so that the spearhead flashed in the sun as Philopoemen twirled it on his fingers like a child's toy. Kineas, already on his hind legs, turned in place under the sparkle of the steel head in the air.

Philopoemen cut Machanandas' thrown spear from the air, and it fell like victory from the tyrant's grasp, to rattle against the stones.

Philopoemen trotted towards the Spartan Tyrant.

Machanandas turned his horse. In between one beat of Alexanor's heart and the next, he was gone over the side.

Philopoemen followed him, Kineas pausing only a moment before plunging for the ditch.

'Damn you,' Alexanor said.

And followed.

It was the bravest, stupidest thing he'd ever done.

Luckily, Pegasus was smarter than he. The big horse stuck out its forefeet and sat back. Alexanor kept his seat; the gravel ripped at his feet and the horse's legs, and then they were at the bottom, and Pegasus was done, shivering at the bottom of a great ditch.

But Machanandas had seen a farmers' path on the other side, and his warhorse was as good as theirs, and scrambled for the top.

Kineas knew his rider. He landed on all four feet at the bottom, and then leapt, gathered his powerful haunches, and scrambled.

Both warhorses crested the great trench together, side by side, perhaps three paces apart. Philopoemen turned in the saddle, angling Kineas by a span ...

He threw.

Machanandas took the spear right through his head. The force of the throw carried him from the horse. He hit the lip of the ditch, and then tumbled all the way to the bottom.

He was very dead.

Philopoemen's horse had hauled itself, by equine will, to the top, and now stood, legs shaking, head down.

'Fuck!' Alexanor said.

He made himself run up the side of the ditch. Gravity ripped at him and he defied it, like the horse Kineas, and forced himself up, scrambling with his hands because every beat of Philopoemen's heart was killing him, the blood flowing out in the red, red sun.

'Raise your fucking arm!' Alexanor managed on his way up.

Philopoemen obeyed dully.

'Over your head!' Alexanor begged.

He was at the top. He got his canteen strap over his shoulder; it caught on his armour and he ripped it free.

'Off!' he yelled. 'Dismount!'

Philopoemen turned and slid from his horse, and the horse sighed.

'Kneel!'

Alexanor didn't wait; he tapped the back of Philopoemen's right knee, forcing the man down, already taking the raised left arm in his own.

He got the strap of his canteen over the middle of the arm and began to twist. He was praying.

In the distance, the Achaeans were singing the *paean*.

'You will not die!' he commanded.

Philopoemen's eyes met his; dull, and yet full of joy.

# EPILOGUE

## Nemea

### HIPPODROMIOS, 207 BCE

The games were opened by the athletes, not by the Achaean army. They came in and were cheered, and the stands were full of men in scarlet *chitons*. A few of the athletes wore their own. But the crowd cheered when men from Elis came, and men from Athens, and Corinth, and Thebes, and far-off Amphipolis. There were wrestlers and *pankration-ists*, runners at every distance, horses and chariots, musicians and poets.

There were even a few men of Sparta, because of the truce. The cheers were subdued, but there were no jeers. The Spartans walked with their heads high, like the champions they were.

The first to compete was the musician Pylades. He chose to sing *The Persians*, the great epic written by Aeschylus, poet and warrior, of the men of Greece standing against the Great King. But as he sang – and he sang brilliantly – he kept looking at the middle of the stands.

'*Worship honour, the helpmate of valour!*' he sang, and the stands cheered. '*Ares is King and Greece fears no foreign gold!*'

Men began to climb to their feet.

In the centre of the stands, a dozen young Achaeans entered, wearing their red cloaks and their scarlet *chitons*, and men were cheering; they were all young men, serious, and every one bore a wound. And in their midst was a man taller than they, his whole left arm bound in white linen; he was dressed exactly as they were.

368

And Pylades stood from his seat, raised his arms, and sang the ancient words of Aeschylus, as if invoking the gods,

'*Under his conduct, Greece was glorious, and free!*'

Every man and woman in the vast theatre turned and looked at Philopoemen, and the applause of ten thousand people was deafening.

Philopoemen smiled, but he raised a finger to his lips and pointed at the singer.

'What a great actor you would have made,' Phila said behind him.

Philopoemen turned as Alexanor began to laugh.

And later, when wine was served, and all their friends were gathering, as well as a new crop of sycophants and flatterers, Philopoemen smiled at Alexanor.

'I have been meaning to ask you,' he said. 'There we were. Exhausted horses. No javelins. And you said, "Let's charge them."'

Alexanor smiled. 'Yes.'

'Why? I think I'm the daring one ...'

'You were bleeding out,' Alexanor said. 'I needed you to be done. It seemed the fastest way to get you to medical attention.'

Philopoemen sat back and raised his wine cup. 'By Zeus!' he said. 'Never, ever tell Phila that tale.'

And later, a little drunk, Alexanor put an arm around Philopoemen's shoulders.

'Are we done?' he asked. 'Is Greece saved?'

Philopoemen sighed. He had a wreath on his brow, and a touch of Phila's rouge on one cheek. He did not look like a god.

'Perhaps,' he said. 'For a generation or two. There is no forever, for men and women.'

Alexanor thought for a moment. 'We did what we could with what we had.'

Philopoemen nodded. He was looking out at Aspasia and Phila, laughing together on a couch, and Dinaeos and Lykortas, Dariush leaning on Kleander, who had his cloak around Kuka-Jaxarta, who was laughing too hard to resist him.

He walked towards the Scythian woman, and Alexanor followed him.

'Why are you two laughing so hard,' Alexanor asked.

'I asked her what her dowry was,' Kleander said. 'She said, "Your life."'

Philopoemen had tears in his eyes.

'We are not the last Greeks,' he said. 'Look at them.'

They were just announcing the day's winners, and crowning them. Pylades was first.

Alexanor stood with Philopoemen and watched the victors crowned. And then the crowd joined together, hand to hand. They sang the *paean*.

Then they raised their hands, all together, and shouted '*Athanatos*' at the heavens.

# PHILOPOEMEN OF MEGALOPOLIS AND HIS AGE

*by Aristotle Koskinas*

ATHENS, APRIL 2018

The novels *The New Achilles* and *The Last Greek*, by Christian Cameron, narrate the tale of Philopoemen – a statesman and general from the Greek city of Megalopolis. It is a story of cities and kingdoms; of kings, generals, priests and philosophers. It is a tale of high adventure filled with dramatic battles, political maneuvering and scheming; of radical political ideas, philosophical enquiries and ethical dilemmas. But it is also the story of Greece and the Greeks during the Hellenistic period, one of the most fascinating and complex periods of ancient history.

**The Era**

We usually call Hellenistic the years right after the death of Alexander the Great (323 BCE) until 30 BCE, when Egypt succumbed to the Romans.

The period is quite distinct from the previous Classical one in several aspects. Within a short decade, Alexander's conquests had brought the Greeks all the way to central Asia, dismantling the mighty Persian Empire in the process. Alexander's short-lived realm stretched from the rocky shores of Greece in the West to the plains of northern India in the East and from the snow-capped Caucasus mountains in the North to the hot Egyptian desert in the South.

Alexander's sudden death sparked infighting among his generals over his throne. The battle of Ipsus, in 301 BCE, and the death of Antigonus the One-eyed spelled the breakup of Alexander's empire into three separate kingdoms: the *Ptolemaic* kingdom of Egypt (comprising Egypt and several other lands on the Eastern coast of the Mediterranean and the Aegean Sea), the kingdom of Macedonia (ruled by the *Antigonid* dynasty and including the old kingdom of Macedonia and its territories in central and southern Greece) and the *Seleucid* kingdom (containing most of the lands of the former Persian Empire as far as the Indus valley). Later, the kingdom of Pergamon proclaimed its independence in Asia Minor, whereas several parts of the huge domain of the Seleucids broke away, forming several smaller independent kingdoms.

All these changes had a huge impact on the Greek world, radically altering its political geography. Overshadowed by the vast kingdoms, the city-states lost their capacity to effectively carry out their own independent policy and experienced various degrees of domination by the great kingdoms. Given their fierce sense of independence, it is unsurprising that the Greeks resented the loss of their sovereignty, a feeling exploited by the different rulers, who promised the Greeks independence in exchange for their services in one conflict or another. Military confrontations in Greece were to a large extent due to the intervention of the great kingdoms, in their endless conflicts.

Ubiquitous war was one of the defining features of the Hellenistic Era. No one was exempt: the great kingdoms fought for dominance or territories against each other, tried to suppress insurgencies within their borders, or attempted to repel barbarians. The smaller kingdoms tried to hold their own against the larger kingdoms or one another. Even the city-states, now reduced to comparative insignificance, still fought against each other over old and new grievances, either alone or, most commonly, in alliances or federations. Even Athens and Sparta, who had lost most of their power and resources, were in an almost constant state of war, either against the kingdom of Macedon or neighboring city-states. This state of affairs lasted until the Roman conquest, when it was replaced by the firm Pax Romana.

In classical times, the fighting armies consisted of free citizens who armed themselves according to their means as cavalry, lightly armed skirmishers or heavy *hoplite* infantry. The *hoplites* carried a large round shield called *aspis* or *hoplon* (with a 1m [3 ft] diameter) and a 2.5m (8.2ft) long spear; they fought in a tight formation called the *phalanx*. Battles were primarily confrontations of these heavy infantry formations, while the cavalry and light infantry played secondary roles – if they participated at all.

In the Hellenistic period, national armies still existed, although it became common practice to employ large numbers of mercenaries. The armies of the large kingdoms comprised regiments of heavy infantry fighting in the Macedonian variation of the *phalanx*, where fighters carried the sarissa (a long pike about 6m [18 ft] long) and a smaller shield (with a 66-74m [26-29in] diameter), with handles that allowed the warrior to hold the pike with both hands. Warriors also carried short swords and wore a helmet and cuirass; it seems that only officers and front-line fighters wore full armor.

The Antigonid army had an elite unit called the *peltastai*, armed with a smaller variety of the Macedonian shield and a shorter pike. Some believe that they were armed like hoplites; whichever the case, they could be deployed in the phalanx, but were versatile enough to fight alongside cavalry or light infantry.

Another feature of Hellenistic warfare was the adoption of the *thyreos*, a long oval shield made of wood and leather with a single handgrip and a central spine. It was introduced to Greece by the Gauls during their invasion of 279 BCE, after which large numbers of Gauls served as mercenaries of the large kingdoms; it was also adopted by the Illyrian and Thracian tribes. In Greece it was adopted by several Greek city-states, including the army of the Achaean League. Fighters equipped with it were called *thyreophoroi* and fought with spears and swords but did not have the capacity to stand against the Macedonian phalanx.

Cavalry played a greater role in Hellenistic armies. In the campaigns of Alexander and some of his successors cavalry was the decisive arm, but later its main task was limited to making certain that the opposing cavalry would not threaten the main infantry formation. Light cavalry was used to screen the flanks of the army, while light infantry continued its role of skirmishing and supporting in conjunction with the other arms.

Hellenistic battles were complex affairs in which multinational armies with variously armed troops were combined to achieve the goal of their commanders. Compared to classical times, the difference in scale was staggering; for instance in the battle of Raphia, in 217 BCE, 143,000 men were deployed.

War became a rather expensive business for all parties involved. The monarchies could generate the necessary revenue through taxation and tribute, but that was far more difficult for the city-states which had to take care of a plethora of war expenses (including the remuneration of soldiers and the construction and maintenance of fortifications) with much fewer resources. In order to make ends meet, cities relied on the revenue generated by custom duties, income from public or sacred lands, but also on the contributions made by wealthy citizens in the form of a *liturgy* (public service) or in the form of extraordinary taxes imposed on wealthy and poor alike. Several communities had to revert to taking loans from wealthy citizens, other cities or even kings. Repaying these loans was also difficult, especially in a time of war; as a result cities had to mortgage their public assets.

Although city-states had lost their capacity to make their own foreign policy, they were flourishing as a system of social, financial and cultural organization. Several new cities appeared, founded by the new kings. These were designed according to the most advanced city-planning protocol of the time, the *Hippodameian system*, with its grid-iron layout and strict zoning of various activities. Each was endowed not only with the sine-qua-non gymnasium, agora and theatre, but also with a system of "democratic" organization, which included a citizen's assembly, a council and public officials.

However, these "democracies" bore little resemblance to the classical ideal. Their function was limited to running the city and their decisions were always subject to annulment by the king. Their systems were more or less democratic, according to what each ruler decreed, and the kings could (and often did) appoint an oligarchy or a tyrant to rule the city, if they so wished. The city officials were elected, not chosen by lot, meaning that public offices were available only to the most prominent citizens; Hellenistic cities were certainly less egalitarian and democratic than Athens; theirs was a democracy of the elites and their outlook was more conservative and geared towards preserving the status and privileges of the powerful few.

The Hellenistic era is one of rampant urbanization. New cities are founded as far as the heart of Asia and they all become administrative centers of their surrounding areas. Urban centers begin to draw ever increasing populations, not merely members of the upper classes, but also merchants, artisans and craftsmen of various trades, mercenaries, dispossessed farmers and more.

This trend is observed not only in the large kingdoms but also in mainland Greece, where recent surface surveys have revealed a considerable drop in the number of rural sites across several regions

(Argolis, Achaea, Sikyon, Megalopolis and Nemea). This could be due to depopulation and warfare, but it may also be attributed to the emergence of larger estates or the enlargement of the cities. In Sikyon, where there is data for both the city and its countryside, the latter seems to be the case. Even Sparta (which had previously been a conglomeration of 4 villages with large tracts of empty land among them) acquired the layout of a city with a unified urban grid.

It is interesting to note that the gap between rich and poor widened in Hellenistic times. Naturally this resulted in social friction, which in turn bred an aversion of the ruling classes to social reforms and a constant fear of potential uprisings. These were amply documented in the alliance treaty between Demetrius Poliorketes and the Greek city states in 302 BCE, clauses of which explicitly forbid writing off debts or redistributing land.

Socially, the focus of the people living in the Hellenistic Era ceases to be the public domain. The majority of the citizens are no longer involved in the decision making process and instead focus their attentions and energies to the private domain, pursuing personal goals, such as advancement or enrichment.

In Hellenistic times the limited experience of the city-state expanded as it became part of a much wider whole in an early version of globalization. Mobility increased across the Hellenistic world, as mercenaries, merchants and philosophers traveled communicating in the Lingua Franca of the time, Greek. Another example of this increased mobility was the doctors from the island of Kos, whose Asclepeion was one of the most famous, and its doctors, collectively called Asclepeiades, traced their lineage all the way to god Asclepius. Such was their fame that the island's doctors were in demand all over the Hellenistic world. City-states and kings would send envoys to Kos asking for doctors and the city would send the appropriate man for the task. If he was successful, he would receive honors by the state he served, like Hermeias, son of Emenidas, who served in Crete during the Lyttian war; inscriptions reveal that his success was such that he received the citizenship of Gortys (among other honors), while he was honored by other Cretan cities too.

It was formerly considered that the Hellenistic Era was simply a time of artistic decline, with classical motifs merely copied and imitated. This view was held by the Hellenistic Greeks themselves, who considered the preceding Classical Era far superior to theirs. And yet, the contact with alien peoples and cultures led to the birth of new forms, which, instead of merely copying the classical ones explored new and original means of artistic expression.

Other aspects of the Hellenistic civilization made their own, significant contributions. For instance, two new schools of philosophy appeared, the Stoic and the Epicurean, while mathematics and astronomy thrived. Mechanical engineering flourished, with several military applications; non-military inventions were early steam engines and immensely complex gearing systems, which accurately predicting eclipses, among other things.

The foundations of modern medicine were also laid at this period; the ideas of Hippocrates of Kos, that diseases have natural observable causes and cures, were beginning to spread. Treatment was sought by means of medical interventions, such as proper diet and surgery, while the properties of medicinal plants were systematically analyzed.

The Hellenistic period was a time of deep contrasts; unprecedented wealth was amassed next to widespread poverty; the sciences began to unravel the secrets of the natural world at a time when mystic cults expanded; technology advanced by leaps and bounds but could not compete with the cheapness of slave labor; travel and trade brought people in contact with one another as never before, yet war remained an ever present threat throughout the period.

## Philopoemen

Philopoemen was born in 252 (or 253) to a noble family of Megalopolis, a large city in the mountainous region of Arcadia, in the Peloponnese. He died about seventy years later. We know nothing of his life until he was about 30 years old, but, as a child of a noble family, he must have received the best education available for his age. He would have studied with philosophers, been instructed on matters of state, while at the same time exercising and practicing for war. It is said that his mentors were Ecdemus and Megalophanes, of tyrant-deposing fame. These two prominent Megalopolitans had been educated in Athens, returning to assassinate their city's tyrant, a feat which earned them a prolonged exile. They also assisted Aratus of Sicyon in deposing the tyrant there. Since they were away from the city, it follows that Philopoemen must have spent at least part of his youth "abroad".

He appears in historical sources in 223, bravely defending his city against the Spartan king Cleomenes III. It is safe to assume that in the continuous warfare that was part of Greek life, he would have taken part in other battles before. Such conflicts would have endowed him with the necessary military experience, as well as recognition by his compatriots. Without these, he would never have taken part in the negotiations that followed after the battle of Megalopolis, between his native city and Sparta.

A mere year later, in 222, Philopoemen is distinguished in the battle of Sellasia, as head of the Achaean League's cavalry, fighting with the Macedonians against the Spartans. He then spent about a decade fighting on the island of Crete, on behalf of its prominent city, Gortys. It is theorized that he was sent there by the Achaean League to defend the interests of the alliance between the League and the Macedonian king Philip V.

In 212 BCE he returned to the Peloponnese and begun his career as an official of the Achaean League whose policies he would influence until his death.

### The sources

Our main sources about the life of Philopoemen are passages from the book *Histories* by Polybius and his biography by Plutarch.

The former was a fellow citizen of Megalopolis who, although quite younger, might have even met Philopoemen in his life. He based his *Histories* to a large extent on firsthand accounts and, being a military man himself, provided accurate battle descriptions. However, his personal biases are made evident by his descriptions of the Achaean League and its foes.

Plutarch, on the other hand is not a historian. He compares the lives of Philopoemen and Titus Quinctius Flaminius with the aim of highlighting their character and morals. He underscores the virtues of Philopoemen and presents him as a worthy child of Greece, who struggled for the freedom of his people.

To conclude, both sources are of great value to the modern historian, but they both paint an extremely idealized portrait of Philopoemen and his character.

Aristotelis Koskinas
Athens, 2018

# HISTORICAL NOTE

There's a great deal that I want to say about these two books. I'll try to keep it to a minimum.

First, to the best of my ability, I have tried to keep to the actual history, including the almost incredible operational pace of this book, *The Last Greek*. I have drawn on nearly contemporary sources for most of it; Polybius, for the most part; Livy, who I like to think preserves some of the Polybius that is lost (like his biography of Philopoemen, which would have been very handy) and a handful of other, later historians; most useful of whom is certainly Pausanias, whose tourist guide to help Romans see the glory that was Greece, written almost four hundred years later, preserves many monuments, statues, and tales not held elsewhere. And I have seen the monument that the Achaeans erected at Delphi for Philopoemen, or at least its base, and felt a thrill to touch it. I have walked the battlefield at Sellasia, sat in Philopoemen's seat in the great theater of Megolopolis, and spent many happy hours at Epidauros.

So ... this is a novel. But it is also my attempt to reconstruct political, military and social events of a lost world. The endless tangles of the Romans, Carthaginians, Italians, Illyrians, Egyptians, Seleucids, Macedonians, Rhodians, Aetolians, Spartans and Achaeans, Cretans and Nubians ...

Second, the philosophies presented are, to the best of my ability, accurate. Stoicism, Epicureanism and Platonism flourished in Hellenistic Greece, and gave birth to most of the philosophical systems we still use to this day. I have chosen to present Philopoemen as a radical Stoic, mostly on the evidence of his foster-fathers beliefs' and his actions when alive.

Phila, Aspasia, Kau-Ippa and Jaxarta are all creations of mine. The fact that Scythian women fought and led other fighters has been proven by archaeology. There were women like Phila, and women like Aspasia. Too often historical novels ignore the roles of women, except as victims. History tends to ignore them as well. But they were there, like the hundred Plataean women who served in the siege against the Spartans, like the Scythian women, like countless others.

Bringing them to life does not make me 'revisionist'. It makes me a good historian.

And I fully confess that I am not a great fan of Sparta. But whether you admire or detest Sparta, the Sparta of Leonidas and the Persian Wars, it was well and fully dead by the time of Nabis and Machanindas. Current classical scholarship has done a great deal to show us the collapse of the *agoge* and the changes in the Spartan homeland after the Fourth Century.

Finally, Philopoemen may not have been a spotless hero, but both Greeks and Romans saw him as one; Plutarch thought he was a greater man than Flamininus. I have met great men and women in my life, and I have very much enjoyed creating one for a novel. I never intended to cover Philopoemen's entire life; I rather like leaving him at the Games in 207 BCE, accepting the plaudits of the crowd and the poet Pylades (this actually happened; like most of my good scenes, it's lifted straight from the Classical sources). He went on to direct the Achaeans for a generation; to lead them in war and peace, to restore Crete to stability, and finally to make an alliance with Rome and Rhodes. Maybe someday I'll write it all, but this was the story I wanted to tell.

Christian Cameron
Toronto, 2019

# GLOSSARY

I am an *amateur* Greek scholar. My definitions are my own, but taken from the LSJ or Routledge's *Handbook of Greek Mythology* or Smith's *Classical Dictionary*. On some military issues I have the temerity to disagree with the received wisdom on the subject. Also check my website at www.christiancameronauthor.com for more information and some helpful pictures.

**abattis** – an improvised barrier made of felled trees, the trunks pointed 'in' towards the defenders and the branches, sometimes sharpened, pointed out

**agema** – elite cavalry unit

**akinakes** – a Scythian/Persian knife or short sword

**andron** – a room, usually in the front of the house or on the street, often with mosaic floors and couches for dinner parties. The 'parlour.'

**archon** – chief or lord

**Archon Basileus** – in many Athens and some other Poleis or city states, the Archon Basileus was the leading Archon

**arete** – honour, excellence

**artemon** – a sail

**Asclepion** – in a general sense, a temple dedicated to Asclepios the healing god. Within a Temple complex, the Asclepaion may have been the building within which a patient was expected to dream of healing.

**aspis** – a round shield, worn double strapped on the arm, and deeply dished

**baqsa** – a Scythian shaman

**Boeotarch** – a military commander within the Boeotian Federation

**Boule** – a city council

**causia** – a Macedonian flat hat, not unlike a modern Afghan Pakol

**chiton** – a garment like a sleeveless tunic, usually a very light wool

**chitoniskos** – a very short chiton, usually worn by the Goddess Artemis and also the length worn by men under armour

**chlamys** – a cloak, usually worn by young men of military age

**daric** – a gold coin

**dekarch** – a military officer commanding ten men

**despoina** – 'lady' or 'mistress' as a form of address

**epilektoi** – a military unit of chosen or selected men. In Athens, the descendents of the elite 'chariot warriors'

**equites** – Roman cavalry

**falcis** – a sword like a reverse-curved saber

**gastraphetes** – a crossbow cocked against the belly

**Heraion** – a shrine to Hera

**hestiatorion** – a guest dining room

**hetaera** – a courtesan (literally a female companion)

**hetaeroi** – Elite cavalry (literally male companions)

**Hipparchos** - the senior cavalry commander of a state; in the Achaean Federation, the second in command.

**hippeis** – cavalry

**hoplamachos** – a weapons instructor in all the arts of fighting as an Hoplite

**hoplite** – the traditional heavy infantryman of the Greek world, carrying an 'aspis' or heavy round shield weighting about 5 kilos and wearing a full *panoplia* of bronze or leather. By Philopoemen's time, the Hoplite was somewhat outmoded. In most states, the hoplites had been replaced by *Theurophoroi* (see below) after the Celtic invasions, and then replaced again by *phalangites* (see below) in the Macedonian manner. In the author's opinion, the hoplite style remained the most flexible but required the highest personal training; Alexander's elite *hypaspitoi* appear to have been armed as hoplites.

**hypaspist** – an elite foot soldier in the Macedonian system; also a sort of military squire

**hyperetes** – a cavalry rank like 'troop sergeant'

**Katagogion** – a pilgrim hostel

**Kerameikos** – the potters' quarter of Athens, noted for its statuary and also a cemetary

**kline** – a couch

**kontos/kontoi** - lance, lances

**krater** – a drinking vessel

**kykeon** – sort of mulled wine

**kylix** – a drinking vessel

**lembi** – small boats

**metic** – a resident alien in a city, subject to a special tax

**naos** – the inner cell of a temple

**neodamodeis** – newly enfranchised men; especially in the Spartan system

**Neoteroi** – the 'new men', a faction in government on Crete

**opson** - 'anything eaten with bread' usually little fish, or just olive oil

**pais** – a patronising form of address meaning 'boy'

**palaestra** – an arcaded space with a sanded floor for wrestling or fencing

**pankration** – 'all-fighting' a martial art that included wrestling and boxing techniques, as well as throws

**Panoplia** – a full set of armour;

greaves for the legs, a thorakes of bronze, leather, or chain for the torso, a helmet and a shield. (Modern 'panoply')

**pelta** – a shield, usually small and round but also small and crescent-shaped

**peltastoi** – soldiers who carry the 'pelta' and fight in dispersed order. However, worth noting that later Macedonian armies had 'elite' units called Peltastoi. Theoretically, light military units used for raiding and partisan warfare may have developed over time into elite heavy infantry; the same process can be seen in the Early Modern period.

**penteres** – a warship with five rows of oars or five men to the oar or some combination thereof

**peplos** – a woman's dress with an overfold for modesty; very old-fashioned by Philopoemen's time

**petasos** – a large, broad-brimmed hat usually worn by horsemen against the sun, made of wool felt

**Phalangites** – the heaviest infantry class, usually well-armoured in bronze *panoplia* at least in the front ranks, carrying pikes in the Macedonian fashion

**Phalanx** – in general, any large body of men. Often used technically to apply to the full body of all the 'phalangites' formed together.

**phylarch** – a military commander commanding a file

**porne** – a prostitute

**pronaos** – the vestibule in front of a temple

**Propylon** – part of the temple complex, usually the outer entrance to the sanctuary

**psiloi** – soldiers, usually the very lightest armed, weather slingers, archers, or nearly naked men throwing rocks. Sometimes slaves or helots.

**quadrareme** – a warship with four oarsmen to the oar. The standard warship of the Hellenistic age, larger then the trireme

**sarauter** – the long bronze or iron butt-spike on a Greek spear or pike. Literally, the 'lizard-killer'.

**sarissae** – long spears or pikes

**skeuotheke** – the sacristy or storage house for sacred vessels

**Synodos** – a council

**taxeis** – a military unit; not unlike a modern company

**Taxiarchos** – a military rank, commander of a 'taxeis'

**thete/thetes** – orig a serf, later the lowest class of voters and citizens

**thorakatoi** – armoured *Theurophoroi*, because they are wearing a 'thorax' (see below *thorax* and *Theurophoroi*)

**thorax** or thorakes – a piece of armour – traditionally, in Ancient Greece, the thorax would be the bronze muscle cuirass. However, sometimes the *spolas* of white tawed leather could be considered a thorax, and by the time of Philopoemen, the first chain maille shirts were appearing fromt he Celtic world and being called 'thorakes.'

**Theurophoroi** – Infantry soldiers between the light *'peltastoi'* and the pike armed, often armoured, *'phalangites'* of the phalanx. Technically, the Roman Legions who fought Hannibal and Philip of Macedon were *'Theurophoroi'* and *'Thorakatoi'* because they fought in a more open order than phlangites and used short spears and swords.

**tholos** – a circular building often found in temple complexes and city capitals

**xiphos** – a sword with a leaf-shaped blade, made of steel. Greek swords, based on archaeology, are made of pattern-welded steel and are of very high quality.

# CREDITS

Christian Cameron and Orion Fiction would like to thank everyone at Orion who worked on the publication of *The Last Greek* in the UK.

**Editorial**
Lucy Frederick

**Copy editor**
Steve O'Gorman

**Proof reader**
Clare Wallis

**Contracts**
Anne Goddard
Paul Bulos
Jake Alderson

**Design**
Rabab Adams
Tomas Almeida
Joanna Ridley
Nick May

**Editorial Management**
Charlie Panayiotou
Jane Hughes
Alice Davis

**Production**
Ruth Sharvell

**Publicity**
Alainna Hadjigeorgiou

**Finance**
Jasdip Nandra
Afeera Ahmed
Elizabeth Beaumont
Sue Baker

**Audio**
Paul Stark
Amber Bates

**Rights**
Susan Howe
Krystyna Kujawinska
Jessica Purdue
Richard King
Louise Henderson

**Sales**
Jen Wilson
Esther Waters
Victoria Laws
Rachael Hum
Ellie Kyrke-Smith
Frances Doyle
Georgina Cutler

**Operations**
Jo Jacobs
Sharon Willis
Lisa Pryde
Lucy Brem

# THE TYRANT
## SERIES

by CHRISTIAN CAMERON

Opening in the setting sun of Alexander the
Great's legendary life, follow the adventures
of Athenian cavalry officer Kineas and his
family. When Alexander dies, the struggle for
power between his generals throws Kineas's
world into uproar. He must fight if he is to
hold on to what is his . . .

Available now from Orion Books

ORION

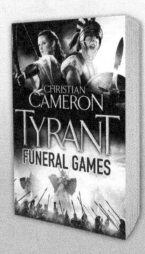

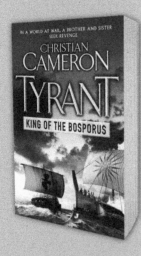

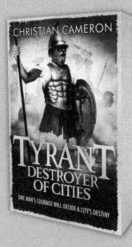

# THE LONG WAR
## SERIES

by CHRISTIAN CAMERON

Arimnestos of Plataea is just a young boy
when he is forced to swap the ploughshare
for the shield wall and is plunged into the fires
of battle for the first time. As the Greek world
comes under threat from the might of the
Persian Empire, Arimnestos must take up his
spear to preserve his entire way of life.

Available now from Orion Books

ORION

'A sword-slash above the rest'
IRISH EXAMINER

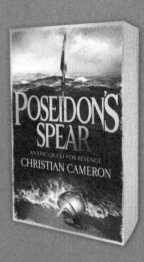

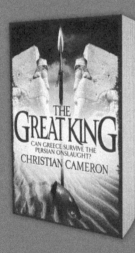